Study in Slaughter

Christopher G. Nuttall

Twilight Times Books
Kingsport Tennessee

Study in Slaughter

This is a work of fiction. All concepts, characters and events portrayed in this book are used fictitiously and any resemblance to real people or events is purely coincidental.

Paladin Timeless Books, an imprint of
Twilight Times Books
P O Box 3340
Kingsport TN 37664
http://twilighttimesbooks.com/

First Edition, December 2014

Library of Congress Control Number: 2014957677

ISBN: 978-1-60619-302-0

Cover art by Brad Fraunfelter

Printed in the United States of America.

Prologue

THE FLASH OF LIGHT WAS, FOR A LONG MOMENT, OVERPOWERINGLY BRIGHT, A SURGE OF magic as well as light. It faded quickly, revealing a tall woman with a harsh, angular face and a long braid of blonde hair that hung down to her waist. The Grandmaster bowed in welcome as she approached, his shorter form contrasting oddly with the newcomer's. They made a study in contrasts.

He spoke. "Welcome back to Whitehall, Lady Barb."

"Thank you, Grandmaster," Lady Barb said. She bowed formally to him. "It's good to be back."

He didn't say another word until they were in his office, surrounded by the most complex and powerful wards in the Allied Lands, and they both had a glass of wine in their hands.

"I understand that you had a chance to observe our Child of Destiny in Zangaria," he said, bluntly. "What do you make of her?"

"A bundle of contradictions," Lady Barb admitted, after a long moment. "She's smart, but she seems to lack practical knowledge and awareness. She's powerful, but she seems almost reluctant to use that power. She's loyal to her friends, to the point where it gets her into very real trouble. Where does she come from?"

The Grandmaster leaned forwards, interested. "What makes you think she comes from anywhere special?"

"Her...attitudes, for want of a better word," Lady Barb said. "I was given to understand that she was brought up in a sorcerer's tower. She simply doesn't *act* like any of the other children I've known who had sorcerers for fathers. At times, she can be more caring and sympathetic than anyone else, but at other times she simply doesn't realize that there is a problem. She acts more like a foreigner than someone who belongs in Zangaria."

"Where she was ennobled, after saving the lives of the Royal Family," the Grandmaster said, dryly. "But you're right. She doesn't come from here at all."

"Lady Emily was kidnapped out of her world by Shadye," he admitted. "She's from another *universe*."

Lady Barb listened, feeling a growing sense of unreality, as the Grandmaster explained.

"Impossible," Lady Barb said, when he had finished. "There are no such things as alternate universes."

"It isn't a very well studied branch of magic," the Grandmaster said, shaking his head. "But yes, alternate worlds do exist—and Lady Emily was taken from one."

"And saved by Void," Lady Barb said, unable to hide the bitterness in her voice. "Do you trust him with a girl of unknown potential?"

"No," the Grandmaster said. He looked down at his desk. "Why do you think I was so quick to agree to allow her to come to Whitehall?"

Lady Barb studied his face for a long moment. "Do you trust her?"

"I think that she is a decent human being," the Grandmaster said. "On the other hand, some of her virtues are also weaknesses. Do you realize that her loyalty to her friends has often overridden her common sense?"

"You mean she might be loyal to *Void*," Lady Barb said, after a long moment. "Do you trust *him...with anything*?"

"With great power comes great instability," the Grandmaster said. "And a certain lack of concern for everyone else."

"That isn't an answer," Lady Barb said.

"We know very little about Emily's life before she was kidnapped," the Grandmaster said, ignoring her. "I believe that it wasn't a very happy one, as she has shown no particular interest in returning home. On the other hand, her life here hasn't been very happy either."

"She's wealthy and famous," Lady Barb pointed out.

"She was targeted by a necromancer for death—and then enslavement," the Grandmaster countered. "One of her father figures is a rogue half-mad sorcerer. Another—Sergeant Harkin—died at her hands. She had no choice, but she still took it badly."

"I'd only heard rumors," Lady Barb said. "Is that true?"

"In a manner of speaking," the Grandmaster said. "She really had no choice."

He explained, briefly.

Lady Barb listened in disbelief. "She *knows* how to perform a necromantic rite?"

"It isn't difficult to master the theory," the Grandmaster reminded her. "Do you like Lady Emily, personally?"

"I could," Lady Barb admitted. "She's a decent person—and I honestly don't think that she intended to cause problems for the Allied Lands. But on the other hand... there's a sense that she thinks she knows what is right, always. She has a touch of Void's arrogance without the willingness to believe that the ends justify the means."

She shrugged. "And when the time came, she slipped into the castle to save Princess Alassa—her friend—and the rest of the Royal Family," she added. "Someone like that shouldn't be dismissed easily."

"True," the Grandmaster agreed. "Will you watch her?"

"I only agreed to stay at Whitehall for a year," Lady Barb said, in some irritation. "You *know* how I feel about Healing. But yes, I *will* watch her."

"Good," the Grandmaster said. "Because, just like her Guardian, she's a rogue element. And rogue elements cause trouble."

Chapter One

THE CASTLE WAS *HERS.*

Emily stood in the chamber underneath Cockatrice Castle and closed her eyes. She'd never had a real home before, not one where she'd felt safe and welcome. Even Whitehall wasn't *hers*, not in the sense that she could stay there permanently. Here, however, there was a home. It might be a cold castle, incredibly hard to heat save through magic, but it was *hers*.

The hearthstone lay in front of her, glowing faintly as energy hummed through the wards protecting the castle from magical attack. Emily could sense, without even touching it, the power that was securely anchored in the stone—and the override King Randor had used to secure Cockatrice Castle. It no longer belonged to the treacherous baron who had plotted against the King—a man whose very name had been stricken from the books—but to Emily, who had saved the King and his family from assassination. And it would belong to her heirs in perpetuity.

She felt a curious mix of emotions as she stepped forward and held her hand over the stone. Part of her wondered what her mother the drunkard would have said, if she'd known what her daughter had become; part of her wondered if there were unexpected surprises waiting for the Baroness Cockatrice in the future. The castle wasn't *free*; being a baroness, one of the highest-ranking nobles in the Kingdom of Zangaria, brought obligations of its own. King Randor had set out to reward her, but he had also had an agenda of his own. Emily had no doubt of it. The man who had set out to ride the whirlwind of political and social change Emily had started needed to think at least two steps ahead.

No time to worry about that now, she thought, as she reached into her belt and produced the silver knife. Holding her hand over the stone, she cut her palm, allowing blood to drip down and merge with the wards. The pain vanished almost as soon as it appeared—the knife was charmed to heal its wounds—allowing her to focus on the wards. Magic billowed forward, waiting for her. Closing her eyes, Emily stretched out and put her hand on top of the hearthstone.

Her mind reached out, accessing the wards. It was a very different experience to touching the wards protecting Whitehall; here, the wards were crude, anchored within the hearthstone and in need of constant renewal. There was no sense that they were alive or adapting to new situations—or watching for young magicians pushing their luck too far. There was a long moment when she felt that the wards were about to reject her, before they recognized their new mistress and opened up for her. If she wanted, she could make them do anything. She was, to all intents and purposes, the administrator of the castle's security network.

Someone did a very crude job, she thought, as her mind flashed through the network. But that shouldn't have been a surprise. Deprived of the raw power that allowed Whitehall's wards to exist, the original creators had needed to limit the reach and power of their creations. There wasn't even a ward intended to track magic used within the castle! Making a mental note to change that as quickly as possible, Emily found the administrative center and issued a handful of instructions, then pulled her mind out of the wards. There was, as always, a brief feeling of disorientation as her mind returned to her body. She didn't want to *think* about what would happen if her body suffered an accident while her mind was drifting around in the wards.

She stepped back from the hearthstone, which was glowing with heavy satisfaction, and walked over to the door. Outside, Bryon, Son of Cheam was waiting for her, as per her instructions. The young man didn't *look* that impressive—he was thin, with short brown hair and soft brown eyes—but he came highly recommended by Imaiqah, one of Emily's best friends. Reading between the lines, Emily suspected that her friend was sweet on Bryon, even though romance would be difficult now that Imaiqah's father had been raised to the peerage. Her friend's marriage would be a political tool, rather than a romantic affair.

"My Lady," Bryon said.

"Come in," Emily said, impatiently. There were times when the formalities annoyed her, even though she understood that they were part and parcel of Zangaria's society, the lubricant that kept it running smoothly. "The wards are waiting for you."

There was no way that *Emily* could remain in Zangaria, even though she knew King Randor would be delighted if she did. *She* had to go back to Whitehall for her second year of study, leaving Cockatrice Castle and the surrounding lands under the control of a steward. Bryon was young and inexperienced, but he *did* understand what Emily wanted him to do, as much as anyone born in Zangaria could understand. She'd made a start by reforming the laws the previous baron had propagated—the man was a scumbag, even if he hadn't tried to overthrow his King—but there was much else to do. Bryon would just have to make a start on her work.

"Hold your hand over the stone," Emily directed, as she cleaned the knife. The charms placed on the blade should have removed all traces of her blood, but she knew better than to take it for granted. Besides, taking care of one's tools and weapons had been hammered into her head at Whitehall. "I'm giving you complete authority over the castle, so be careful. If I have to come home to sort out a mess, I will *not* be pleased."

Bryon winced—and Emily cursed herself, inwardly. As baroness, she held the power of Middle and Low justice in Cockatrice—and High too, if King Randor didn't wish to deal with it personally. She was effectively judge, jury and executioner...if she'd wanted to lop off Bryon's head, it was unlikely that anyone would care enough to stop her. Save perhaps Imaiqah, of course, and *that* wasn't something most of the locals would take into account, not when their friendships were often nothing more than political expediency.

She took his hand in hers and cut his palm, just enough to allow the blood to drip onto the stone. The wards hummed loudly enough to be heard for a long moment, before falling back into the background magic pervading the castle. Bryon would have near-complete authority over them, save for a handful of areas that Emily had reserved for herself. For one, he wouldn't be able to use spell-controlled slaves in the castle itself. The practice might be very secure, although Emily knew how easy it was for the spells to be rewritten by a competent sorcerer, but it still disgusted her. There was no way that she was going to allow anyone under her command to use them.

"I can *feel* them," Bryon said, in shock. "I...I don't think they like me."

Emily smiled. Bryon came from a merchant family, one step above peasants grubbing in the soil, at least according to the previous baron. The wards had probably picked up a great deal of their owner's personality, even though he hadn't been the one who had built the castle or forged the wards. They respected Emily because she was now their lord, but it would take them time to grow used to Bryon.

"They'll come around," she said, dryly. "Until then, do you think you can control them?"

Now that Bryon's blood had been linked to the wards, he should be able to control them mentally, no matter where he was in the castle itself. It had taken Emily nearly a week to master it, although she'd had a considerable disadvantage. The time she'd touched the living wards protecting Whitehall had spoiled her, giving her preconceptions that the wards of Cockatrice Castle hadn't been able to meet. Bryon should find it easier to control the wards, even though he wasn't a very powerful magician. He had less to unlearn.

Besides, Emily thought, *the last baron wasn't a magician either.*

She led the way up to the baron's chambers, shaking her head at how the previous baron had decorated his castle. He had been a great hunting enthusiast; there was scarcely a room that didn't have a handful of mounted animal heads placed on the walls, all carefully displayed so they looked as savage as possible. There were hundreds of paintings too, each one showing the baron and his family in heroic poses—and a single painting of the Royal Family, which hung in the baron's Reception Room. In hindsight, anyone who looked at the man's castle would have known that he had dreams of kingship. Nothing else made sense.

He'd also had a staff largely composed of young and pretty girls. Emily had told them that they were free to go, if they wished, but most of them had refused to leave, even though it was clear that the previous baron had abused them. The pay was better...and besides, young women were less useful on farms than their brothers, particularly if they were no longer virgins. Emily found that sickening and hoped she would *always* find it sickening. The day she didn't, she'd told herself, was the day she'd been in Zangaria long enough to go native.

Emily's own quarters would be off-limits to everyone while she was away, naturally; the castle's wards wouldn't permit entry. She'd put Bryon in the next set of chambers, which had belonged to the previous baron's Castellan. The man had vanished after his master had been killed. No one quite knew what had happened to him, but Emily had taken the precaution of erasing all of his access permissions from the wards, just in case. Inside, the room was hot and stuffy; the maids had lit a fire in the grate to warm it.

"Thank you, Milady," Bryon said, once the door was closed. "I won't let you down."

"Good," Emily said. "I look forward to reading your regular reports."

She had to smile at Bryon's expression. Unlike most locals, he had actually been able to read and write before Emily had arrived and taught everyone Arabic numerals and Latin letters, but writing out regular reports would still have been difficult. The Scribes Guild had made itself fantastically wealthy by providing a reading and writing service before Emily had inadvertently destroyed them. Now, over half the Kingdom could read and write using the system she had imported from Earth... but there was still room for scribes. Besides, Imaiqah had assured Emily that Bryon wasn't as bad as some of the others.

"I'll send them weekly," he assured her.

Emily thanked him, then walked back to her own quarters and stepped inside. The rooms *still* struck her as insanely big—the bed alone was big enough for five people to share—but they gave her privacy, as well as plenty of space to work. She picked up a set of opened letters, dropped them into her borrowed trunk—her previous trunk was on its way to Whitehall, containing a very angry Cockatrice—and then glanced around to be sure that she hadn't left anything behind. Unlike Alassa, the Crown Princess of Zangaria, Emily always travelled light. She'd never had the opportunity to develop bad habits.

She shook her head as she rang the bell for the maids. It bothered her that she hadn't heard anything from Jade; he hadn't written to her once since she'd been raised to the peerage. Had he decided that she was too good for him now, even though her reputation as the Necromancer's Bane made her more dangerous and forbidding than the average Royal Princess? Or was he busy with his new master? His last message had spoken of new lessons, although he'd been very vague. Vows of secrecy were taken seriously by the magical community. Someone who broke a vow would almost certainly be killed or lose their magic permanently.

The maids appeared and curtseyed to her, something that still made Emily feel rather silly, even though she *was* their baroness. She directed them to take the luggage down to the coach, then followed at a rather more sedate pace. There had seemed little point in holding a grand farewell ceremony, not when she would be back in nine months to take a full accounting from Bryon of what had happened in her absence. Besides, she might have been rich, but she didn't *feel* rich. Her early life hadn't prepared her for sudden wealth.

She checked the wards on the carriage before she climbed in, then issued orders to the driver. The carriage lurched into life a moment later, the horses pulling it out of the courtyard and onto the badly-maintained road outside the castle. If it hadn't been for the spells on the carriage, Emily knew that she would probably have felt motion sick within five minutes—and besides, she certainly wouldn't be able to get any reading done. Still, she pushed the book aside and stared out of the window. The land surrounding the castle were all hers too.

The previous baron had been a dominating guy, she'd come to realize; he'd rarely allowed his peasants a chance to buy their own land and start growing whatever they wanted to grow. Emily had changed that, to some extent, but making so many changes so quickly would have almost certainly unhinged the local economy. Luckily, the influx of people into the nearby city—taking advantage of Emily's looser laws—had balanced the increase in food production quite nicely. She hadn't been so lucky with other matters...

It still struck her as absurd that *she* was the mistress of all she surveyed. Back on Earth, she would have been trying to scrape up the marks to go to college on a scholarship, hoping that it would give her the background she needed to escape her mother and stepfather once and for all. Here, she was the baroness...and a single word from her could change the lives of thousands of people. She'd learned that the hard way.

Settling back in her seat, she opened a book and started to read. The previous baron had been a collector of expensive books, although Emily had a private suspicion that it had been more for the pleasure of ownership than out of any intellectual habits. He'd probably felt that *intellectual* was a dirty word. Some of the books were on magic, including several that made Emily's skin crawl whenever she touched them. She'd placed them all in her trunk for Lady Aylia to examine, once she reached Whitehall. The librarian might be able to tell her more about their history.

It was nearly two hours before they reached the outskirts of Alexis, the capital city of Zangaria. Unlike Emily, Alassa couldn't hope to leave without a major send-off, even though she was only riding to the portal outside the city, where she would step through and reach Whitehall. Emily waited until her coach had come to a stop, then jumped out and pointed the coachman towards the portal. After what had happened the last time she'd used one, she would have preferred to be with her friends when they went through the next portal. At least Alassa already knew how badly portals affected her.

"Lady Emily," someone shouted, as Emily walked towards the Royal Carriage. "Are you going back to Whitehall?"

Emily did her best to ignore them. The combination of the new printing presses and the relaxation of most censorship laws had created a flourishing newspaper industry. Most of the newspapers would be gone within six months, she suspected—the economy probably couldn't support over six hundred new publications within Alexis alone—but that didn't stop them from being annoying. The society pages alone seemed to be ruder than anything she recalled from Earth.

She placed her hand against the wards surrounding the Royal Carriage, waited for them to recognize her and then climbed up, into the cool interior. Alassa, as perfectly poised as ever, gave her a smile; Imaiqah, who seemed a little overwhelmed by all the attention, looked relieved to see Emily. Given how badly the two girls had gotten on before Emily had arrived at Whitehall, she wasn't entirely surprised. Now, after Imaiqah had helped save Alassa's life and kingdom, she was nobility too. It was depressing to realize that made the girls get on better.

"It's good to see you," Alassa said, once the door was closed. "I hope that everything is prepared in Cockatrice?"

"I hope so," Emily said, unsurprised by her discretion. This world offered all sorts of ways to spy on someone—and the new newspapers printed whatever their snoops found out. She had a private suspicion that King Randor already regretted giving the editors so much freedom. "And yourself?"

"They spend most of their time complaining that I didn't choose a husband," Alassa said, ruefully. "But after everything that happened..."

Emily nodded in understanding. Alassa's planned engagement had been pushed to one side by an attempted coup—and, after that, most of her suitors had been recalled home so their parents could consider the new situation in Zangaria. Alassa hadn't been too upset, although she'd made a show of moping whenever she'd known she was being watched. She hadn't really wanted to get married so quickly, even if she *was* the Crown Princess.

"Don't worry about it," Emily advised. "You have plenty of time before you take the throne."

She shaped her defenses in her mind as the carriage lurched forward, approaching the portal. The nexus of magic seemed to reach out for them, pulling the vehicle onwards...and then Emily gasped in pain as the magic threatened to overwhelm her. There was a long moment when she felt she was about to die, or have her soul sucked out of her body, and then the feeling was gone. Compared to the first time she had passed through a portal, it was nothing.

Thank you, Lady Barb, she thought.

"Welcome to Whitehall," Alassa said, quietly. "And it's snowing."

Emily nodded, peering out of the window as the spires of Whitehall came into view.

Somehow, she couldn't escape the feeling that she was coming home.

Chapter Two

THE COLD GRIPPED THEM AS SOON AS THEY CLIMBED OUT OF THE CARRIAGE AND STARTED to walk towards the main entrance. Emily shivered and drew her cloak closer around herself, half-wishing that she was back in Zangaria. It had been warmer there. A handful of students were tossing snowballs around, despite warning glances from the staff and servants who were assisting the coachmen to unload the carriages. Emily shook her head, remembering just how much she'd hated school on Earth, even if it *did* get her away from her stepfather. The students at Whitehall seemed to love coming back to school.

Inside, it was mercifully warm. She allowed one of the servants to take her cloak, then walked towards the Main Hall, where the other students were gathering. Most of them looked familiar—they'd been told that the different years would return on different days—but a handful were strangers. Quite a few pupils had been withdrawn from the school after Shadye had attacked it, bringing Whitehall's invulnerability into question. She was surprised to see that others had been transferred *to* Whitehall.

"Lady Emily," Mistress Irene said, as they stepped into the Main Hall. "Welcome back."

"Thank you," Emily said. She *liked* Mistress Irene, even though she was strict. "It's good to be back."

"They all say that," Mistress Irene said, but she was smiling as she said it. "Take a seat, anywhere you like. There will be some speeches and then there will be food."

Emily nodded and found a seat next to Alassa, gritting her teeth when she saw other students throwing nervous glances at her. No one quite knew what to make of a girl who had bested a necromancer in single combat—and, because they didn't know precisely *what* she had done, they thought that she might be a necromancer herself. It was frustrating, sometimes, to look into a classmate's eyes and see fear looking back at her. In some ways, she was almost as alone in Whitehall as she had been on Earth.

But I have some friends here, she reminded herself, firmly. *I didn't really have friends on Earth.*

Mistress Irene had been right, she realized; most of the students *did* seem delighted to be back at Whitehall. But perhaps that wasn't too surprising. Whitehall was staggeringly luxurious by the standards of most in this world, even if they *weren't* allowed any individual servants or fancy clothes. Hot and cold running water alone was a vast improvement over what they would find elsewhere, enough to weaken their ties outside Whitehall. By the time they graduated, they would be used to a life of luxury they might have considered unimaginable. It would keep them loyal to Whitehall even after they completed their sixth year.

She looked up towards the high table as a ripple of silence ran through the air, calling their attention to the Grandmaster. He stood just in front of his table, flanked by Mistress Irene and a dour-faced man Emily didn't recognize. She couldn't help thinking, as she took in his bald head and dignified features, that he looked a little like Captain Picard. The thought made her smile inwardly as silence settled over the vast room.

"Welcome back to Whitehall," the Grandmaster said. He was a short, wizened man, who wore a cloth wrapped around his eyes, but there was no mistaking the power in his voice. "Let us hope that we have a less exciting year this time."

Emily felt her cheeks burning as several pairs of eyes glanced in her direction.

"The Allied Lands have decided to station several additional regiments of troops in the nearby lands, even pushing forward into the territory formerly occupied by Shadye," the Grandmaster continued. "Most of the orcs and goblins have been rousted out of the mountains, but there remains a danger that they may attack unwary travellers—or students—as they grow desperate. If you go outside the wards, go in a group and make sure you inform the staff before you leave."

His sightless eyes swept the room. "You should all understand the realities of the threat we face. I urge you all to be very careful. There are forces out there that would love to reduce our graduating classes—and not all of them are as unsubtle as a necromancer.

"On a different note," he added, "I would like to welcome a handful of students who have transferred to Whitehall from Mountaintop Academy." He nodded towards a handful of strangers, sitting at the rear of the room. "I hope you will make them all very welcome."

There was a long pause, then he nodded towards the Captain Picard lookalike. "This is Master Tor, Master of Law and Head of Second Year," he said. "I will leave you now in his capable hands."

Master Tor stepped forward, his eyes moving from student to student. They seemed to linger on Emily longer than she would have expected, although perhaps it shouldn't have been a surprise. Master Tor had presumably heard all about her, even if he hadn't seen her in class or in the library.

"Your first year at Whitehall was somewhat chaotic," Master Tor said, bluntly. "That is inevitable, simply because we need to start training newly-discovered magicians as soon as possible. Students come into schooling at all times and have to run through a series of classes to teach them basic skills. It is very disorderly.

"That is not true of second year," he added. "Your second year serves as the basis for your third and fourth years, where you will complete the first level of training and either go on to fifth and sixth year or leave to find employment outside the school. We attempt to keep second year as orderly as possible, while giving you a chance to experience as much as possible. You will need that experience in order to determine which subjects suit your particular talents."

Mistress Irene didn't look too pleased, Emily realized, as Master Tor paused long enough for them to take it all in. But he was right; her first year at Whitehall *had* been rather chaotic, even without Shadye's attack. With new students arriving at unpredictable intervals, it would be impossible for the staff to follow a regular syllabus. Students had to gain the basic skills before they could advance into second year.

"During the next week, you will have the opportunity to attend a sample class from each of the elective subjects," Master Tor said, breaking into her thoughts. "Attendance in these classes, if you wish to take up the subject, is mandatory. The tutors will give you a brief introduction, demonstrate the value of the class and discuss what they hope to accomplish over the coming year. At the end of the week you will be able to decide what classes you wish to take over the year. I would advise you to consider what kind of career you intend to follow, once you leave Whitehall. Certain positions require high qualifications from Whitehall or another magical academy.

"Once term starts next week, you will have the opportunity to change classes for up to one month before becoming locked into them. If you realize that you have made a mistake *after* that, you may find yourself marked down or being forced to repeat the year. In any case, you will be listed as having failed the original class. I advise you all to be very careful in choosing your electives. A single bad choice can blight the rest of your term.

"In addition, you will be expected to choose an advisor," he continued. "You'll find a complete outline of the role that advisor is expected to play in your welcoming packet, but in general the advisor is supposed to act as a mentor. Should you fail to choose one, you will either be assigned an advisor or allowed to operate without one. This would mean, among other problems, that you would have no one to assist you if you got into trouble."

He smiled, rather bleakly. "I strongly advise you to find one as soon as possible," he warned. "The good advisors are often overwhelmed by requests."

Pity I can't ask Void, Emily thought. But after what she'd discovered about Void from Lady Barb, she was no longer sure that she trusted him completely. She looked up at the other tutors, wondering which one of them she should ask. Professor Thande was fun, but also slightly insane; right now, he looked as if he had died and had then been dug up and put back to work. What had he been *doing* over the holidays?

"On a slightly different note," Master Tor informed them, "*Ken* tryouts will be held in the latter half of the week and next week, should there be enough interest. Team Captains will post the schedules in the common rooms; if you're interested in trying out, you may attend their sessions and see if you manage to impress them. Alternatively, if you wish to form your own team, you may do so. A copy of the rules and regulations for new teams can be found in your common rooms."

There was a sudden surge of interest—mainly from the boys, Emily noted. *Ken* was a sport that seemed to combine football, basketball and dodge ball, not something her life had encouraged her to enjoy. Most of the students, however, loved it and attended every match religiously. Emily just found it tedious.

Alassa elbowed her. "We should found a team," she said, mischievously. "And then we could just sit around in the arena devising new ways to cheat."

"No, thank you," Emily said, quickly. *Anyone* could found a team, if they could find enough players. There had been nineteen different teams last year, most of them composed of players from second to sixth year. Every year, the teams would have to look for new blood or risk being disqualified. "I don't have the time anyway."

"How true," Alassa agreed.

Emily wondered, absently, what King Randor would make of his daughter playing in the arena. Would he approve or would he fear that she was placing her life in danger? *Ken* could and did turn nasty, particularly when the referee was looking the other way. Magic offered thousands of ways to cheat and many of the players were inventive enough to think of new ones on the fly. But it might be good for Alassa to learn to take orders before she gave them.

"But I could found a team," Alassa added. "It wouldn't be *that* hard to round up a handful of other players."

"Oh," Emily said. Of *course* Alassa wouldn't want to enter a team at the bottom. And she might well be able to round up enough players to enter a new team. "Maybe you should start recruiting from first years."

Alassa gave her a questioning look. "But they wouldn't know what they were doing," she pointed out. "Students in later years would know more spells and..."

"They can't form a team on their own," Emily pointed out. "If you were to invite them, however, they would be able to join—and then you would have a steady team for the next four years. Think of how many pupils leave each year."

She left Alassa to think about it as Master Tor started to speak again.

"There will be a visit to Dragon's Den this coming weekend," he said. "If you are interested in traveling to the city, I suggest that you add your name to the lists in the common rooms. We may not be able to provide enough security to take *everyone*."

Emily nodded, making a mental note to add her name to the list. Her trunk had disgorged the Cockatrice she'd captured, but it was now effectively useless. She'd been lucky to be able to recover most of her property before trapping the beast for the second time. The trunk would have to be taken back to Dragon's Den, where she'd bought it, in hopes that the enchanter who'd constructed it would be able to make repairs. If not, she would have to buy a second trunk.

"Finally, there has been a change in policy. As you are all second years, you may wear something apart from robes outside classes," Master Tor concluded. "Bear in mind, *please*, that the standard rules are still in existence. Those who break the rules will have the right to wear something apart from robes revoked."

"That's good," Alassa muttered. "I can wear those dresses mother sent for me."

Emily was less sure that allowing students to wear their own clothes was a good idea. Everyone wearing the same robes ensured that the richer students couldn't purchase incredibly expensive outfits to show off their wealth. Back home, those who had been able to afford designer clothes had lorded it over those who couldn't—like Emily. Now, she was wealthy by local standards, but she still didn't want to wear anything apart from robes. The dresses she'd worn in Zangaria had been uncomfortable, to say the least.

She caught sight of Melissa and her cronies chattering away about what they would buy in Dragon's Den. The announcement hadn't been made earlier, she realized, because it would force the students to buy new clothes at Dragon's Den—at least until they arranged for some of their clothes to be sent from home. Maybe someone at Dragon's Den had bribed the school to make the announcement just before the first weekend visit...no, that didn't seem too likely. Whitehall was far richer than Dragon's Den.

The Grandmaster stood up again. "Thank you, Master Tor," he said. No one, thankfully, seemed to be expecting applause. "There are a handful of minor matters that I need to cover and then we can eat."

He seemed rather amused at the relief that swept through the hall. "As you know," he continued, "we allow you students to practice certain kinds of spells on one another as pranks, believing that it encourages you to learn how to counter such spells without assistance from outside. Provided such behavior does not get out of hand—and provided that you have mastered the spells sufficiently—we do not intervene."

Emily winced, remembering just how close she had come to killing Alassa. The locals might regard certain spells as little more than practical jokes, causing embarrassment and humiliation at worst, but she could never see them as anything other than loaded weapons in the hands of children. But they did have a point. Nothing provided incentive to learn cancelling spells like being turned into a frog by another student. Melissa was alarmingly inventive with transformation spells.

"However, you are now second years, with a year of experience under your belts," the Grandmaster said. "You are absolutely forbidden to start *any* sort of prank duel with first years. They are unlikely to be able to counter your spells, or match you—and if they can, you should be ashamed of yourselves. If any of you start it, you will be severely punished; if they start it, we expect you to show restraint. Remember that you are older than the new students, remember that you should know much more magic and protections than they do—and if you can't remember that, remember what it feels like to face the Warden."

"Good piece of advice," Alassa muttered.

Emily nodded. She *had* cast spells on her seniors—in Martial Magic, where she'd been the youngest pupil in the class. But they'd been under the watchful eye of the sergeants, who would have hammered anyone who acted badly. Outside the classrooms, she could easily imagine older pupils trying to dominate the younger ones...if they'd been allowed the chance. After what had happened to the three of them when they'd used magic on one of the servants, she had no doubt that the teachers kept a sharp eye on them through the building's wards.

"There are also certain pranks which are on the banned list, at least in public," the Grandmaster continued. "You'll find the current list pinned up in the common rooms; I suggest that you study it carefully and remember not to use them, at least unless your life is in grave danger. Those who *do* use them, on *anyone*, will regret it."

He smiled, pressing his hands together as if he were in prayer. "And with that completed," he concluded, "we can eat."

Emily smiled at the cheers that echoed through the room. A small army of servants emerged from the concealed doors, carrying giant platters of food. She felt her smile growing wider as one of the servants placed a large roast chicken at one end of the table and started carving it up into slices, which were then passed down the table to the students. Another started carving up roast beef, while a third cut up a faintly greasy meat she didn't recognize. Others passed out potatoes, vegetables and steaming jugs of gravy.

Once, she would have been lucky if she'd had enough to eat. Now, eating too much was a very real problem.

Alassa went on happily about *Ken* teams throughout the meal, while Emily listened as politely as she could. It was odd to see her chatting to Imaiqah about something that didn't involve Emily, but it boded well for their future. Besides, Imaiqah had been ennobled along with her father in the wake of the coup attempt in Zangaria. No one could claim that she wasn't an aristocrat now.

The servants finally removed the plates and replaced them with cakes, ice cream and a jelly-like substance Emily had tried once and resolved never to try again. Instead, she took a piece of chocolate cake and munched it thoughtfully, wondering why the cooks had never thought of baking a carrot cake. She'd always loved them on Earth...

She looked up in surprise as a hand fell on her shoulder. Mistress Irene was standing right behind her.

"Stay behind," she ordered, as the Grandmaster started to dismiss the staff, signaling that the students could leave at any moment. "We need to talk to you."

Chapter Three

IT HAD BEEN SEVERAL MONTHS SINCE EMILY HAD LAST SET FOOT IN THE GRANDMASTER'S office, but it didn't seem to have changed at all. The room was empty apart from a desk, a handful of chairs and a single crystal ball in one corner. High overhead, a glowing ball of light provided oddly-tinted illumination. The Grandmaster's blindness, Emily realized as she sat down, made it harder for him to produce light globes. And he wouldn't need decorative elements either.

"Wait," Mistress Irene ordered, when Emily opened her mouth. "The others are on their way."

Emily felt herself squirming against the hard wooden chair. In her experience, unexpected summons to a teacher's office meant trouble; the last time she had been summoned to a teacher's office had been when she'd made a mistake while writing an essay for Advanced Charms. Professor Lombardi had pointed out, in great detail, that if she'd tried it in real life, the results would have been disastrous. He'd made her write her own critique and then rewrite the entire essay. But she hadn't even *been* at Whitehall for months.

The door opened, revealing the Grandmaster, Master Tor and Sergeant Miles, who shot Emily an encouraging smile. It was easy to forget that Miles was one of the most powerful magicians in Whitehall; he looked friendly, almost reassuring. But Emily had seen him casually working spells that were well beyond her.

"Thank you for coming," the Grandmaster said. He sat down behind his desk, motioning for the others to take seats of their own. "As you are no doubt aware, your status changed over the last few months."

Emily flushed. King Randor had sprung her ennoblement as a surprise, making it impossible for her to turn it down. Maybe she would have turned it down anyway, if it had just been him, but Alassa had been there too. The King, she suspected, had counted on that to ensure that Emily did what he wanted. And she had.

"This presents us with a unique set of problems," the Grandmaster continued. "Your guardian insisted that you receive full training as a sorceress of the Allied Lands, a person owing allegiance to the White Council and the Allied Lands as a whole. However, your ennoblement makes you a subordinate of King Randor of Zangaria—and you are assumed to be compromised, no longer able to judge fairly in disputes between the Allied Lands."

Emily opened her mouth to protest, but he held up a hand, silencing her.

"As such, we are caught between two different sets of demands," he added. "King Randor has made no demands, but his rivals may insist that you never be allowed to serve the White Council. If so, it would be difficult to deny the justice of their request. Your guardian, however, may take exception to that."

"And that might have been what King Randor had in mind," Master Tor said.

The Grandmaster shot him a sharp look, then continued.

"We will continue to train you, for now," he said. "However, you should be aware that you may not be permitted to take fifth and sixth year courses. The political situation may well have shaken itself down by that time."

Emily scowled, inwardly. There was no way to know what to say or do.

"There is a second problem," the Grandmaster added. "You have received almost no training in estate management, for the very simple reason that such courses are almost *never* offered at Whitehall or any other academy. Normally, estates are passed from parents to children; the parents generally ensure that their children know what they are doing before they pass on and leave the estates to their heirs. You, however, have inherited an estate with almost no background knowledge at all. King Randor may not have appreciated your ignorance when he gave you the estate."

"I had to learn quickly," Emily admitted.

"I would be surprised if you had done more than scratch the surface," the Grandmaster said. "It is also possible that King Randor intended to *rely* on your ignorance. As you should have learned by now, a Baron of Zangaria is capable of acting independently and eventually challenging his sworn overlord for power. An ignorant baron, one dependent on the King for advice, might suit him perfectly. You need to be aware of that possibility."

He pressed his fingertips together. "We will be arranging for someone to teach you the basics," he added. "However, this needs to remain a secret. Even if King Randor doesn't object, others will see it as threatening Whitehall's neutrality. Once the classes are arranged, we will come up with a cover story—and I strongly suggest that you don't even tell your best friends."

Emily nodded in bitter understanding. Alassa *had* to answer any question put to her by her father—and King Randor was Imaiqah's monarch. Telling either of them would ensure that it would eventually get back to King Randor. She felt a pang of guilt at keeping something from her best friends—and another pang when she remembered that she hadn't told Imaiqah about her origins—and pushed it aside. The Grandmaster was right, but she didn't have to *like* it.

"Second, you passed your first year of Martial Magic with decent marks," the Grandmaster continued. "As you have more schooling to do, it was decided that you should move into the advanced class, rather than apprenticing yourself to a combat sorcerer or allowing your skills to atrophy over the next five years. However, this causes other problems."

He nodded to Sergeant Miles, who smiled at Emily. "Your origins make it difficult for us to track the process of your magical development with any actual reliability," he said. "You are also young, the youngest pupil to join the class since it was founded. There are spells covered during the advanced classes that you will probably be incapable of casting yet, no matter how practiced you are. Accordingly, you will receive special instruction from Lady Barb or myself. Furthermore, as there is no point in allowing you to attend Defensive Magic, you will spend that time practicing with us or older students. We will work out a timetable once we know your electives."

"Thank you," Emily said, softly.

"This will not be an easy year," Master Tor said. "Second Year is rarely easy, even for the best of us. *Your* life is absurdly complicated."

Emily glanced at him and saw...*something* in his eyes. Dislike? Disappointment? It was impossible to be sure. But she'd never met him, although she dimly recalled seeing him once or twice last year. They'd never talked, not even to exchange greetings.

"But I have faith that you will learn to handle it," the Grandmaster said. "Thank you for your time, Lady Emily."

"Thank you," Emily said, standing up and bobbing him a curtsey.

Outside, she found herself in an unfamiliar corridor. The school must have been reconfiguring its interior again, she decided, just to ensure that they remembered how to cast the spell to find their way around. She'd had enough practice last year, once she'd mastered it, to allow her to cast it easily. A tiny ball of light materialized in front of her and started to drift off down the corridor. Emily followed it until it halted in front of a blank wall. Once she put her hand against it, the blank wall opened up, revealing a hidden passageway. Like the first year rooms, it was a long corridor, studded with doors leading into private rooms. Hurrying forward, Emily saw the light float to a halt in front of a single door and flicker out of existence. Shaking her head, she put her hand against the door and it opened.

She expected to see Alassa and Imaiqah. They'd certainly requested to share rooms. Instead, two strangers looked back at her.

"I think I'm in the wrong room," Emily stammered. The spells on the doors shouldn't allow any other student to enter without at least one of the roommates accompanying them. "I'm sorry..."

She started to back out of the room, only to run into Madame Razz.

"I'm afraid not," Madame Razz informed her. "This *is* your room."

Emily stared at her. "Madame...I requested to share with Alassa and Imaiqah," she said. "We *all* made the same request."

"And it was overruled by Master Tor," Madame Razz said, bluntly. "He *insisted* that you receive different roommates."

There had been a time when she would have accepted that meekly. No more.

"Why?" She demanded. "I..."

"I would advise you not to speak to *anyone* in that tone of voice," Madame Razz said, coldly. "And I would suggest that you ask him yourself. You will be able to find him in his office tomorrow morning. Until then, sleep here and refrain from unpacking."

She caught Emily's arm before she could step back. "And I would *also* suggest that you apologize to your new roommates," she added. "Feuds can get *very* nasty when they are between people sharing the same room."

Emily flushed as she turned and stepped back into the room. Her trunk—the spare she'd borrowed in Zangaria—had been neatly placed by her bed. Unusually, the bed sheets were already made up for her, although she suspected that she'd have to do it herself in future. A trio of desks had been placed against the far wall, one of them already covered in books and paper, rather than parchment. She couldn't help smiling at the evidence of her own work. Paper had been unknown in the Allied Lands until she had arrived. It was still hideously expensive, but that would change.

"I'm sorry," she said, addressing the room as a whole. "I didn't expect to be here..."

"Nor did I," the first roommate said. There was something oddly inhuman about her voice, something that made Emily's hair prickle. "But I failed second year."

She turned, allowing Emily to see her clearly. Her body was human, although strongly muscled, but there was something serpentine about her face and her hair was a teeming mass of snakes. Emily almost stumbled backwards in shock at the overwhelming *wrongness* of it all, even though she'd seen weirder things. She'd heard of Gorgons, the intelligent cousins of medusas, but she'd never come face-to-face with one.

"Most people have that reaction," the Gorgon said, dryly. Up close, Emily could see hints of *scales* under her skin. "Gorgons that can perform magic are quite rare—apart from the standard magic the faerie built into us. I can turn you into stone two different ways."

Emily hesitated, then extended her hand. "Emily," she said, simply. "Pleased to meet you."

The Gorgon took her hand and shook it. There was something faintly dry about her skin, as if it were flaking off very slowly.

"My name is"—she made a hissing sound, with the help of her snakes, that Emily couldn't have hoped to repeat—"but humans can't actually pronounce it. You may as well just call me *Gorgon*...and if you call me Snake Face I'll turn you into stone."

"I'll bear that in mind," Emily said, dryly. She'd met the *real* Snake Face; a medusa kept by the Sergeants as a particularly unpleasant surprise for the students. Medusas looked humanoid, but they weren't really intelligent. "Why did you have to repeat the year?"

The Gorgon shrugged. "I failed three of the final exams," she admitted. "There was no way I could proceed into the next year, so they ordered me to repeat the year."

"I'm sorry to hear that," Emily said, sincerely. She looked towards the other roommate, who was lying on her bed. "And you?"

The girl rolled over and looked up at Emily. She was short and slight, with brown skin, dark eyes and very black hair. "My name is Lin," she said, softly. Her voice was so quiet that Emily had to strain her ears to listen. "I came from Mountaintop."

Emily smiled at her. "A transfer student?"

"Happens from time to time," the Gorgon said. "It's supposed to promote understanding between the different magical schools and institutes."

"Oh," Emily said. "What's Mountaintop like?"

"I can't really say," Lin said, still very quietly. "We don't talk about the school outside the wards."

"Bit more particular who it takes in," the Gorgon supplied. "There are no shortage of rumors about it too."

Lin didn't seem disposed to argue. She merely lay back on the bed and closed her eyes again.

"I've been hoping to speak with you," the Gorgon said, turning back to Emily. "Did you *really* beat a necromancer?"

"Yes, I did," Emily said, tiredly. It had been a very long day. "But I can't really talk about it."

"Of course not," the Gorgon agreed. She sounded rather rueful. "I would like to discuss it at some point, however. Necromancers are a persistent problem for my tribe."

Emily frowned. She'd studied orcs and goblins and a handful of other semi-human creatures, all seemingly created by the faerie for reasons beyond human comprehension, but she'd never actually considered Gorgons, beyond the basic fact that they existed. Most humans were scared of them, not without reason. Their unintelligent cousins could cause real trouble if they were allowed to run around without any supervision.

"I know almost nothing about your society," she admitted. "Why are necromancers a problem?"

The Gorgon smiled, rather inhumanly. Emily could have sworn that she saw sharp teeth in her mouth.

"My tribe lives on the outskirts of the Desert of Death," the Gorgon explained. "We don't need as much water as you do, so we built our society there, well away from humans who might want to kill us. On the other side of the desert, the necromancers lurk. Ever so often, they come to try to kidnap a few of our children. You don't want to know why."

Emily could guess. The petrification spell the faerie had worked into their bodies would have altered their flesh radically, allowing them to serve as ingredients for potions and other alchemical products. She couldn't see the necromancers considering the moral shortcomings of harvesting intelligent creatures for their flesh and blood, not when they were already sacrificing vast numbers of humans to keep their magic under control. And children wouldn't really be able to fight back.

"If you could give us something we could use against them," the Gorgon added, "we would be very grateful."

"I wish I *had* something," Emily admitted. The trick she'd used on Shadye might not be workable, outside Whitehall. It had drawn on the vast power of the nexus point under the school, something that wasn't available elsewhere. But there were other tricks. "I'm working on it."

"Work harder," the Gorgon advised. "By the way, I think that's your timetable on the bed."

Emily turned and saw a parchment envelope lying on the bedding. It was addressed to her, so she broke the seal and opened it up. Inside, there was a large sheet of parchment detailing the various taster classes—and a stern reminder that attendance at one of the taster classes was mandatory before deciding to attend the class for the rest of the year. Emily couldn't help smiling as she realized that Lady Barb's class in Healing would probably be her first. She had little interest in Magical Artwork. It would be good to see Lady Barb again.

Perhaps she would be my advisor, she thought, as she skimmed the rest of the parchment. She *had* said that she was only going to be at Whitehall for a year, but perhaps she could offer advice from a distance. Or maybe she would consider staying if teaching worked out for her. Emily made a mental note to ask, then planned out her week. A handful of classes threatened to be as boring as Artwork, but most of them looked mildly interesting.

"Master Tor is incredibly boring when it comes to law," the Gorgon said when Emily asked, "but it is quite an important class. Sorcerers are not always bound by local law, but they are bound by the laws written and upheld by the White Council. You would probably need it in any case."

Emily scowled, remembering the laws that her baronetcy had built up over the years since Zangaria had been founded. Many of them were completely contradictory. Others were so poorly written she couldn't help wondering if the clerks had deliberately sought to sabotage their lord's work.

"Probably," she said, sourly. She couldn't escape the sense that Master Tor simply didn't *like* her, which was worrying. What had she done to *him*? "I see I'm still stuck with Alchemy."

"It gets more interesting as you go on," the Gorgon assured her. "But if you slip behind, you find it very hard to catch up. Professor Thande does classes for students who are smart enough to admit that they need help, but you really need the knack for Alchemy to become an alchemist."

"And I don't have it," Emily muttered. She tapped her trunk, checking that the protection spells remained intact, then started to undress. She'd sleep in her underwear for once, then move into the next room...if Master Tor allowed her to move. "Hey—do *you* have to retake all of your classes?"

"Not really, but I have to work on the subjects I failed and retake the exams," the Gorgon explained. "And I may forget half of what I knew over the coming year."

Emily scowled. "You mean you have to retake *all* of the exams?"

"I'm afraid so," the Gorgon said. She rubbed her forehead, causing the snakes to hiss ominously. "It isn't going to be a fun year."

She glanced over at Lin. "I think she's a little surprised to meet you," she added. "But she'll get over it."

"I hope so," Emily muttered. She'd never really wanted to be famous. Now, an entire world knew her as the Necromancer's Bane—and didn't really know her at all. "Goodnight."

She climbed into bed, then closed her eyes and cast a basic sleep charm. Moments later, she was asleep.

Chapter Four

THE ROOMS WERE SUPPOSED TO BE SOUNDPROOFED, BUT EMILY WAS AWAKENED THE FOLLOWING morning by the sound of Madame Razz giving a student a sharp lecture on bringing *everything* on the list of required items. Opening her eyes, Emily realized that the door was propped open and Lin, her new roommate, was the recipient of the lecture. Swinging her legs out over the side of the bed, Emily stood and staggered towards the shower. A hot wash would wake her up.

Madame Razz had thankfully finished lecturing Lin when Emily emerged. Madame Razz might have had a heart of gold—Emily still remembered her showing kindness to homesick girls, who might never have left their home villages before—but she was also intolerant of mistakes, foolishness and horseplay. Or, as Emily had good reason to remember, mistreating the servants. Still, Lin didn't look to have been in *real* trouble.

"I left a pair of robes behind," Lin admitted, tearfully. "Madame Razz was not pleased."

"I think they have supplies of everything," Emily reassured her, as she pulled her robe on and checked her appearance in the mirror. Everything *looked* fairly normal—or as normal as possible, in a place like Whitehall. "I had my robes issued when I arrived last year."

Lin nodded, then opened her trunk. "She said she would bring me something," she said, flatly. "She won't report it to Master Tor, will she?"

"I don't think so," Emily said. "But she will probably remind you about it, ever so often. She won't let you make the same mistake again."

She glanced at her watch, then walked out of the bedroom and down to the common room. Unsurprisingly, it was empty. Most of her fellow students, she suspected, would have stayed up half the night chatting away and would try to sleep in as much as possible. They were in for an unpleasant surprise if they kept trying to sleep in when term properly started, she knew; Lady Barb had told her that the beds automatically evicted anyone who was still asleep when the first bell rang for class.

One wall held a set of parchment sheets. The first told her that the Night Stompers, a *Ken* team with seventeen years of history, was holding tryouts later in the afternoon. All were welcome, apparently. Emily glanced over a handful of other parchments, which repeated the same message for different teams, until she found something different. The list of banned hexes and jinxes was surprisingly short, although there was a blanket prohibition on anything that was either lethal or would do serious injury.

She rolled her eyes as she took in the short list of banned spells. One of them caused a person's clothes to fall off—she could just imagine the chaos *that* could cause in the dining hall—while another caused instant diarrhea. She hadn't wanted to know that was even *possible*. The others were just as bad; one, a small love charm, could be abused easily, if the caster was completely unscrupulous. At the bottom, there was a short note that if anyone attempted to use them, at least without the victim's permission, they would be lucky if facing the Warden was *all* that happened.

Shaking her head, Emily walked through the common room, out of the living quarters and down the corridor towards where the Head of Year was commonly housed. If Master Tor was anything like Mistress Irene, he would have an office near the dining hall, where he could eat and work at the same time. She hesitated outside Mistress Irene's office, then walked onwards until she saw Master Tor's name on a door. It was glowing faintly, informing her that he was inside. There were dark rumors about what happened to anyone who tried to break into a tutor's office while they were absent.

She tapped the door and waited. A moment later, it swung open, allowing her to enter the room.

Master Tor's office was large, larger than the Grandmaster's office. All four walls were covered with bookshelves, groaning under the weight of thousands of texts, each one large enough to be difficult for a single person to carry. Two desks were covered with pieces of parchment and paper, while a third was almost completely empty, apart from a tiny textbook and a mug of kava. Apart from the chair Master Tor was sitting in, behind the third desk, there was nowhere for anyone else to sit.

"Lady Emily," Master Tor said. The look of vague dislike on his face was still there. "What can I do for you?"

Emily bit down on her temper. Shouting at him wouldn't help.

"I applied to share a room with Alassa and Imaiqah," she said. It was fairly certain that he would know Alassa—and probably Imaiqah as well. "All *three* of us made the same request. I would like to know why we did not wind up sharing a room."

"Because I changed the room assignments," Master Tor said. There was something flat, utterly emotionless, in his tone. "As, I believe, Madame Razz was kind enough to explain to you last night."

Emily felt her temper flare, forcing her to focus her mind to damp it down. There was something about his attitude that made her want to lash out at him, even though she knew that it would be disastrous. Assaulting a teacher wouldn't be taken lightly, even at Whitehall. And Master Tor was almost certainly far more powerful and capable than her...

"I would like to know why you did it, then," Emily said, as carefully as she could. "We *all* made the request."

"Yes, you did," Master Tor agreed. "But I *did* change it..."

Emily glared at him. She was *not* going to let him push her around, teacher or no. "I would be prepared to file an official complaint," she said, although she had no idea of the procedure for complaining about a teacher at Whitehall. Did she address the Grandmaster, the Board of Governors or the White Council itself? "I would appreciate a *proper* explanation for your decision."

For a long moment, he held her gaze, staring into her eyes as if he could peer into her very soul.

"You are a noblewoman of Zangaria," he said, finally. "Your two friends are *also* noblewomen of Zangaria. However much we may regret your ennoblement, we must recognize it as fact. And we must also recognize that Whitehall serves more roles than merely teaching immature little girls about magic."

Emily flushed at his scorn, but held her tongue.

"In particular, Whitehall serves as a place for you to make contacts and familiarize yourself with the people who will be high-ranking nobles and powerful sorcerers after they graduate," he continued. "You will have to work with these people, no matter where you end up; meeting them here, without the strict protocol of official functions, allows you to form personal bonds that will last your entire lifetime.

"Allowing you to remain with your friends will not encourage you to make other friends and contacts," he concluded. "Hence, all three of you have been assigned to different rooms—with different roommates. I trust that makes a certain kind of sense?"

"Put that way," Emily said, bitterly, "it sounds almost logical."

"I'm glad to hear it," Master Tor said, dryly. "And I suggest that you learn to moderate your tone before you speak to me again. I have no patience for spoilt brats."

He looked down at the small textbook on his desk. "I have a lesson plan to complete," he added. "The room assignments will stay as they are. I suggest that you learn to make friends with your new roommates, rather than staying with a small group. It is not good for your future development."

It was clearly a dismissal. Emily nodded her head to him, turned and walked towards the door, which opened as she approached. She felt his gaze boring into the back of her head until the door closed behind her. What he'd said *was* logical, she couldn't deny it, but she couldn't escape the sense that it hadn't been his *only* motive. He seemed to dislike her and she honestly had no idea why.

She stopped outside Mistress Irene's office and considered asking her, then shook her head, dismissing the thought. No doubt she would find out why Master Tor hated her soon enough; she would have to attend a lecture on law within the week, just so she could decide if she wanted to stick with the subject. She didn't want to, but she had to admit that it might be useful to know what the rules were, at least before she broke them. Heinlein's advice still held true, even in a magical world.

The dining hall was almost deserted, not entirely to Emily's surprise. A pair of students from Sixth Year—Emily recognized one of them from Martial Magic—were sitting in one corner, pushing pieces of paper around while making pointing and shoving gestures. Two more looked to be wrapped up in each other, while the person sitting next to them was studiously ignoring their antics. Emily snorted inwardly and walked over to the buffet table, finding a large caldron of porridge and a pile of fresh fruit. No doubt after the feast last night, the cooks had decided to go for the healthy option. Normally, they served bacon and eggs.

She was midway through her breakfast when Alassa walked in, wearing a long blue dress that set off her eyes nicely. Emily felt a flicker of envy—no matter what she wore, she would never be as stunning as Alassa—and then pushed it aside as her friend picked up a breakfast tray and sat down next to her.

"I got a pair of girls from the Western Isles," she said, by way of greeting. "How about you?"

"A Gorgon and a transfer student," Emily said, noticing a slip of paper in Alassa's hand. "What's that?"

"A list of players for *Ken*," Alassa said. "My roommates were interested, although I did have to explain that they couldn't fight while they were playing or we wouldn't stand a chance. I asked around the common room while everyone was reading the lists and rounded up nine more names."

Emily blinked in surprise. "Nine?"

"Everyone who joins an established team will start at the very bottom," Alassa explained, ruefully. "Someone like me will have to wait at least four years before getting a shot at being Captain, let alone a chance to build up a reputation. But if I establish the team myself, I can become Captain immediately."

"I see," Emily said. "What about equipment?"

"It's all in the school's stores," Alassa said. "Once we have a team set out, we can draw supplies from the stores to outfit the players. We're not allowed to bring in equipment from outside the school, sadly. I could have purchased the very best of everything."

"Probably for the best," Emily observed. "People would wonder if your victories came from superior training or superior equipment."

"True, I suppose," Alassa agreed. She looked up at Emily, suddenly. "Do you want to join?"

"I'm lousy at games," Emily replied. "I used to be the last person picked..."

But was that true any longer? Between the sergeants, who had never met an exercise routine they didn't like, and Lady Barb, she was fitter than she'd ever been in her life. And she'd learned how to run, climb and crawl through tight spaces, all in the interests of turning her—eventually - into a combat sorceress. Jade had been fond of running through the assault course with her...

The thought gave her another pang. Where *was* he? Why wasn't he writing to her?

Maybe he found someone else, she thought. She couldn't really blame him. They'd never made a formal—or even an informal—agreement before she'd been ennobled.

"Come and try," Alassa urged. "At the very least, you can help us think of new ways to discomfort the opposition."

Emily must have looked puzzled, because Alassa launched into a long and complicated explanation. Most of the second year students, male and female, were fans of the game, but they were rarely allowed to try out for high positions in the older teams. Even if they got *on* the teams, they weren't invited to the planning sessions—and any good ideas they might have had were either stolen or ignored. Alassa, however, intended to allow *all* of her players to contribute suggestions. Between them, they might build up a truly formidable team. They wouldn't have the experience of the other teams, but they could build that up over the coming months.

Or they might end up embarrassing themselves.

Emily didn't *want* to play. She disliked team sports, even though she had taken part in team activities when she'd been in Martial Magic. But Alassa was keen on it and perhaps she should at least *try*...

"I'll do my best," she said, ruefully. "I spoke to Master Tor."

Alassa listened as she outlined what Master Tor had said, then nodded when Emily had finished.

"Father could have warned me," she said, crossly. "But Master Tor is probably right. Blast."

Emily scowled. Last year, Alassa had shared a room with two noblewomen from different kingdoms, while Emily had shared with Imaiqah and Aloha. But then, she had literally had no ties to *anyone* in Whitehall or the rest of the world. Now...now she was a baroness and had thousands of people underneath her...and the Grandmaster had been right. She really *wasn't* prepared for such responsibility.

"Still, there will be plenty of time to get used to new roommates and we can meet up outside of classes," Alassa continued. "And you can try playing *Ken* with us."

"If I have time," Emily said. She fumbled through the pockets of her robe and produced her timetable. "I'm going to be attending Lady Barb's introductory class at noon, just before lunch, then Subtle and Ritual Magic this afternoon. Tomorrow, there's a special class for Martial Magic..."

"It clashes with Herbology," Alassa observed, consulting her own timetable. "Do you want to go there?"

"Not if I can help it," Emily said. She knew which plants could be eaten safely from Martial Magic—and she had no real interest in farming and agricultural magic. "Besides, there's another four introductory classes, one per day."

"I've got Defensive Magic tomorrow," Alassa said. "I think the course is really meant as a primer for Martial Magic..."

Emily scowled, remembering Aloha's reaction to discovering that Emily had been put into Marital Magic. Aloha had worked *very* hard to enter the class during her Second Year, but Emily had just jumped ahead, pushed by Void and the Grandmaster. She'd threatened Emily with a fate worse than death if Emily let her down, although she'd calmed down after Emily had beaten Shadye. Emily couldn't have done much more to prove herself.

"My father won't let me take Martial Magic," Alassa supplied, a moment later. "Too much chance of serious injury—or death."

"True," Emily agreed. She'd been injured more than once during Martial Magic, where a mistake could have ghastly consequences. "But if you do well on Defensive Magic, you might be able to get him to change his mind."

"Maybe," Alassa said, doubtfully. She looked down at the timetable for a long, thoughtful moment. "Law is something I probably need, sadly. I studied the law in Zangaria, but not the law elsewhere in the Allied Lands. And things are changing quite rapidly, thanks to you."

Emily flushed. Many of her changes had already started having unintended consequences.

"Animal bonding might be fun, but father probably wouldn't let me put it into practice," Alassa continued. "Imaiqah was talking about Artwork; she thinks she might enjoy it. Construction and Warding are definitely worth taking—I think they're actually taught by the same teacher. And then there's more formal etiquette lessons. You probably need them."

"Not if I can get out of it," Emily said, quickly.

Alassa gave her a droll smile. "You're a baroness," she said, dryly. "Every time you pick up the wrong fork, you are diminished in the eyes of everyone watching you. Make enough mistakes and people will think that you are going soft and start plotting against you."

"I think I preferred it when you taught me," she admitted. Most of the etiquette she'd been taught made no sense, but Alassa had managed to hammer it into her head somehow. "You were patient."

"That's true," Alassa agreed. She looked oddly pensive, recalling her childhood. "My mother was patient too."

Emily poured herself another cup of kava and then settled back in her chair. "Are you going to be coming to Healing?"

"I think it might be useful to know the basics," Alassa said. "Father might have other ideas for my future classes, of course. He wouldn't want his daughter to be a healer, bound by Healer's Oaths. At least he knows and respects Lady Barb. I hear she was a very strict teacher. Imaiqah would probably want to go too."

"I should go to the library later," Emily said, thoughtfully. She'd missed Whitehall's vast library almost as much as she'd missed everything else. "It's been too long..."

"There won't have been time to mess up the books," Alassa assured her. "Why don't we go for a swim instead? There won't be anyone in the lake at this hour."

Emily laughed. "You do remember that it's snowing out there?"

"Heating charms," Alassa said. "I checked it out last year. During wintertime, the lake is warmed by magic. We will probably need additional spells on us too, just in case, but we should be fine."

"Or we could go for a snowball fight," Emily suggested. She'd never actually had one in her life, ever. Proper snowball fights required friends. "Or see what magic can do to snowballs."

"Turn them into walking, talking snowmen," Alassa hazarded. She looked contemplative for a moment, then shook her head. "But swimming would be preferable. It's good exercise and it would be *warm*."

Emily sighed and gave up. "All right," she said, "but I don't think we should be late for Lady Barb's class. I think she would be very strict indeed."

Chapter Five

"THERE'S NO ONE HERE," ALASSA SAID, AS THEY ENTERED LADY BARB'S CLASSROOM. "I told you that we were leaving too soon."

Emily shrugged. She'd enjoyed the swim, even though the lake had been surrounded by snow and flakes had dropped into the water from high overhead, but she didn't want to be late for her first class. They'd had to climb out of the water, use charms to dry themselves and then dress rapidly—and, somehow, the charms never left her feeling completely dry. Her robes were still threatening to cling to her body.

The classroom was massive, easily large enough to hold fifty students at once. There was a single large metal table in the center of the room, surrounded by desks and chairs. The walls were covered in parchment drawings of human anatomy, including a surprisingly detailed chart of the human skeleton. Others were explicit enough to make Emily blush and look away. High overhead, powerful light globes orbited, casting brilliant white light down on the table below. Emily realized, as she found a desk and sat down, that the room was spelled to allow them all to see what was being done at the center.

This is partly a practical class, she recalled, and shivered.

The classroom slowly filled up as the other students filed in. Emily smiled at Imaiqah as she entered, carrying a large roll of parchment under one arm. Several other students were carrying their own parchment; Imaiqah explained, when Emily asked, that she'd been in Artwork and the parchment was her very first drawing. When she unfurled it, Emily saw a sketch of Imaiqah's mother and father. She felt a flicker of envy as she realized that Imaiqah had a genuine talent for Artwork.

"There was plenty of your paper there," Imaiqah muttered. "We spent almost the whole class drawing. This"—she tapped the parchment—"was my final piece of work for the day."

"It's very good," Emily said, sincerely. "You should stick with it."

"I'm certainly going to try," Imaiqah said. "But father wasn't sure what use it might be in the future."

Emily and Alassa exchanged glances. If Imaiqah hadn't been ennobled, a talent for drawing and painting might have taken her far, particularly once they started infusing magic into their artwork. But it would be a lower-status occupation for her now, even if her father hadn't wanted her to remain involved with the family's growing business. He was planning to sell steam engines to the world once they had improved on the design.

"It might give you some personal fame," Emily pointed out, finally. Imaiqah's father could start the ball rolling by promoting his daughter's work, just like artists had had noble patrons before the internet and art journals. "Or..."

She was interrupted by a loud bang as Lady Barb strode into the room, closing the door firmly behind her. Emily watched Lady Barb march up to the desk and turn to face the class, her face set in a grim expression that reminded Emily of Sergeant Harkin. Lady Barb had donned a white jacket and pair of trousers that set off her blonde hair nicely, but utterly failed to conceal that she was a very dangerous person. And she looked thoroughly unhappy.

"It is now five chimes past the bell," Lady Barb said. Her voice was very cold, very composed. "In future, the door will be locked at the precise moment that class is due to start. Should any of you be *late* and find yourself unable to gain entry, you can save me some time by reporting directly to the Warden. And you will also be marked as absent from the class, which may lead to your eventual removal if you make a habit of it."

Emily winced. She wasn't the only one. *That* didn't sound fair. What if the student had a very good excuse?

Lady Barb's gaze swept the room. "This is a very important class that requires absolute concentration and dedication," she continued. "Many of you will not have the talent or dedication to become a healer. This lesson will assist you in discovering if you *do* have a talent for it—and to save you from spending the rest of the year here, should you not have a talent. As you should have been informed, you may leave within a month without repercussions."

She smiled, but it didn't quite touch her eyes. "How many of you have used standard healing spells?"

Emily put up her hand, joined by almost all of the class.

"Very good," Lady Barb said. For a moment, her gaze rested on Emily, then moved on to the next student. "Do you also understand their *limitations*?"

There was a long pause.

"Clearly not," Lady Barb said. She clasped her hands behind her back, as if she were at parade rest, and carried on. "The standard healing spells are understandably crude, as they are designed for people who may not know what they are doing. Repairing a broken bone sounds like a laudable goal—and it is—but the standard spells can cause additional damage to the person undergoing treatment. *That* is why you are all told to ensure you see a qualified healer as soon as possible.

"More complex work requires more than a standard spell," she continued. "Repairing a person's eyes, for example, is beyond any pre-designed spell. Purging poison from a person's bloodstream can go horrifically wrong unless the magician is directly involved with the process from start to finish. Learning to direct the magic that is necessary for carrying out more complex healing sessions is an important part of this course. Those of you who do not have the talent for it will be removed very quickly.

"Completing the first year of Healing will give you the ability to treat a wide range of injuries and diseases, as well as a firm grounding in medical magic. You will not, however, be bound by Healer Oaths, nor will you be considered qualified healers. Should you have the talent and inclination to go onwards, you will have to take the oath, even if you don't wind up serving as a healer. Those oaths are magically-binding and they *will* bite if you end up abusing your position."

She paused, looking around the classroom. "Do any of you want to leave now?"

No one moved.

"Good," Lady Barb said. "I will now give you a brief overview of what we will be looking at over the year.

"First, we will be looking at more complex healing spells. You will learn how to manipulate the spells in response to feedback from the injury and how to compensate for unexpected responses. This is not an easy skill to master, but once you have mastered it you will be able to perform proper healing magic, *without* having to worry about finding a qualified healer afterwards. Those of you intending to become combat sorcerers or court wizards will find it a very useful skill indeed."

She moved, pacing around the room. No one said a word until she started to talk again.

"Second, we will be looking at curse-breaking and other counters to magically-inflicted injuries. You will know, of course, just how easy it is to get injured while practicing magic—or how easily a mundane can be cursed by a magician. Healing such damage is an important part of your training. Again, it will be a very useful skill, once mastered.

"Thirdly, we will be looking at mundane healing methods," she concluded. "As you may well expect, healing magic can be very draining. Mundane methods, healing without magic, may be nowhere near as convenient, but they may be all you have to use when you've drained your magic completely. Those of you who faint at the sight of blood are not advised to stay in this class, because there *will* be blood. And guts. And gore. Ideally, you will never have to actually *use* these skills, but they are an important part of becoming a healer."

She paused. "Are there any questions?"

Emily hesitated. Something was missing, but it had taken her several seconds to realize *what*. Lady Barb had said nothing about any form of mental care or psychiatric treatment. Physical injuries were one thing; mental injuries were quite another. A knock on the head, she knew, could have effects that standard healing spells couldn't cure. Indeed, they'd been told to avoid using the standard spells on skull injuries. It would be far too easy to accidentally disrupt someone's mind.

But it was something she was going to have to ask later. She wanted to stay behind in any case.

"We've already looked at curse-breaking," one of the other students said. She was one of the transfer students, Emily guessed, if only because she didn't even vaguely recognize the girl. "Why are we going to look at it again?"

"Curses that attach themselves to the human body can have very nasty long-term effects," Lady Barb said, simply. "There is, for example, a cutting spell that is completely impossible to cure using the standard healing spells. The designer of the spell actually wanted to ensure that the damage would get worse if the standard spells were used—and he succeeded, far too well. People have died because well-meaning magicians tried to use the standard spells to save their lives.

"In such cases, the curse must be removed *before* any form of healing can take place," she added. "Failing to remove the curse would, at the very least, make healing impossible.

"There's also the danger of the curse migrating from the victim to anyone else in the area, including the healer. Better to get rid of it as quickly as possible."

She gave the girl a droll smile. "Does that answer your question?"

"...Yes," the girl said.

Lady Barb clicked her fingers over the metal desk and a humanoid figure appeared. Emily stared, wondering how she'd managed to make the teleport spell work within Whitehall—and then realized that the figure had always been there, just hidden under an invisibility spell. No wonder she hadn't seen him when she came into the room.

"This is Paddy," Lady Barb said. "As you may have deduced, he is a homunculus, a copy of the human body. Paddy was created by a team of the most capable and dedicated healers in the Allied Lands to allow youngsters such as yourself a chance to practice without actually killing anyone. His responses to your spells will be identical to an actual human. Should you injure Paddy too badly, however, he will simply switch into regeneration mode and start rebuilding himself. So far, no students have ever actually managed to *destroy* him."

There were a handful of nervous chuckles.

Emily studied the homunculus carefully. He had skin tinted a very odd shade of brown, no hair and wore nothing, not even a piece of underwear. She couldn't tell if he was anatomically correct or not from her angle, but she had the feeling that the designers would have reproduced as much as they could. He would have been far less useful if he wasn't as close to humanity as possible.

"Later on, you will be practicing certain spells on each other—as well as volunteers from the other classes," Lady Barb continued. "However, for the moment, we will stick with Paddy, as you will be unable to cause permanent harm to him."

She paused, her gaze moving from person to person. "I will be operating under the assumption that Paddy is a *real* human being," she added. "If I think you're cutting into him for the hell of it, or if you're being careless because you think he isn't important, you *will* regret it. A sadistic attitude to Paddy may lead to a sadistic attitude to one's patients and that leads to a dangerously unstable healer. Or worse. I will not hesitate to kick you out of the class if I feel that you will prove a danger to others or...yourself.

"Healers have the most important job in the Allied Lands. It is vitally important that we do nothing to tarnish their good name. A healer who abuses his or her powers will be hunted down and executed, if they are not killed by breaking their oaths. Healing is serious business. If you're here because you think the class will let you have a chance to look at naked bodies, think again.

"There are plenty of other courses you can take at Whitehall that you can actually turn into a career—or a vocation—if that is all you want. You do not need to feel that you are wasting your time here.

"I will tolerate nothing less than your *complete* concentration, dedication and focused study," she concluded. "We have a *lot* of ground to cover, all of which will be mentioned on your exams—and tested, extensively. Students have been known to break under the pressure of healer exams. I know I felt myself pushed right to the edge when I was a student."

Emily nodded in understanding. Her last set of exams had been nerve-wracking, even though Mistress Irene had hinted that the school might have given her a free pass, after she'd beaten Shadye. Somehow, it just hadn't seemed right to accept the offer. *And* she'd wanted to know just how well she was doing, compared to the other students.

Lady Barb looked down at Paddy, then back up at her students. "If you don't want to be here, you may leave now," she said. "Everyone else, stand up and gather around Paddy."

Emily watched in some amusement as a handful of students headed for the door and escaped out into the corridor, then she stood and walked to the main table. Up close, it was easy to see that Paddy was male; she blushed furiously when she saw his manhood between his legs. She wondered, absently, how they were going to practice working on a female body, then pushed the question to one side. It was something she could ask later.

"Feel free to touch his body," Lady Barb said. "You'll notice that it feels *human*."

She was right, Emily realized, as she touched Paddy's leg. It felt rougher than her own leg, but it was warm and very human. If his skin color hadn't been so unnatural, he could easily have passed for a human being. But then, creating homunculi that could pass for a specific human was banned by the Allied Lands. The thought of being replaced by a copy was probably one of the nightmares that kept King Randor up late at night. Would anyone realize if the King were no longer himself?

Presumably, she told herself, the homunculus would be unable to *act* like the King—but there might be spells to ensure that wasn't a problem. Or perhaps the entire court could be replaced, quickly and efficiently. Or perhaps the King's brain-waves could be copied and used as a template for the homunculus...

Lady Barb produced a small knife and jabbed it into Paddy's chest. The homunculus let out a cry of pain and everyone jumped.

"Human reactions," Lady Barb said, flatly. "You'll be expected to master spells that can cancel out pain, but there are some curses that counteract them—and situations where using them is dangerous to both parties involved. Paddy and I will be simulating such situations for you over the next few months and you will learn from them. By the time exams roll around, I expect you to have mastered the basics. If you haven't, there will be no point in going for the exams.

"There are other spells that you are also expected to master," she continued. "One spell cuts down on your own...emotional reactions, which can interfere with your work. Another prevents further infection, although there are dangers involved with casting the spell. A third is a very basic truth spell. You'll discover, if you go into healing, that quite a few people lie about what happened to them. This can be dangerous, particularly if knowing the cause of the injury is required to fix it."

Alassa stuck up a hand. "Can you give us an example of that, please?"

Lady Barb didn't look pleased at being interrupted, but she answered the question anyway.

"Quite a few curse wounds come from trying to break into a magician's property," Lady Barb explained. "In that case, speaking with the magician who created the spell can be quite useful—but the victim may not want to be publicly identified as a would-be thief. Other curses, including those used by angry husbands or wives, need the active cooperation of the caster to break. And then there are the diseases that are spread through sexual contact, where we need to heal everyone involved."

She smiled, rather dryly. "Healing is a dirty job, no matter the prestige that comes with it," she warned. "Those of you who wish to stay in this class can read *An Introduction to Healing*, which you will find in the medical library next door, over the rest of the week. You will find it a good introduction to what we are going to cover—and where it will lead. If you decide that you don't want to carry on after reading the book you may leave. No one will hold it against you."

Emily watched as Lady Barb cast a handful of healing spells on Paddy, all more complicated than the spells Emily had learned last year. Some of them seemed automatic, others required careful fiddling...rather like dismantling a set of charms, she realized. Maybe the two disciplines were closer than she'd thought.

"Formal classes will begin on Monday," Lady Barb concluded. "If you don't come back, I honestly don't mind." There were some chuckles from the students. "But if you do, I expect you to work."

Alassa tugged at Emily's arm as the students began to disperse. "You coming to dinner?"

"I need to talk to Lady Barb," Emily said, quickly. She should have mentioned it to Alassa earlier, but there hadn't been an opportunity. "I don't know how long I'll be."

"We'll see you at dinner then," Alassa said. She winked, mischievously. "I have teamwork to plan."

Emily rolled her eyes. Alassa's new obsession might be fun for her, and those who enjoyed team sports, but not for anyone else. But then, Emily had never actually played...

"Good luck," Alassa said. "See you at dinner."

Chapter Six

"Emily," Lady Barb said, when they were alone. "What can I do for you?"

Emily hesitated. Lady Barb...was a complex person, someone who had seemed to dislike her at first, but had also helped her to overcome some of her demons. Her lessons in combat, both magical and physical, had been painful, yet they had also been very welcome. And she'd never known Lady Barb to be less than completely honest with her. No one else, even the Grandmaster and Void, had been so honest.

And there was her resemblance to Sergeant Harkin...

"I need to ask you a favor," Emily said. She wasn't sure *what* to say. "And I need some advice."

Lady Barb quirked an eyebrow, then nodded and strode over to a desk in the far corner of the room. It must have had some aversion spells on it, Emily realized as she followed her tutor, because she hadn't realized it was there until Lady Barb had drawn her attention to it. There were two chairs, one on either side, both covered with books. Lady Barb motioned for her to take one of the chairs and started to transfer the books on the other to the table. Emily hesitated, then did the same for her chair.

"Be careful with that book," Lady Barb advised, as Emily reached for the final book. "You cannot open it until you have spoken the Healer's Oath."

Emily nodded, feeling her fingertips skittering over the cover. "Why not?"

"There are spells that...that can create obligations between those involved," Lady Barb said, shortly. "One of the aspects of the Healer's Oath is to put aside all obligations that might otherwise be assumed. Those who refuse to take the oath are not supposed to know how to cast the spells."

Her expression darkened. "Which may not have stopped them from leaking out," she added. "But it's difficult to know for sure."

She sat down on the chair and rested her elbows on the desk. "So," she said. "What sort of favor can I offer you?"

"I need an advisor," Emily said. She knew that bluntness would get her further with Lady Barb than being coy. "And I need some advice."

Lady Barb studied her for a long moment. "Do you understand the obligations and rights of an Advisor?"

"I think so," Emily said, carefully.

"You could come to me at any time, if you needed advice," Lady Barb said, flatly. "I wouldn't be able to share whatever you told me with anyone else, unless I believed that you posed a clear threat to others. But you would also have to *listen* to my advice on any subject...given your rather curious legal position, you might be better off without an advisor."

Emily considered it. Unlike Alassa and the other aristocrats in the school, she had complete control over her own wealth, rather than drawing a stipend from her parents. In absolute terms, Alassa was far richer than Emily, but she couldn't control all of that wealth. And there were limits to what she could do, limits that Emily simply didn't have. If she wanted to spend her entire fortune on ponies, there was no one to say no.

"I was under the impression that it was a requirement," she said, finally. "Is that actually true?"

"It depends," Lady Barb said, slowly. "There are some students who come to Whitehall when they're much older, even though they would probably learn more from private study or an apprenticeship. *They* don't really form the same relationships with their advisors. There are certainly no legal obligations there."

She shrugged. "I'd have to check with the Grandmaster," she added. "But I would certainly be willing to give you *advice*."

Emily nodded. "I have a lot to talk about," she admitted. "Do you know Jade?"

"I believe you might have mentioned him once or twice," Lady Barb said. They'd talked quite a bit while they'd been sparring in Zangaria. "What's wrong with him?"

"He hasn't sent a letter for months," Emily confessed. It was bothering her and she wasn't even sure why. "I don't know what to make of it."

Lady Barb stroked her chin, contemplatively. "Do you like him?"

"I don't know," Emily said, feeling the old frustration welling up inside of her. She did like Jade as a friend; it had honestly never occurred to her that a man five years older than her would ask her out, let alone propose to her. "I just don't know."

"You *have* become a baroness," Lady Barb pointed out. "Your social station is much higher than his now, isn't it?"

Emily flushed. "He isn't mailing me because he thinks I'm too grand for him?"

"It is a common problem, although you do seem to do things to the extreme," Lady Barb said, lightly. "Right now, it would be seen as presumptuous of him to court you, no matter how he—or you—felt. If he becomes a qualified sorcerer, he may be able to pick up matters again..."

"Oh," Emily said. "Men are impossible to understand."

She snorted at the age-old complaint. "Am I allowed to swear off marriage forever?"

Lady Barb snorted too. "You're a baroness," she said. "Having children to carry on the family line is one of your obligations now. And you would *have* to marry before you could get pregnant."

Emily shook her head in tired disbelief. If King Randor hadn't sprung it on her as a surprise...she might well have turned it down. But he'd timed it perfectly and now she was trapped in a gilded cage, a prison that was no less a prison just because most of the bars were invisible. And anyone who'd been *born* in Zangaria would be *delighted* to uphold the obligations, if they became a baroness in exchange.

"If you want my advice," Lady Barb said, "write to him. Maybe you can build up a friendship again. But he may not be able to reply immediately in any case."

"True," Emily agreed. "Can we talk about something else?"

"You *did* start it," Lady Barb pointed out. "What else can we talk about?"

Emily considered, briefly, asking about Master Tor, before deciding that was her problem to solve. Instead, she reached into her pocket and found a handful of notes she'd scribbled down during her return to Alexis.

"Void gave me an old spellbook," she said, as she smoothed out the sheets of paper. "And I was slowly deciphering parts of the book. I came across some old spells I was planning to try out."

"I hope you deciphered everything," Lady Barb said smoothly, although there was an undercurrent of concern in her voice. "Some of the older sorcerers had a nasty habit of deliberately mixing up the details, just to annoy their successors."

Emily nodded, ruefully. One large passage in the book, when she'd finally managed to decipher it, had turned out to be a recipe for beef soup. As far as she had been able to tell, there was nothing particularly magical about it at all. A second passage read like an extract from a badly-written pornographic novel. But she was slowly making progress on deciphering the rest of it.

"I think so," she said. "One of them involves bilocation, being in two places at once."

"That's an old spell," Lady Barb said. "Most sorcerers won't risk using it, though. If they happened to move too far apart, they wouldn't be able to reintegrate themselves and they would become two separate entities. Or they might fade away. I'd advise you not to try it. Even if you succeeded in using it, it could cause permanent damage to your mind."

"Oh," Emily said, a little deflated. She'd hoped, despite herself, that the book's secrets would be unique. "I meant to ask. Why doesn't healing include dealing with damage to a person's mind?"

Lady Barb gave her a sharp look, as if she had expected her to be able to figure it out for herself. "Mental instability is associated, in general, with a particular kind of magician," she said, sardonically. "I believe you killed one of them, once."

"Necromancers," Emily said, flatly. "But surely not everyone who has a mental problem becomes a necromancer...?"

"Any sort of mental problem carries a huge stigma," Lady Barb explained. Her tone suggested it should have been obvious. "If someone in the family was insane, the entire family would be held accountable for his actions—even if magic wasn't involved. When it is...well, suffice it to say that smart magicians, no matter how unstable, go out of their way to appear stable. Those that aren't are often treated as pariahs by everyone else."

"So there's no attempt to cure them," Emily said, flatly. "And they're allowed to sink further into madness."

"Trying to work with an unstable magician is very dangerous," Lady Barb said. She looked up into Emily's eyes. "Something you ought to bear in mind."

Emily cleared her throat, carefully. "I will," she said. "Another spell was teleportation. I was hoping that you could help me to learn how to teleport."

"You don't have the power reserves to manage it yet," Lady Barb said. "You really shouldn't be experimenting with teleporting at all until you reach sixth year."

Emily blinked. "Why not?"

"Because you don't have the power," Lady Barb repeated, patiently. "It takes years of training and experience to build up the reserves necessary to teleport—even then you'll be completely drained when you materialize at your destination. Casting the spell isn't all that is required; you need power and discipline to keep your destination in mind at all times. A teleport spell that goes badly wrong could easily kill you outright."

"Or plunge you into the middle of a mountain," Emily muttered, and shivered.

"Precisely," Lady Barb agreed. "You need to spend more time flexing your muscles and building up your power reserves before you start teleporting. And even the most capable magicians have never managed to do more than two or three hops in quick succession. Those who tried to go further often drained themselves completely."

Emily considered it, carefully. It sounded as though a magical battery was required, but there was no such thing, not really. Sure, wards could be anchored in metal or stone—and human flesh—but they didn't hold power indefinitely. And stealing someone else's power through necromancy meant insanity. She hadn't seen Shadye teleport—the only sorcerer she had seen teleport was Void—but the price was too high to risk it.

Why *couldn't* raw magical power be stored? What happened to it when someone tried?

It fades away into the background, she recalled. It had seemed such an obvious solution, too obvious not to have been tried in the past. But building up a reserve of raw power seemed impossible...as long as the power had somewhere to go. A thought struck her and she opened her mouth, then closed it again as she decided to do some research. She wanted to prove that it worked first, before sharing it with anyone else.

"There was a third spell," Emily said, changing the subject. "But none of the descriptions made sense. The only thing I was clear on was the *name.* What is a Pentagram Spell?"

Lady Barb's eyes went very hard. "I would like to take a look at that book," she said. "Would that be possible?"

Emily hesitated. Part of her suspected that Lady Barb could be helpful, part of her felt that showing it to anyone else would be a really bad idea. And besides, it would ruin the fun of cracking the code for herself. Now that she *had* started to unravel it, she didn't want to pass it on to someone else, at least until she had copied down all of the interesting spells.

"I would prefer not to show it to anyone," she said, finally. "I'm sorry..."

"I see," Lady Barb said. There was a long, uncomfortable pause. "A Pentagram Spell - *the* Pentagram Spell—is a spell used to deal with rogue magicians. It effectively destroys their magic completely, leaving them powerless. If a sorcerer was convicted of magical misdeeds, the spell could be used to punish them—and prevent them from posing a danger to anyone else."

Emily shuddered, then asked the obvious question. "Why wasn't it used on Shadye?"

Lady Barb snorted. "Because it takes five sorcerers to cast the spell and the victim has to be tied down," she said, dryly. "And because getting five sorcerers to cooperate is about as easy as herding cats, with the added disadvantage that they might turn you into a small hopping thing if you annoyed them."

Her eyes narrowed. "I would strongly advise you never to suggest to *anyone* that you read the instructions for the spell," she added. "It *will* be held against you."

"Thank you," Emily said. She could understand why the other students would be horrified. Not all of them were aristocrats; it was magic and magic alone that had brought them to Whitehall. "Do you have any other words of advice?"

"Be careful," Lady Barb said, simply. If she was offended at Emily's tone, she didn't show it. "And if you need advice, my door is always open."

Her lips quirked. "Although if you waste my time," she added, "you *will* regret it."

"I understand," Emily assured her.

"Do you?" Lady Barb said. She looked down at the desk for a long moment. "Do you know what dark magic really is?"

"Evil magic," Emily said.

"Define *evil*," Lady Barb countered. "Almost all of the spells at this school can be turned to evil purposes, given a little imagination. Don't you know that by now?"

"Yes," Emily said. Just because a spell was intended to counteract gravity and make it easier to move heavy boxes from one room to another didn't mean that it couldn't be used for pranks. "I know what you mean."

"Dark magic is never an easy subject to define," Lady Barb allowed. "The simplest definition is magic used with bad intentions. The problem is that people rarely wake up one morning and decide that they're going to become evil. Instead, they inch towards the darkness step by step, justifying their actions until they reach a point where they no longer even feel the *need* to justify themselves. There are certain spells that are darker than others, true, but even the simplest of spells can cause real trouble if used with dark intentions."

She stood. "Power brings its own temptations," she added. "Watch yourself."

"I will," Emily assured her. "And thank you."

"Thank me by being a diligent student," Lady Barb said. "My last experiment with teaching was not a great success."

Emily nodded and left the classroom, walking back towards the dining hall while mulling over what Lady Barb had told her. Casting the teleport spell wasn't the problem; the problem was summoning and directing enough power to make it work. It required intensive mental discipline, she realized, which might be why the necromancers didn't simply teleport over the mountains and into the Allied Lands. They lacked the discipline to make it work.

But they store vast amounts of power in their wards, she mused. *I wonder what might happen if...*

She tensed as she spied Melissa at the other end of the corridor, but the young sorceress merely scowled at her before stepping into the dining hall. *That* was a pleasant change, although Emily didn't expect it to remain that way for long. Melissa and her coven had jinxed and hexed Emily, Alassa and Imaiqah over the last year and no doubt they'd do it again *this* year. Some of their pranks, if taken too far, might have been truly dangerous.

Which might have been what Lady Barb was talking about, Emily thought, as she stepped into the dining hall herself. It was crammed with students, all trying to eat and talk at the same time. Alassa and Imaiqah sat at one end of a table, joined by two dark-skinned girls Emily didn't recognize. They were probably Alassa's roommates. The thought made her glance around for the Gorgon and Lin, but she didn't see either of them.

"We're just sorting out the team," Alassa explained, as Emily picked up a plate of food and sat down next to them. "We actually have more volunteers than I expected, so we'll be trying out tomorrow night—I wanted tonight, but the older teams have priority at the arena."

"And more practice at cheating," one of the two dark-skinned girls said. She held out a hand to Emily. "I'm Sam, by the way, and this is Song."

Emily shook her hand, then Song's. Up close, the girls seemed to come from different ethnic groups, even though they both had dark skin. Sam seemed African, while Song appeared to have some Chinese blood in her. But then, racism against humans didn't seem to be part of Whitehall's world. There were too many non-humans around to make racism against humans very practical. It struck her, suddenly, that the Gorgon must have had a very hard time of it.

"Pleased to meet you," she said, seriously. "Are you *Ken*-mad too?"

"Of course," Song said. "Who wouldn't be?"

Emily hesitated, noticeably

"You can try out, and then say you tried," Alassa told her, quickly. "Besides, you might enjoy it."

Emily took a bite of her food, controlling her reaction. If Alassa became a completely sports mad fanatic...

She'll still be your friend, she told herself, firmly. *Besides, learning how to run a Ken team will probably be good training for being queen.*

They finished their lunch, then checked their timetables. "I don't know anything about Professor Eleas," Song said. "Is he one of the tougher teachers?"

Emily shrugged. She hadn't heard of him either.

"Better not be late," Alassa said. "The notes on the timetable say that we need to be there on time or we need not bother coming at all."

"Sounds tough," Song agreed. She pushed her plate aside and stood. "Let's go."

Chapter Seven

PROFESSOR ELEAS WADDLED INTO THE CLASSROOM FIVE MINUTES AFTER THE LESSON WAS supposed to begin—and, like Lady Barb, closed the door firmly behind him before marching up to the front of the room. Emily found herself staring at him as he turned to face them; unlike most of the other tutors, he wore nothing more than a simple loincloth, exposing his chest...which was covered in blue tattoos that seemed to have been carved into his skin. In fact, she couldn't see a single part of his body that *wasn't* covered in tattoos. Even his bald head seemed to have runes carved into its flesh.

He was short, his head barely coming up to Emily's shoulder, with a potbelly and bright, twinkling eyes. Emily found herself liking him on sight, even though she suspected that, like Sergeant Miles, his affable exterior was intended to hide great power. His gaze swept across the room and, if anything, his eyes grew brighter with suppressed amusement. Emily honestly couldn't see what he found so amusing.

"Good afternoon," Professor Eleas said, calmly. "Before we start, I have a simple question for you. Why do you have your hands on your heads?"

Emily jumped as she realized, to her horror, that her hands *were* resting on her head. The entire class was the same...and no one had noticed. When had it even happened? She pulled her hands down and stared at them, then looked up at the teacher. She'd experienced compulsion spells before, but nothing so...subtle. There hadn't even been a *hint* that something had been wrong.

"Try looking under your chairs," Professor Eleas said, dryly.

Emily, along with the rest of the class, stood and picked up the chair, looking underneath. Carved into the wood were three runes, barely visible to the naked eye. The last vestigial traces of magic surrounding them were flickering and fading away, leaving the runes—she hoped—harmless. She turned the chair back over and sat down, carefully. This time, she felt the subtle magic pushing at her mind. If she hadn't been watching for it, she would never have realized that it was there.

"Believe it or not," the professor said, "that was not a particularly *subtle* magic."

He cleared his throat as the remaining students returned to their chairs. Now that they knew about the runes, it was easier to resist their compulsion, although Emily saw a number of hands twitching, as if they were about to go up again before the student caught the motion and held them down. The whole trick was thoroughly nasty.

"There were three runes involved," Professor Eleas explained. "The first one was a basic command, the second two pushed you into missing the effects of the first command—and the odd behavior of your fellow classmates. However, the runes would not have lasted for very long, once you activated them when you sat down. Nor, for that matter, would they have been effective if you had been watching for them. Even something as simple as knowing that they are there can negate their effects."

Emily scowled. She hadn't thought to check under the seat before she sat down, nor had anyone else. The whole notion of being manipulated so easily was terrifying, which was probably why the professor had introduced them to it so bluntly. They had to learn to take it seriously.

The professor smiled at their expressions. "How many of you," he asked, "have used a transfiguration spell?"

Emily hesitated, then raised her hand. So did almost everyone else.

"The important detail about such spells is that they demand that you be as precise as possible," the professor said. "You cannot cast a spell intended to cause random transfiguration. Instead, you have to determine just *what* you intend to turn someone into, along with the other factors. Failing to be precise may prevent the spell from working—or it might produce unexpected effects.

"Subtle magic, however, works *better* when it is imprecise. The runes I used to demonstrate such power to you are about as blatant as the magic becomes—ever. Indeed, the mere nature of the compulsion meant that there was a possibility that some of you *would* notice it and, in doing so, allow others to realize that they too were being controlled. A more subtle rune might go completely unnoticed. For example, you might not be assured of success if you tried to use the runes to give someone a broken leg, but you would be almost certain to succeed if you merely aimed at an injury.

"There are other dangers. A standard compulsion spell leaves the victim in little doubt of what has actually happened to him, while the less powerful spells can be unreliable. Subtle magic, on the other hand, can push someone into doing something—and encourage them to invent their own justification for their actions. It is a great deal harder to realize that one is being influenced through subtle magic, particularly when one has almost no experience with magic at all.

"Most importantly of all, a transfiguration spell requires power and discipline to cast it," he concluded. "All a subtle magic rune requires is a low level of ambient magic in the vicinity. What, do you think, are the implications of this?"

There was a long pause. It was finally broken by Imaiqah.

"Ah...*anyone* can use the magic runes," she said.

"Correct," Professor Eleas said. "There is no reason why a mundane couldn't learn to draw the runes himself in an attempt to cast magic. It might work—or it might not. It can be incredibly difficult to determine if such attempts have actually worked or if the 'success' is really nothing more than a coincidence. Those of you intending to go on to a career in law enforcement will need to bear that in mind."

Emily held up her hand. "What happens if the runes are drawn poorly?"

"It depends on how they are drawn," Professor Eleas said. "We will be covering that later, but they can simply fizzle out—or do nothing at all, or produce unexpected effects."

He paused and gazed around the classroom. "In this class, you will learn the basic runes and how to read and use them," he said. "Should you stick with the class until fourth year, you will master the complete runic alphabet; if I haven't scared you away by then, you will learn how to craft your own runes in fifth and sixth year." His smile grew wider. "There are plenty of people who will argue that subtle magic and runes are not really magic, but such people are short-sighted. Used properly, subtle magic can be devastating."

Emily listened with interest as he outlined a number of cases he had handled before coming to Whitehall to teach. There had been an elderly woman who had used subtle magic against her neighbours, several cases of secret admirers trying to make the objects of their affections fall in love with them and one case of a powerful lord being cursed by one of his subjects. Emily found it hard to blame the subject; the lord had taken the man's sister into his castle and used her as a concubine, then discarded the girl when he had tired of her. The lord had been withering away by the time someone found the runes and destroyed them.

"Destroying the runes can cancel out the long-term effects of the magic," Professor Eleas explained, when Sam asked. "However, the effects that had already taken root proved immensely hard to destroy. They had blended with the person's mind."

Alassa had a different question. "Is it possible to protect yourself against such magic?"

Emily frowned. From what she recalled of the Royal Bloodline, it stood to reason that such protections would already be part of Alassa's package. But the runes had clearly affected her too...unless the professor had somehow keyed them to overcome the Bloodline. Maybe they were just powerful enough to do that. Sooner or later, wouldn't she have wanted to use her hands?

"We will be covering that in later classes," the professor promised. "However, there are several steps that need to be covered first."

He picked up a set of tablets from his desk and held them up in front of the class. "The precise design of the rune is merely one aspect of the whole," he informed them. "You have to be careful in choosing precisely what material you use to harbor the rune, as different materials produce different effects. A rune scratched out in the earth might work very quickly, but it also wouldn't last very long. In contrast, a rune carved into metal can take weeks or months to take effect, yet those effects can last indefinitely."

Building up a charge, Emily guessed, thoughtfully. Outside Whitehall and the other nexus points, the level of overall magic in the air wasn't very high. *And the easier it is to destroy the rune, the lesser the effect.*

"You will have noticed runes carved into the stone of Whitehall, helping to channel the power of the nexus point," Professor Eleas said. "Those runes have to be very carefully placed, as a single mistake can render the whole process worse than useless. Once built up, the network needs to be left intact. Removing a single rune could cause the whole network to fall apart.

"Furthermore, you can carve runes into your own flesh," he added, one finger touching the tattoos on his chest. "Doing this is immensely dangerous; you have to carve the important runes out yourself, rather than allow someone else to do it for you. And you have to do it without painkilling potions or anything else that might interfere with your concentration. A single mistake would be disastrous."

Emily shuddered. It had been hard enough removing a splinter with a pair of tweezers; she honestly couldn't imagine carving runes into her own flesh and watching the blood dripping to the ground. And if she couldn't use an anaesthetic...she couldn't imagine managing to keep the rune so perfectly precise. How had the professor managed to carve so many runes into his own flesh?

She frowned as the professor turned slightly. How had he managed to carve them into his *back*?

"You are *not* to experiment with carving runes into your own flesh," the professor informed them. "If you are caught trying, you will be expelled for gross stupidity. But if you're *not* caught, you may wind up wishing that you *had* been caught and expelled. The consequences of making a mistake can be shattering."

He launched into another series of cautionary tales. Emily shivered as she listened to the story of the man who had accidentally ensured that he would never fall in love, the woman who had blinded herself, the children who had killed their own parents through drawing out runes in their house...the list went on and on. She honestly couldn't understand why *anyone* would experiment with such power. But if they had nothing else, why not?

"I have a question," Melissa said, suddenly. "How did you manage to carve the runes into your back?"

"I had a friend to assist me," Professor Eleas said.

Emily blinked. "But you said..."

"The *important* runes are the ones that have to be carved out personally," the professor explained, patiently. He twisted around, showing them the carved runes on his back. "You will study these in greater detail later, but the ones on my back channel power, rather than collect it. I had to make the decision to carve *this* rune"—he tapped a rune just above his heart—"myself, then do it."

Emily felt her blood run cold. Shadye had told her to stab Sergeant Harkin there with a necromantic knife, trying to pull his magic out of his body and into her wards. It would have killed her, or driven her insane, if the Sergeant had *possessed* magic. Instead, the absence of any power had rocked Shadye back enough for her to break free. Was there any significance in the rune's location? Had Professor Eleas performed a necromantic rite when he'd finished carving runes into his own flesh?

But there was nothing particularly *difficult* about the rite, Emily knew. As long as the magician was prepared to go insane, it was fairly simple to perform. But what did it mean if someone was trying to draw on their own power? Was that really nothing more than what she and every other magician did?

Imaiqah poked her. "Emily? Are you all right?"

Emily nodded, hastily.

Professor Eleas seemed not to notice. "For self-carving to work, you have to make the decision, in full awareness of the possible consequences, to actually proceed with the carving," he explained. "Should someone try to carve a rune into your flesh without your permission—let alone with your participation—it is unlikely to last very long. Bodies tend to resent cuts and bruises at the best of times, so once the rune heals its effects start to fade away. Naturally, some aspects may linger for a long time, but they can be overcome."

Emily silently considered what *else* could be done with runes. If they served to direct magic, even to reshape it, what could she do with them? Store and redirect magic? But if channelling vast amounts of magic was that simple, the necromancers would never have to channel the magic through their own minds, driving themselves insane in the process. She'd read enough history books about people who thought they could play with necromancy without going insane to know that hundreds of ideas had been tried. They had all ended in disaster.

"You will be pleased to know that there are limits to runes and the subtle magic they can work," Professor Eleas said. "The runes on your chairs, for example, were designed to affect the person who sat down—they were not targeted on any of you specifically. Placing the rune, therefore, is a serious problem. If you craft a rune intended to help one of your friends, you have to make sure that the rune doesn't affect someone else. Indeed, the more people who can be touched by the rune, the less effective it will be. We shall discuss other ways to target the runes and subtle magic later on in the year."

Blood, Emily thought, remembering Shadye. Blood was the easiest way to influence or control a person—or even to find someone, if they were hidden away. They could never be completely severed from their blood, at least not without performing the charms to do so right away.

"In addition, we will be covering ways of *finding* runes," he added. "As you can imagine, if someone suffers a run of bad luck, it might be possible that their enemies have crafted a rune and hidden it nearby. However, given the right spells, the rune can be tracked down and destroyed. We shall be working on that and other protections throughout the year because they are vitally important skills. Failure to master them will leave you exposed to hostile rune-crafters.

"There are books in the library you will need to read," the professor concluded. "I have written out a full reading list, which you can pick up from that desk over by the door. If you decide you wish to continue with this class, you should make an attempt to have the basic texts read by the end of the week and the remainder by the end of the month. I would also advise you to invest in a dictionary of runes. This new-fangled printing press makes copying such books so much easier."

Alassa tossed Emily a mischievous look, then winked. "I bet he wrote the textbook," she muttered, deadpan.

"Stay behind after class, Lady Alassa," Professor Eleas said, crossly.

Emily stood up with the rest of the class, then headed outside to wait for Alassa. Sam and Song said goodbye and headed off to the library, carrying their reading lists with them.

"It looks longer than I thought," Imaiqah said, as she skimmed the reading list. "When are we going to have time to do *anything*?"

"Good question," Emily agreed. Lady Barb's reading list would already take up too much of her free time...and she was sure that the other tutors would have their own reading lists. If there were other books being produced on the printing presses she'd inspired, they might even be expected to *buy* new copies. "I don't know."

Alassa emerged before Imaiqah could say anything. "He *did* write the dictionary," she said, as they fled down the corridor. "But he says it's a very good one."

Emily started to laugh. "We can go to the library now and have a look, then get an early night's sleep," she said. "Tomorrow..."

"Defensive magic," Alassa said, rubbing her hands together. "That should be fun."

"Martial magic," Emily said. Thankfully, it was the only class she had on Tuesday—and it started late, after lunch. She'd have a chance to browse through the library and write down her ideas before they faded from her mind. "Good luck with yours."

"It would have come in handy last month," Alassa pointed out. She pulled her timetable out of her pocket and scowled at it. "Law on Wednesday; Animal Bonding on Thursday, followed by Polite Death Threats..."

Emily snorted. "Etiquette lessons?"

"Yep," Alassa said, sardonically. "How To Insult Someone's Mother Without Actually Allowing Him To Take Offense."

Imaiqah giggled. "How do you do that?"

"I haven't the slightest idea," Alassa replied. "Insulting someone's mother is normally a good way to start a fight."

"Maybe you just dress it up in flowery phases and run while he's still trying to work out what you meant," Emily said. She'd received a note from a baron in Zangaria a week after she'd been ennobled. Four pages of expensive parchment and expensive handwriting had boiled down to a handful of insults and dark suggestions concerning what she had done to earn her new rank. "You can look it up in the library."

Chapter Eight

Alassa and Imaiqah had gone to Defensive Magic when Emily finally came down to the dining hall, so she chatted with the Gorgon while eating breakfast, then walked up to the library to look for the books on her first two reading lists. Unsurprisingly, several copies were already out on loan and others had been marked down for short loans only, but she was able to take out enough books to allow the three of them to read up on both Healing and Subtle Magic. Once she'd had the books issued to herself, she searched the shelves for anything on enchantment, then studied the runes used for channelling magic.

One thing became clear very quickly. Runes simply weren't capable of channelling vast amounts of magic, no matter how precisely they were drawn. Magic destroyed the runes as it flowed through them—and even a minor degradation could prevent them from working properly. Emily made a list of notes anyway, then resumed the search for books on enchantment, finding almost nothing. Most of them, according to Lady Aylia, had been taken out by students who'd attended the first taster class for Construction. Emily herself wouldn't be attending that class until later in the week.

She was still mulling it over when she left the library and ran down to the armory, where she changed into her uniform for Martial Magic. Half of the students she recalled from last year had gone on to private apprenticeships, like Jade, but the remainder smiled at her in welcome as she joined them on the field. Snow lay everywhere; she hastily cast a warming charm to keep her teeth from chattering as they lined up and waited for the sergeants. A snowball hit her in the back of the head and she swung round to see Cat, who was picking up a second snowball. Emily ducked down, intending to make a snowball of her own to throw back, then there was a loud cough as Sergeant Miles strode onto the field, followed by another man wearing the same uniform. The students rapidly lined up properly and came to attention.

"Welcome back," Sergeant Miles said, gruffly. He didn't have quite the same powers of intimidation as Sergeant Harkin, but everyone knew just how powerful a sorcerer he was. It was hard to imagine anyone giving him any trouble, at least more than once. "You seem to have been neglecting yourselves during the summer months."

Emily felt herself flushing as his gaze passed over her, then moved on to the next students. Cold water trickled down her back from where the ice had lodged in her hair. She cursed Cat under her breath, not daring to say anything out loud. The sergeants didn't like interruptions.

"This is Sergeant Bane," Sergeant Miles continued, indicating his companion. "After a long and illustrious career in the military, he has agreed to help me whip you into shape. I suggest you treat him with respect."

Sergeant Bane was tall, muscular and scarred, his hair cropped close to his skull. He looked surprisingly like Sergeant Harkin, although there was a very definite sense of magic surrounding him that Harkin had lacked. But then, few people had realized that a tutor at a magical school might lack magic himself. The secret had only come out when Shadye had tried to force Emily to kill Harkin and take his power—his non-existent power—for her own.

"And seeing that it is freezing cold," Sergeant Miles continued, making a gesture with his hand, "we'd better do some exercise to warm up."

Emily felt her warming charm flicker out of existence. The cold struck her a second later; judging by their reactions, she hadn't been the only person to use a spell to warm herself. Sergeant Miles chuckled at their expressions, then turned and started to jog across the field, towards the forest. The students hesitated, then followed him. Sergeant Bane brought up the rear, snapping and snarling at anyone who moved too slowly.

She'd expected to run around the field, but instead Sergeant Miles led them into the forest. The evergreen trees seemed to close in around them as they ran down the track, falling into single file as the pathway narrowed. Emily kept her eyes firmly on Cat's back, knowing from experience that dwelling on the distance they were covering only made it worse. At least they weren't going on a ten-mile hike this time.

They reached a clearing in the middle of the forest and Sergeant Miles called a halt. Ahead of them, there was a large gothic-style mansion, completely hidden from the outside world. Emily had explored the forest and mountains with Jade, but she'd never realized that the mansion was even there. It must have been concealed with misdirection spells, she decided, or maybe there were only one or two ways to reach it. There were parts of the forest that were inaccessible, either because the trees were so tangled together or because they were infested with dangerous creatures.

"Stand at ease," Sergeant Miles ordered. "Are you feeling warmer now?"

Emily nodded, feeling sweat trickling down her back. She hadn't done enough physical training over the last couple of months, she realized; the sergeants had warned her that it was easy to lose one's physical condition, but there had been too much else to do. Maybe she *should* join Alassa at *Ken*, if only to keep herself in shape.

"This"—he indicated the building—"is Blackhall. It was built by a grandmaster a couple of hundred years ago who turned out to be secretly evil. He intended to drain Whitehall's power and use it to turn himself into the most powerful magician alive, which shows a certain level of imagination lacking in the average necromancer. Thankfully for Whitehall, he was exposed and defeated before he could work out the kinks in his insane plan. His mansion was passed on to those responsible for training new combat sorcerers at the time."

He smiled at their expressions. "They spent months removing all of the booby traps and other nasty surprises the madman set up to welcome uninvited guests," he added. "Don't worry. We're fairly sure that we got them all."

Emily shivered. Sorcerers were allowed to ward their homes however they pleased, including using lethal wards to kill anyone who tried to break in. It hadn't taken her long to realize that most sorcerers spied on other sorcerers, looking for their secrets and testing the limits of the Sorcerer's Rule. Legally, anything a sorcerer did to a thief was permitted. He could kill or transfigure or enslave and no one would say a word against it. She could understand the impulse to punish someone for violating one's privacy, but she did wonder if they went too far.

"Now, we have set up hundreds of traps of our own," Sergeant Miles continued. "This whole house is a death trap—metaphorically speaking, of course. Over the coming year, you will be entering the house several times and trying to recover various items from inside—all the while avoiding traps and tricks that will disqualify you. When the year is finished, you will have plenty of experience in detecting and neutralizing booby traps. These skills are very useful for combat sorcerers. If nothing else, you will learn how to ward your own homes effectively."

He smiled at them. "Some of the traps are ones you can escape, through quick thinking and careful use of magic," he added. "Others, I must admit, will stun you—or simply evict you from the house. In both cases, we will assume that you failed and were killed. That will be very unfortunate for you."

Emily snorted, inwardly.

"You should know by now that the brute force approach rarely works when confronting a sorcerer holed up in his own house," the Sergeant concluded. "The necromancers might be able to blast down the wards, but they might accidentally destroy the entire house in the process. Instead, you will be forced to learn how to avoid, trick or dismantle wards—ideally without alerting their master to your presence. Should you be caught...well, I don't think you need me to spell out the possible consequences."

His gaze seemed to rest on Emily for a long moment, then he looked away. Emily shivered, remembering—once again—just how much experience the other students had, experience she lacked. Aloha had worked like a demon to enter Martial Magic in her second year; Emily had had almost no experience at all when she'd joined the class. It was clear that their current exercises should have drawn on lessons in Construction and Subtle Magic, lessons that Emily had only just begun. Just how far behind *was* she?

She gazed over at the windows, spying small bushes that had been planted beneath them, crawling up the walls. Was it her imagination or were the plants actually *moving*? There were walking plants, she knew, but she had thought that they were only found well away from civilization. But then, they would have made excellent guard dogs. Someone might well fail to notice them until the plants caught hold and *pulled*.

I may end up repeating this year, Emily thought, and shook her head. Oddly, it didn't feel like it would be a failure. More experience would definitely help her...she made a mental note to spend more time in the library, looking up defensive wards and ways to avoid or counter them. The sergeants possessed *years* of experience to rig Blackhall so that the students would have a difficult challenge. Doing something as simple as touching the doorknob with her bare hand might trigger a nasty surprise.

The cold started to seep in again and she shivered, resisting the urge to hug herself or cast a second warming charm. Sergeant Miles gave them all one last grin, then led them away from Blackhall, back towards the school. Emily forced herself to jog faster as Cat and Bran ran past her, leaving her at the rear. Sergeant Bane swiped at her with his baton, barely missing her rear. Gritting her teeth, she pushed herself onwards until they ran back onto the field and came to a halt.

"You will also attend private training sessions," Sergeant Miles continued, showing absolutely no signs of exhaustion. Neither he nor Sergeant Harkin had seemed taxed by their exercises. They'd always given the impression that they could go on forever. "Combat sorcery requires one-to-one tuition, particularly for those of you who have not practiced magic for three to four years. Those sessions will be held in the last period; speak to your tutors if they want to put you in a different class at the time. We can fiddle around, to some extent, but you don't want to have to go to another class after a long training session."

Emily nodded in understanding and relief. Last year, every training session had ended with her exhausted and soaked in sweat. Going anywhere but bed had seemed an impossible task. Now, with more advanced magic and exercise, she had the feeling that it would be even worse. She might not have the energy to have a shower before collapsing into bed for a quick rest.

"And there will be additional physical training," Sergeant Miles added. "You need to keep your strength and endurance up, or you will be in for a nasty surprise when you are called upon to fight."

He looked at Emily for a long moment, meeting her eyes. Lady Barb had to have told him that Emily had frozen when confronted with a potentially deadly threat. Even after Shadye, even after the cockatrice...she'd frozen. If Lady Barb hadn't been there, Emily and Imaiqah might well have ended up dead. Or worse.

"There are a handful of spellbooks in the Armory marked out for your attention," Sergeant Bane said, gruffly. "Do *not* take them out of the room, just read and master the spells."

It was the first time Emily had heard him speak. His accent was thick, as if he'd barely learned how to talk; where, she asked herself, did he come from? On Earth, she would have pegged him as coming from Eastern Europe. Maybe one of the distant lands across the ocean, where the Empire had never been so powerful? It would make sense, she decided thoughtfully. The Empire might have shared a common language, but it wouldn't have taken such firm roots somewhere thousands of miles from the Empire's heartlands.

"But there is another matter we must discuss," Sergeant Miles said. "Follow me."

Emily and the rest of the students obeyed, following him as he jogged up to Whitehall's walls and led the way through a door that hadn't been there moments before. Inside, there was a large hall—it reminded her of a gym hall, but with weapons and equipment dangling from the walls—with enough room for all of them to duel. At the head of the room there was a large glass box, lined with rocks, plants and a small pool of water.

"Look inside the box," Sergeant Miles said. "What do you see?"

It took several moments for Emily to see the snake, curled up beside one of the rocks. She'd never liked snakes, but she had to admit that this one was beautiful. It was bright blue, with a golden pattern on its scales that contrasted sharply against the rock. She couldn't understand why she hadn't seen it at once. It should have been immediately obvious.

Aloha coughed and turned pale. "Is that a...?"

"Correct," Sergeant Miles said. The humor was gone from his voice. "This is a Death Viper. A single drop of poison is almost *always* fatal. There is only one recorded case of a person surviving—and that was only because he cut off his leg to prevent the venom from spreading through his bloodstream and into his heart. Everyone else died within two minutes.

"You'll notice that the beast has no natural camouflage," he added. "It does not even *try* to blend in with its surroundings. This is because its scales also carry poison, although a slightly less venomous kind than its fangs. Should you pick up the snake with your bare hands, you will be lucky if you *only* have to have them amputated. The venom is not called the Rotting Death for nothing. It is often used to inflict a particularly unpleasant and agonizing death."

The Death Viper opened its eyes and reared up. It seemed tiny, Emily realized, hardly even as long as her forearm. But it didn't have to be huge to be dangerous. It opened its mouth, showing sharp fangs; its beady eyes seemed to suggest endless malice. Emily caught herself taking a step backwards, then realized that she wasn't alone. Almost everyone had reacted badly to the colorful snake.

"I mention this because a third year student was dumb enough to find this particular snake in the forest yesterday and pick it up," Sergeant Miles said. "Luck, it would seem, favors the fools. The snake seemed to accept his petting without trying to bite him, leaving the poison on its skin to spread through his hands. That fool of a student is now in the infirmary. One of his hands will probably need to be removed permanently, unless the healers can patch it back together. There may also be long-term damage to the rest of his body.

"If you see a snake like this, *don't* try to pick it up. If you see a creature you don't recognize, don't try to do *anything* with it, no matter how harmless it seems. In fact, give all creatures a wide berth unless you need to hunt—and if you do, be careful what you chose as your target. I expect all of you to review the books on dangerous creatures—Mistress Kirdáne, I am sure, will be happy to go over it with you."

He looked down at the snake, which had lowered its head and gone back to sleep. "The idiot who found this snake will be lucky if he manages to return to classes by the end of next year," he added. "His future career prospects have been shattered, if only because there are spells that depend on the caster making the right hand movements. One stupid mistake almost killed him. I expect all of you to avoid the same fate."

Emily shivered as she looked down at the Death Viper. Its lack of natural camouflage made sense, she told herself. Any creature that tried to eat it would end up being poisoned and eaten itself. She wondered, briefly, just how smart the snake actually was, before deciding that it didn't really matter. The snake would have evolved a hunting pattern that suited it—or it would have died out.

"These snakes are often used in alchemy," Cat said, breaking the uncomfortable silence. "What's going to happen to this one?"

"I believe that the Grandmaster intends to show it to everyone in the school," Sergeant Miles said. "After that, we will kill it and Professor Thande can turn it into something more useful."

Aloha nudged Emily. "Would you want to drink something you knew had been made from a Death Viper?"

Emily shook her head.

"It's really too dangerous to keep around," Sergeant Miles explained. "If it managed to escape, it could kill other students before we hunted the beast down and destroyed it."

Emily winced, inwardly. She *knew*, intellectually, where most of the ingredients for alchemy came from. As Professor Thande preferred to assign detentions rather than send students to the Warden, she'd spent several of her detentions chopping up various small animals and preparing them for the older students. But it was still hard to realize that the creatures had been living once—or that they might have been very dangerous.

The Sergeant clapped his hands. "Now," he said, "back to work. We have another hour and I don't want to waste it."

Chapter Nine

Emily was still mulling over what they'd been told in Martial Magic—and what she'd read from the private stockpile of books the sergeants had shown them—when she joined Alassa and the others in the arena. Like the swimming pool, it was charmed to keep it warm and deflect the snow away. There wasn't even any water dripping on them as they gathered outside the main gate.

She hadn't been sure how many students Alassa would manage to rope into the tryouts, but there were nearly fifty pupils gathered in front of her. Alassa was standing on a small stool so that everyone could see her, waving and smiling at everyone. Emily almost turned and walked away; she disliked large crowds at the best of times, and if there were so many potential players her friend hardly *needed* her. But it *was* important to Alassa that Emily at least *tried* to play.

"Welcome," Alassa said, in her best regal manner. "How many of you have played before?"

Several hands went up. Emily blinked in surprise, then understood. She had been excused Whitehall's counterpart to PE because she did Martial Magic, but just about everyone else would have taken part in gym class. Or, as Calvin had put it, studies in state-sponsored terrorism. Emily had never liked the experience. The only people who did were the ones who would have done it anyway.

"Excellent," Alassa said. She gestured towards a small pile of balls just outside the arena. "We'll start with a simple exercise. Twelve of us"—she jabbed her hand at eleven students, including Emily—will run through the arena. Everyone else will throw balls into the cage and we'll try to dodge them. We won't bother with the advanced settings this time, we'll just see how we fare when dodging balls."

Emily looked up at the arena, silently admiring the spellwork that had gone into its construction. From the outside, it seemed to be little more than a faintly translucent cage; inside, it was a network of tunnels, hallways and climbing frames. The local gravity was twisted around too, ensuring that there would be times when the students would be upside down. It wasn't quite as impressive as Whitehall itself—and she suspected that it would be impossible to duplicate away from a nexus point—but it was striking.

"Here we go," Alassa said, as she opened the gate. "Come along inside..."

Emily stepped into the arena and felt her foot sink slightly. The interior of the arena was semi-visible, but it didn't *feel* quite right, almost like one of the safety wards surrounding the spellwork chambers she'd used when they'd been experimenting with hexes and jinxes. She poked the wall with one finger and felt it pushing back. If she crashed into it, it would protect her from the force of the impact—and throw her back. The few games she'd watched had included several players using it to best advantage.

She felt uneasy as she walked further into the arena, as if she were balancing on top of an unstable boat. The floor kept shifting between her feet, making it harder to concentrate. No doubt she would get used to it eventually—she'd gotten used to quite a few things in Whitehall—but it was still disconcerting. The realization that the outsiders could throw things *into* the arena was just as worrying.

"They've put a labyrinth spell on the arena," the Gorgon's voice said. "We might not be able to leave unless we *wanted* to leave—or were forced out."

Emily twisted around, wondering why she hadn't realized that the Gorgon was there. She wore a headscarf that covered her snake hair; without them, her face wasn't *too* inhuman, or scaly. Emily couldn't help thinking of the Death Viper and wondering what would happen if one of the Gorgon's snakes bit her, before deciding that she was being silly. There were more important things to worry about.

Alassa blew her whistle and the outsiders started throwing balls into the arena. There must have been a spell on them, Emily realized, because the balls simply kept going. Sometimes, they bounced off the walls and something they went right *through* the walls; there was no reliable cover inside the arena at all. Emily snatched out at a ball that flashed past her, only to miss and land sprawling on her face. The Gorgon landed beside her, helped her back to her feet and winked. It wasn't very reassuring.

"If you get hit by a ball," Alassa said, using a spell to magnify her voice, "go stand in the penalty box for a minute. And don't lie about it."

Emily rolled her eyes, then concentrated on dodging the next two balls that came in her general direction. She'd never been very good with ball games, even when the games didn't warp the laws of physics. Catching the balls seemed impossible, despite everything they'd done in Martial Magic. She made a grab for a third ball, only to have it slam into her chest and send her falling over backwards on her ass. Red lights lit up as the outsiders jeered.

"Penalty box," Alassa said.

Emily felt her face burning red as she pulled herself through the arena and into the penalty box. The sadist who'd crafted the arena had placed it right at the top, where she could be seen by everyone in the stands. Thankfully, the outsiders were too busy throwing balls into the arena to take much notice of Emily, but during real games the spectators would point and laugh—and sometimes throw things, when the referee wasn't looking.

She scowled at Alassa, who seemed to be having no trouble dodging the balls or catching them and hurling them at the nearest target. Why had her friend suddenly become a sports-mad fanatic? Maybe King Randor had urged her to take on the job of crafting a new team for Whitehall...it would certainly make a change from jousting or rugby. But then, Alassa had never been allowed to do either in Zangaria. Perhaps she'd come up with the idea of founding a new team on her own.

"Hey," Song called. "I'm in, you're out."

Emily nodded and allowed Song to take her place in the penalty box. Alassa's roommate looked to be enjoying herself; Emily almost offered to stay there and let her go free, before she decided that it was probably against the rules. She wasn't clear on the precise details, but ideally the better players should be trapped in the penalty box as long as possible. Or hexed, when the referee was looking in the other direction. Teamwork was more important to *Ken* than she'd realized.

And we haven't even started including traitors yet, she thought, ruefully. *When that happens, things are going to get worse.*

Alassa finally blew the whistle to end the game after what felt like hours. A quick check of her watch revealed that it had barely been fifteen minutes. Emily left the arena gratefully, feeling sweat trickling down her back again. She sat down on the bench and watched tiredly as Alassa organized the next set of players to go into the arena. It was hard to see how Alassa would make the final decision on who would play and who wouldn't.

As long as she doesn't want me, Emily thought. *She must have noticed that I didn't play well.*

Watching the second match was slightly more interesting than actually taking part, she decided, even though it *looked* thoroughly odd. The arena's walls seemed to shimmer in and out of visibility, then reshape themselves at will. Emily wondered, as one of the other players started to run upside down, if she'd done that without even noticing. The constant shifts had rapidly made it impossible for her to keep track of her own orientation.

Imaiqah sat down beside her. "I think I did all right," she said, reluctantly. "But I never liked playing it before."

"I guess it's better if you're playing with friends," Emily said. Perhaps she would have enjoyed herself more if Alassa hadn't been so determined to found her own team. But then, she'd always been happier by herself—or with one or two friends. "How do you decide who's better?"

"Alassa was saying that it was the ones who stayed in the game the longest who won," Imaiqah explained. "But someone could just hide..."

Emily nodded, watching as the second game came to an end. A handful of students stumbled off, looking tired and dispirited, but there were still enough players to form three whole teams. It struck her that some of them might form their own teams too, following in Alassa's footsteps—there was certainly no rule against it. But would the older, more established teams try something to deter them?

She rolled her eyes. Life was definitely much simpler when she hadn't even *thought* about team games.

"Good work, all of you," Alassa said. "Third match, now; sudden death. If you get hit with a ball thrown by another player, you're out. The remaining players when we get down to twelve will be the first team. And then we start practicing in earnest."

Emily sighed and climbed to her feet, looking over at the Gorgon. "Didn't Lin want to come?"

"She was studying in our room," the Gorgon explained. "She didn't even want to go down for dinner."

The arena opened up in front of them, even though there were nearly three times as many players this time. Alassa tossed balls upwards, where the magic fields caught them and started to project them into the arena at random. Emily wasn't sure what happened if a player was hit by a ball thrown by the arena itself, but she didn't want to find out. It was probably something that fans like Alassa considered obvious.

She picked up a ball that rolled past her and looked around. The arena seemed determined to make it harder for her to *see* the other players this time; she caught sight of the Gorgon, briefly, but when she hurled the ball it ricocheted off an invisible wall. A loud chime rang through the arena as the first player was knocked out, followed rapidly by a second. Emily saw something moving out of the corner of her eye and ducked, sharply, as a ball flew over her head. She grabbed the ball as it bounced back at her and threw it at a young male student she vaguely recognized from Advanced Charms. He caught it neatly, grinned at her, and then launched the ball towards her with all of his might. Emily started to dodge, but it caught her in the side before she could escape. Another chime rang through the arena as the magic reconfigured itself, creating an invisible slide that evicted her from the playing field.

"Hard luck," a voice said. "Happens to us all.

Emily looked up to see Cat. "What are *you* doing here?"

"Checking out the competition," Cat explained, without a hint of shame. "You never know; your royal friend might just be the ideal player for *my* team."

Emily looked over at Alassa, who was doing an impression of Sergeant Harkin while preparing to throw a ball at the next target, and then looked back at Cat. "You're *talent-spotting*?"

"Of course," Cat said. "I'm a sixth year now, don't you know? I won't even be *here* next year. If I can find the teammates who will take the team further—after I'm gone, of course—it will look very good on my resumé."

He gave her a smug smile that made Emily want to hit him. "Some people here with talent," he noted happily. "What will your friend say if we lure them away?"

Emily shrugged. "Is that even legal?"

"There's no rule against it," Cat said. "Of course, the original rulebook was lost years ago, so it is possible that there *was* such a rule..."

"And someone junked the book so they could break it," Emily said. She had a private suspicion that Ken, the wizard who had created the game and then named it after himself, had actually pulled several different games together, but there was no way to know. "What can you actually offer the players?"

Cat shrugged. "Fame and glory?"

Emily laughed. She *had* fame and glory—and they weren't really what she'd *wanted*. Alassa was a Royal Princess. Neither of them could really be boosted by playing *Ken*. And if someone else decided to leave Alassa's team to join an older one... well, it wasn't as if she were short of volunteers to play.

"Best of luck," Cat said, as he turned away. "You'll need it."

Emily snorted as the final chime rang out, signaling that the number of players in the game had been reduced to twelve. Alassa had made it, naturally, as had the Gorgon, Alassa's two roommates—and Imaiqah. Emily felt an odd pang as she realized that her friends were going to be spending their evenings practicing the game, rather than spending time studying with her. After finally making friends...she was going to be left alone again.

Maybe I should have tried harder, she thought sourly, as she walked over to where Alassa was handing out practice schedules. *But I tried as hard as I could.*

"You four will be in the reserves," Alassa said, to the last four students to be evicted from the arena. "If one of the players can't make it, you can take their place."

She looked over at Emily as the rest of the players started to head towards the showers. "I can still put you on the team..."

Emily hesitated. She hadn't enjoyed the game, not really. And yet, the thought of being left alone was...unpleasant.

"I think it would be obvious that you were showing favoritism," she said, finally. It was true, after all. "I didn't make the team fairly."

"I suppose not," Alassa said. She reached out and took Emily's arm, leading her back towards the school. "And thank you for trying. You're welcome to help with planning, if you want."

She leaned closer. "Or is there something from your home that can help?"

"Probably not," Emily said. It wasn't as if she'd spent time following sports on Earth. "And I don't qualify as a cheerleader."

Alassa blinked. "A cheerleader?"

Emily hesitated, then tried to explain. "They're girls who dress up in skimpy clothes and cheer for the team," she said, after a moment's thought. There was probably more to it than that, but she hadn't bothered to follow the cheerleaders either. *She* had certainly never been considered to join the team—and wouldn't have wanted to if she had. "I think it's meant to encourage the players."

Alassa snorted. "And distract them so they run into the walls and suchlike?"

"Probably," Emily said. "I really don't know much about them."

"Maybe not something we need," Alassa said, after a moment. "Would the spectators be cheering on the team—or the girls?"

"I honestly have no idea," Emily said. It was easy to think that the spectators might be watching the girls, rather than the players. But the first requirement for being a cheerleader, at least in her opinion, was being brainless...and it was hard to think of anyone at Whitehall who qualified. Brainless magicians, she had been told, never lasted very long. "What else can I do?"

"Help me think of tactics," Alassa said. She put on a wheedling tone. "Or you could do my coursework while I play."

Emily gave her a sharp look. Last year, Alassa had bullied Imaiqah into doing her homework—before Emily had nearly killed her, accidentally.

"Not a chance," she said, finally. "Besides, do we have the *same* coursework?"

Alassa shrugged as they entered the shower. "I've noticed you reading books on everything," she said, dryly. "I think you probably know more than I do about some things—and I was born here."

Emily flushed. She *had* spent plenty of time in the library, just learning as much as she could. There was no shortage of interesting books in Whitehall, although most of them were written on the assumption that their readers didn't come from a different world. She had already run into several problems caused by her lack of background knowledge, knowledge that any child born near Whitehall would gain instinctively.

"Maybe," she said, as she started to remove her tunic. Three showers in a day—thankfully, Whitehall didn't have any restrictions on how much water they could use. There were students, she knew, who came from hovels and had to go back to truly disgusting conditions when term ended. It separated them out from their families, creating a gulf that would be near-impossible to surmount.

Maybe Master Tor has a point, she thought, reluctantly. *They have to get to know their new family, because they won't have much in common with their old one.*

She washed and dried herself, then pulled on her robes, wincing slightly as her body started to ache. Between playing *Ken* and Martial Magic, she had used muscles she hadn't used in far too long. The sergeant had been right, she realized. She had allowed herself to slip.

"Come and eat," Alassa said. Somehow, she always managed to look beautiful, even after a communal shower. "And then we can plan how we're going to win the next game."

"Cat was watching," Emily said. She explained quickly. "He even *admitted* that he was talent-spotting."

Alassa looked pensive for a moment, then shook her head. "He can't offer slots on his team to everyone, or he'd destroy it," she said. "It isn't really something we need to worry about."

"True," Emily agreed. Cat's team probably had three open slots for new players, after the previous players had graduated. He could only steal three players at most, from people who probably wouldn't be interested. "Let's see how it goes."

Chapter Ten

"IT IS LAW," MASTER TOR SAID, "THAT IS THE TRUE EMBODIMENT OF SOCIETY."

Emily listened, fighting down the urge to rub her eyes. Instead of going to bed early after the *Ken* game and dinner, she had stayed up with Alassa and the other girls, listening as they brainstormed ideas and tactics for their first formal match. In hindsight, she realized, she should have left them and gone to bed herself, but she'd forgotten that she had an early class the following morning. Thankfully, Master Tor didn't seem to have noticed her tiredness as he swept into the room and took control of the class.

"You will be aware, no doubt, that there are different laws in each of the Allied Lands," he continued. "One kingdom may forbid something that is enthusiastically practiced in another, which in turn may forbid something that is a vital part of the third's economy. You are not expected to be familiar with the intricacies of separate kingdoms, at least unless you intend to spend the rest of your lives practicing law. However, you *are* expected to be familiar with the shared law upheld by the Allied Lands. Can anyone tell me which field that law covers?"

There was a long pause.

"Magic," Alassa said, finally.

"Correct," Master Tor said. "Sorcerers are not always bound by local laws, but they are obliged to follow the shared laws of the Allied Lands, which are upheld by the White Council and the Mediators. You are expected to be at least loosely familiar with those laws, as well as a handful of others. Those of you who go on to serve as Mediators will be expected to know the laws *thoroughly*. Judging will be a vitally important part of your career."

He paused, tapping one finger against his cheek. "When magic is involved, the White Council has the right to take the lead," he added. "This can include dealing with magicians, but also with magical creatures and magically-binding contracts. If you serve as a Mediator, you will be called upon to create such contracts—or to try to break one, if it was created illegally. Such tasks also require an awareness of both human and magical law.

"A secondary aspect of your career will include meditating disputes between the different Allied Lands. Most of you, I suspect, will be aware that there *are* clashes between the Allied Lands on a regular basis. I might direct you, for example, to the endless skirmishes between kingdoms and city-states, or commercial disputes that threaten to turn into wars. It is the task of the Mediators to attempt to moderate such disagreements and maintain a united front against the necromancers."

For a long moment, he gazed at Emily—and then continued. "For the remainder of this lesson, I will give you a brief overview of the basics and a reading list for further study," he concluded. "Should you wish to remain in this class, you will be expected to research precedents and cases that date all the way back to the foundation of the Allied Lands themselves—and be ready to quote them when necessary. Many of you will find them tedious and boring, but they are vitally important. Attention to detail matters even outside learning magic.

"We will also be practicing debating and rhetoric," he added. "You will be expected to present evidence in support of an assertion—or to counter it. This is excellent training for law-related work—and also for writing essays, if you haven't mastered it by now. I intend to hold a debate every Friday afternoon, using topics chosen by you. You may pick anything you like, as long as you are prepared to argue for it—or against it."

Song put up her hand. "Are you saying, sir, that I might have to argue against something I support?"

"Precisely," Master Tor said. He held up a hand before she could object. "A frequent problem in arguments is that both sides are incapable of seeing the other's point of view, which ensures that they see each other as monsters who need to be fought, tooth and nail. If you try to look at the argument from the other person's point of view—if you try to uphold their side of the argument—you will come to understand it. You may then be able to look for a workable compromise."

Emily wasn't so sure that she agreed. It was true that political debates and internet discussions back home had degenerated into shouting matches rather than reasoned discussion, but there were subjects that could *never* be upheld. *She* couldn't put together an argument that supported the suppression of human rights or forced marriages, even though there were people who did both with enthusiasm. How could she be forced to *defend* them?

"Alternatively, you may be able to determine that there is truly no justice to their claims," Master Tor added. "In that case, you can win allies by proving it—rather than simply asserting it to be true. The power to convince people to support you willingly can often be more powerful than the strongest—or subtlest - of mind-control spells. It is a technique that requires absolutely no magic to make it work, just training and discipline."

He gave the class a thin smile that didn't quite seem to reach his eyes. "However, we are moving slightly off topic," he said. "How many of you are familiar with the Sorcerer's Rule?"

Emily put up her hand. A dozen others joined her.

"The Sorcerer's Rule states, specifically, that a sorcerer who makes a new discovery in the field of magic cannot be forced to share it with other sorcerers, even by the White Council," Master Tor said. "That isn't quite the impediment that you might imagine. Once a new magical technique is proved to be possible, research wizards and sorcerers will start attempting to duplicate it. They do, in fact, have a very high success rate. Only a handful of spells remain the exclusive property of their developer."

He shot Emily a quick glance and then addressed the classroom as a whole. "That is but one of the laws enshrined by the White Council of the Allied Lands," he told them. "There are others that, like the Sorcerer's Rule, apply only to sorcerers. A sorcerer can do whatever he likes to protect his home, as long as it doesn't conflict with the other laws. The only real requirement is a clear line marking his property—a ward or a wall. And if he happens to catch a criminal breaking in, he can do whatever he likes."

Emily nodded impatiently. She'd known that for a long time.

"The only exceptions to their general freedom are spells that are classed as the Black Arts," Master Tor continued. "Demon summoning is specifically forbidden, as is any form of magic intended to drain a person's magic and life force and use it—necromancy, in other words. A magician who chose to create a homunculus would be bending the rules; legally, such creatures can only by created by direct permission of the White Council. And creating one that can actually pass for human is completely forbidden."

He scowled around the classroom, his eyes flickering over Emily and moving on. "You may be called upon to judge a fellow magician—and to stop him, if he is breaking the law," he explained. "In that case, knowing what is actually forbidden can only help you."

Emily shivered as she realized what he meant. A sorcerer like Void would be incredibly hard to control—or stop. No wonder they had so much freedom; the local City Guard wouldn't want to go out on a limb to stop them unless they were getting completely out of hand.

She listened as he ran through a series of laws and examples, outlining what they would have to deal with if they became Mediators. It was illegal in almost all kingdoms for non-magicians to experiment with runes and other forms of subtle magic, no matter the justification. Animal and inanimate object transformation was perfectly *legal*, provided the victim was allowed to keep their human mind. Depending on the exact circumstances, it was either a cruel practical joke or assault. Turning someone so completely into an animal that they lost their human thoughts, however, was classed as murder.

It made a certain kind of sense, she decided, reluctantly. She'd been an object—one of Melissa's nastier tricks—and she'd hated it, but she'd also managed to return to human form. Destroying her mind completely, on the other hand, would have killed her...

"You are also required to be familiar with laws governing various magical creatures," Master Tor continued. "Gorgons, for example, are barred from most human settlements, as are werewolves. Mermen and mermaids are welcome in coastal towns, but rarely welcome elsewhere. Vampires and Night Stalkers are to be exterminated wherever they are found..."

Emily found her voice. "Why?"

Master Tor turned to scowl at her. "Why *what*?"

"Why," Emily asked, "are Gorgons and Werewolves barred from human settlements?"

"They are often dangerous," Master Tor said, finally. "A werewolf is not a man who becomes a wolf, but a wolf who becomes a man. Even in human form, their conduct is more animal than human. They can never be trusted completely."

His eyes met Emily's. "Have you ever met a werewolf?"

Emily shook her head, mutely.

"As you seem determined to demonstrate your ignorance in front of the class," Master Tor said, "you can give me an essay on Werewolf culture and society—such as it is—before the end of the weekend. I think three to four scrolls should be enough."

Emily scowled at his back as he turned away. She already had a long reading list—and writing even three scrolls of parchment would take hours, once she'd done the research. As punishments went, she decided, it was brutally efficient. And educational.

But the Gorgon seemed a decent person, once Emily had managed to overcome her reluctance to look her in the eye. How could someone condemn *all* Gorgons, even if a few of them were bad people?

Easily, her own thoughts answered her. *Racists have been doing it for hundreds of years.*

"Should you discover a magical creature out of its tribal lands," Master Tor continued smoothly, "you may be required to push it back into its territory—or destroy it. We will be discussing the precedents for each individual decision later in the year."

He turned to his desk and picked up a piece of parchment. "Would any of you like to hazard a guess and tell me what this is?"

"A magically-binding contract," Lin said. It was the first time Emily had heard her new roommate speak in class. "I think..."

"You are correct," Master Tor informed her. He held it up in front of his face, pretending to read it. "This contract stipulates that I will take Mistress Kirdáne to eat in Dragon's Den this weekend. If I choose not to go, I will have itchy feet for the rest of the day."

There were some giggles from the students. Master Tor scowled at them.

"This may be a very basic contract, but there are few limits when it comes to writing them," he said, tartly. "And the consequences may be a great deal worse.

"At base, a contract is an agreement that one person will do something—or suffer the consequences," he added. "A magically-binding contract uses the signer's own magic to *enforce* the agreement. The consequences can be far worse than itchy feet; a person can suffer dreadful pain, or death—if, of course, the contract does not attempt to *enforce* the agreement directly. I could insist that you all sign a contract that you remained silent in class and you would find yourselves unable to speak, if those were the terms of the agreement.

"There are four principle rules when it comes to crafting magically-binding contracts. First, they must be entered into *willingly,* with a full awareness of both the terms of the agreement and the punishment for breaking them. Second, they must be crafted as carefully as possible, to avoid loopholes and misjudgements. Third, one must not ask for the impossible—or for a person to die. Fourth, and finally, you cannot make a magically-binding contract with a mundane. They simply lack the magic to make it work.

"Magically-binding contracts are prevalent in many areas of our society," he explained. "It is not uncommon for marriage agreements to be magically-binding, particularly among the greater magical dynasties. However, asking someone to sign a contract is often seen as clear proof of mistrust. It has been known to lead to fighting—and worse."

There was a long pause, then he started to rattle off examples. Emily listened, remembering the deal she'd made with the fairies. She hadn't exactly had much choice, even if she hadn't been mind-controlled into making the agreement. Did it count as a magically-binding contract? All of her research suggested that it did, but the only way to be sure was to test it. And *that* could prove fatal.

"Crafting a contract is not difficult," Master Tor said, once he'd finished the examples. "I dare say that most of you, with a little research in the library, would be able to do it. That will, however, ensure that you are expelled. A poorly-designed contract is not a laughing matter. Outside Whitehall, only accredited sorcerers are permitted to design contracts and to offer their services to other magicians who might want to use them. Unfortunately, that doesn't stop rogue magicians from crafting their own and selling them to the less scrupulous elements of our society."

Emily looked down at her notes, resisting the urge to rub her eyes again.

"I have a question," Imaiqah said, after she had raised her hand and been acknowledged by the tutor. "Could someone write out a contract in a different language, then lie about its contents?"

"Not in practice," Master Tor said. "If someone believed—honestly believed—that the terms of the contract were different from what they truly were, their magic would go by what they believed to be true, rather than what is *actually* true. Breaking a contract isn't easy because you would have to *believe* that you weren't actually breaking the agreement."

Emily considered it as he offered them more examples. A contract-breaker would have to lie to himself—and do it so well that he wasn't even aware that he was trying to fool himself. It wouldn't be easy to do that, not without endlessly chasing his own tail. But if someone erased his memory of signing the contract, or revised the terms and conditions he thought he was following, he could break the contact. Yet he would never *know* what he'd done...and could never know. The results might be disastrous.

"We will cover all of these in more detail later," Master Tor concluded. "Are there any final questions?"

Emily remembered *Harry Potter* and raised her hand. "Could you create a game where the players were bound to compete –and couldn't back out, at least without giving it an honest try?"

"Easily," Master Tor said. He didn't seem irked by the question. "Indeed, I believe that is actually done, in certain *Ken* matches. There was a big scandal over players being lured away by other teams and the captains started insisting on proper contracts."

Alassa snorted. "What were the terms of the agreements?"

"If the contracts were broken, the players were never able to play again," Master Tor said. "This led to situations where players deliberately played badly, because the only way they could escape the contracts was to have them torn up by the captains."

Emily was still following her first line of thought. "But you couldn't *force* someone to play, could you?"

"No," Master Tor said, shortly. "A person can only enter into a contract if they have full awareness of the terms and conditions—and accept them."

A student Emily didn't know put up his hand. "But someone could sign the contract without actually intending to keep it," he pointed out. "What happens then?"

"The contract is written on charmed parchment," Master Tor said, with surprising patience. "If you didn't *want* to uphold your word, the contract will not activate itself. It's as simple as that."

He smiled, dryly. "To answer what will probably be your *next* question," he added, "the contract is really lodged in a magician's magic. Merely destroying the parchment will not destroy the contract."

Emily shuddered as she realized the implications. It would be easy to get wrapped up in a morass of contracts and agreements, each one with nasty penalty clauses. Master Tor was right; the class might be boring, yet it was also vitally important. Maybe he didn't like her—and she had no idea why he'd taken such an instant dislike to her—but she had to learn from him, even if it meant spending *much* more time doing research.

"You'll pick up the class schedules from my desk," Master Tor concluded. "If you wish to remain in this class, the first formal lessons are on Monday and Tuesday. Sort out your timetable and come to me if you have a problem balancing your classes."

His hand fell on Emily's shoulder as the class started to vacate the room, holding her back.

"Ignorance isn't a sin," he said, when the room had been cleared. His disapproving gaze bore down on her. "But making pronouncements from ignorance isn't a virtue either."

"Yes, sir," Emily said. It wasn't fair—she hadn't made any pronouncements—but there was no point in arguing. She just wanted to get away. "I..."

"Three to four scrolls," Master Tor reminded her. "And I suggest that you read widely. Far too much information on werewolves is inaccurate."

Emily nodded, then fled the room. Alassa and Imaiqah met her outside.

"Nice guy," Alassa said, sardonically. "What does he have against you?"

"I have no idea," Emily said, tiredly. She wanted to sleep so desperately. "But it really doesn't matter."

Alassa snorted, but held her peace.

Chapter Eleven

THE REST OF THE WEEK WENT SURPRISINGLY QUICKLY IN A WHIRLWIND OF TASTER CLASSES and a handful of social engagements. Emily discovered that she enjoyed Construction and Warding, although the tutor told the class—rather bluntly—that it might be years before they were ready to start building their own houses and warding them against all comers. Apparently, there were more advanced studies to be done after they graduated from Whitehall, particularly if they wanted to work with the nexus points. Animal Bonding, on the other hand, proved a waste of time. If there was a creature out there willing to bond with her, it wasn't in the small zoo Mistress Kirdáne demonstrated to the class. The fact that Imaiqah had picked up a hamster, of all things, was a minor irritation.

Etiquette was tedious, even though the tutor explained that they would be touching on swordsmanship and penmanship as well as basic manners. Artwork was thoroughly boring; Emily tried, mainly for Imaiqah's sake, and discovered that her drawing and painting hadn't improved over her work when she'd been a young child. The only other class—New Writing and New Math—had made her laugh when she'd realized that it taught the letters and numbers she had introduced. Clearly, the Grandmaster had decided that the students needed to know them as well as the older script.

Unsurprisingly, she spent most of her evenings in the library. Each of the classes had a long reading list, mostly composed of books that were specific to the individual class. Emily had a feeling that Subtle Magic, Law, and Construction and Warding were linked together, but it didn't seem that way from the reading lists. And she had a long essay to write on werewolves from Master Tor. By the time the weekend rolled around, she was exhausted and just wanted to sleep.

"Don't forget we're going to Dragon's Den," Alassa said, on Saturday morning. "You need a break."

"Five days," Emily muttered, tiredly. "Five days and I already need a holiday."

"You should be spending more time just relaxing," Alassa informed her, blithely. "Come and watch us play, even if you don't play yourself."

Emily snorted. Alassa could never be a combat sorceress, or anything apart from princess and later Queen of Zangaria. In one sense, it didn't really *matter* what degrees she brought home—or if she qualified as anything at all. Her blood had already determined her future. Emily, on the other hand, needed qualifications...at least if she wanted to be anything more than Baroness Cockatrice. But it was tempting just to go back to her castle and hire tutors, rather than coping with the pressures of Whitehall. Last year hadn't been so stressful, at least when Shadye hadn't been attacking the castle.

But you spent last year learning the basics, she reminded herself. *Now you have to learn all the tedious little background details.*

Imaiqah nudged her. "Did you complete your essay for Master Tor?"

"I did," Emily said. It had been fascinating, although most of the books on werewolves had contradicted one another. They seemed to act like pack animals most of the time, even when in human form, but the writers weren't sure if they *were* animals or if they were merely taking refuge in animal behavior. Maybe the latter made sense. Werewolves found outside their tribal lands were summarily executed, as if they were wild beasts. "I'll give it to him later."

"Nice of him, giving you an essay so early in the year," Imaiqah said, sarcastically. "What does he have against you anyway?"

"Probably wants to establish that he's not scared of the Necromancer's Bane," Alassa said, dryly. "Or maybe he thinks..."

"Don't worry about it," Emily said, seriously. "We survived Shadye. We can certainly survive Master Tor."

Alassa grinned, then took a final sip of her kava. "Come on," she said. "The coach leaves in ten minutes and I don't want to be late." She rubbed her hands together with glee. "Clothes shopping!"

Emily rolled her eyes, but didn't bother to argue. She'd never been fond of shopping for clothes on Earth, even though most girls her age had been happy to spend hours in the shops, just trying on outfit after outfit. Now, she had enough money to outfit the entire school in the local version of designer brands...and it still seemed like a waste of time. But she did need some new outfits, including working clothes.

"I have to visit the enchanter," she reminded them, as she finished her juice. "After that, I'll meet you in the clothes store."

The ride to Dragon's Den was almost as she remembered, although the carriage seemed to have problems on the icy road, despite all the charms protecting it. Outside, the fields were covered in snow for as far as the eye could see. Some of the townsfolk were building snowmen or having snowball fights; several of them launched snowballs towards the carriages, then fled before the occupants could hurl jinxes or hexes in their direction. Emily waved cheerfully after them, then smiled as the city itself came into view. It looked as if hundreds of people had been clearing snow from the streets.

"Remember the rules," Master Tor said. He'd ridden in the lead carriage. "If you need help, signal."

Emily smiled. The first time she'd come to Dragon's Den, she and Alassa had wound up being kidnapped—but that was very much the exception. Normally, the worst danger any student of Whitehall had to face in Dragon's Den was high prices and shopkeepers who knew more about bargaining than most of the students. Emily had a private suspicion that the presence of Whitehall—with hundreds of rich students—was actually driving prices in Dragon's Den upwards, although it was hard to be sure. It was possible that the locals got lower prices.

She removed her old trunk from the carriage, cast a pair of lifting spells on it to make it easier to carry, then turned and followed Alassa as she led the way towards the shops. Hardly anyone noticed her on the streets, she was glad to see. Everyone knew her in Whitehall, even the upper classes who generally had very little to do with the younger students, but in Dragon's Den she was just another student. She pulled the robe tighter around her as they stepped into a long street crammed with shops and smiled as she saw the hawkers, who were offering everything from food to cheap clothes and alchemical ingredients. Professor Thande had warned them, quite specifically, not to risk buying any of the latter until they were qualified alchemists. It was hard to tell where the ingredients had really come from—or how it had been harvested.

"That's Yodel's store," she said. "I'll meet you in the clothes store."

Emily stepped into the cluttered store and looked around, remembering everything she'd seen the first time she'd visited. There was a Hand of Glory, a magical device made from a human hand, sitting on one table; another held a shield emblazoned with strange runes. After what she'd learned in Subtle Magic, she had a feeling that the runes were intended to help the shield hold firm, no matter what struck it. A third table was covered with metal arrows, each one charmed to fly directly to its target. The fourth held a silver necklace that glittered under the faint light from high overhead. Emily reached out to touch it, only drawing her hand back when she realized that it was enchanted.

"I wouldn't touch that if I were you," Yodel said. He stepped out of the shadows and bowed politely to her. This time, he was wearing protective gear that kept his face and hands thoroughly covered. "That necklace is charmed."

Emily frowned. "To do what?"

"Private commission," Yodel said, bluntly. He looked her up and down, then removed his mask, giving her a moment to realize that he hadn't changed at all since their first meeting. "You have become someone *interesting* since we last met."

"Yes," Emily said, flushing. She'd been new to Whitehall when she'd first visited Dragon's Den. Since then, she'd beaten Shadye *and* been ennobled by King Randor. "And I may have broken my trunk."

Yodel lifted an eyebrow, then stepped past her to examine the trunk floating in the air. "And what, exactly, did you do to it?"

Emily felt her flush grow brighter. "I put a Cockatrice in it," she said, and explained briefly. "There was no other choice."

"I am...reassured to hear it," Yodel said. He tapped the trunk with one finger. "Is the beast still in there?"

"No," Emily said, feeling a stab of guilt. She hadn't gone to see the Cockatrice since it had been decanted from the trunk and installed in Whitehall's zoo. It had already become the star attraction for Mistress Kirdáne's Magical Creatures class. "It had to be removed."

"A good thing too," Yodel said, dryly. He started to cast spells Emily didn't recognize over the trunk. "You did pretty shoddy work. You're lucky that the safety features weren't triggered, throwing everything you stored in the trunk out into the open."

Emily nodded. She knew, better than most, what happened if a pocket dimension snapped out of existence. Trunks and other dimensionally transcendent artefacts were designed to expel their contents if the dimensions were on the verge of collapse, which would have been disastrous if the trunk had still been holding a very angry cockatrice. Thankfully, the spells had held long enough to get the beast back to Whitehall, rather than forcing her to kill it and use the body for alchemical ingredients.

"If you were my apprentice, I'd sack you for this," Yodel added. "You really *were* incredibly lucky. I don't think the trunk could have lasted much longer, not the way the spells were slowly starting to unravel. If I hadn't anchored them so firmly..."

"I know," Emily said. "Can you fix it?"

"You might be better off buying a new trunk," Yodel advised. "The spells have been warped, making it difficult to be sure that they *were* completely fixed. I don't know anyone with the kind of precision required to inspect each and every one of the charms worked into the trunk, let alone ensure that they work together properly. Most of the more advanced features would be disabled in any case. They simply couldn't be trusted."

Emily winced. The trunk was the first item she had bought with money she had earned, rather than cajoled from her mother or stepfather. And it was where she had hidden her books, including Void's spellbook. It held a special place in her heart.

But if it broke down completely, she risked losing everything.

It crossed her mind that Yodel might be lying, that he might want to sell her a new trunk rather than go to all the effort of repairing the first one, but she knew that he was probably telling the truth. She'd had to improvise desperately when she'd turned the trunk into a trap and she'd almost certainly damaged the trunk quite badly in the process. In hindsight, she might have done better if she'd sent it directly to Whitehall, rather than keeping it with her.

But then I wouldn't have had a secret weapon, she thought, remembering the crow-sorcerer and how close he had come to killing her and enslaving Alassa. *I was very lucky.*

"I think I'd better buy a new one," she said, reluctantly. "Do you have one like this one?"

"I have two in stock, both just as good," Yodel assured her. "And I am currently putting a third together that includes extra space for books. The reading lists at Whitehall seem to have tripled since last year and students want more space for books."

It took Emily a moment to realize *why.* Producing books had been difficult and expensive...until she'd introduced the printing press, along with a number of other concepts from Earth. It hadn't taken long for the printers to start copying as many books as they could, including spellbooks and educational textbooks. In the long run, literacy was going to skyrocket...

And my classmates will kill me if they discover that I expanded their reading lists, Emily thought ruefully. Talk about unintended consequences! Maybe the forbidden tomes wouldn't be copied, but everything else could be...what would *that* do to the world?

She pushed the thought aside for later contemplation and looked up at Yodel. "I think I'd want one of those," she said. "And I need to ask you for something else."

Yodel's eyes glittered. "As long as it isn't an apprenticeship," he said. He tapped the trunk meaningfully. "Maybe you'll be a capable enchanter in five years, but you have a great deal to unlearn."

Emily smiled, weakly. "I was wondering if you had a book on enchantment," she said. "I couldn't find one in the library."

"*That* isn't too surprising," Yodel said. "Enchantment can be a very rewarding career, if you have the mindset to make it work."

He stared at her for a long moment. "Is there a reason you want to borrow one of my books?"

"I could buy it outright," Emily said, avoiding the question. She certainly didn't want to tell him the *truth*. "I do have money..."

"Books like this are rarely *sold*," Yodel said, flatly. "And even if they were, I might not be able to find another copy. I do not know if the printers have started producing books on enchantment yet."

He looked down at the trunk. "On the other hand, loaning you the book might stop you from wrecking another trunk in the future," he added. "But I'd want something in exchange."

Emily hesitated, then lifted an eyebrow.

"Four hundred gold coins," Yodel said. His voice was still flat, emotionless. "Or a place in your estate."

"Four hundred gold coins is a staggeringly high price," Emily said. "Besides, I don't carry that much on me."

She smiled at the thought. Credit and debit cards allowed someone to draw on their funds while reducing the risk of having the money stolen and spent by someone else, but there was no such thing in the Allied Lands. Yet, at least; she did have a plan to found a bank with something akin to debit cards. It would still take months for it to start working properly.

"You are a baroness," Yodel pointed out. "You could easily offer me a place in your estate."

Emily frowned. It seemed simple and cheap—which probably meant, in her experience, that there was a sting in the tail. She might have never been the consummate haggler that Imaiqah was, but she *had* learned a few things about bargaining. Why did Yodel even *want* to move?

"The City Fathers are threatening to raise taxes or otherwise conscript magicians into their service," Yodel explained, when she asked. "Events last year scared the hell out of them."

Emily didn't blame the City Fathers, even if they had seemed a pack of condescending assholes when she'd met them. Shadye's army had been stopped at Whitehall, but he could easily have left a force behind to keep Whitehall sealed and sent the rest of his monsters to pillage the surrounding lands. Dragon's Den was walled, but she knew better than to think that would stop a necromancer. Or a force willing to take as many casualties as necessary to win the day. They might pile up their own bodies in front of the walls and scramble over them to break into the city.

"Besides," Yodel added, "I might be of more help to you there."

That, Emily had to admit, was true, even if her theory *didn't* pan out.

"Very well," she said, finally. "You loan the book to me; I keep it for the rest of the term and return it to you during the spring holidays. In exchange, you will have my permission to leave Dragon's Den and immigrate into my lands, provided that you behave yourself. Does that make sense?"

Yodel smiled, making her wonder just who had gotten the better part of the deal. "Perfectly suitable," he said, simply.

Emily narrowed her eyes. "In addition, you will give me help and advice when I need it," she added.

"While you have the book," Yodel countered. "And if you should lose the book, you have to pay me the full four hundred gold coins."

"Very well," Emily said. She could afford it, if necessary. "When can I expect my new trunk?"

"I can have it ready within the week," Yodel said. He turned and led her into the next room, where a handful of wooden trunks sat on benches. They all looked crude and unfinished, without the varnish and designs—runes, perhaps—that had been carved into her first trunk. "The interior dimensions are largely anchored; I just need to reshape the charms that allow you to remove whatever you want from the trunk, then decorate the exterior. Do you have any particular request? I could do your coat of arms, if you wanted."

Emily shook her head. "Nothing that should tell someone who owns the trunk," she said, flatly. "Just like the other one, basically."

"I'll copy the permissions from the old trunk to the new one," Yodel said, "and have the new one shipped up to Whitehall. If there are problems, bring it to me on your next weekend here and I'll fix it for you."

He pushed a curtain aside, revealing a small bookshelf. "This is the standard introduction to enchantment," he said, picking up a small book bound in black leather. "My master used to say that if you couldn't handle everything in this book, you had no business pretending to be an enchanter. It took me six months before I could perform everything to his standards."

Emily took the book, pressing her fingers against the cover. "Thank you," she said. "I won't lose it."

"See that you don't," Yodel said. "It may be a long time before the printers start producing copies."

Chapter Twelve

EMILY WOULD HAVE PREFERRED TO GO BACK TO WHITEHALL AT ONCE AND START READING the book, but there was no point in even trying. Both Alassa and Imaiqah were determined to find new outfits for themselves—and Emily—and she reluctantly allowed them to suggest several new outfits for her. Two pairs of light trousers that reminded her of jeans, although they were a little tighter than she would have preferred, would come in handy when she was jogging, while a simple dress would suffice for etiquette lessons and the promised dances later in the year.

"They'll all be staring at you," Alassa assured her, as Emily studied her reflection in the mirror. The white dress set off her brown hair nicely. "And all you need is a pretty necklace to direct their gaze to your face."

"They already stare at me," Emily reminded her, tartly. "And they stare at you."

"So they should," Alassa said, unrepentantly. "It's just something you have to get used to as a baroness. Everyone who is lower on the social scale—which is just about everyone—will be taking their cue from you."

"So if I went into the library instead of hosting dances," Emily said, "they'd go into the library too?"

Alassa giggled, then sobered. "Or they'd think you weren't keeping your eye on the ball," she warned. "That's a good way to get booted out of the arena."

Emily nodded. Alassa might have wanted to found her own *Ken* team because it would give her a chance to lead, but it would also help prepare her for life as queen, where taking her eyes off the wrong ball might lead to worse than a few minutes in the penalty box. The ever-shifting patterns of allegiance and loyalty in court were exactly like the arena, where a wall might be there one moment and gone the next. It took more than physical skill to play *Ken* and win.

"Come on," she said, as they paid for their purchases. "It's time to go have something to eat."

Dragon's Den, like most of the city-states, had food stalls that included cuisines from all over the Allied Lands. Emily enjoyed eating at Whitehall, but the food rarely strayed from what the cooks thought enterprising young students should be eating to maintain their health and happiness. Eating in Dragon's Den, on the other hand, allowed her to try foodstuffs that were never served at Whitehall. She didn't always like it—one place had nearly made her throw up, after serving something that had smelt like rotting fish—but it was definitely an adventure.

They found a small grill and sat down. There were no printed menus yet; instead, the menu was written on a blackboard with chalk. Emily selected the mixed grill, while Imaiqah and Alassa ordered two different meals. They could share them so they all had a taste.

"I was looking for an outfit for the team," Alassa said. "Maybe just something to mark us. But there wasn't anything suitable."

"It might not be legal either," Emily reminded her. "Aren't you supposed to draw your equipment from the stores?"

"Yes, but we are allowed to design our own uniforms," Alassa said. "But I couldn't find anything *original*."

The food arrived before Emily could say anything else. It smelt spicy; she was relieved to see the small jugs of yogurt and other condiments, as well as the bread. The food seemed almost Indian, but the waiter seemed so pale as to be almost translucent. That, she vaguely recalled from her studies of geography, suggested that he came from the Ice Kingdom to the far north.

Or his family did, she reminded herself. The Empire had encouraged trade and resettlement before its fall and, because everyone spoke the same language, fitting in hadn't been too difficult. No wonder racism had barely existed in the Empire, at least racism against human beings. The racism against magical creatures seemed just as illogical.

"Not too bad," Alassa concluded, as they finished the meal. "I'll have to see about importing this into Zangaria."

Emily snorted. The meals in Zangaria had been even less imaginative than the meals in Whitehall...at least at the formal receptions. She'd heard that private parties were much more imaginative, but she'd never been invited to any. Rumor had it that hostesses, desperate to keep themselves in the public eye, kept pushing the limits of what they could decently serve to their guests. Stuffed dormice and roast cat were the least of it.

"I received a request to immigrate today," she said, and outlined briefly what Yodel had said. "Why would he want to move?"

"Could be that he expects great things from you," Alassa said. "You've already reshaped the tax laws in your territory. What *else* might you do in the future?"

Emily scowled. The tax laws the previous baron had written—or enforced—seemed designed to spark off an eventual uprising and civil war. It wasn't a question of what the baron would take, but what he would let the peasants *keep*. A single bad harvest could wipe out an entire village, particularly if the baron didn't let them off their taxes. And it hadn't taken long to realize that part of the reason takings were so low was because the baron's henchmen all took their share—and more. Removing them had been necessary, just to ensure that she gained *something* from her holdings.

"I have no idea," she said, tiredly. She looked down at her empty plate and smiled. "Perhaps I'll introduce the burger or pizza to the world. Or fries."

Alassa nodded and stood, leaving a handful of coins on the table. "Time to get back to school," she said. "We have another practice session this evening."

"Oh," Emily said. "And how are you doing?"

"We're learning," Alassa assured her. "And we're evolving our tactics."

Imaiqah caught her arm. "You will come to our first game, won't you?"

Emily hesitated, then nodded reluctantly. She didn't want to waste her time watching a game when she could be reading or studying, but both of her friends deserved her support. Besides, it might give her a chance to relax.

"I'll come," she said. "Who are you playing?"

"We're not sure yet," Alassa admitted. "One of the older teams is having difficulty recruiting new players, so they're trying to convince the tutors to give them additional time. If they don't, the first set of games should be played in a week or so."

Emily nodded. She hadn't been interested, but she'd picked up a great deal of information about scoring anyway, enough to know that each team would play the others, then the scores would be somehow tabulated and a winner announced at the end of the year. It seemed confusing to her, but the simple solution—eliminate each team that lost a game—was probably cruel and unnecessary.

"Good luck," she said. "I'll be there."

The drive back to Whitehall was hair-raising; more snow had fallen on the road, making it very hazardous. Emily couldn't help wishing that they'd decided to walk instead—she'd walked further for Martial Magic—but neither Alassa nor Imaiqah took the class. By the time they pulled up in the courtyard and saw the line of animated snowmen forming up in front of the door, she was very relieved to be back.

"Look out," Alassa snapped, as the snowmen started to throw snowballs towards the carriages. "Who made *those*?"

Emily ducked as a snowball thudded into the carriage, just above her head. "I don't know," she said, concentrating on raising a shield. The lecture on Construction had mentioned animation, but the tutor had explained that they wouldn't touch on it until fifth year. "How do you get rid of them...?"

There was a flash of red light from Master Tor's carriage and the snowmen started to melt with terrifying speed. Emily thought she heard groans as they faded into puddles and drifted away, even though she ***knew*** that they weren't truly alive. Master Tor stepped over the water and led the way into the school, then stopped just inside. He caught Emily as soon as she entered the building herself.

"I'll review your essay tonight at seven bells," he informed her. "I hope you have it ready."

"Yes, sir," Emily said, shortly. She didn't need to eat dinner after eating in Dragon's Den, which would give her time to review the essay before she took it down to him. She knew from experience what happened if the punishment essays were unsatisfactory. "I'll be there."

Alassa squeezed her shoulder as they made their way past him and up the stairs to the dorms. "Don't worry," she said. "You're much better at writing essays than I am."

Emily shrugged. It had taken her far too long to master the techniques she needed to use at Whitehall, even though she'd written essays on Earth. There were no computers, no spellcheckers...and a single mistake could force her to rewrite the whole sheet of parchment out again and again. It did teach precision, she had to admit, but it was also very frustrating—and torturous. Writing with a pencil for so long left her hands feeling numb.

"Let's hope so," she said. "But you probably know more than I do."

She waved goodbye and stepped into her room. The Gorgon was absent—Emily hadn't seen her in Dragon's Den, which might not have been surprising—but Lin was lying on her bed, reading a large textbook on law. Emily wondered absently if Master Tor had written textbooks too. He certainly *looked* the type of professor who would force his students to buy books he'd written.

But he should know what he's talking about, she thought, as she sat down at her desk. *You can't fake competence here.*

She found her essay and read it over for the final time, looking for problematic areas. There weren't any that she could see, but she had a suspicion that there was plenty of common knowledge that had been left out of the books. No one apart from her, the sole immigrant from another *world,* had questioned the exclusion of werewolves and other magical creatures from human settlements. There had been more antislavery campaigners in the American South than that!

Shaking her head, she pushed the essay to one side and opened Yodel's book. Unlike most textbooks, it seemed to be written with the completely ignorant in mind; it started with baby steps and went upwards from there. Emily sucked in her breath as she realized why; enchantment was fantastically complex, even when creating a basic pocket dimension. If she hadn't had Whitehall's nexus point to draw on, back when she'd fought Shadye, it wouldn't have worked so well. Raw power had compensated for the shortcomings in her spellwork.

And it wouldn't even work outside a nexus point, she thought, slowly. Trapping the Cockatrice had been straightforward, if risky, but trapping another necromancer might be much harder. The imitation black hole she'd created might not be practical outside Whitehall...or require so much power that a single magician, even a necromancer, couldn't duplicate it. And that meant...

Shadye's lands on the other side of the mountains hadn't been taken by another necromancer, Emily had heard. That was...*odd*; despite their madness, they had to believe that Shadye had been killed directly, rather than the more traditional method of poison or trickery. She'd intimidated them all...but she was effectively bluffing. What would happen when they called her bluff?

She muttered a curse under her breath and started to parse out a basic spell for crafting a pocket dimension. It was much harder than she had assumed; there were so many separate sections in the spell that making them all work together would be a nightmare. No wonder, she decided, that Yodel had been so horrified by her makeshift modifications to her trunk—or why they had rendered the trunk almost completely useless. Altering one variable might cause the entire spell to collapse.

Lin put down the textbook with a loud thud and headed off to dinner. Emily started, then rolled her eyes. It was easy to forget that Lin was there; the girl seemed to spend her time in classes, the library or the dining hall, nowhere else. Emily had tried to talk to her, but it had gone nowhere. Maybe she just needed more friends.

She stored Yodel's book in her borrowed trunk, then stood and changed into a clean set of robes. It was a rule—a stupid one, in her opinion—that students visiting their tutors after normal school hours still had to wear their robes, even though the blanket ban on wearing anything else had been rescinded. She picked up her essay and a small bound notebook she'd been sent by Imaiqah's father, then walked out of the room, feeling her heart starting to pound inside her chest.

Master Tor's office door opened when she approached, beckoning her inside. Bracing herself, Emily walked into the room and nodded politely to Master Tor, who held out a hand for the essay. Emily kept her face as expressionless as possible as she passed it to him and stood at parade rest, silently grateful that the sergeants had insisted that they spend so much time standing to attention. Before she'd come to Whitehall, she would have been fidgeting within minutes.

"Werewolves become extremely dangerous when the full moon is up," Master Tor said, when he had finished reading her essay. "If you happen to encounter a werewolf during that time, you will be very lucky to survive—and if you are bitten, you will become a werewolf yourself. There is no cure for lycanthropy, nor is there any way to moderate the hunger and lust of born werewolves. In packs, at least, they turn their aggressive tendencies on each other."

Emily shuddered. The packs seemed to be dominated by the rule of might making right. An alpha male could never rest, even when in human form; another male could issue his challenge at any time, demanding control of the pack. And such duels were always to the death. The victor would gain power and unrestricted access to the pack's females, who had their own hierarchy. It made the power struggle in Zangaria looked genteel by comparison.

"In human form, they *still* act as a pack," Master Tor added. "When alone, they may seem human, but they are very far from it. You can never trust them completely."

He put the pieces of parchment down on the desk, then looked up at her. "Did you learn something from this essay?"

"Yes, sir," Emily said, shortly.

Master Tor studied her for a long moment. "And do you have any *questions* about this essay?"

Emily hesitated, then nodded. "Why are Gorgons excluded from human settlements too?"

"They do tend to scare people," Master Tor said. "Do you know that Gorgon petrification is almost impossible to reverse? The Gorgons themselves can do it; human sorcerers can rarely cure someone who has been turned to stone by a Gorgon. They were created by the faerie—and, like all such creatures, they have unpleasant surprises running in their bloodstream. And they *worship* the faerie.

"A deal was made in the closing days of the Empire," he added. "If they stayed in their own lands, we wouldn't try to destroy them. They are not really part of the Allied Lands—your roommate wouldn't be here at all if she hadn't developed an independent talent for magic. And when she finishes her education, she may not be able to *use* it."

Emily scowled. "But why is that a *problem*?"

"The Gorgons worship the faerie," Master Tor reminded her, shortly. "What would happen if they tried to bring them *back*?"

"I see," Emily said, slowly.

But she didn't, not really. The Gorgons could surely have called the faerie back by now, if that were possible—and if that was what they wanted to do. And if they were constantly treated like dirt by the nearby humans, they might well want to upend the balance of power once again. It just didn't seem *right* to treat them as animals.

"I have checked your timetable," Master Tor said, changing the subject. "You should have no problems with the rest of the term, although I am obliged to warn you that you only have a month to switch or drop classes without repercussions. I have also reviewed your curriculum for Martial Magic. I would advise you to concentrate heavily on wards, booby traps and other passive defenses. Your expertise in this is shockingly low."

Emily nodded, surprised that Master Tor was trying to be helpful. Each Martial Magic class drew in students from several different years, but Emily was still the youngest—and least experienced—of them all. Aloha would have mastered Construction and Warding in her second year, while also taking the first year of Martial Magic. Jade would have had five years of experience and education under his belt before joining the first class himself.

"Yes, sir," she said, finally.

"They will be testing you first, on Monday afternoon," Master Tor added. An odd little smile played over his lips. "I suggest that you spend the rest of the weekend researching in the library. You're going to need it."

Or wind up completely humiliated, Emily thought, ruefully. *Just like playing Ken.*

"Thank you, sir," she said, out loud.

Master Tor marked her essay quickly, then passed it back to her. "There are some aspects you need to research more," he said, "but you can leave that until the end of the month. It doesn't really need revising."

The door swung open behind her. Taking it as her cue, Emily nodded to him and turned, walking out of the room. The door swung closed, allowing her to look at the notes he'd written at the bottom of the essay. He insisted that she did more research.

"Fine," Emily muttered, as she started to walk towards the library. "I'll *do* some more bloody research.

Chapter Thirteen

"SO," SERGEANT MILES SAID, ON MONDAY AFTERNOON. "ARE YOU READY FOR THIS?"

Emily looked up at Blackhall and shook her head. If anything, the small mansion looked even more sinister in the twilight. Darkness would fall completely, she suspected, before they returned to Whitehall. There were no lights in the darkened windows, suggesting an unfriendly welcome. If anything, the windows seemed to absorb the light.

"Smart answer," the sergeant said. As Master Tor had warned, he'd pulled her aside as soon as she had changed and taken her to Blackhall, while the others went with Sergeant Bane to jog around the school. "Have you mastered the emergency spell?"

Emily nodded and cast it into the air, careful not to actually move her hands. The instructions for casting the spell had been very clear on that point. All it did, she'd learned while studying the spellbooks, was create a surge of magic, one that could be detected by a trained sorcerer or pre-programmed wards. Sergeant Miles nodded as the spell shimmered into life and then faded away. They'd been warned that it wouldn't last very long.

"Should you find yourself stuck, cast that spell and I will come to the rescue," he said, giving her a reassuring smile. "That will, of course, result in you being marked down for the day—should you wind up knocked out or otherwise helpless, you will *also* be marked down. Don't use the spell unless there is no other choice."

Emily nodded, feeling her throat constrict. She'd faced worse than a haunted house, hadn't she? But two trained combat sorcerers had spent months devising tests for students, all of whom were more experienced than herself, and she knew that it wasn't going to be easy. Just touching the wrong thing might cost her the whole exercise.

Better than costing you your life if you have to do it for real, she thought, remembering the days of chaos in Zangaria. Sneaking through the castle's wards had been difficult—and if she hadn't had a sample of Alassa's blood, it would have been impossible. She was ruefully aware that a trained sorcerer would probably have done a far better job.

Sergeant Miles reached into his pocket and produced a small glowing orb, barely smaller than Emily's fist. "Your task is to find this orb's counterpart in the house and then remove it from the property," he said. "You may take as long as you believe necessary, but *do* bear in mind that the longer you stay inside, the weaker you will become. Next time, you might want to bring water and foodstuffs with you."

Emily flushed. She hadn't been told to bring water and food, but she hadn't been told that it was forbidden either. And if she had, the worst that would happen was that it would get confiscated before she went into the house.

"Good luck," the Sergeant said, taking a step backwards. "And be *careful.*"

"Wait," Emily said. "How should I enter the house?"

"Any way you please," Sergeant Miles said. "It's up to you."

Emily turned back and faced the house, then slowly walked towards it until she was only a meter from the stone wall. She could sense hints of magic crackling through the stone, almost certainly basic protective wards firmly embedded within the rock. Breaking them required more force than any magician had, short of a necromancer. A team effort might work, she knew, but it would certainly alert the person who had put the wards together. She wouldn't have put it past the sergeants to have someone *inside* the house, reconfiguring the wards to trap unwary students.

She stopped in front of the main door and cast the basic magic detection spell. The doorknob lit up with an ugly red color, so bright that it took her a moment to realize that the entire door was glowing red. Touching the doorknob would probably mean instant failure. Shaking her head, she walked around the house, checking each of the windows. They were all warded, several quite imaginatively. One of them actually looked unprotected until she was almost close enough to be caught. The rear door was just as heavily protected as the front door.

Picking her way through the wards might be possible, she told herself, but she knew she should look for a simpler solution first. Carefully, she checked the walls themselves; if *they* weren't so heavily protected, maybe she could blast her way into the building. She certainly hadn't been forbidden to do that either. But there were loose traceries of magic running through the stone, grounding the wards. Knocking the wards down might be impossible.

Emily exclaimed in frustration and took a step or two backwards, staring up at the rear of the house. There *had* to be a way in somehow...she walked around the house, looking for the solution, dimly aware that the sergeant was watching her. And then it hit her. There was a gap between the rear door and the stone floor. It didn't seem to be protected. Emily walked up, shaped a shrinking spell in her mind and cast it on her own body. The door seemed to expand in size rapidly as she shrank.

Her mind spun as her perspective altered. Instead of being a footstep or two away, the door seemed to be miles from where she was standing—and the gap underneath the wood seemed impossibly huge. Emily fought down the sense of dizziness—being shrunk messed with a person's mind, even if there *were* protections woven into the spell—and ran forward. It still seemed to take a long time before she passed under the door and into the house.

She heard a scuttling sound in the darkness and hastily undid the spell, staggering as she returned to normal size. A spider or cat might be harmless to a normal-sized human—although she'd seen films where the enemies were tiny but poisonous spiders—but they would be lethal to her if she remained barely five centimeters tall. The darkness inside the building fell around her as though it were a living thing; gritting her teeth, she cast the spell for a light globe and sighed in relief as it burst into life, illuminating the long corridor.

It was simple, almost completely unfurnished apart from a handful of portraits. The walls were made of cold stone, tingling with magic running through them. There were no obvious threats, which only made her more suspicious. The sergeants wouldn't have created obvious threats, but ones that would try to take their students by surprise. Emily cast the revealing spell and saw nothing, apart from a faint glow from the walls. *That* bothered her. It didn't seem likely that *all* they'd done was ward the walls.

Carefully, she cast a seeking spell into the air, concentrating on the image of the orb the sergeant had shown her. An arrow appeared in front of her, pointing upwards. The hidden orb was on one of the upper levels. Emily had only used the seeking spell twice, but the spellbooks had been clear on its limitations. It might point directly towards the hidden object, yet it wouldn't take account of walls or ceilings that might be in the way. And it could be fooled, if the wards were configured to do so.

She felt a tingle at her feet and looked down—and swore. Dark shapes were clustering around her boots, while the carpet was starting to feel as if it were turning into quicksand. Emily tried to yank her boots free, only to discover that the carpet had a firm grip on them and all that happened was that she fell over. Her bare hand touching the carpet seemed to make the effect worse; she forced herself to scramble forward, not daring to keep her hand anywhere for more than a few seconds. Desperately, she cast a practical joke spell—it undid shoelaces—at her own boots, then pulled her feet out of them. They vanished into the carpet moments later.

Emily ran down the corridor until she reached the end of the carpet and jumped onto the stone floor, realizing—a moment too late—that might have been a dreadful mistake. But the floor seemed solid and reassuring...she looked back at the carpet and cast the revealing spell, wondering why the magic hadn't shown up the first time she'd looked for it. It took her a moment to realize that the magic had actually been buried under the hallway and had come crawling up when she'd stepped onto the carpet for the first time. The spell hadn't found anything because the magic had been out of range.

Devious, she thought, looking around. There was a rickety stairwell ahead of her, looking barely strong enough to hold her weight. Carefully, she tested it and discovered a handful of obvious spells, each one ready to throw her down the stairs and back into the hallway. Putting her foot in the wrong place could be disastrous...she looked around, but the only other options were a pair of locked and charmed doors. Breaking the charms holding them closed was beyond her abilities. Inch by inch, she picked her way up the stairs, avoiding each of the hidden charms. When she reached the top, she almost relaxed as she triggered the seeker spell again. This time, the arrow pointed towards a blank wall.

Emily gritted her teeth, then cast the revealing spell yet again. The entire wall lit up with red light, practically *daring* her to take her best shot. She stepped backwards instead, looking down the corridor. It ran in the opposite direction, but there might be a way around the first wall if she looked around. The only other alternative was to go back down the stairs and try to find another way up. Shaking her head, she walked down the corridor, casting the revealing spell every fifth step. The walls kept lighting up with red light. But a door, when she found it, was completely free of magic. Suspicious, Emily used a spell to open it from a distance and peered inside. There was nothing but absolute darkness.

She looked back down the corridor...to discover that it was gone. The walls had *moved* when she wasn't looking. There was no way out, apart from walking into the darkness. She summoned another light globe and directed it ahead of her as she walked through the door, one hand ready to cast a protective spell. For a moment, she saw blank walls and another door at the far end...and then her light globe simply blinked out of existence, leaving her trapped in the darkness. It should have been silent, but she could *hear* something moving in the room. Desperately, she cast the spell again, but nothing happened. The wards were interfering with her magic.

All right, she thought, as the first flickers of panic began to run through her mind. *I keep walking forward and then I reach the door...*

She moved forward, but her fingers touched nothing. The room couldn't be *that* large, could it? But it was easy enough to create a magical trap that acted just like a hamster wheel; the victim could run as fast as they liked, but the ground would keep shifting beneath their feet and they would never actually get anywhere. Or perhaps it was a pocket dimension...she pushed the panic aside and knelt down, feeling cold stone beneath her fingers. The sound, whatever it was, seemed to be coming closer.

"Emily," a voice snapped. "You're retarded, girl!"

Emily stood and spun around to see her stepfather, drunk and staring at her with wild eyes. Everything she'd learned at Whitehall simply faded from her mind as the memories bubbled up inside her. His rages, his tantrums, the moments she'd caught him staring at her...he had never *hit* her, but there were times when she would have thought that would have been preferable. She had never quite dared shower or even wash when he was in the house. He advanced forward, his breath stinking of beer, forcing her back.

"You'll never amount to anything," he bellowed, waving his meaty fists in the air. "You won't ever..."

It was an illusion, Emily told herself, but it was so hard to actually *believe* it. The scene felt so *real,* a composite of a hundred different memories. Somehow, Blackhall had pulled them out of her mind, then flung them back at her. The confidence she had built up over a year in Whitehall faded away, leaving her the scared little girl who had hidden in her room, praying desperately that her stepfather would leave her alone for one more day. It would be so easy to collapse...

She was thirteen again, her body slowly starting to flower into womanhood. It hadn't been a pleasant time. Her mother had never told her anything about her own body. It had been a dreadful shock when she'd started to bleed for the first time, let alone grow breasts. And then her stepfather had started to *look*...She'd hidden, cowering in her room, knowing that the thin door would provide no protection if he came for her. Her life had been a nightmare...

And yet she hadn't really *known* it was real. She saw, now, that she had been subjected to mental abuse, but she hadn't known *then* that it was real. Who could she go to and ask for help? What if they didn't believe her? Fear had kept her prisoner far more effectively than ropes and chains. She'd long since lost the urge to trust any adult.

Emily gritted her teeth so hard they hurt, fighting to control her emotions as they threatened to overwhelm her. She wasn't that person any longer.

She forced herself to think and cast the cancellation spell, yet it took four tries before her stepfather's image snapped out of existence. Her panic forced her to push so much power into the spell that the magic trapping her in the room also vanished. The next light globe worked perfectly, revealing an empty room with a single door, right ahead of her.

Emily sank to the floor, staring at where her stepfather's image had been. No one knew him in Whitehall; the image had to have been pulled right out of her mind. There *were* spells that did just that, she knew from her reading, even though she had never used them herself. What did it say about her, she wondered absently, that her greatest fear wasn't the power-mad necromancer Shadye, but her powerless stepfather? Tears prickled at the corner of her eyes; it was all she could do not to break down and sob her eyes out. The reminder of where she had come from had torn away all of her carefully prepared mental defenses.

Somehow, she pulled herself back to her feet and staggered through the door. There was nothing outside but a long corridor; she cast the seeker spell and saw that the orb was directly ahead of her. The cold stone against her bare feet felt reassuringly solid as she kept moving, a droll reminder that her whole encounter with her stepfather had been an illusion, a particularly nasty one.

Good thing no one saw that, she thought, before remembering that they were probably being monitored by the sergeants. At least they probably wouldn't share what they saw with the other students. She was fairly sure that she wasn't the only person to come from an unpleasant family—Alassa's aunt had planned to either kill or enslave her—but it wasn't something she wanted to talk about, even with her closest friends.

She reached the door at the end of the corridor and checked it, thoroughly. There were no spells that she could detect, but when she tried to open it the door refused to budge. Someone had not only locked it, they'd jammed up the lock to make it impossible to pick. She glanced down, wondering if she dared shrink herself again, then realized that she couldn't make herself small enough to fit through the cracks. Shrinking spells had their limits; too small would prove immediately fatal, they'd been warned. Bracing herself, she triggered a blasting spell and watched the door explode into the room.

Emily peered inside—and frowned. It looked exactly like her room in Whitehall, at least in basic outline; there were no hints that someone was actually *living* there, apart from the chest on the floor. It looked like a pirate's treasure chest, right down to the golden padlock on the front. A golden key lay right next to it. She cast the seeker spell and nodded in approval when the spell firmly indicated that the orb was inside the chest. All she had to do was open the chest. She picked up the key...

...And felt a powerful transfiguration spell taking hold of her body. She tried to dispel it, but it was already too late. Her body shivered and melted into its new form...and she was stuck, utterly unable to move. Some such spells could be broken, but this one was too tough to break easily. And she couldn't even move her hands to help focus the spell.

"Well," Sergeant Miles said, from behind her. "That could have gone better, couldn't it?"

He moved into Emily's field of view and held up a mirror. She saw a small golden statue of herself, perfect in every detail, without a trace that it had once been human. The sergeant let her take a good long look, then cast the counter-spell. Emily staggered; she would have fallen over backwards if he hadn't caught her. Between seeing her stepfather and making a simple mistake, she felt as if she were at the end of her endurance.

"Yes," she muttered, reluctantly.

"You didn't do too badly, for a first time," Sergeant Miles said. "Some of your fellow students might try to get through the walls rather than risk walking into a mysterious room, but you didn't really have much choice. And you did manage to dispel the phobia spell, even though it had caught on to your mind. Losing your boots...you'd get marked down for that, but if you'd been trapped it would have been the end. Overall, not a bad first attempt."

His voice hardened. "Picking up the key, on the other hand, was careless," he added. "You should have known better than to assume it was safe—if you thought that much at all."

Emily felt herself flushing. She *hadn't* thought at all. In hindsight, she could have just cast the revealing spell and discovered that the key was booby-trapped. But she'd just been so relieved at the thought of completing her task and getting out of Blackhall she hadn't realized that the ordeal wasn't entirely over.

Sergeant Miles patted her on the shoulder. "You go back to Whitehall and get some sleep," he ordered, holding out a hand to help her to her feet. "Tomorrow, someone else gets run through the maze. The next time you get in, it will be a little harder."

Emily nodded.

"I'd suggest taking a sleeping potion too," Sergeant Miles added, as he put the key back where she'd found it. "The phobia spell often brings back old memories—and they are often stronger at night. Tell Madame Razz I ordered it, if she protests."

"I won't argue," Emily promised. "And thank you."

Chapter Fourteen

"PROFESSOR LOMBARDI IS MAD AT YOU," ALASSA SAID, THE FOLLOWING MORNING. "YOU missed his class."

Emily nodded, blearily. The sleeping potion had worked, but not well enough. She'd slept, she thought, yet she had also had vague nightmares that had kept snapping her in and out of sleep. By the time the first bell of the day rang, she still hadn't been able to get out of bed, let alone go down for breakfast. Professor Lombardi was definitely not going to be pleased.

"I know," she said, resisting the urge to rest her head on the desk. There was no point in irritating Lady Barb as well as Professor Lombardi. As it was, Emily knew she could look forward to another punishment essay—or worse. "I'll go speak to him before lunch."

Imaiqah reached across and put a hand on Emily's arm. "What happened to you?"

"Long story," Emily muttered. The sergeants hadn't told her to say nothing about her experience in Blackhall, but she didn't *want* to talk about it. Even Alassa, who had seen images from Emily's memories, didn't know the full story of her upbringing. "I overslept."

"That's bad," Alassa said, although she didn't sound convinced. "He *really* won't be pleased with you."

Imaiqah smiled. "How did you stop the bed from tossing you out in the morning?"

"I don't know," Emily said. Maybe Madame Razz had ordered it to let her stay under the covers until the sleeping potion had worn off completely. "I..."

Lady Barb swept into the room, closing and locking the door behind her. The class straightened up as she marched to the front of the room and turned to face them. Emily couldn't help noticing that a third of the students who had attended the taster class hadn't shown up; clearly, they'd decided that a career in Healing wasn't for them. They didn't even want to learn the basics.

"Welcome back," Lady Barb said, sardonically. She'd probably noticed the missing students too. "Stand up and gather round Paddy."

Emily stood and followed the other students to the front of the class. "We will start today with a very simple exercise," Lady Barb said, as she produced a silver knife from her robes and held it over Paddy's chest. "Watch carefully."

She plunged the knife into Paddy's body. Several students let out cries or stumbled backwards as blood—a shade too bright to be real—appeared around the wound, trickling down Paddy's chest and pooling on the table. Emily felt sick, even though she knew that Paddy wasn't human—or sentient. Lady Barb had done it so casually.

"This blade is cursed," Lady Barb said, conversationally. "I would like one of you to try a simple healing spell as I pull the knife out of the wound. Any volunteers?"

Song raised her hand.

"Very good," Lady Barb said. "On three...one, two, *three*."

She pulled the knife out of the wound. Song cast the healing spell...and the wound, instead of closing, opened wider. Blood spewed upwards, as if it were projected out of a fountain, forcing the students to jump backwards to avoid getting any on their robes. Seconds later, Paddy let out a disturbingly human-like cry and fell limp.

"The curse drew on the power of the healing spell and perverted it," Lady Barb said, into the appalled silence. She clicked her fingers and the wound started to heal. "Do you see what would have happened if Paddy had been a real human?"

Emily nodded. It was amazing what one could live through, the sergeants had pointed out more than once, but even a necromancer would have had trouble surviving having his chest ripped open. Healing spells had their limits, even without curses intent on making healing impossible. A human would have died before the magician had time to realize that something had gone badly wrong.

"You'll find cursed blades everywhere," Lady Barb added, dryly. "Even the ones that are not charmed to be instantly fatal can be disastrous, if not checked properly. And, as they are wired into the person's body, they are often far harder to remove than a standard curse."

She looked directly at Song. "How might you have handled it better?"

Song flushed. "Remove the curse first?"

"A very good idea," Lady Barb agreed. "You start by casting the most precise revealing spell you know"—she demonstrated; the knife lit up with an unholy red light—"and then you dismantle the curse as quickly as possible. *However*, it is vitally important that you don't allow yourself to panic. Curse-breaking, as you should have learned in first year, can be very complex."

Emily scowled, remembering the advanced exam they'd given her when she'd tested out of Basic Charms. Some curses could simply be dispelled, but others had to be dismantled very carefully or they might lash out at their victim before they fell apart completely. The nastier ones had to be taken apart in a specific order. Anyone looking at the curse might not have long to work it out before it was too late.

Lady Barb stabbed the knife into Paddy again. "This time, try to remove the curse first," she said. "Go."

Song cast the revealing spell, then a series of counter-curses. Emily watched as the curse faded away into nothingness, although she could tell that it wasn't a particularly *complex* curse. Paddy made sounds of distress as Song worked, causing her to bite her lip as her work proceeded. Finally, she cast the healing spell and pulled out the knife. The wound closed, but Paddy seemed to be no better. Moments later, he shuddered and expired.

Lady Barb reset him and took back the knife. "The standard healing spells are not capable of fixing such damage," she said. "You need more complex spells to save someone who has been stabbed. The body *wants* to heal, but it needs direction and those directions provided by the standard spells are...insufficient."

She looked up, eying her students. "Determining which kind of spell is required to deal with the wound is a vitally important part of your task," she added. "Standard healing spells require little power, beyond the first casting. More complex healing spells can leave you drained. Yet using the standard ones can be disastrous, if the wound is too deep or the body is too badly mauled. If you don't know for sure, use the more complex spells—but be careful that there are no hidden curses. You don't want to start doing two separate tasks at the same time.

"This"—she waved her hand in the air, causing a line of spell components to appear in front of them—"is the most basic form of advanced healing spell," she continued. "You'll notice that it bears a strong resemblance to curse-breaking spells, particularly the sections that allow you to control it directly, rather than allowing it to operate on its own. As you can probably imagine, these spells require a great deal of concentration."

She smiled, then returned the knife to Paddy's chest. "Princess Alassa, why don't you try to cast it first?"

Alassa nodded and stepped forward. She removed the curse first, then carefully cast the healing spell. There was a moment when magic flared around her, then Paddy let out a cry and blood splashed everywhere. Alassa jumped backwards, too late. Bright red blood stained her robes and hair.

"Too much power," Lady Barb said. The blood vanished a moment later. "Healing requires skill as well as power."

She held up a hand. "For those of you who look sick, I should remind you that healing is not a very clean art," she added, dryly. "Blood, guts and gore will be common if you go into healing. Grow a strong stomach or give up now."

Emily had seen horror ever since Shadye had dragged her into a whole new world, but there was something different about working on a living body. Two other students tried, both getting a little further than Alassa before Paddy expired. Lady Barb didn't seem angry at the failures, although she lectured the third student on not repeating the same mistakes as the prior students. When it was Emily's turn, she stepped forward, cast the spell and her mind plunged into Paddy's body.

The experience was deeply disconcerting. Curse-breaking allowed her to see the curses; healing, it seemed, allowed her to see everything inside the simulation of a human body. It felt almost as if she had placed her head under the water. Everything was so loud that she couldn't help wondering if she had plugged into Paddy's nervous system, at least to some extent; she was aware of the damage to his body without quite knowing *how* she was aware of it. But actually *healing* the damage was much harder. Basic healing spells would simply have knitted the wrong parts back together and caused worse problems in the future.

She concentrated, but the wound refused to heal properly.

Careful, she reminded herself. But it didn't get any better.

"None of you managed to heal him," Lady Barb said, when they had all finished. "I cannot say that I am surprised. Making the spell work is one thing, actually *healing* someone is quite another. By the end of the term, however, I expect you to have mastered the art."

Alassa stuck up her hand. "You *expected* us to fail?"

"It takes months of experience to perform an advanced healing spell successfully," Lady Barb said, flatly. "I did not expect you to heal him on your first try."

She motioned for them to return to their desks, then stood in front of the classroom at parade rest. "You will realize, of course, that the experience of working inside a person's body is rather hard to master," she said. "For your homework, you are to practice exploring each other's bodies—using the spell, I shall add quickly—and getting used to the sensations that come from being inside someone else."

Emily had to fight down a giggle. She wasn't the only one.

"Yes, we sniggered at it too," Lady Barb said. "And it *is* funny. Failing to master the spell, on the other hand, will cause you to fail this class. Is that so funny?

"You are *not* to attempt to wound each other so that you may practice healing," she added, tartly. "None of you are anything like ready to actually *heal*. I would also suggest that girls work with girls and boys work with boys. It's often easier to heal someone of the same sex as yourself, if only because you will have an instinctive understanding of how their bodies work."

There was a loud groan from the rear of the room. "Detention," Lady Barb said, aiming her words at one of the transfer students. "Healing is serious business. How many times do I have to repeat myself?"

Emily scowled, inwardly. She disliked being naked in front of someone else, even her closest friends. Alassa, for all her regal dignity, had no real problem undressing in front of servants, male or female. The idea of undressing in front of someone she barely knew...luckily, she could practice with Alassa and Imaiqah. Practicing with the Gorgon might have been possible, but her body might be significantly different from a normal human. She'd have to check before she asked.

Come to think of it, she asked herself silently, did she even *need* to undress?

"You will also look up case studies of cursed weapons and precisely what they did to their victims," Lady Barb continued. "I will expect five rolls of parchment from each of you at the end of the month, covering the most common ways to curse a weapon and how they can be detected and countered. There is, alas, no shortage of material."

Emily winced. *Another* essay?

"Now," Lady Barb said, once they'd written down the essay title. They knew from experience that having to ask for it later in the month would not be well-received by the tutors. "We will take a look at mundane ways to deal with injuries, all of which you *will* be tested on later in the year."

She launched into a long lecture on basic sanitation that, apart from a few odd points, seemed workable. Emily listened, fascinated, as she talked of tiny monsters in the air that spread disease—germs, in other words—and how they could be stopped. Even something as simple as making sure that everything was *clean* and washed regularly in boiling water, Lady Barb pointed out, would cut down on the risk of infection. Emily had known, intellectually, that some people in Whitehall knew about germs, but she had never looked at *what* they knew before. There just hadn't been time to look at everything.

They could have shared this knowledge with the world, she thought, sourly. *I didn't have to tell them anything about germs. They already knew.*

But the knowledge didn't seem to be very common, outside Whitehall. Some of the city-states she'd seen had been remarkably clean, others had been ghastly—and the conditions of the peasants in some of the kingdoms was appalling. Even King Randor had to use toilets that Emily wouldn't have installed in a prison. The stench alone should have been lethal.

She stuck up her hand and waited for Lady Barb to call on her. "Why don't you tell everyone about the...little monsters?"

"Because there are limits to what we are allowed to tell people," Lady Barb said. She couldn't have missed the accusation in Emily's tone, but she didn't respond to it. "And because even when we do, there is so much nonsense out there that it is hard to make any headway."

That, Emily decided, made no sense. She could see kings or other aristocrats deciding that the great unwashed should *remain* the great unwashed, even if they *did* catch diseases and drop dead in terrifying numbers, but why would they want to deny *themselves* the chance to live healthier lives? But then, they did have better food and drink than the peasants—and access to healing magic. They might reason that they didn't *need* to take better care of themselves, like a girl Emily had once known who went for liposuction every year.

But *Emily* had introduced the concept of basic sanitation and it had spread wildly...

She mulled it over for the rest of the class, while Lady Barb talked about the dangers of trying to transfer blood from one person to another. They didn't seem to know about the different types of blood; Emily made a mental note to use the memory spells to recover what she'd heard and forgotten about them. She could write it all down and give the information to Lady Barb.

"While healing," Lady Barb concluded, "you must remember that a person's life is in your care. A single mistake could kill him."

She smiled at the class, then clicked her fingers at the door. It opened with an audible *click.*

"Master the first part of the spell as quickly as possible," she ordered. "Once you have it mastered, we can proceed."

Emily waited until the rest of the class was gone—she didn't share Alassa and Imaiqah's next class—and then stood. "I need to ask for some advice," she admitted. "I overslept this morning..."

"Careless," Lady Barb said. "Which classes did you miss?"

"Advanced Charms," Emily replied.

"That's bad," Lady Barb said, dryly. "Annoying an expert in Charms is *never* a good idea, I'm afraid. Do you have a good excuse?"

Emily blinked, then explained. "I took a sleeping potion last night," she said, and outlined what had happened in Blackhall. "It didn't work perfectly..."

"The phobia spell is very good at getting under the victim's skin," Lady Barb said, when Emily had finished. "Luckily, it wasn't a Nightmare Curse. Those things are damn near impossible to remove without a great deal of luck. I'm impressed you threw it off as well as you did."

"I don't feel that I did well," Emily said. "I failed the test."

"You'll learn from the experience," Lady Barb grunted, in a manner that suggested grudging approval. "I would suggest going to see Professor Lombardi now and explaining what happened. He will probably insist that you review the material for today. He's much more easy-going than the one who taught me."

Emily winced at the thought. Professor Lombardi didn't seem to have the abiding sense of dislike that pervaded all of Master Tor's dealings with Emily, but he was a fussy precisionist who didn't hesitate to strike his student's hands when they made a mistake. Emily could see his point—a single mistake could be disastrous—yet part of her also resented the public humiliation. Visiting the Warden was almost preferable.

"Oh, yes," Lady Barb assured her. "Old Professor Shanks liked to use naughty students as test subjects. He'd have the victim stand at the front of the class and everyone else would practice their hexes on him."

Emily gulped.

"I'd go see Professor Lombardi now," Lady Barb said. "And Emily?"

Emily looked up at her, questioningly.

"You did very well yesterday, whatever you may think," Lady Barb assured her. "Pushing the limits is always a good idea. Even when you fall flat on your face, you learn something from the experience."

"Thank you," Emily said. "I'll try to do better next time."

"By the end of the year, you should be walking through Blackhall without problems," Lady Barb said. "And if you can't...you have quite a few years of schooling ahead of you. You could repeat that class without problems."

Emily thought, briefly, of Jade. If he'd failed Martial Magic's first year, he wouldn't have had a second chance. His hopes of an apprenticeship would have been dashed. Why hadn't he done it earlier? It wasn't something she felt comfortable asking him.

"I'll do my best," she promised. She turned and walked towards the door. "And thank you."

Chapter Fifteen

THE REST OF THE WEEK WENT BY VERY QUICKLY AS THE STUDENTS FELL BACK INTO THE comforting routine of classes, homework, eating, sleeping and using whatever time they had left for more entertaining pursuits. Alassa and Imaiqah spent most of their free time practicing with the team, leaving Emily to work on her homework as well as her private research project. It was frustrating, at times, trying to figure out how the enchantment spells went together, but she refused to surrender and ask her professors for advice. She wanted to solve it on her own.

Her new trunk arrived on Saturday, along with a note from Yodel asking for written permission to emigrate to Zangaria. Emily wrote out a note for Bryon, then signed it with the seal she'd been given by King Randor. Only Emily or her heirs, she had been assured, could actually *use* the seal. Alassa had demonstrated by trying to stamp it on a sheet of parchment, only for the seal to be completely illegible. Emily sent the note back down to Dragon's Den, then started transferring her books, clothes and other supplies from her borrowed trunk to the new one. There was so much room in the trunk, Yodel's instructions assured her, that she could hide an entire library inside and no one would be any the wiser. She had just completed the transfer when Alassa opened the door and stuck her head into the room.

"Aren't you coming to the game?"

Emily sighed inwardly, but stood. She'd half-hoped that Professor Lombardi's revision notes from the class she'd missed would provide an excuse, yet all he'd really done was revise some of the charms they'd studied last year and made sure that their spellwork hadn't slipped while they'd been on holiday. Emily had already mastered the basic charms, although she'd gone through them all one by one, just to make sure. She didn't want to irritate the professor again so soon.

"Coming," she said, as she sealed the trunk. She cast a wistful look at the notes on her desk, then decided to leave them till later. "Are you facing Cat's team?"

"No," Alassa said, as they left the room and headed down to the arena. "I think we're facing the Stompers. Gar's team. At least there will only be one set of opponents."

Emily smiled, ruefully. Gar had been a fifth year when she'd come to Whitehall, but he hadn't been in her first Martial Magic class. She only knew of him because everyone kept pointing him out as a great *Ken* player and nothing else. A jock, in other words. Emily wasn't even sure what someone like that could *do* outside Whitehall, not when there were few championship games outside Kingmaker. And Kingmaker was a Chess-like board game.

But Ken requires some skill and cunning, she reminded herself. *Maybe he excels in other areas too.*

The arena seemed even larger than she remembered as Alassa pointed her towards the stands. There were hundreds of students there, chattering happily amongst themselves as they waited for the game to begin. A number of students were tossing balls around *inside* the arena, although it looked like a piece of harmless fun rather than an early game. Alassa winked at her, then headed off towards the changing room. Emily, wishing that she had bought a book, found a seat and sat down, waiting for the game to begin.

It seemed like hours before the referee finally blew the whistle, evicting the students from the arena. Emily covered her ears as his magically-amplified voice bellowed out over the stands, announcing the Stompers and their new challengers, the Upstarts. Emily had to laugh; she'd known that Cat and his fellow Captains had termed Alassa's team the Upstarts, but she hadn't realized that Alassa had taken it for her own. If they won, the joke would be on their opponents.

The arena seemed to sparkle to life as the two teams marched inside. Alassa's face was set in a firm expression of grim determination, while most of the others looked rather nervous. It was impossible to blame them. The game they'd played during the tryouts was simplicity itself, compared to the regular version of *Ken*.

"Take your places," the referee ordered. "Captains...shake hands."

Emily watched as Alassa and Gar shook hands, both of them trying to do as much harm as possible. Alassa was good at hiding her feelings, but Emily could tell that she'd been hurt; Gar looked too thick-headed to notice if someone had crushed his hand into a pulp. Emily briefly considered what sort of spells she could throw at him, before realizing that it would be futile. The arena wouldn't allow outsiders to do more than point and laugh at the players. It seemed, she decided, that cheating was only permissible if it was done by the players—and if they weren't caught at it.

"On five," the referee said, as the Captains returned to their places. "Here come the balls!"

The spectators cheered as twenty balls plummeted down into the arena, their colors already flickering between green, yellow and red. Several players moved to trap balls, but no one tried to pick them up. Being hit by another ball while carrying one could mean being removed from the game completely, depending on the precise color. Emily smiled as the referee blew his whistle, marking the start of the game. Immediately, the Upstarts grabbed balls and started to throw them at their opponents.

It was lucky, Emily realized, that there *was* only one opposing team. If there had been four teams in the arena, she had a feeling that the three older teams would gang up on the Upstarts and try to force them out of the arena. Even with only one team, it was clear that the Upstarts were badly outmatched by the more experienced players. Or were they? Gar's team seemed to be largely composed of show-offs, while Alassa had worked hard to convince her players to work together.

Even so, the Stompers were brutally aggressive. They pushed through the corridors, trying to overrun the Upstarts. Their main target seemed to be Alassa herself, unsurprisingly, but that had clearly been anticipated. While Alassa was dodging balls, several of her teammates managed to score. The Stompers, irritated by the fact they might lose, redoubled their efforts, including throwing a handful of jinxes towards the opposing players. One of them was so blatant that the referee blew his whistle and sent the offending player off the field.

Emily sighed as the game went on and on. There was no set time limit; the game ended when all of the players from one team were pushed out of the arena. It could go on forever, she realized, even though she knew that the players couldn't play eternally. The Stompers would probably have the edge in raw endurance. She looked around at the spectators, wondering just how they could spend the entire afternoon watching the game. It might take hours before one team came out ahead.

And she wanted to experiment with Yodel's book.

I'm sorry, she thought, and left the stands. No one seemed to notice as she walked back towards the school and in through one of the side entrances. Unsurprisingly, the building almost seemed deserted; the students who weren't watching the game would probably be in the library, frantically looking up spells, case studies and precedents for their classes. There was more homework and private study in Whitehall than she'd ever had on Earth.

No one was in the bedroom as she stepped inside and sat down in front of her desk, looking down at the spell she'd composed. She'd scrawled the components out carefully, as Professor Lombardi had taught her, then checked them one by one to see how they interacted *before* she tried to actually cast the spell. Creating a pocket dimension, even a relatively simple one, was fiendishly complex. If she hadn't had some insights from her own universe, Emily suspected that it would have been impossible without many more years of schooling.

Maybe I can make a TARDIS next, she thought, as she checked the spells one final time. It should work, she assured herself. Every step seemed to fit together perfectly.

Carefully, she reached for the iron hoop she'd borrowed from the armory and placed it on the desk, positioning it so it stood upright. The instructions for actually *casting* the spell had told her that a solid inanimate object –preferably made of metal—would make the best anchor. Creating a pocket dimension that was attached to *her* seemed tempting, but the spellbook seemed to think that was a very bad idea. It didn't go into details. Emily had puzzled over it at first, then realized that if something went wrong and the pocket dimension expelled its contents back into the normal world it might well kill the magician who created the spell. It was far easier to abandon a trunk if necessary.

Concentrate, she told herself. The instructions insisted that she *visualize* the edge of the universe inside the hoop, as if it were a soap bubble. She closed her eyes and held the thought in her mind, then swore mentally as she realized that she would need to be looking at the spell while she cast it. There *were* treatments to ensure a perfect memory, but the permanent ones were dangerous. She would never be able to forget *anything.*

Bracing herself, she struggled to hold the image in her mind as she looked down at the spell, understanding finally why enchantment wasn't taught until fifth year. The kind of mental discipline it took to cast the spell was far greater than anything she'd ever tried, even the healing spell Lady Barb had taught the class. And to think that it had seemed *easy*! But it had been, with the power of the nexus behind her. *This* spell couldn't draw on the nexus, or it would be completely useless outside Whitehall.

She cast the spell, focusing on the image. There was a spark of magic...then nothing. Emily glared at the hoop of metal, then tried again. This time, there wasn't even a spark.

Emily shook her head and focused her mind. Yodel had probably had years of experience in memorizing and casting complex charms before starting to work on enchantment; *he* could probably cast the spells with his eyes tightly closed. Emily, on the other hand, had to do two things at once—and they tended to cancel one another out. She gritted her teeth, focused on the spell, and ran through it again. This time, the spark of power shimmered into life. The interior of the hoop was glowing with an eerie translucent light. A second later, it popped out of existence and the magic faded away.

"Well," Emily said, out loud. "At least that was *something*."

But it felt *odd*. Either the spell should have worked or it should have failed. Instead, it had clearly done something...and then collapsed. Shaking her head, she looked back down at the sheet of parchment, trying to see what she'd missed. Perhaps she'd messed up one of the spell components and the power had simply dissipated into the ether. But no matter how she looked at it, she couldn't find anything wrong.

She ran through the steps in her head. First, visualize the exterior of the pocket dimension where it connects to the main dimension. Second, blow out the dimension like a soap bubble, taking care not to exceed the level of magic and destroying the entire spell. Third, link the gateway to the hoop and seal the dimension. Done properly, it would be difficult for someone to even *find* a trace of its existence, let alone break into it.

But she honestly couldn't see where she was going wrong.

It was possible, she knew through experience, to drain her magic, but she didn't *feel* drained. She cast a light globe spell, then banished it; her magic seemed to be working perfectly. And yet the spell wasn't working quite right. Putting more power into it, according to the notes, shouldn't be necessary at all. Still, the only alternative was swallowing her pride and asking Yodel. It crossed her mind, briefly, that she could ask Void, but she didn't want to share her thoughts with anyone until she knew if it actually worked.

The hoop was warm to the touch, she realized, as she repositioned it on the desk. That was...*odd* too. She looked down at the book, but saw nothing about the anchor growing hot—or risking its own destruction. The book *had* advised her to pick something solid, yet it hadn't said why. That, in her experience, was alarmingly common in spellbooks. She cast a cooling charm, then closed her eyes, visualizing the edge of her pocket dimension. Maybe it would work better now she had a handle on how the magic was supposed to flow.

She opened her eyes, trying to keep the visualization in her head, and looked down at the spell once again. It seemed to come easier this time, now that she'd cast it several times; there was a surge of magic and the faint shimmer fell over the hoop once again. And then it just snapped out of existence. There was a wave of heat so strong than Emily pushed her chair back from the desk, feeling as if her face was starting to burn. She yanked the papers away from the desk before they could catch fire, ignoring the heat. The hoop was glowing so brightly that she was surprised it hadn't exploded.

The door burst open.

Emily spun around and saw Master Tor, storming into her room. He looked furious, far too like her stepfather for comfort; Emily recoiled, feeling somehow violated. She hadn't even *known* that male teachers could get into the bedrooms, although it did make sense. He *was* their Head of Year, after all. Behind him, she saw a nervous-looking Madame Razz.

Master Tor glared at her. "What the..."

He saw her notes and glanced down at them. A moment later, his face turned purple with rage. "You..."

Emily cringed back, expecting a blow at any moment. For a chilling moment, she thought she saw the face of her stepfather, drunk and furious, overlaying Master Tor. He gathered himself, then caught Emily by the ear and dragged her out of the bedroom. Emily gasped in pain, then forced her legs into motion as he pulled her down towards his office. The handful of students they passed on the way stared at them in astonishment—and horror.

"In," Master Tor said, pushing her into the office. He pointed towards the corner. "Stand there and *wait*!"

Emily found her voice. "I..."

"Shut up," Master Tor snapped. He pushed her into the corner. "Stay there, don't move and don't leave the office. If you do, I'll damn well see to it that you are expelled."

Emily staggered as she heard him leaving the office. She wanted to look around, or to run, but she knew that it would be useless. The office was probably warded to let him know what she did while she was inside, or to keep her from leaving. Besides, she needed time to think and calm herself. She'd thought that the effects of the phobia spell had worn off, but it was clear that they were still lingering in her mind.

And they don't have any mental health professionals here, she thought, bitterly. Naturally, a world where certain kinds of magic could drive one mad wouldn't want to develop cures, would it? And nothing in her life had convinced her that psychologists actually knew what they were talking about. But she would have been very grateful if someone had erased the phobia spell from her mind.

She cursed herself under her breath, wishing that she'd stayed at the arena, no matter how boring she'd found it. It might have saved her from getting into trouble... but she'd intended to run the experiment anyway. She might just have done nothing more than put the trouble off for a few days—or even hours. And Master Tor had practically threatened to expel her...

It felt like she was alone for hours before Master Tor finally returned to his office, giving her plenty of time to worry about what he was doing. Searching her trunk? It should have been impossible, but she knew better than to assume that breaking Yodel's enchantments was beyond Professor Lombardi—or the Grandmaster. Or was he shouting at the Grandmaster and trying to convince him to expel Emily, risking Void's wrath—and King Randor's? Or was he merely taking his time to make her sweat? Or searching for an extra painful cane? It was almost a relief when he returned to his office and closed the door behind him.

"Stay there," he grunted. "Hands on your head, where I can see them."

Emily obeyed, and waited. She heard the rustle as he worked his way through the papers—her papers or essays; she didn't know—and waited, as best as she could. The sergeants were fond of telling her that military service was mostly boredom, with fleeting moments of terror, but it didn't seem to compare with waiting for the hammer to fall. Or perhaps it was entirely the same thing.

"Turn," he ordered, finally.

Emily shifted around, not daring to take her hands from her head, and met his eyes. He was *furious*—and all of that anger was directed at Emily herself. It struck her, suddenly, that she had been very careless. He hated her and now she'd given him a reason to demand that she be expelled. And she didn't even know why!

"So tell me," he ordered, after a long chilling moment that had Emily half-convinced that he was going to kill her on the spot, "just *what* were you thinking?"

Chapter Sixteen

Master Tor went on before Emily could say a word.

"Did it penetrate whatever you use for a mind," he demanded, "that Whitehall is largely constructed within a pocket dimension? Your spell, as limited as it was, could easily have interfered with it."

Emily stared at him in horror. She'd known, but she hadn't considered the implications—and the book hadn't bothered to mention them. But it wouldn't have done, she suspected; nexus points were rare and required different techniques to harness and control.

"Did it occur to you to wonder," Master Tor added, "*why* enchantment isn't taught until fifth and sixth year? Why most enchanters learn their trade through apprenticeships? Why your class on Construction and Warding barely touched on it? The spells themselves cannot be practiced in Whitehall. Those spells have to be taught *outside* the school."

His eyes bored into hers. "The wards protecting the school automatically shut down any spells intended to create pocket dimensions," he snarled. "Under the circumstances, you're very lucky that you didn't accidentally start a fire too."

Emily found herself torn between relief and fear. Relief that her spell had been fine—it had been the wards that had prevented it from working properly—and fear for her future. Master Tor was quite right; it *had* been stupid of her to experiment in Whitehall, particularly when a few questions would have told her why it was stupid. And she had thousands of square miles of land in Zangaria she could have used to carry out her experiments.

"This piece of work"—Master Tor waved her parchment at her—"is crude, unformed—and could have done serious damage, if you'd lost control of it. I would appreciate knowing just *what* you were *thinking* when you started your little project."

"I wanted to learn how to make my own trunks," Emily said. It was partly true, after all—and she didn't want to share her other idea with anyone, at least until she knew if it would work. Once she'd created the pocket dimension, she would have embarked on the next stage of the project. "I've already lost one..."

"You are one of the richest students in Whitehall," Master Tor snapped, effortlessly overpowering her voice. "If you wished, you could buy trunks for every single student without straining your resources."

"Yes, but they wouldn't be *mine*," Emily said, frantically. She wanted to run and hide, not stand there and face him. "And I don't have *that* much money..."

Master Tor gave her a furious look. "Do you have enough money to replace an entire school?"

His voice hardened. "What you did was criminally irresponsible," he added. "I shudder for the poor peasants of Cockatrice, living under a baroness who thinks nothing of the danger to others when she works her magic. And you do realize that most peasants cannot leave their lands? They'll be exposed to you until the day you die."

That *stung.* Emily recalled the sort of brat Alassa had been before Emily had almost killed her; she'd shown a complete lack of concern for those she considered her social inferiors. But Emily ***hadn't*** been like that...or like some of the others she'd heard rumors about, during her time in Zangaria. The less said about Princess Lucinda the better.

"I didn't mean to put anyone in danger," she said, trying to control her voice. "I..."

"You didn't mean to put anyone in danger," Master Tor repeated. His voice became mocking. "I do believe that is almost worse! You didn't even ***think*** about the possible harm you could have done before you started messing around with pocket dimensions."

He looked her right in the eye. "That book is only available with a permission slip from the Head of Construction," he said. "Where did you get it?"

Emily hesitated, then confessed. "I borrowed it from Yodel, in Dragon's Den," she admitted. "I..."

Master Tor interrupted her. "And he loaned it to you, just like *that*?"

He went on before Emily could admit to making a deal with Yodel. "I shall insist that the Grandmaster have strong words with him," he snapped. "Taking on apprentices is one thing, but actually giving out books...you stupid girl! Why didn't you ask him to teach you on weekends? You could have performed the spell safely in Dragon's Den."

Emily shuddered, remembering her stepfather. He'd been fond of calling her a stupid girl too.

"Stop snivelling," Master Tor ordered. "Do you have the slightest comprehension of just how far the repercussions could have reached if you managed to actually ***damage*** the school?"

"...Yes," Emily said. She felt very small and stupid. If Whitehall had been damaged, if the nexus point had been warped...there were cautionary tales about what happened to people who meddled with nexus points. None of them ended well. "I'm sorry."

"You're *sorry,*" Master Tor repeated. "You're lucky you didn't accidentally start a fire and burn yourself to ash and you're *sorry*?"

"There aren't any rules against it," Emily said. "I..."

"Very few people would be stupid enough to start experimenting with pocket dimensions without reading up on them first," Master Tor said. "Or were you so determined to see if you could master the spell that you didn't even think to ask a few questions? Lady Emily, this is a place of *education*! Had you bothered to *ask,* we would have explained to you why trying to build your own pocket dimensions inside Whitehall was an immensely foolish idea. It's hard enough to convince the wards to accept trunks and other dimensionally-transcendent artefacts that are created outside the building. Why didn't you *ask*?

"Or weren't you told, back when you started, to be careful what spells you cast?"

His eyes bored into hers. "The most ignorant Hedge Witch would be aware of the danger," he sneered. "Why weren't ***you***?"

Emily gritted her teeth, but said nothing. Like so much else, it was something that would be immediately obvious to a native of this universe, but utterly unknown to someone from Earth, where pocket dimensions were the stuff of science fiction and fantasy. But hadn't there been an episode of *Doctor Who* where the TARDIS had been twisted around so that there was no way out?

"I have spoken with the Grandmaster," Master Tor added. "He is not happy."

Cold ice ran down Emily's spine as he continued. "He doesn't intend to expel you," Master Tor added. "He does, however, intend to ensure that you receive a very severe punishment. There may also be punishment for Yodel. Giving that book to anyone was not wise."

"It wasn't his fault," Emily said, quickly. "I borrowed the book..."

"And you seem to be alive and human," Master Tor sneered. "Dear me—did you manage to steal the book without being caught and punished? Or did you think that your status as the Necromancer's Bane was enough to save you from the consequences of your actions?"

Emily did her best to ignore his tone. "I made a deal with him," she said. "He didn't know what I wanted to do with the book and..."

"Do you think," Master Tor enquired archly, "that makes it any better?"

Emily remembered what he'd said earlier and flushed.

"The Grandmaster will talk to him," Master Tor said. "After that...we shall see."

It was on the tip of her tongue to point out that Yodel had wanted to move to Cockatrice, but she held it back. If Yodel was forced out of Dragon's Den, he could just go directly to Cockatrice and set up shop there. Even without any further patronage, an enchanter could find work anywhere. There was no shortage of demand for their skills. Master Tor didn't need to know that Yodel had options. Besides, it *wasn't* fair that he should suffer the consequences of Emily's misdeeds.

"Professor Lombardi will be talking to you later on," Master Tor said. He looked down at the piece of parchment. "I think he will want to go over, again, the sheer folly of a second-year student trying to craft a pocket dimension. What would you have done if it had started to expand uncontrollably? You would have been lucky if you'd *only* lost everything you put inside it."

Emily fought to keep her face blank. That was alarmingly close to what she'd done to Shadye.

"Luckily for you, the Grandmaster is merciful enough *not* to have your stupidity publicly announced at dinnertime," Master Tor added. "We would prefer that others didn't get ideas. Still, you are to avoid using magic in Whitehall without supervision—and you are *not* to be alone in your room, at least until we rescind the ban. Your roommates will not be happy with you."

Good thing Whitehall doesn't have house points, the irreverent part of Emily's mind whispered. *They'd have to make up some new numbers...*

She sobered. It wasn't going to be pleasant. All three roommates suffered if one of them was caught misbehaving in the rooms. The Gorgon and Lin would be furious when they found out that Emily was under restriction. They'd have to stay in the room with her or chase her out when they left. It wasn't going to be pleasant at all.

"No magic at all, unless you're in immediate life-threatening danger," Master Tor clarified. "I would suggest that you kept *that* part of the punishment to yourself."

Emily felt her stomach twist uncomfortably. Melissa and her cronies hadn't done anything so far, but she had a nagging feeling that once they had grown accustomed to the stresses of second year they would return to their favorite sport of hexing Alassa and her friends. Not that she could entirely blame Melissa for wanting a little revenge—Alassa had treated her badly, back when she'd been a royal brat—but it could go too far. And it would be worse if she wasn't allowed to retaliate—or even to cancel the hexes that caught her. She'd *have* to tell her friends...

...And they would be mad at her too.

"I'll do my best," she said, sourly. "I..."

"You might also want to ask yourself why Yodel didn't mention this to you when he loaned you the book," Master Tor said, nastily. He tapped the cover thoughtfully. "Did he assume that you already knew or did he want to get you in trouble?"

Emily hesitated. It wasn't uncommon for Whitehall students to be charged high prices when they went to Dragon's Den—and one shopkeeper had tried to sell her fake dragon's blood—but she couldn't see Yodel doing it deliberately. For one thing, Emily would certainly remember—and he would be living in *her* territory. Setting her up would be an incredibly foolish thing to do. And he might have assumed that she knew what she was doing...just because she was seventeen—she thought—didn't mean that she was in second year.

"I don't know," she said, finally.

"Perhaps I will ask," Master Tor said. He leaned forward. "You will report to the Warden, immediately. He is expecting you. Once you have finished with him, you will go to the library and study—I would suggest that you reread the safety precautions and rules that apply to all students in Whitehall. I will summon you later to discuss the rest of your punishment."

Emily gritted her teeth. It was far from uncommon to see punished students heading back to their rooms, but it was very rare to see one of them going to the library afterwards. Word would be all around the school before the hour was up. Everyone would wonder if she was trying to show off how tough she was...or if there was another reason why she hadn't returned to her room to hide until she felt better. In a school of thousands of students, she suddenly felt very alone—and exposed.

"This was incredibly stupid," Master Tor concluded. "If it were up to me, you would be expelled before you accidentally got someone killed—which, if memory serves, you nearly did once already. As it is...if you do something else like this, no one will be able to stop the Grandmaster from expelling you and sending you back to Zangaria. Do you understand me?"

"Yes, sir," Emily said, meekly.

"Remember what I told you," Master Tor said, sternly. His gaze bored into hers for a long moment, then he looked down at the parchment on his desk. "No spells. No alone time in your room. And *behave*.

"Oh, and as for the book?"

Emily leaned forward, despite herself. It wasn't *her* book.

"I shall return it to Yodel personally," Master Tor informed her. "I suggest that you keep whatever your side of the agreement was. It might make it up to him."

He pointed at the door. "Go."

Emily took her hands off her head and marched through the door, trying to keep her head held high. She sagged the moment the door closed behind her, feeling utterly defeated. He'd been right; she *had* been stupid, too stupid to even *think* about the possible consequences. And she could have asked someone...he was right about that too. Instead, she'd just bulled ahead and almost caused a minor disaster. The wards wouldn't have stopped her incinerating the room and everything inside it, including herself.

She dawdled as much as she could as she walked towards the Hall of Shame. There was hardly anyone in the corridors, apart from a pair of first-year boys who stared at her with open admiration. It was the Necromancer's Bane they were looking at, she knew, not a young and inexperienced girl who had made a stupid mistake. She was tempted to hex them before remembering Master Tor's admonishments. There was to be no magic at all without supervision, which effectively meant outside class. When Melissa found out...

The next corridor held a crying third year, who was being comforted by a sixth year girl who was clearly out of her depth. Emily remembered just how *she'd* felt while taking exams on Earth, even though they had been increasingly worthless as the years rolled on. Third year pupils, apparently, weren't eased back into their education, but expected to start studying intensely as soon as they returned to school. Those who failed to get back into harness were often forced to repeat the year again and again until they got it right. Emily could understand why one of the students would be crying...

She briefly considered helping, but what could she say? All she really wanted was to delay her visit to the Warden, not help a student who was a year ahead of her. The sixth year girl shot her an annoyed look and Emily walked on, not wishing to attract more trouble. She caught sight of her own reflection in one of the suits of armor lining the corridor and shuddered, inwardly. She looked as though she had been crying herself. Bitterly, she wiped at her eyes, then strode onwards. She would definitely be crying after she faced the Warden.

Emily gritted her teeth as she walked into the Hall of Shame. It was empty, apart from a sixth year boy—Travis—she knew from Martial Magic. He had never been teamed with her, which might have been why he seemed to dislike her. Jade, at least, had been willing to give her a chance...but the ones who didn't know her might well resent her. And, she realized numbly, the student was also a keen *Ken* player. Being assigned to supervise students waiting for punishment meant he'd miss the game.

Travis looked up at her. "How goes the game?"

"I don't know," Emily admitted. She didn't want to talk about it to anyone. "I left early."

"And got in *real* hot water," Travis taunted. He smirked at her, unpleasantly. "I have never heard Master Tor shouting so loudly in my entire life."

Emily shuddered. Had he really calmed down before coming back to face her?

Travis's grin widened. "I dare say the Warden will let you have it all right," he said. His face twisted into a leer. "I even think it's going to be on the bare."

"No," Emily said. She'd already cursed the decision to wear the trousers instead of her robes, even if they did look flattering. The cane would hurt more when it struck her bottom. "He can't..."

She saw his expression and realized that he was trying to make her panic. Jade had once told her that the only students who got caned on the bare were the ones who tried to don extra padding before reporting to the Hall of Shame. The Warden, it seemed, had an uncanny ability to tell when someone was trying to cheat.

Her temper flared. "You..."

"Have a care," Travis interrupted. "Insulting a sixth year could mean *another* session with the Warden. Or worse. Do you know how many transformation and compulsion spells I know?"

Emily bit down on what she wanted to say and started to walk towards the wall.

"You might as well go in," Travis said, airily. The previous ice was suddenly gone from his voice, replaced by mockery. "Fewer students come here for punishment when there's a game on."

His chuckles followed her as she pushed open the door and peered inside, her eyes slowly adjusting to the semi-darkness of the Warden's lair. She'd never quite worked out why he seemed to like to live in darkness, unless it was part of his reputation. For all she knew, he was a real party animal when he wasn't disciplining students.

"Hi," she said. Behind her, she heard the chuckles growing louder. It *had* been a stupid thing to say, but how did one address the Warden? Mr. Warden? "I'm here..."

She stopped and stared, feeling cold horror taking a firm grip of her heart. The Warden was seated, but his head was cocked to one side as if someone had snapped his neck.

And a silver dagger had been plunged into his chest.

Chapter Seventeen

EMILY RAN FORWARD, HEARING THE DOOR SLAM CLOSED BEHIND HER, AND LOOKED DOWN at the Warden's body. Bright red blood was trickling down from where the knife had been stabbed into his chest, while his neck was very definitely broken. She reached out to touch the knife, then caught herself at the very last second. Lady Barb had warned them that cursed blades could sometimes curse anyone foolish enough to touch them. And there was no point in trying to save him. If his neck was broken, the Warden was very definitely dead.

She spun around and ran back to the door. "Travis," she called. "The Warden is... come and look."

"This had better not be a joke," Travis muttered, as he stood and walked towards her. "You don't seem to have been..."

His voice drained away as he looked past her—and caught sight of the Warden. A moment later, he touched the sixth year badge he wore and then cast revealing spells over the protruding knife. Nothing appeared. Travis poked him in the chest and used a couple of spells Emily didn't recognize, then he looked over at her, his eyes burning with accusation.

"How did you do that?" He demanded. "You *killed* him?"

Emily stared at him in horror. How could he think that she had killed the Warden?

"I didn't," she protested. "You were *watching* me!"

"I wasn't watching you once you stepped inside and closed the door," Travis sneered. He waved his hand at her and she felt an invisible force fixing her shoes to the floor. She suspected, judging from the power, that removing her shoes wouldn't allow her to escape. "I'm calling the Grandmaster."

Emily fought down the urge to cry as he tapped his badge again and again, all the while keeping one eye on Emily as if he expected her to pull out another knife and stab him in the chest. What was *wrong* today? Everything seemed to be falling down around her. There was a bustling noise behind her and she tried to turn, only to discover that she was still stuck.

"Good grief," Mistress Irene's voice said. "What happened to him?"

"Lady Emily must have killed him," Travis said. "She was alone in the room with him..."

"For a few seconds," Emily snapped, finding her voice. "I found him like that..."

"Shut up, the pair of you," Mistress Irene ordered. She knelt down beside the Warden, then tapped the blade carefully. "Dead. Dead and gone."

"Yeah," Travis said. "He was alive while Master Tor was speaking to him..."

"I told you to be quiet," Mistress Irene said. She pulled the blade out of the Warden's body and examined it. "A silver dagger. Interesting. Sergeant Miles will need to look at it..."

She stood and walked over to Emily. "Come with me," she ordered. "Now."

"I can't," Emily said. Tears welled up in her eyes. "My feet are stuck."

"I didn't want her to escape," Travis said, self-righteously. "She could have..."

Mistress Irene waved her hand, cancelling the spell. Emily stumbled as the magic around her feet faded away; Mistress Irene caught her with one strong hand and gently steered her towards the door. Professor Thande appeared, as wild-eyed as ever, and stared in horror at the Warden. Mistress Irene nodded to him, then pointed to Travis.

"Take him to a private study cell and keep him there," she ordered. "The Grandmaster will want to talk to him."

"But I didn't *do* anything," Travis protested. "I..."

"It is standard procedure," Mistress Irene snapped, her patience clearly exhausted. "And if you have problems remembering it, perhaps your position of power should be revoked."

Professor Thande beckoned for Travis to accompany him. "Come with me, lad," he said, grimly. "There's no other choice."

Emily watched Travis, still muttering protests, being escorted out of the room, then Mistress Irene took her hand and led Emily out, closing, locking and warding the door behind them. There were a handful of onlookers already, gathered at the far end of the corridor, but there was no sign of the Grandmaster. Surely *he* would know that Emily couldn't have killed the Warden? Why would anyone want to kill the Warden?

The entire school, her own thoughts answered her.

She couldn't help feeling as if she were in handcuffs while she was escorted through a confusing network of corridors. If the other students had already seen her with Master Tor, God alone knew what sort of rumors were going to start when they realized that she'd been with Mistress Irene later. Even if they didn't know about the Warden...but they would, she knew. Even if Travis kept his mouth shut, it was rare for a day to go by without *someone* being sent to face him. Who would take over his duties now that he was dead? Someone would realize that Emily might have been the last person to see him alive...

And there had been a knife in his chest. Necromancers used knives...and quite a few students already believed that she *was* a necromancer. If they heard about her experiments with pocket dimensions, they might have wondered if it was the first sign of instability.

Mistress Irene stopped in front of a wooden door and waved her hand in a complicated gesture, disengaging the wards holding it closed. The door unlocked, revealing a small bedroom illuminated by a magical light set within the ceiling. There was a bed, a toilet and little else.

"I need you to stay here," Mistress Irene said, as she gently pushed Emily inside. "You have to wait here until you are summoned."

Emily looked around the bare stone walls. "Why?"

"Because we have to investigate what happened to the Warden," Mistress Irene said. "And because the alternative is taking other steps to...immobilize you."

"I understand," Emily said, bleakly. There weren't even any books in the tiny room. "Can I have something to read?"

"I can't let you have anything," Mistress Irene informed her. "And Emily?"

Emily looked up, frowning.

"*Don't* try to leave this room," Mistress Irene said. "There are people who would take it as a sign of guilt."

She closed the door, leaving Emily alone.

Emily stared at the bed for a long moment, then stepped over and lay down. It was a harder mattress than the one from the bedroom she shared with her roommates; she couldn't help wondering if the room was supposed to belong to the servants—or a prisoner. Whitehall *was* effectively a military school, at least to some extent, and she was sure that military schools had something resembling a prison for *really* rowdy students. Or maybe they were just expelled. She'd never been to such a school on Earth.

She stared up at the blank ceiling, trying to meditate. The sergeants—and later Lady Barb—had been keen on meditation as a mental discipline, but Emily still found it very hard to focus and calm her thoughts. Her emotions were spinning around; Master Tor's row had been bad enough, but discovering that the Warden was dead...she didn't know how to cope any longer, even though it had only been a day. Part of her just wanted to curl up and die.

They couldn't blame her for the Warden's death, could they? She'd been in Master Tor's office while he'd spoken to the Warden—if Travis had been telling the truth, Master Tor had been the last person to see the Warden alive. Had *he* killed him in a clumsy attempt to frame Emily? But the Grandmaster had already agreed to her punishment for crafting a pocket dimension and surely Master Tor wouldn't risk his position to try to punish her further. Besides, she knew that he had a great deal of latitude when it came to determining the rest of her punishment. He could have made Emily's life thoroughly miserable without risking his own career.

But would everyone *listen* to her?

No one had taken her seriously, not until she had come to Whitehall. Even then, there were people who thought that she was strange, or a very real danger. She remembered the reactions of some of Alassa's suitors and their families to the changes that Emily, however inadvertently, had wrought. They might well ignore all the evidence and demand that Emily be charged with murder, just to discredit her. And what sort of punishment would she receive for murder? Somehow, she doubted that it would be time in jail.

Maybe they give the keys to their jailhouse to unscrupulous creatures, the irreverent part of her mind whispered. *What could possibly go wrong?*

Somehow, the thought was not really amusing.

She ran through the first three calming exercises the sergeants had taught her, trying not to think about the Warden's dead body. But no matter how she concentrated, it just kept coming back into her mind. She'd barely known the Warden—outside of punishment sessions, she'd never even *seen* him—but he hadn't deserved to die, had he? And why *him*?

Maybe he didn't have any magic too, she thought, remembering Sergeant Harkin. But that didn't seem too likely. She hadn't really known what was about to happen the first time she'd visited him, yet surely the other students *would* have known. If someone had panicked and started to lash around with magic, it could have been disastrous. No, the Warden would have to be someone with *real* power, just to keep himself alive. But his magic had clearly failed him at the last.

And if someone had managed to use a necromantic rite to kill him, that meant that a necromancer was wandering the halls of Whitehall, probably already going insane.

Emily shivered, looking over at the wooden door. She *had* to tell the Grandmaster, she had to warn him, but Mistress Irene had told her not to leave the room. It was funny; once, she could have spent hours on her own, yet the moment she was told not to leave she *wanted* to leave. But the room was empty, without anything to distract her from her own thoughts. It was definitely a prison cell.

She reached into her pockets, looking for something to distract her. There was a small notepad, one of the ones created in Zangaria using the improved paper-making process, a couple of pencils and little else. Emily felt an odd twinge as she held one of the pencils in her fingers; designing an ink-filled pen had been relatively simple, but they hadn't caught on in Whitehall. She wasn't quite sure why.

But if literacy levels explode over the next few years, they'll get in, she thought, remembering the school she'd visited in Zangaria. The New Math and New Writing, as they called it, was spreading like wildfire. By the time she graduated—if she was allowed to remain in the school for the next five years—it would be everywhere. And the implications of *that* were staggering.

Imaiqah and Alassa had both known how to write in the empire's script; Alassa had been a royal princess, while Imaiqah had been expected to do the bookkeeping for her family and her husband's family, whenever she finally married. *Emily* had had to write in English, using a translation spell, at least until she had mastered the empire's script herself. Even with special tuition and memory-enhancing potions, it hadn't been simple. But now...what would happen if everyone learned how to read and write?

The thought failed to distract her for long, so she pulled the notepad out of her pocket and started making notes about gunpowder weapons and tactics. Her quiet research program in Zangaria hadn't yet produced anything more dangerous than primitive cannons, but she knew that it was only a matter of time before they graduated to flintlocks, muskets and rifles. The basic concepts had come from her mind, yet they'd taken them and worked like demons to build something new. And once they had pistols and revolvers....

They complained about stirrups, Emily recalled. The simple invention had turned some societies upside down. Noblemen had been the only ones with any training to ride horses, but stirrups eliminated most of the required training. Or something like that; Emily had learned to ride, from Alassa, but she'd never fallen in love with the beasts. The sooner the railways were running all over the Allied Lands, the better. *What will they say when they realize what gunpowder can do?*

She shook her head. It was impossible to concentrate for more than a few minutes without remembering the Warden—and the lecture Master Tor had given her. She closed the notepad, returned it to her pocket and lay back on the bed. If she could only clear her mind...

...But her mind refused to stop focusing on the dead man.

"I know I didn't kill him," she said, out loud. "I *didn't*."

There was a loud tap on the door, which opened a moment later. Emily half-expected to see Master Tor, coming to shout at her some more; it was a relief when she saw Sergeant Miles, even if he looked coldly furious. He hadn't looked so angry when he'd shown them the Death Viper and told them just how it had entered the school. But the anger, thankfully, didn't seem to be directed at Emily.

"Good afternoon," he said, as he closed the door. "How are you feeling?"

Emily stared at him, fighting down the urge to burst into tears. "I don't know," she admitted, finally. Untangling her feelings would take weeks. She wanted a stronger sleeping potion and a few days to relax and rest, but she knew she wasn't going to get it. "I just..."

"Too much stress can do that," Sergeant Miles said. He held a hand out to her. "On your feet, soldier."

Emily obeyed, even though part of her mind pointed out that he was unlikely to help another soldier to his feet. Lady Barb had told her, in brutal detail, that combat sorceresses had to work twice as hard as the combat sorcerers to be accepted—and they had to suppress their femininity completely while they were in the field. Given how many students Emily had overheard muttering about how attractive Lady Barb *was*, Emily couldn't help wondering how successful she had been. But then, Lady Barb *was* a combat sorceress and power was always attractive.

"I'm afraid they're going to ask you a great many questions," Sergeant Miles said, as he led her towards the door. "Just do your best to answer truthfully and you should be fine."

It struck Emily, suddenly, that *he* knew she hadn't killed the Warden. She could have kissed him in that moment, even though it would have started off a whole new series of rumors if anyone saw them. Instead, she allowed him to lead her up towards the Grandmaster's office, through a series of deserted corridors. The entire school seemed to be empty.

"Everyone has been sent back to their rooms," Sergeant Miles explained, when she asked. "The staff is searching the entire building, thoroughly."

For a murderer, perhaps a necromancer, Emily thought. Her blood ran cold. *Or for proof that I killed him.*

Sergeant Bane, wearing a suit of silver rune-covered armor and carrying a large broadsword, met them just outside the Grandmaster's office. The faint shimmer of magic behind him suggested that he wasn't alone. Emily had no idea who would come into Whitehall and remain invisible, but maybe it was a test for her. If she had been intent on fighting her way out, she might think that the odds were better if she faced only the two Sergeants. Her lips quirked with bitter humor. Either of the sergeants could have snapped her in half with one hand tied behind his back.

But if I were a necromancer, she added, in the privacy of her own mind, *I would have enough power to kill them both before they could react.*

"I'm afraid we have to search you," Sergeant Bane said. He looked uncomfortable, rather than nervous. "Are you carrying anything we ought to know about?"

Emily shook her head, silently grateful that she hadn't copied Alassa's habit of carrying a dagger everywhere she went. Alassa might have used it to save her life—and Emily's life—but it would have looked damning right now. A similar dagger had been used to kill the Warden. She gritted her teeth as Sergeant Bane frisked her, quickly and efficiently, then cast a revealing spell over her body. It found nothing.

Would it find a necromancer? She asked herself. Very few necromancers, according to her research, had ever bothered to try to hide. Even when they did, their madness was quite capable of making them think that a false accent and a wig was enough to fool everyone else. But there was no way to know, not when she didn't dare ask.

"Nothing of great interest," Sergeant Bane said, finally. "Leave the pencils with me, if you don't mind."

Emily fought down the urge to roll her eyes, then passed him the pencils, keeping the notepad within her pocket. She had no idea what they would have made of her notes and diagrams—she'd written them in English, but a translation spell would be able to decipher them—but she didn't want to find out. Not now.

"Don't worry," Sergeant Miles said, placing a hand on her shoulder. "Just tell them the truth and you should be all right."

There was the sound of someone clearing his throat from one of the shimmers. Sergeant Miles glared at it, then pushed Emily towards the office door. There was a flare of magic and it opened, allowing her to step inside. It was all she could do to take the first step over the threshold. If it hadn't been for the reassuring presence of the sergeant, she might have turned and fled.

Inside, the Grandmaster was waiting for her.

And he wasn't alone.

Chapter Eighteen

THE OFFICE SEEMED LARGER SOMEHOW, EMILY REALIZED, AS SHE WILTED UNDER SEVERAL accusing stares from the gathering. Sergeant Miles kept his hand on her shoulder, quietly reassuring her, as he steered her towards a chair that had been placed in front of the Grandmaster's desk. The Grandmaster himself had a perfect poker face—not being able to see his eyes made it harder to read him—but the others seemed less inclined to hide their feelings. She recognized Master Tor, Mistress Irene and Professor Lombardi; the others were strangers. It crossed her mind that they might have been brought to Whitehall because of the Warden's murder...

She felt a tickle of magic as she sat down on the chair, a spell that sparkled around her and then faded out of existence. She frowned as it vanished completely, wondering just what it had been intended to *do*. It hadn't even stuck her to the chair. The Grandmaster frowned too, sharing a brief glance—insofar as he *could* glance—with Mistress Irene.

"We had planned to question you on what happened when you entered the Warden's office," he said, flatly. "But the truth spell seems to have slipped away from you. Why?"

For a moment, Emily's mind went blank. And then she remembered.

"Void gave me a spell to prevent my secrets from being taken from me," she said, grimly. She'd hesitated when he'd given her the spell, but not for very long. It would have been easy for someone to pull her knowledge from her mind without it. "I don't know if it would affect the truth spell."

"It did," the Grandmaster said. His tone hadn't changed at all. "Which is inconvenient, as you have no way to prove your innocence."

He cocked his head, slightly. "Tell us what happened from the moment you entered the Hall of Shame," he ordered. "And be as detailed as possible."

Emily flushed, but outlined everything from Travis's taunts to opening the Warden's office and discovering his body. The spectators listened, then bounced questions off her when she finished, some of which puzzled her. What did it *matter* what Travis had said to her, precisely? Or how she'd entered the Warden's office?

"If she wasn't called in, he might well have been dead before she entered," Mistress Irene pointed out. "It isn't as if the Warden gives—gave—them much time to stew before administering punishment."

"But he was definitely alive when I spoke to him," Master Tor objected. "The Warden must have died after that...was anyone else sent there between then and Emily's arrival?"

"Travis says no," one of the strangers said. "And the truth spell worked on him."

Emily grunted, inwardly. If Travis had told her that the sky was blue, she would certainly have insisted on checking before accepting his statement. But if he'd been under a truth spell...she knew quite a bit about them, mainly through reading Master Tor's lecture notes and background reading. The strongest of them *compelled* the subject to talk, while even the milder ones prevented the subject from actually lying. But could a strong sorcerer push the effects aside without making it noticeable?

"She could have slipped past Travis after I left and staged finding the body to throw off suspicion," Master Tor said.

"I was in your office," Emily protested. "I..."

"Quiet," one of the strangers snapped. "You will..."

"*You* will not talk to one of my students like that," the Grandmaster interrupted. His tone was mild, but Emily heard the sheer power behind it and shivered. "You were saying, Emily?"

"I was in Master Tor's office," Emily said, wondering if they would bring up the whole matter of pocket dimensions. "I couldn't have gone anywhere else."

"The wards would certainly have noticed your exit," Mistress Irene said. She cast an ironic look at Master Tor. "Did you think to check before you made wild accusations?"

Master Tor looked embarrassed. "I do not bother to record people who leave my office," he admitted. "But she might have been able to fool the wards and slip back into my office after destroying the Warden."

Emily blinked. *Destroying* the Warden?

Mistress Irene snorted. "Are you suggesting that a second year student, even one with an excellent grade in Charms, was capable of breaking into your office *without* leaving any evidence behind?"

Professor Lombardi coughed. "I do not believe that Lady Emily is capable of breaking into the offices at all," he informed the room. "Doing it without leaving a trace would be far harder. I can examine the wards to see if they have been tampered with, but that would be spellwork well above her current level."

"But she does know how to perform a necromantic rite," Master Tor pointed out. "That makes her the prime suspect."

Sergeant Miles cleared his throat, loudly. "It does not require more than a passing grade in charms to reinvent the basic necromantic rite," he said, darkly. "And there is clear proof that whoever was responsible for the destruction of the Warden *didn't* know as much as Emily knows."

"And how," Master Tor demanded, "do you know that?"

"The knife," Sergeant Miles said, simply. "Necromancers use stone blades because they can channel the magic, once properly prepared, without destroying themselves. A necromancer who used a silver dagger as a tool would be lucky if it didn't explode in his hand. At worst, there would be a sudden surge of magic and the necromancer would be vaporized. In fact, I am inclined to wonder if this really *was* a necromantic rite at all."

"Breaking the Warden's neck and stabbing him with a silver blade would not be enough to destroy him," Mistress Irene said, simply. "*Something* else had to be involved."

"Yes," Sergeant Miles said. "But what?"

He was right, Emily realized. If someone had tried to perform necromancy with a silver blade, the consequences would have been disastrous. And yet...the consequences hadn't materialized at all. That suggested...what?

She looked at the Grandmaster. "Was the Warden a magician?"

The Grandmaster looked surprised at the question, but some of the others seemed to find it funny. Master Tor's lips twisted into a sneer, while Mistress Irene seemed determined to hide a smile and several of the strangers weren't even *trying* to hide their amusement. Emily opened her mouth to demand to know what was so funny—Shadye's attempt to use Sergeant Harkin as a power source had failed because he hadn't been a magician—but Sergeant Miles tightened his grip on her shoulder, warning her to be quiet.

"That is an interesting point," Master Tor said, smoothly. "Would a necromantic rite even *work* on the Warden?"

"Possibly," the Grandmaster said, reluctantly. "No one has ever tried."

He looked around the room. "In order to destroy the Warden, Lady Emily would have had to slip out of Master Tor's office, slip past Travis in the Hall of Shame, destroy the Warden and make her way back to Master Tor's office before he returned. Does anyone really believe that she could have done all of that in the time she had?"

Emily shivered. If Master Tor had gone to the Grandmaster first, *then* to the Warden, she would have had only a few minutes to do all that without being detected. No, there just wouldn't have been the time she would have needed to do it, even assuming that the Warden didn't put up a fight. She couldn't imagine him not having the power—or the protections—to deal with uppity students who didn't want to take their punishments.

"It looks rather more like a clumsy frame up to me," Sergeant Miles said, bluntly. "The one person we are supposed to blame is the one person who can prove her innocence."

"But she had a motive," Master Tor pointed out, smoothly.

"I dare say that there isn't a student in Whitehall who *doesn't* have a motive," Mistress Irene said, equally smoothly. "Can anyone name *any* student here who didn't face the Warden at least once?"

"But she has an immediate motive," Master Tor said. "Her unauthorized experiments..."

The Grandmaster held up a hand. "Have nothing to do with this, I believe," he said. He looked down at Emily, his blindfold twitching. It took Emily a moment to realize that he'd *winked* at her. "There is no proof that Lady Emily was anything other than the person who discovered the body."

"Hell of a coincidence," Master Tor grumbled.

"Students don't often face the Warden on weekends," Sergeant Miles pointed out. "The destroyer, whoever he was, might have assumed that the body would remain undiscovered for hours."

Emily wondered, inwardly, if that was actually true. If the murderer had been close enough to move in and kill the Warden, he would have had to do it just *after*

Master Tor had left. She'd dawdled on her way down to the Hall of Shame, but had she given the murderer enough time to kill the Warden and vanish?

She looked up at Master Tor and wondered if *he* was the murderer. He'd certainly had the opportunity to set it up and frame Emily for the deed...but it would be clumsy—and stupid, when she had an alibi he'd provided himself. No, no matter how much he disliked her, it was hard to see any conceivable scenario where he was the murderer. There would be just too many things that could go wrong. Master Tor's insistence on precision, she suspected, wasn't just related to the law.

But why had he looked at her and decided to hate her?

One of the strangers had a different question. "Where did the knife actually come from?"

"We don't know," Sergeant Miles said. "Silver blades are not uncommon; they're used against both werewolves and vampires. I have checked the stockpiles in the armory, but none of our blades are unaccounted for."

Emily nodded. The students who took Martial Magic were allowed to sign weapons in and out of the armory, but they'd been warned that taking a weapon without leaving a paper trail would have dire consequences. Jade used to insist that they carry swords when they left Whitehall for their hikes in the mountains; Emily hadn't taken anything out since she'd come back to Whitehall. She just hadn't had the time.

"I did a forensic spell on the blade," Sergeant Miles added, "but found nothing. The person who used it, I suspect, ordered it new and wore gloves whenever he touched it. This was a premeditated murder."

"Which renders the whole issue of Lady Emily's involvement even more suspect," Master Tor said. "Did she deliberately plan to be sent to the Warden so that..."

"*Enough*," Sergeant Miles snapped. Raw anger—and power—cascaded through the room. "I have had the pleasure of training Lady Emily over the past year. She would know better than to rely on a half-baked scheme that requires everyone to act their part to perfection. The odds suggest that her involvement was nothing more than a coincidence."

He let go of Emily's shoulder and leaned forward. "I don't know why you seem so determined to blame her, but simple logic rules her out as a suspect," he added. "Unless you find more proof, I insist that you stop throwing around wild accusations..."

"Lady Emily has shown a capacity for being grossly irresponsible," Master Tor insisted, angrily. "I..."

The Grandmaster held up a hand. "There isn't enough evidence to blame her and a great deal of evidence that suggests she is innocent," he said, flatly. A sharp look from him quelled Master Tor before he could resume the argument. "I am satisfied that she is an innocent in this matter. And, in this school, my word is law."

"Unless the White Council sees fit to remove you," one of the strangers said. "Last year, there was a necromantic attack that somehow broke through your wards. Now, the Warden has been destroyed. Both incidents took place after Lady Emily, who seems to specialize in causing chaos and disruption, entered your school."

Emily found herself caught between two different waves of emotion. Relief that the Grandmaster believed her, that he knew she hadn't killed the Warden—and a paralyzing fear that the stranger might be right. She *had* been to blame for Shadye entering the school, even though she hadn't intended to harm anyone. Was she somehow responsible for the Warden's death too? But she honestly couldn't see *how.*

"That is the decision of the council," the Grandmaster said. "I would suggest, however, that using *this* as the charge will raise a great many uncomfortable issues in the process."

He looked directly at Emily for a long moment, then towards the door.

"Sergeant Miles, please wait outside to escort Emily to Lady Barb," he said. "I will speak with her—alone."

Master Tor gave her a dirty look as he left the room, followed by the others. Emily watched them go, then looked back at the Grandmaster. His wiry frame suddenly looked very tired and old. She had no idea just how *old* he actually was, but if Void was well over a hundred years old...why couldn't the Grandmaster be just as old?

"I owe you an apology," the Grandmaster said, after he had cast a privacy ward into the air, ensuring that no one could spy on them. "It is far too easy to forget the truth of your origins—or what you might never have been told, simply because everyone assumes that someone else told you. And you had good reason to think that constructing pocket dimensions was safe."

Emily stared at him, then nodded in understanding. She'd *done* it, after all, when she'd defeated Shadye. In hindsight, her willingness to create additional pocket dimensions might have stemmed from her already having *done* it. And her trunk—and countless others—had entered Whitehall without problems. She had never realized that actually *constructing* pocket dimensions inside Whitehall's interior could be dangerous.

She looked at the Grandmaster, wondering just how much he knew about how Shadye had been defeated, then looked away. It had been a very long day.

"If I thought that you had known the dangers and proceeded anyway, I would not have hesitated to expel you," the Grandmaster added. "Master Tor, who is unaware of your origins, had good reason to be furious—and to be angry at me, for insisting that you be allowed to remain in the school. I cannot really blame him for being outraged."

Emily swallowed, but said nothing. Somehow, the Grandmaster's gentle rebuke felt worse than Master Tor's shouting. Part of her just wanted to curl up and die, part of her wanted to run—but there was nowhere to go. Besides, she'd been told that she was never to be alone in her bedroom. Did that mean that she had to ask the Gorgon or Lin to stay with her? Or would her friends count as an escort?

She cringed, inwardly. She was going to have to explain it all to her friends.

"Master Tor saw a student die through one of his fellows pushing the limits," the Grandmaster added, softly. "He took it badly, even blamed himself for not seeing the problem and dealing with it before it turned lethal. It wasn't his fault, but it still torments him. Your experiment, if you had *really* pushed it, could have damaged the entire school."

Emily nodded, fighting back tears. A caning would have been better than this gentle, but firm lecture.

"And it does seem odd that the Warden died today, just after detecting your experiments," the Grandmaster mused. "Was it really a coincidence or is something more sinister afoot?"

He looked up at Emily, his hidden eyes seeming to peer through the blindfold. "I cannot—I will not—countermand his punishment for you," he said. "However, I will insist that you spend some of it in detention with Lady Barb. She knows your origin and will be happy to talk to you about other pieces of knowledge you might have missed—and yet been expected to know."

"Thank you," Emily said, very quietly.

"I'd ask you not to talk about what happened," the Grandmaster said, "but the rumors will be all over the school by now. Try not to make them any worse."

Emily scowled, remembering how the rumors about her—and other students—grew in the telling. Mostly, they vanished just as quickly, but a few stuck. How many students believed that she was secretly a necromancer?

She looked up at him. "Grandmaster," she said, "what if there *is* a necromancer in the school?"

"If there is," the Grandmaster said, "he's a very stupid one. Using a *silver* knife and picking on the Warden...?"

Emily felt her scowl deepen. One thing that had been hammered into her head time and time again was that stupid magicians rarely lived very long—but she'd just learned that ignorance could be twice as lethal.

"Sergeant Miles will take you to Lady Barb," the Grandmaster said. "I'll speak to the visitors myself, but if any of them try to speak to you insist that I have to be present. They do not have the legal right to interrogate students in Whitehall without my permission, which will not be forthcoming."

Emily stood, feeling her legs wobbling under her, and made her way to the door. Sergeant Miles took one look at her and held out a hand, helping her down the corridor towards Lady Barb's classroom. The interior of Whitehall felt oddly silent, as if the entire building were *completely* deserted. All she could hear were her own footsteps—and the pounding of her own heart.

"Emily," Lady Barb said, as Sergeant Miles opened the door. "What happened?"

Emily felt her last reserves begin to crack, then shatter. Lady Barb caught her as she staggered, then held Emily in her arms as she started to cry.

Chapter Nineteen

THE NEXT THING SHE REMEMBERED WAS LADY BARB PASSING HER A GLASS OF WATER AND motioning for her to drink. It tasted slightly odd; she realized, too late, that Lady Barb had added a hint of calming potion. But it worked; slowly, her sobs died away and she found that she could breathe normally. She hadn't dared to break down and cry since her mother had found more comfort in a bottle than in her daughter's arms. Lady Barb held her, rocking her body slightly. Slowly, Emily started to feel the tension drain out of her mind.

"Relax," Lady Barb said, firmly. "You've had a terrible day, but it's over now."

Emily shivered, feeling oddly comforted in Lady Barb's arms. She hadn't had a *real* mother, not since the woman who had given birth to her had remarried when Emily was five...did she still *want* a mother? Or was she just looking for comfort wherever she could find it? Her thoughts were so twisted up and confused that she honestly wasn't sure.

Lady Barb patted her back. "I shall have cross words with Master Tor," she promised, darkly. "Baroness or not, you're still very young and he pushed you too far."

But that will make it worse, part of Emily's mind objected. Every time someone had remonstrated with her stepfather, he'd just grown worse and worse. Was Master Tor the same kind of person? It was hard to see his face without seeing her stepfather's face overlying it.

She fought down the urge to start crying again. "Why...why does he *hate* me?"

Lady Barb pursed her lips in a manner that promised trouble for Master Tor. "It's... it's political," she said, finally. "And it isn't really something you could *help*."

Emily stared at her. "Did I unseat his patron in Zangaria?"

"If only it were that simple," Lady Barb said. "I think he had decided to dislike you even before you were ennobled."

She laughed, humorlessly. "King Randor should have made sure that you had a proper set of lessons on how our world actually works," she added. "He's marked you out as a target without telling you *why*."

Emily looked at her. "Why?"

"It's political," Lady Barb repeated. "How much do you actually *know* about the White Council?"

She went on before Emily could speak. "On the face of it, the White Council exists to coordinate the Allied Lands in battling the necromancers," she explained. "But it's more than just a simple council of kingdoms. There are independent city-states, magical dynasties and trading networks that also have vast influence. And then there are the independent sorcerers like your guardian. It's all a terribly confusing mess."

Emily nodded, remembering how the great trading families of Europe had exercised an influence out of all proportion to their size. And someone like Void, vastly powerful, would also have considerable influence, if he saw fit to use it.

"There are three...call them *factions* within the White Council," Lady Barb continued. "The first faction wants to maintain the *status quo,* while the other two wish to rebuild the empire and reunite the Allied Lands completely." She snorted. "The only real difference is who they want to put on top. One faction wishes to support a king as High King, blurring all the monarchies together, while the other wishes a looser structure, led and guarded by the Mediators. Master Tor is a strong proponent of the third."

Emily remembered his lectures on the rule of law and nodded. "He thinks that the Allied Lands should have a federal structure?"

"The concept isn't fully developed," Lady Barb explained. "That faction is largely made up of independent magicians and traders. I suspect that it will fracture if it ever managed to get into power and start bending the rest of the Allied Lands to its will."

"While the other faction just wants to stay with aristocracy," Emily deduced. "Why...?"

"Just after the empire fell, there were several attempts to reunite the world by force," Lady Barb explained. "None of those attempts succeeded, but many aristocrats still hold dreams of total power. I would not expect King Randor to hesitate if he was offered the position of High King—or emperor. But every other monarch would oppose him on principle."

"Because *they* want to be High King," Emily said. "But what does that have to do with *me*?"

Lady Barb snorted, rudely. "You came into this world and changed it," she said. "Not just beating a necromancer, but by introducing all kinds of minor improvements that have started to spread out of control. And then King Randor offers you a position that, just incidentally, binds you to him. Just what do you think Master Tor's faction thinks of you now?"

Emily felt her blood run cold. "They think I'm going to help him conquer the world?"

"Yes," Lady Barb said, simply.

She smiled at Emily's shocked disbelief. "You are the greatest force for change this world has seen since the first necromancers," she said, dryly. "Or didn't you *realize* that? If King Randor has you in his corner, or at least has people *thinking* that you're his powerful ally, he can boost his own status within the Allied Lands. Tell me...what *didn't* happen during the holidays?"

Emily hesitated, then saw it. "Alassa didn't get married," she said. "But that wasn't my fault..."

Lady Barb shrugged. "Alassa is your friend and your future liege," she said. "How much do you think that has improved her status when it comes to marriage?"

She shook her head. "I suspect that Master Tor considered you a potential ally for *his* faction before you became Baroness Cockatrice," she added. "Instead, you've threatened to upset the balance of power in favor of monarchy."

"I didn't mean to," Emily protested. "But..."

"That doesn't always matter," Lady Barb reminded her. "And now he had another demonstration of what he thinks is your gross irresponsibility."

"I didn't kill the Warden," she said. "I..."

She stopped as a thought struck her. "Why did they keep saying that someone had *destroyed* the Warden?"

Lady Barb chuckled, lightly. "What made you think that the Warden was *human*?"

She nodded towards the table where Paddy lay. "The clue is in the name," she said. "*Warden*; linked to the wards. The Warden was the embodiment of the monitoring functions built into the wards that supervise you and your fellow students. Like Paddy, he was a homunculus, if rather older and more capable than any other."

"Because he drew power from the wards," Emily guessed.

"Yes," Lady Barb agreed. "Think about what the Warden *does*—did. He was created to be an impartial judge and punisher. Or didn't it occur to you to question that either?"

Emily shook her head. "But Paddy...you stabbed him a dozen or more times," she said. "How could the Warden be killed so easily?"

"That is indeed the question," Lady Barb said. "Stabbing him should not have killed him; breaking his neck should have taken mere moments to fix. A necromancer might have been able to slash through the protections and vaporize him, but we could hardly have failed to notice the sudden surge of power. No, we are left with a mystery. What can kill someone like him?"

She shook her head. "A disturbing mystery," she added. "Someone in the school capable of such a feat...and remaining completely unknown."

Emily shuddered. "And tried to frame me," she said. The potion must have been stronger than she'd realized, she decided, for she found it easier to think about it now. "Or was that sheer luck?"

"Could be," Lady Barb agreed.

"Right," Emily said. "Can the Warden be repaired?"

"I don't know," Lady Barb said. "Professor Lombardi will be looking at him, but I have a feeling that the magical core that powered him will have been shattered beyond repair. It should have been impossible, inside Whitehall. Trying to use him as a source of power for necromancy...either it would have failed or the entire school would have been wiped out in a giant explosion. Necromancers are rarely *that* stupid."

Emily nodded. "Could you plug Paddy into the wards?"

"Perhaps," Lady Barb said, "but I doubt it. Paddy was designed to be a simulation human, not a semi-autonomous entity in his own right. I'll mention the possibility to Professor Lombardi, just in case."

She looked at Emily, her eyes suddenly sharp. "Tell me," she said. "What exactly were you *thinking* when you started meddling with pocket dimensions?"

Emily hesitated. "The Sorcerer's Rule..."

"I'd advise you not to cite that too often," Lady Barb said, dryly. "Or have you forgotten what happens to magicians who insist on pushing the limits a little too far?"

"Professor Thande told us," Emily admitted. "They get sent off to isolated places and told to do their experiments there."

"Master Tor won't be the only staff member demanding your expulsion if you keep doing experiments and refusing to talk about them," Lady Barb warned. "What were you doing?"

When Emily hesitated, she held up her right hand. "I, Lady Barb, swear upon my magic that I will not deliberately share anything Lady Emily discloses to me in confidence without her permission," she said, tartly. "You *do* recognize the oath, don't you?"

Emily nodded, mutely. If Lady Barb deliberately broke it, she might die—or lose her magic.

"And now *that* is done," Lady Barb added, once she had cast a series of privacy wards into the air, "perhaps you could tell me just what you had in mind?"

"You told me that I needed more power to teleport," Emily said, after a long moment. Perhaps it *would* be a good idea to talk about the idea first, before she experimented again, somewhere outside Whitehall. "I started thinking about how I could *store* magic. You can anchor shaped magic in wards, but raw magic seemed to drift away into the background *mana*. It rarely stays still."

"Or controlled," Lady Barb said. "Which is why so many of your peers are discovered when they start to perform random acts of magic. The magic seeps out of them."

Emily nodded. *She* hadn't performed any random magic, but she'd been on Earth where magic didn't exist—or was so low that it was barely noticeable. Imaiqah, on the other hand, had nearly scared the life out of her brother when she'd come into her magic. If she hadn't gone to Whitehall, she might have accidentally done much worse.

"Yes," Emily said. "The magic level evens out, like pouring water into a bathtub. There's no way to concentrate it safely unless it's firmly anchored—and then it's not easy to use it for anything else."

"That isn't exactly unknown," Lady Barb said. "It takes years of training and practice to build up the channels to muster vast amounts of magic."

Emily nodded. "I started thinking," she said. "What would happen if the magic had nowhere to go?"

"If you tried to hold it in your wards," Lady Barb said slowly, "it would eventually drive you insane."

That, Emily *did* know. Mistress Irene had warned her to make sure that she tried to perform at least some magic every week, cautioning her against allowing it to build up inside her mind. Eventually, it would burst out—or damage her. Suddenly, the insanity shown by all surviving necromancers made a great deal of sense. They didn't *dare* let go of the power they had stolen.

"So I thought that I could put it somewhere else," Emily continued. "If it was pumped into a pocket dimension, it would have nowhere to go, so it would remain concentrated. And it wouldn't have to be shaped because it was just resting there, not helping to maintain the dimension. I could then draw upon it at any time..."

"You..." Lady Barb had gone very pale. "Do you have *any* idea what that could do?"

Emily started at her expression. "Power a teleport...?"

"Power a necromancer," Lady Barb said, sharply. "How long would they be able to remain semi-sane if they could put the power *outside* their own minds?"

Her eyes narrowed. "Could you even channel the power when you accessed it?"

Emily hesitated. "I was thinking that I could use carved runes to help direct it into my spells, without actually pushing it through my mind," she said. "Like Subtle Magic, but it would take effect immediately—the runes would collapse, but the magic would already be completed. I could teleport..."

"Or unleash hell," Lady Barb said, stiffly. "Do you have *any* idea just how dangerous you are?"

She stared down at Emily, who fought the urge to jump backwards. "There are... rituals for sharing power," she explained. "They're rarely used because most sorcerers will not cooperate enough to lower their guard around their *fellow* sorcerers. It's quite possible that research into such rituals accidentally paved the way for the discovery of necromancy. This...*trick* of yours might make them workable, with only *one* sorcerer.

"Or a necromancer could funnel magic into a pocket dimension, storing it elsewhere," Lady Barb added. "This could upset the entire world."

Emily nodded, miserably. And to think that it had seemed such a tempting prospect...

"I'd *strongly* advise you to destroy all your notes and to ensure that you never mentioned it again to *anyone*," Lady Barb said. "You could trigger an earthquake if you had enough magical power, even without a nexus. Luckily, even a necromancer would have trouble gathering enough power...unless someone shares your idea with him."

"I will," Emily promised, softly.

"I should make you swear an oath," Lady Barb said. "Or sign a contract."

She reached out and caught Emily's shoulder. "You don't think small, do you?"

"But this could be used against the necromancers," Emily pointed out, desperately. "It would allow us to match their power."

"Maybe," Lady Barb said, slowly. "But I think you should realize, right now, that you do *not* need more enemies. You already have people advocating your murder in the White Council—or in the rest of the kingdoms. How many more do you want to hate you?"

It's going to get worse when they realize the implications of gunpowder, Emily thought, grimly. *But that genie is firmly out of the bottle.*

"I understand," she said, finally. "I won't play with it again."

"Wait for a few years, then we can think about it," Lady Barb suggested. "But it might be best not to tell everyone the truth."

Emily bowed her head.

"King Randor set me up," she said, softly. "Didn't he?"

"He certainly played on your ignorance," Lady Barb agreed. "Of course, he *did* have to reward you. Kings who don't reward their friends tend to run out of them when it really matters. And he clearly intends to ride the tidal waves you've created rather than just let them swamp his kingdom. And if it won him the High Kingdom...he'd be happy to let you change the world to your heart's content."

She pointed a long finger at Emily. "I would be happy to talk to you, under whatever oaths of secrecy you require, about any new...*ideas* you have," she added. "But I would suggest that you *didn't* try any experiments before sharing them with me."

Emily nodded.

"Master Tor sent you to the Warden," Lady Barb added. "What else did he say?"

"That I couldn't use magic outside class," Emily confessed. "I..."

"That's going to be bad, if your enemies find out," Lady Barb said. "I'll escort you back to your bedroom. And I would strongly suggest that you went straight to sleep. You can talk to your friends tomorrow. No doubt plenty of idiots will want to thank you for destroying the Warden."

"But I didn't," Emily said.

"That makes it harder—much harder—for the staff to monitor the interior of the school," Lady Barb added, smoothly. "You might want to remember that."

Emily frowned. What was Lady Barb trying to tell her?

"Just be careful," Lady Barb warned her. "You don't want to get *seen*."

Emily smirked in sudden understanding.

"Master Tor will probably insist on other punishments," Lady Barb said. She reached out, swung Emily around and smacked her bottom several times. "Should he ask, tell him I punished you. I suggest you don't go into details. Just look embarrassed and grimace every time you sit down."

"Thank you," Emily said, rubbing her rear. The sting was fading already. "I..."

"Don't mention it," Lady Barb said. "*Ever.*"

Emily nodded. She had the feeling that next time, if there was a next time, would be a lot harder. "What are they going to use now the Warden is gone?"

"Someone will probably have to take over his duties," Lady Barb said. "I don't know how long it will take them to produce a new one. It could be quite some time."

"I did touch the wards, back when I was facing Shadye," Emily pointed out. "I could help..."

"I'll suggest that to the Grandmaster," Lady Barb said. She hesitated, then continued. "But you may not have *quite* known what you were doing. They don't normally let anyone but qualified professors work on those wards. There are some secrets to them that no one else is allowed to know."

She led the way out of the door, up the stairs and into the dorm. It was dark and silent, apart from the looming presence of Madame Razz at the far end. She didn't seem pleased at all.

"Lie down on the bed," Lady Barb said, before Emily could say a word. She pushed open the door to Emily's room. The Gorgon looked up from her desk, her snakes hissing as they were disturbed. Lin was lying in bed, pretending to be asleep. "I'll have a word with your roommates."

Emily wanted to hear that conversation, but somehow she felt herself dropping asleep as soon as her head touched the pillow.

Chapter Twenty

SHE WAS AWOKEN THE FOLLOWING MORNING BY SOMEONE SHAKING HER, NONE TOO GENTLY.

"Wake up," Alassa's voice hissed. "What *happened* yesterday? Where *were* you?"

Emily opened her eyes and looked up, blearily. Alassa was wearing a white nightgown that set off her blonde hair nicely and she looked...deeply worried. Behind her, Imaiqah was wearing a more demure outfit, but she looked worried too. Emily felt her stomach rumble as she sat upright, remembering that she hadn't eaten anything since breakfast yesterday. So much had happened that she hadn't had time to eat.

"They're saying you destroyed the Warden," Imaiqah said. "What *really* happened?"

"Someone killed him," Emily said. It was still hard to think of the Warden as anything other than a living being, even if he hadn't been human. *Paddy* couldn't pass for human; the Warden, it seemed, *could*. Or perhaps she'd been the only one fooled. "I found the body."

Alassa scowled. "What *else* happened?" She added. "They're also saying that you're going to be expelled."

Emily shook her head, bleakly. "Master Tor wanted me expelled," she said. "The Grandmaster said no."

"I should think so too," Alassa said, crossly. She stamped her foot, then repeated the question. "What happened yesterday?"

"Long story," Emily said, and outlined as much of it as she dared. "I think they thought I'd killed him at first too."

"I don't see you doing that," Imaiqah objected. "You're not a killer."

"Shadye would disagree," Emily said, numbly. She'd snapped him out of existence. And then there had been the crow-sorcerer. *And* a number of orcs and goblins during the running battle they'd fought in the mountains. How many more had she killed indirectly because of all the innovations she'd introduced to the Allied Lands? "But I didn't kill the Warden."

"They should have called me when they dragged you in front of an inquest," Alassa said, sharply. "I shall have angry words with my father. You are effectively aristocracy now and part of my family..."

"Don't," Emily said. "I...they know I didn't do it."

"Inquests aren't always about finding the truth," Alassa warned her. "Sometimes they're just looking for someone to blame." She shook her head, sending golden ringlets shimmering everywhere. "Outside Whitehall, it would be illegal to put you in front of an inquest without my father's permission. Or mine."

Emily rubbed her forehead, feeling a dull ache inside her temple that was probably caused by hunger—or stress. "The killer might have been trying to frame me," she said, grimly. "I...they used a knife to kill him."

"There isn't a shortage of suspects," Alassa mused. She grinned, suddenly. "Who would want to destroy the Warden?"

"They'd have problems fitting all of the possible suspects into the Great Hall," Imaiqah agreed. "The entire school would have a motive."

Emily nodded. As far as she knew, the Warden's only responsibilities had been to monitor the wards and administer punishment to misbehaving students. It was easy to imagine someone resenting their punishment and wanting to kill the Warden, perhaps even a would-be necromancer trying to practice on the person who would detect him when he started playing with necromancy. There was no shortage of possible suspects.

But what could they do? Master Tor had promised to discuss the laws surrounding evidence and truth spells later in the term—absently, she found herself wishing that she had paid more attention in his class—but this was serious. It was quite possible that the Grandmaster would insist on questioning the entire school. And if *that* happened...how many others had used a spell to make it impossible to drag information out of them?

"Hey," Alassa said, slapping Emily's shoulder. "There will be people who will call you a hero."

"But I didn't do it," Emily protested. "They *know* I didn't do it."

"When has rumor ever paid attention to facts?" Alassa asked. "Do you know how many rumors there are at any one time?"

Emily nodded, bitterly. She'd *wanted* to be special, she'd wanted to be famous...but now she knew just how irritating it could be. Or worse, if people really *believed* the rumors about her being a necromancer-in-training, one who had somehow slipped under the radar and hidden in Whitehall. Come to think of it, she realized, anyone who believed that might think she had a *very* good reason to want to get rid of the Warden. If she were feeling the necromantic lust for power, the Warden might notice...particularly if she tried to murder one of her fellow students.

Imaiqah put her hand on Emily's arm. "What else happened?"

"I'm in deep trouble," Emily admitted.

"You should have stayed in the arena," Alassa pointed out, tartly. "If you had, you wouldn't have seemed a plausible suspect."

Emily flushed. Alassa was right.

"We were still playing when they cancelled the game and ordered everyone back to their rooms," Alassa continued. "We looked for you, but we didn't see you. Why did you leave?"

A dozen excuses ran through Emily's head, but she pushed them all aside. "I got bored," she admitted, "and I had work to do..."

"You should have stayed to support us," Alassa said, angrily.

"Not that we were *winning*," Imaiqah said. "We were behind by twenty points and we'd lost two players through fouls."

"The referee was on their side," Alassa grumbled. "But we could have caught up, eventually."

"Maybe," Imaiqah said. "But we were tiring fast..."

Alassa shook her head, impatiently. "Never mind that," she said. "What sort of trouble are you in?"

She peered at Emily. "You don't *seem* to have any trouble sitting upright."

Emily felt her flush deepen. "He died before he could...you know," she said, embarrassed. "I'm on restriction until Master Tor says otherwise."

Alassa's blue eyes showed a flash of sympathy. "That's going to be ghastly," she said, grimly. "No magic means that you can't fight back if someone hexes you. I *hated* it."

Imaiqah looked at her, sharply. "When were *you* on restriction?"

"After..." She rubbed her jaw, meaningfully. "I wasn't allowed to do magic outside class for a week. Luckily, no one realized."

Emily scowled. How long would it be before someone realized that she couldn't do magic outside class indefinitely? If Master Tor *really* hated her—and he did, it seemed—all he would have to do to make her life hell would be to let that fact slip out. Melissa and her cronies weren't the only people who might want to take a shot at the Necromancer's Bane, particularly if they blamed her for ruining yesterday afternoon.

She swung her legs over the side of the bed and looked around for her trunk, where she'd stashed some food. It was gone.

"They came yesterday and took it," the Gorgon's voice said. Alassa stepped to one side, allowing the Gorgon to look at Emily. "They searched everything, even *my* trunk."

Emily winced at her tone. The Gorgon sounded *furious.*

"What were you *doing*?" The Gorgon demanded. "Do you know how many rules they broke just to search our rooms?"

Emily nodded, silently. The Sorcerer's Rule wasn't the only one that allowed magicians some privacy. Breaking into a magician's house—or his trunk—was considered a dreadful mistake. Legally, as Master Tor had taken some delight in pointing out, a magician could do whatever he liked to a thief. Searching her trunk was pushing the rules as far as they would go; searching the Gorgon's trunk snapped them into a thousand pieces. And she assumed that Lin's trunk had been searched too.

"My people *value* their privacy," the Gorgon hissed. Her face suddenly looked very inhuman. For a long chilling moment, Emily was convinced that she was about to be turned to stone. "Do you think that I take their violation of my privacy lightly?"

"No," Emily said. She could barely look the Gorgon in the eye. Somehow, she'd not only been put on restriction, but also destroyed her relationship with one of her roommates. And Lin wasn't going to be very happy either. "I'm sorry."

"You *will* be," the Gorgon said. Her snakes hissed in unison. "And *don't* expect me to spend much time in this room."

It took Emily a moment to realize what she meant. If she—or Lin—wasn't in the room, Emily couldn't be there either. She'd effectively be a guest in her own room. Whitehall's wards didn't allow someone to enter the room or stay in it without one of the original roommates also being there. The Gorgon could force her out just by leaving the room and spending most of the day in the library.

The Gorgon started to turn away, then looked back at Emily. "Your trunk is with Madame Razz," she added. "If you happen to want anything from it, you'll have to ask her for permission to open the trunk. I don't think they trust you any longer."

She stalked back to her own bed, then started to pull on her robes. "Come on, Lin," she called. "I think we should be somewhere else."

Emily stared at her back in helpless rage. "Don't worry about it," Alassa said, quietly. "You can always stay in my room."

"Unless your roommates hate me too," Emily said, bitterly. "Did your room get searched too?"

"I don't think so," Alassa said. "Besides, that would be a gross breach of protocol."

Emily nodded. Alassa *was* a royal princess, after all.

A loud chime rang through the air, interrupting her thoughts. "Attention, all students," the Grandmaster's voice said. "You are to make your way to the Grand Hall immediately. Do not delay."

Emily stood upright and scowled. She was still wearing the trousers and shirt she'd donned yesterday. After sleeping in them, they smelt thoroughly unpleasant. She needed a shower before class, but somehow she suspected that the Gorgon and Lin weren't going to allow her to stay in the room long enough to wash. She tore off the shirt and trousers, then grabbed a robe and pulled it over her head. If there was one advantage to wearing the strange outfits, she'd realized long ago, it was that she could wear much less underneath and no one would be any the wiser.

"You can shower in my room," Alassa muttered, as they walked out into the corridor. "It wasn't your fault that the Warden was destroyed."

"Their possessions being searched *was* my fault," Emily muttered back. "I can't blame them for being angry."

She wondered, as they joined the flock of students heading down towards the Great Hall, if Master Tor hadn't inadvertently done her a favor by not letting her room with her friends. If she'd been responsible for Alassa and Imaiqah having their property searched, would they have been just as angry as her new roommates? Probably...and that might have destroyed their friendship. Alassa had so little privacy in Zangaria that she valued what she had. Imaiqah, a merchant's daughter who had grown up in a very cramped environment, would feel much the same.

Rumors had definitely spread throughout the school, she realized, as other students glanced at her, their faces torn between awe and fear. A number of students grinned at her, rubbing their rears to suggest that they were pleased the Warden was gone, others seemed to shrink away from her, as if they believed that Emily would explode at any moment. She held her head as high as she could, fighting the urge demanding she run for her life and hide.

Maybe I should just go, she thought, as they walked into the Great Hall. *I could go back to Zangaria—or Void.*

The thought reminded her that *Void* hadn't attended the inquest either. She knew nothing about the laws governing such bodies, but she was fairly sure that if Alassa felt she should have been there, Void would feel the same way. Hadn't the Grandmaster called him? Or had he felt that matters would proceed more smoothly without his presence? What would Void have to say to Master Tor?

You can't keep relying on him to hold your hand, she told herself, sternly. *He isn't going to do everything for you.*

The glances and muttered whispers seemed to grow louder as she found a seat and sat down. She locked her eyes on the stage, where she knew the Grandmaster would stand, and refused to give anyone the satisfaction of looking at them. Somehow, as she caught sight of Mistress Irene and Sergeant Miles, it was hard to keep her face under firm control. Everyone seemed to be staring at her.

There was a subtle shift in the wards as the Grandmaster entered the Great Hall and stepped up onto the stage. Now she'd had a moment to think, Emily could tell that the ever-present sense of the wards had changed, fading slightly. Without the Warden, was it even *possible* to maintain the wards? Lady Barb had as good as told her that monitoring the interior of the school would be much harder without him. And she'd seen enough in the Construction and Warding textbooks to know how difficult it was to produce even a basic ward without the near-limitless power of the nexus.

The Grandmaster looked tired, she realized, as silence fell over the Great Hall. He looked utterly drained, as if he'd been up all night. Perhaps he had, Emily decided; they would have needed to take control of the wards and replace the Warden as quickly as possible. If they *could* replace the Warden. How long did it take to produce a homunculus anyway? Lady Barb had implied that it could take a very long time...

"Yesterday afternoon," the Grandmaster said, in a quiet voice that somehow seemed to echo over the Great Hall, "the Warden was destroyed by an unknown person. The Warden appears to be beyond repair."

A low rustle ran through the hall. Emily felt dozens of eyes turning towards her, then looking away.

"We have been unable to determine the identity of the person responsible for the act," the Grandmaster continued. "Nor have we been able to rule out the possibility that he or she might strike again. The Warden's destruction opens up far too many possibilities for someone with bad intentions."

This time, the gazes felt darker. Emily fought down the urge to cower.

"Accordingly, we will be taking immediate steps to assure ourselves of the safety of those within these walls," he said. "Classes will be cancelled for the next few days"—there was another rustle, as if some of the students wanted to cheer, but didn't quite dare—"while we carry out our investigation. We may wish to speak to some of you concerning where you were when the Warden was destroyed. You may wish to start thinking about how you can prove where you were at the time."

Alassa has hundreds of witnesses to prove that she was playing Ken, Emily thought, as the Grandmaster's sightless gaze panned over the gathered students. *So does Imaiqah and the rest of the team—both teams. But everyone else?*

"We strongly suggest," the Grandmaster said, his voice breaking into her thoughts, "that you try to avoid being alone. Stay in groups when outside class—and go from room to room as quickly as you can. If you feel the urge to go some place alone, ask your teachers or older students to walk with you. They *will* provide the escort."

He paused. "If any of you know or suspect anything about the person who destroyed the Warden," he concluded, "please tell us as quickly as possible. Hiding the truth, out of loyalty or fear, will only make the matter worse. Consider the safety of everyone in the school before you decide what to say."

Emily nodded, inwardly. Whitehall had at least one thing in common with schools on Earth: the students disliked sneaks, students who betrayed their secrets to their tutors. Even now, the students would hesitate to tell the Grandmaster anything, even if they knew that one of their fellow students was a murderer. But surely they'd report it if they saw someone making a stone knife? It wasn't as if they didn't *know* that the only magicians who used them on a regular basis were necromancers...

But would they want to *sneak*?

The Grandmaster gave them all a dour look. "Are there any questions?"

A fourth-year girl Emily didn't know put up her hand. "Are you going to send us home?"

"Not yet," the Grandmaster said. "Your schooling is still of primary importance. If matters grow worse, however, I will not hesitate to take firm action."

Emily scowled. The killer might not have committed *murder* by killing the Warden—she doubted that the Allied Lands saw him as human, not if they didn't accept Gorgons as human—but the next target might well be a student. If there *was* a next target. Maybe the killer had been frightened by the Grandmaster's speech and had decided to keep his head down in future.

"Go eat breakfast," the Grandmaster ordered, finally. "If any of you wish to talk to me, my office is always open."

Alassa nudged Emily as the students stood and started to make their way towards the dining hall. "That was interesting," she said. "Do you have any idea who they might have as a suspect?"

Emily shrugged. "Travis? Master Tor?"

She thought about it, briefly. If *she* was ruled out, the last person to see the Warden alive would have been either Travis or Master Tor. Simple logic—which might not apply in a world touched by magic—suggested that one of them had to be the killer. Assuming, of course, they *had* been the last people to see the Warden. There were plenty of ways to turn invisible in Whitehall.

Travis was a jerk, yes. But was he a killer? And what about Master Tor? Was *he* a killer?

"But if the Warden wasn't human," she muttered to herself, "his death might not be taken as *murder*."

Chapter Twenty-One

The dining hall was filled with excited chatter as Emily stepped inside, following Alassa and Imaiqah as they made their way to the second year table. She forced herself to keep walking forward as students stared at her, some of them so distracted that they forgot to chew their food. A handful looked terrified; the moment she sat down, several others stood and walked away. Emily watched them go, wondering if they thought that she was contagious—or a murderer. No doubt the rumor mill wouldn't have bothered to take account of her innocence.

"They'll be talking about something else soon enough," Alassa assured her, as the maids brought trays of food. "Just you wait until the next game."

Emily snorted as she picked at her food. It was unusual to have breakfast served, rather than being allowed to take whatever they wanted to eat; the Grandmaster must have decided to ensure that everyone had a proper breakfast for once. The bacon and eggs tasted like ashes in her mouth, even though she was *very* hungry. It took her a moment to realize that her plate had been subtly hexed. The realization almost made her stand up and run out of the dining hall.

"Toads," Alassa said, as she cancelled the spell. "And they *will* be toads, when I find out who did it."

Emily gritted her teeth as she ate, wondering just who had managed to hex her plate without being noticed. They'd had to have been very lucky to get the right person—or had they just been hexing every plate...She shook her head, bitterly. None of them used food testing spells in Whitehall, normally. There had never been any need.

She looked up at the high table and saw Master Tor, staring at her. Had *he* hexed her food? Surely, a tutor with years of experience could do it without anyone noticing. But it seemed too petty to be him. Besides, he was sitting next to Mistress Irene, who might have been harder to fool. Emily knew from experience that she was almost as good with charms as Professor Lombardi.

"They'll interrogate anyone who cannot prove where they were when the Warden died," Alassa said, clearly trying to distract Emily from her thoughts. "And then...I don't know what they'll do, if they can't find the killer that way."

Emily shrugged, wishing she'd spent more time reading true crime stories while she'd been on Earth. But then, she suspected that most police techniques wouldn't be much use in Whitehall. Some of the cases studies Master Tor had given them had included locked room murder mysteries where—literally—a wizard had done it. Forensic testing wasn't much good if there was nothing to use it on.

But she had to admit that Alassa was making sense. Logically, the killer would be someone who couldn't account for himself during that time...

"Thank you," Emily said, softly. She'd helped teach Alassa how to be more...caring and thoughtful. It had definitely been worth it. "But I don't know what will happen next."

She looked back at her plate, then took a piece of bread from the nearby basket and used it to mop up the remains of the egg. Whoever had hexed her first plate didn't seem inclined to try again, thankfully. She wanted to eat more—she hadn't realized just how hungry she actually was until she had started to eat—but she knew better. It wasn't as if she was going to be doing much exercise later in the day.

A hand tapped her shoulder and she jumped, spinning around to see Master Tor.

"Report to my office at ten bells," he ordered, flatly. "And wear working robes."

He marched off before Emily could say a word. She watched him go, then glanced at her watch. She had barely twenty minutes before ten bells, hardly enough time to wash, dress and run back down to his office. Alassa shot her a sympathetic glance as she pushed the plate into the center of the table, where the maids would recover it, and stood.

"He really has it in for you," Alassa said, as she stood up herself. "I'll let you use our shower."

Emily wanted to hug her as they walked out of the dining hall and ran up the stairs towards the dorms. She tested her door as they passed, but discovered—unsurprisingly—that it wouldn't allow her access without either of her roommates. The Gorgon had been at breakfast, while Lin...Emily shook her head. Where Lin was hardly mattered, as long as she wasn't in the bedroom they shared. No doubt the Gorgon had convinced her to spend the morning in the library or somewhere else instead.

Alassa's room wasn't any different to Emily's, apart from the addition of a wardrobe that was just as dimensionally transcendent as the trunks. Emily took the towel her friend offered her gratefully, then went in to shower. Normally, she would have luxuriated in the water, but she didn't feel *right* using someone else's facilities. They brought back bad memories from her time on Earth. Besides, she had a feeling that being late to Master Tor's office would just make it worse.

"I could come with you," Alassa said. "If he *was* the person who destroyed the Warden..."

"I think you'd just wind up in trouble too," Emily said. "I'll be fine."

She scowled at the thought. No matter how much he disliked her, surely Master Tor wouldn't have gone to all the trouble of trying to frame her if he intended to simply kill her instead. Besides, the more she thought about it, he would have been very stupid if he thought that such a clumsy frame would work. It suggested that someone else was involved.

But who? And why?

"This is one of the robes I bought for messy work," Alassa said, passing it to her. It was a dirty brown robe, surprisingly unstylish for Alassa. Normally, everything she wore was carefully tailored to show off her body to best advantage. "You're a little shorter than me, but you can still wear it and you won't have to go begging to Madame Razz—or your roommates."

Emily felt tears prickling in her eyes as she pulled the robe over her head. It smelt faintly of paint, probably from when Alassa had taken the Artwork taster class.

People were rarely *nice* to her and, somehow, she found it impossible not to be almost pathetically grateful. Alassa gave her a hug as she tied the sash around her chest, then nodded towards the door. Emily hesitated and stepped outside.

The short walk to Master Tor's office was disturbing. A handful of students saw her and stared, or headed away from her as quickly as possible. Emily couldn't help thinking of some of the repulsion charms mentioned in the book of practical jokes she'd found back in first year, or the spells that worked like stink bombs. She felt eyes boring into the back of her neck as she reached Master Tor's office, although when she looked around she saw nothing. But that didn't mean she was imagining it...not in Whitehall. Invisibility spells were relatively simple.

"Lady Emily," Master Tor said, as she entered. He looked pleased to see her, which didn't bode well. "Take a seat."

Emily sat on the chair he indicated, careful to wince when her bottom touched the hard wood—and to hide her reaction when he smiled at her expression.

Pervert, she thought, darkly. Suddenly, using a homunculus to administer punishments made a great deal of sense.

"You will be serving an hour of detention every day for the next two weeks," Master Tor said, without preamble. "Should you have classes that leave you physically or mentally exhausted, you may approach me about moving the detention to another day. Failure to attend your detentions will result in dire punishment."

And you said nothing about actually agreeing to move the detention, Emily thought, feeling cold rage pulsing through her soul. Martial Magic left her feeling shattered afterwards—and so did several other classes. What did he have in mind for her detentions? She'd never served one before, not in Whitehall.

Master Tor stood. "Come with me," he ordered, and strode out of the office. "Now."

Emily followed him up three flights of stairs and down a long series of corridors that she had never explored before. Whitehall's interior was just as confusing as the TARDIS, with its own network of secret passages and hidden chambers. Some of the passageways she knew, from their explorations of the castle, but others were completely unknown. She sometimes wondered if the *Grandmaster* knew all the castle's secrets.

He stopped, just inside a set of corridors. "This used to serve as a barracks for guards, back after the Fall of the Empire," Master Tor said. Oddly, he dropped into lecture mode. "The Grandmaster of that era was less convinced of his ability to manipulate the nexus point than some of his predecessors and insisted that the school also serve as a garrison. When the nexus point was fully under control, the troops were withdrawn and the barracks were abandoned."

Emily peered inside. It was larger than she'd expected, consisting of four large rooms crammed with metal bunks, two giant bathrooms that could hold dozens of men at once and one completely empty room. Dust was everywhere, lying on the floor like snow; wooden shields and swords hung on the walls, mounted on rusty handles. She could see a handful of footprints where someone had moved in and out of the room in the past. It was impossible to tell just how long it had been since the section was last visited.

"The Grandmaster has decided, in the wake of recent events, that we should play host to a garrison once again," Master Tor informed her. "Your task, for the duration of your detentions, will be to clean this entire compartment and get it ready for human habitation. You will expel the dust, you will clean the floors, you will check the pipes and you will prepare bedding, all on your own. You may not use magic—and you may not ask anyone else to use magic on your behalf."

Emily stared at the dusty floor in horror. Whatever he might have thought of her, she *had* been the only one doing the cleaning back home on Earth; she wasn't too proud to clean the floors or do anything else domestic. But without magic it would take *hours* to clear out the entire section, even if the dust was the worst of it. She saw something moving in the semi-darkness and shuddered. Spiders...God alone knew what *else* was lurking in the abandoned section.

"Cleaning equipment has been provided," Master Tor added. "You may draw it from the cupboard down the hallway. The servants have been ordered not to assist you." He gave her a long considering look. "The sooner you complete the task, the sooner you will be free of these punishment duties. I would suggest that you start right now."

Emily scowled at his back as he walked off down the corridor, then turned to gaze into the compartment. It looked worse than ever, she realized as she stepped inside; quite apart from the dust, there were unpleasant-looking stains everywhere and the room smelt faintly of too many unwashed bodies in close proximity. She took a breath, then sneezed as the dust tickled her throat. The sneeze set more of the dust spinning through the air.

Magic could clean this up in moments, she thought, bitterly. *How long will it take to do it by hand?*

She walked through the entire compartment, avoiding the spiders and other insects as best as she could. What was she supposed to do with *them*? Kill them all? Somehow, she found the thought unpleasant, even though she disliked spiders. They hadn't been doing any harm. She remembered the Death Viper and shuddered. Knowing her luck, the spiders were deadly poisonous.

The bathroom was dank and dirty, smelling faintly of something Emily would have preferred not to think about. She tested the pipes and discovered, not entirely to her surprise, that they had been disconnected from the rest of the school. There was no way to know how to *reconnect* them; given Whitehall's ever-shifting interior, it was possible that she would need to ask someone to help link them back into the plumbing. It would have to wait until the rest of the compartment had been cleaned.

Shaking her head, she walked back out into the corridor—and swore out loud as she realized just how grimy she was already, before she had even begun cleaning the compartment properly. There was so much dust on her shoes that she was leaving footprints behind her as she walked. She found the cupboard Master Tor had mentioned and looked inside. There were brooms, dustpans, buckets, cloth bags and mops. No matter how hard she looked, she didn't see anything resembling cleaning liquids.

She took one of the brooms and bags and walked back to the compartment. There was so much dust that the only way to get rid of it would be to stuff it into the bags and then dump it in the incinerator, she decided. Magic could get rid of it instantly... she briefly considered trying to use magic anyway, then decided it wasn't worth the risk. Master Tor might just come and supervise her while she worked, even if he didn't think of a worse punishment.

The dust proved surprisingly resistant when she started to sweep it into a corner. There was so much of it that it felt like sweeping sand, rather than anything else. Emily scowled, fighting down her anger; she knew from bitter experience that using too much force would only make it worse. She was gently removing the dust when she heard the door opening behind her. The hex hit her a moment later.

Emily felt her legs start to jerk around madly. She fell over backwards and landed in the dust, coughing as it got into her mouth. Her legs kept twitching; one of her shoes flew off and landed somewhere in the corner of the room. Moments later, her hands started to flail around as well as the hex reached them, causing a dust storm to blow up around her. She had to fight down the urge to use magic to cancel out the hex, or strike back.

"Well," a familiar voice said. "I guess you *can't* use magic."

Melissa, Emily thought. Her arms and legs were starting to ache, but the hex kept pushing them onwards. It was a simple hex to counter...if she used magic. Not for the first time, it struck her just how vulnerable someone without magic would be in Whitehall. They would be the butt of everyone's pranks and jokes.

She gritted her teeth as she felt the hex finally starting to wear off. Maybe, if Melissa got any closer...

"I think I like seeing you being a servant," Melissa added, lightly. She smirked down at Emily, running a hand through her long red hair. "It suits you, I guess. What would your subjects say, *baroness*, if they saw you grovelling in the dust?"

Emily opened her mouth, then swallowed what she wanted to say.

"I think they wouldn't be very impressed," Melissa teased. "But then, *magic* is the only true source of power. What are you *without* it?"

She stepped closer and Emily lunged, remembering everything that she'd had hammered into her head by the Sergeants and Lady Barb. Melissa yelped and jumped backwards, then cast another spell. Emily found her hands and feet suddenly falling to the floor and locking themselves there, bound by an invisible force. She'd missed her opportunity to hit Melissa before she could react.

"Yes, I *definitely* think I like you there," Melissa sneered.

She turned and walked towards the door, wriggling her bottom as she moved. "Bye, bye," she called. "Have fun explaining why you did nothing for an hour."

Emily groaned as Melissa shut the door, then waited until she was sure that Melissa had just walked off, leaving her stuck to the floor. Bracing herself for a reaction from the wards—or Master Tor—she cast the counter-spell and almost sagged in relief when it worked perfectly. If she hadn't been able to use magic at all, she would have remained trapped until the spell wore off—or until someone came to find her. The hour would have been completely wasted.

She pulled herself to her feet and got back to work, resisting the temptation to use magic to speed up the task. It was bad enough that she'd already had to break the restriction once—and while she thought Master Tor might accept freeing herself as an excuse, she knew that he wouldn't allow her to cheat on her assigned task. Instead, she resumed pushing the dust into the corner, wishing she had a vacuum cleaner. Or even...

A thought struck her and she smiled. Maybe she couldn't use magic directly, but there were other options.

She made a note in her pad, then resumed her task, wondering who had told Melissa that she couldn't use magic. Neither Alassa nor Imaiqah would have given her the time of day...but the Gorgon might have let it slip. No, she *would* have let it slip. She'd been furious with Emily.

But how can I blame her? Emily asked herself. She would have been just as angry, if their positions were reversed. *I got her trunk searched.*

She scowled, fighting down another cough as dust billowed everywhere. It was going to be a very long two weeks.

Chapter Twenty-Two

THE NEXT FEW DAYS WERE AMONG THE WORST IN EMILY'S LIFE. WHEN SHE WASN'T IN CLASS, or accompanied by her friends, almost everyone seemed willing to launch a hex or two at her unprotected back. She rapidly lost track of the number of times someone had stuck her to the floor, turned her into a small animal or object...or befuddled her mind. In the meantime, she was still working on cleaning the barracks. There was little time for anything else.

It didn't help that the Grandmaster and his staff made absolutely no progress, as far as anyone could tell, in tracking down the Warden's murderer. The students who couldn't account for themselves on the day of his death were questioned, but nothing was discovered apart from a handful of student rivalries and an underground ring producing large batches of numbing potion for the students. Alassa pointed out, when she heard about it, that they were the *last* group of students who would want to remove the Warden. He had ensured that they did a roaring trade.

None of the tutors seemed any happier than their students. They snapped at students who stepped out of line and seemed to be competing to see who could assign the worst detentions imaginable. Emily kept as quiet as she could—she already had one endless detention - but other students found themselves balancing books, standing on their heads or even serving as test subjects for interesting alchemical experiments carried out by Professor Thande. No one seemed to be in a very good mood—and they all blamed Emily. It was a relief to be walking towards Blackhall for the second time, accompanied by Aloha.

"I need you to do something for me," Emily said, as they walked. Sergeant Miles had gone on ahead—to prepare the mansion, Emily assumed—and Sergeant Bane had just told them to walk to Blackhall, rather than taking them there himself. "Can you produce a sucking spell?"

"It's second-year charm," Aloha said, dryly. She hadn't joined in the torrent of accusations—and hexes—that had been thrown at Emily, but she had kept her own counsel. "You should be able to do it for yourself."

"I want one that funnels through a hoop," Emily said, carefully. She dug into her pockets and produced a diagram she'd drawn earlier. Reverse engineering a vacuum cleaner hadn't been that difficult, at least on paper. The real question was how well it would work with magic. "Can you do something like this?"

Aloha frowned. "I suppose I could," she said, shortly. "What's in it for me?"

Emily sighed. "What would you like?"

"Twenty gold pieces, plus whatever I have to spend to obtain the hoop," Aloha said. "And why do you need it in the first place?"

"To suck up dust," Emily said. Master Tor had forbidden her from using magic, but he hadn't said anything about charmed objects. "I have far too much dust to remove from a room."

"I heard," Aloha said. She put the piece of paper in her pocket as Blackhall came into view. "Just don't let me down this time, all right?"

Emily nodded. Aloha was *much* better at charms and other forms of detection and defensive magic than Emily, at least for the moment. Aloha had successfully taken the first orb from Blackhall, one of only three students who had succeeded on the first try. After that, Sergeant Miles had said, the test was going to get harder. Much harder. And Emily hadn't even passed the *first* one.

Sergeant Miles waved to them as they walked up to the mansion. "This time, you will be going in together," he said, as if they hadn't already guessed it. "Your objective is to recover another orb from the building and get it outside. Should you be trapped or stunned, you will have failed..."

"We understand," Aloha said. They'd all heard the same lecture several times by now, but the Sergeants never seemed to refrain from repeating it. "We won't screw up."

"You were nearly caught in the infinity trap." Sergeant Miles reminded her, tartly. "Don't make the mistake of thinking yourself invincible."

He nodded towards the door. "You may as well go in through the front door," he said. "Good luck."

"We'll check the rest of the doors and windows first," Aloha muttered, as they walked towards Blackhall. "We don't want to take his word for anything."

Emily nodded. It would be annoying if they discovered that there was an easier way into the house around the back. But when they checked, they discovered that the rear door and windows were absolutely crawling with spells, while the door had been altered to make it impossible to get inside by using a shrinking spell. The front door was heavily warded too, but at least it seemed *doable.*

"Let me take the lead here," Aloha ordered, casting a series of detection spells. "You watch what I do and stand ready to assist if necessary."

"Most of them seem odd," Emily said, as the spells became visible. "They're not stopping us from opening the door."

"Yeah," Aloha said. She touched the doorknob carefully. Nothing happened. "That's what bothers me."

She stepped backwards, picked up a stick and carefully edged the door open. Emily braced herself, expecting something to leap out of them, but there was nothing apart from a long corridor stretching away into infinity. Aloha stepped inside, one hand raised in a defensive gesture, then nodded for Emily to follow her. None of their detection spells showed any sign of unpleasant surprises.

"No carpet," Emily muttered, as she edged her way past Aloha. If there was a problem ahead of them, Aloha would have a better chance of helping her than the other way around. "And no magic at all."

"Make a light globe," Aloha suggested. She cast a detection spell as soon as Emily obeyed. "The detection spells are working perfectly. There isn't any magic in the corridor at all."

They shared a long glance. If there was no magic, what else did the sergeants have in mind?

Aloha cast the seeker spell into the air and frowned. "Upstairs, again," she said. "It can't be *that* easy, can it?"

"I doubt it," Emily said. "Let's go."

They inched their way down the corridor, casting new detection spells every few seconds. Nothing showed up at all, not even a hint of magic in the walls. It made no sense at all; last time she'd been in Blackhall, the whole building had been glowing with magic. She took another step forward, and another...and then the floor dropped out from under them and then fell. Emily heard Aloha cry out as they plunged into darkness and landed on something soft.

She cast a light globe into the air and looked around. They had landed on a pile of cushions, carefully placed to catch the people who fell through the trapdoor. She looked up, but saw nothing apart from a stone ceiling that seemed completely solid. The walls were solid stone too; the only way out, it seemed, was a large metal door directly ahead of them.

Aloha pulled herself off the cushions and cast a light globe of her own. "It looks like a prison," she said, softly. She marched over to the door and checked it for magic. "I don't even *recognize* half the spells keeping this door closed."

Emily couldn't disagree. One set of spells seemed determined to prevent them from opening the lock, while the others protected the door, preventing it from being broken down by force. They were tangled so closely together, she realized, that unlocking them might be almost impossible, certainly for anyone other than the designer. From the look on her face, Aloha had come to the same conclusion.

"Trapped," she muttered. "But there has to be a way out."

Aloha looked over at the chains. "Maybe one of us is meant to be hooked up," she mused. "If the wards think that one is a prisoner..."

Emily snorted. "Do you think that's likely?"

"Secret lairs created by sorcerers can be thoroughly weird," Aloha pointed out snidely. "Can you think of anything else?"

Emily looked around. The walls seemed solid—she cast detection spells anyway, just in case one of them was an illusion—and there was no way to open the trapdoor in the ceiling. She was tempted to start hurling spells at the lock, hoping to break it through brute force, but it would be a good way to exhaust herself even if she succeeded. And then she took a careful look at the door and burst out laughing.

Aloha glared at her. "What's so funny?"

"The hinges," Emily said, as she walked up to the door. "The hinges are on the *inside*."

It took several moments to use a manipulator spell to unscrew and remove the hinges, but when they were gone the door just fell inwards, allowing them to escape. Outside, there was a dark corridor and a ladder leading upwards. There didn't seem to be any way up apart from using the ladder, so they checked it carefully and removed a number of hexes before clambering up into the next level. Even a simple hex could have stopped them both if they'd been caught on the ladder.

"We need to go up another level," Aloha said. She nodded towards a second staircase, leading up to the upper levels. "And *look*! It is absolutely crammed with hexes."

Emily heard the exasperation in her voice and smiled, tiredly. "Maybe we can climb up the banister," she said, after a moment. "Or..."

Aloha looked at the rotting wood. "I wouldn't care to try," she said, as she cast a second set of detection spells. "Let's see what we have here."

It took nearly twenty minutes to remove enough of the hexes to allow them to make their slow way up to the next level. This time, there were three possible directions to go, but only one of them seemed to lead them towards the orb. Emily hesitated, wondering if the sergeants would have *expected* them to take the direct path, but Aloha strode onwards before she could find the words to suggest that they do something else. The moment she joined Aloha in the corridor, the door slammed shut, cutting off their line of retreat.

"Drat," Aloha said, out loud. "And the spells are back in the walls."

Emily nodded, casting detection spells of her own. Someone was quite determined that they make their way down the corridor to face whatever was lurking at the far end. Aloha created a light globe and sent it drifting down the corridor, hoping to spring whatever trap waited for them before they got too close. But nothing happened. Carefully, they inched their way down the corridor...and inched their way down the corridor...and inched their way down the corridor...

Aloha bit off a nasty word in a language Emily didn't recognize. "Stay here," she said, and walked ahead of Emily into the darkness. A moment later, Emily heard someone behind her and spun around...to see Aloha. "They've rigged the entire corridor with some kind of labyrinth spell."

"A hamster wheel," Emily muttered. No matter how far they walked, they wouldn't get anywhere. It was a very neat trap. "Cast a dispersal spell?"

"On three," Aloha muttered back. "One...two...three!"

They cast the spell together, feeling a long moment of resistance as the spell on the corridor struggled against it...and then shattered. Emily felt her head spinning and closed her eyes; when she opened them, there was a wooden door at the end of the corridor. It seemed as though it had never been any more than five meters from end to end.

"Follow me," Aloha said, as she checked the doorknob—and then opened the door. Eerie green light washed out. "I..."

She stopped, dead.

Emily stared, unsure of what had happened. Something seemed to have captivated Aloha, holding her spellbound...and utterly mesmerized. If Emily hadn't been behind her, she might have been caught too. There was something about what little she could see of the light that was almost hypnotic. If she looked at it for too long, she would be trapped too.

Bracing herself, she came up behind Aloha and pushed her hand over her friend's eyes. Aloha started, then twisted around until she had her back to the light. Emily pushed her gently forward until they were close to the source of the spell, then cast the strongest dispersal charm she could. The eerie light vanished, revealing another treasure chest, positioned in the center of the room. Sunlight was streaming in through a large glass window.

"I...thank you," Aloha said, as she staggered to the floor. She sounded disorientated—or drunk. "I...I just couldn't break free."

"If it had been just one of us," Emily said, "we would have been caught and trapped."

Aloha nodded. "Thank you," she said. She sounded stronger, thankfully. "Why... why do you want the suction spell anyway?"

"To suck up dust," Emily said. She was sure that she had already explained. "I can't use magic..."

"Use runes," Aloha said, flatly. "There are quite a few that repel dust. Draw them on the floor with chalk, then let them do their job. It's slow, but it will work."

"Master Tor said no magic," Emily said, slowly. "I thought an enchanted hoop wouldn't count..."

"Neither would runes," Aloha insisted. "Draw the runes in the right place and the dust will inch towards the corner. Done properly, it will even start cleaning the rest of the floor."

"I could get rid of the spiders that way too," Emily mused. "There are runes to repel insects..."

"You might want to check with Mistress Kirdáne," Aloha warned. "If the spiders have been there for decades, they may object to being moved."

Emily nodded, wordlessly.

"Master Tor seems to be *really* mad at you," Aloha added. "He wasn't so bad to me last year, even when I messed up an essay. I just had to redo it and then look up various examples to justify my case."

"Wonderful," Emily muttered. "It's political."

"I hate politics," Aloha commented.

"No...ah, *combat sorceress* can afford to be a virgin where politics are concerned," Emily misquoted. Trying to explain the origin of the quote would be a waste of time. "Politics is the root of wars."

Aloha snorted. "Really? I thought it was power-mad necromancers."

She pulled herself to her feet and walked towards the chest. "The key's in the lock," she commented, dryly. "Does that mean it's safe, do you think?"

"No," Emily said, sharply. Although, she supposed, if one of them was caught by a hex, the other could free the victim. "Check it for surprises first."

"Nothing," Aloha said, after a moment. "Check it yourself."

Emily ran through the detection spells, but found nothing, either on the key or on the chest. Aloha flipped open the chest and saw the orb sitting on a velvet sheet, waiting for them. They exchanged glances—surely it couldn't be so easy—and then Aloha reached for the orb and picked it up.

"Well, we got it," she said. She sounded as puzzled as Emily felt. It wasn't like the sergeants to just let them waltz out with the orb. "Why..."

There was a dull rumble behind them. Emily swung around to see the walls starting to close in on them. The door was gone. They stared around, looking at the window. It seemed impossible to get out in time to escape before they were crushed into pulp...

She remembered what Sergeant Miles had said and grabbed for the orb. Before Aloha could stop her, she threw it at the window, smashing it through the glass and out of the building, satisfying the terms of the challenge. Moments later, the walls stopped advancing and started to retreat. The door reappeared in front of them.

Aloha stared at her. "How...?"

"He told us that the orb had to be outside the building," Emily said. She was just relieved it had worked. "He *didn't* say we had to *carry* it out ourselves."

"It seems to have succeeded," Aloha said, slowly. She sounded rather doubtful. "Are you always looking for ways to cheat?"

"If you're not cheating," Emily said, quoting Sergeant Harkin, "you're not trying."

She smiled at the thought as they made their way down the stairs and out of the house. Magic was all *about* cheating, she'd come to realize, all about finding shortcuts to power and fame—or simply to get things done. Whitehall was designed to *encourage* them to master their powers and think of new applications...

"Well done," Sergeant Miles said. He was holding the orb in one hand, studying it thoughtfully. "Quick thinking to get out of a lethal trap. You'd be surprised how many people go to pieces or freeze when they think there's no way out."

"It was Emily who saw it," Aloha admitted. She sounded annoyed with herself. "I missed it completely."

"But I wouldn't have gotten through all of the traps without you," Emily said. She'd frozen in Zangaria and it could have gotten her and Imaiqah killed. "I..."

"You'd better practice," Sergeant Miles said. He passed Emily the orb. "The next test will involve much more teamwork..."

He turned to see Lady Barb running towards them. "Emily," she said, "where were you for the last hour?"

"She was in Blackhall," Sergeant Miles said, before Emily could say a word. "Why?"

"They just found a body," Lady Barb explained. "Travis is dead."

Emily stared at her in horror. "Travis is dead?"

"Yes," Lady Barb said. Her tone was very grim. "And it seems that it was the work of a necromancer."

Chapter Twenty-Three

"Get them back to the school," Sergeant Miles said. "I need to go to the Grandmaster."

"He's ordered a full lockdown," Lady Barb explained. "The students are being chased back into their dorms."

And they'll find a way to blame me for it, Emily thought, bitterly. *Or...*

She stopped. "So where is he?"

Lady Barb scowled at her. "Who?"

"The necromancer," Emily said. "If he just sucked in power, he should be easily noticeable..."

"Good question," Lady Barb said. "We don't know."

She nodded towards the path leading back to Whitehall. "That way," she ordered. "Now."

Emily mulled it over as they were chivvied down the path through the darkening forest. She'd been allowed to read books on necromancy and most of them agreed that a newborn necromancer was immediately noticeable. Even if they didn't go insane at once, there should still have been a colossal surge of power. It would take an experienced necromancer to dampen the surge—and most of them saw no *reason* to hide.

And Travis was dead.

She'd never *liked* Travis; he'd been a jerk, abusing his power for his own amusement. But he hadn't deserved to die. But...he'd also been a strong magician and student of Martial Magic. What sort of inexperienced necromancer would target him? Or had he been tricked somehow...

Lady Barb slowed as they approached the armory. "Aloha," she said, "I'm going to take you to Mistress Irene's office. She'll escort you back to your room."

Emily blinked in surprise. She wasn't entirely sure where Aloha was sleeping—they were no longer roommates—but she had thought that her room wouldn't be too far from Emily's bedroom. In Whitehall, of course, that didn't always mean anything. The interior just kept shifting around. But she took one look at Lady Barb's grim face and kept her thoughts to herself. Lady Barb was good at concealing her feelings, but Emily was sure that she was deeply worried.

Mistress Irene didn't look any better. She motioned for the two girls to wait while she had a brief discussion with Lady Barb, concealed behind a privacy ward. Emily couldn't hear a word and she had never leant how to lip-read, but from their expressions and gestures it seemed that they were having a major disagreement. Finally, Mistress Irene cancelled the privacy ward and nodded for Aloha to accompany her. Emily watched her go, then turned to face Lady Barb. She looked quietly furious.

"You were in Blackhall for over an hour," Lady Barb said. "It is unlikely that they can blame this on you."

Emily sagged in relief. She'd been with Aloha in Blackhall—and Sergeant Miles could verify that they'd been inside the mansion—but it would have been harder to prove where she was earlier. There had been a free hour; Emily had been forced to use it to make more progress on cleaning the wretched barracks. The sooner she looked up some cleaning runes, the better.

She concentrated, trying to remember what little she could of police procedure. "Who found the body? And where?"

Lady Barb gave her an odd look, but answered the question. "Danielle," she said. "Travis's girlfriend. They were planning a quiet rendezvous in the upper levels of the North Tower; when she arrived, she found him dead."

Emily felt a moment of pity for the girl, even though she had some problems imagining *anyone* wanting to date Travis. But then, many of the girls on Earth had dated absolute jerks too. It had never made any sense to her. Luckily, none of the boys had ever tried to ask *her* out. Jade had been the first to see her as a desirable person.

"She was very upset," Lady Barb said darkly, "and went screaming through the castle. The entire school heard before the Grandmaster put the castle into lockdown."

Emily nodded. They'd *definitely* try to blame her.

Lady Barb led her out of the office and through a twisting series of passageways that seemed to go up and down at random, finally coming out in a deserted corridor. Emily could hear someone speaking at the far end as she glanced out of the window and realized that they were in the upper levels of Whitchall. Lady Barb caught her arm and gently pulled her down into the tower room, where—rumor had it—older students were allowed some degree of privacy. Travis's body lay on the ground, a stone knife stabbed through his heart.

Emily shuddered as she took in the condition of the body. Travis looked utterly desiccated, as if something had sucked all the life out of his body. It seemed to be on the verge of crumbling into dust; Emily was mildly surprised that it was even recognizable. She checked the blade protruding from his chest and frowned, inwardly. It was definitely a stone knife.

But there was no sense of necromantic power surrounding the corpse.

"Strange," she said, out loud. She looked around, but none of the walls were scorched. "I don't know *what* happened."

"Neither do I," the Grandmaster's voice said. He was standing in the shadows, his expression grim. "The knife is stone, but there is no trace of power."

"Or blood," Lady Barb said. "There should have been some blood."

Emily tuned them both out as she stared at the body. If there *was* a necromancer somewhere in Whitehall, he might well have killed the Warden to ensure that he remained undetected—and then started preying on the students. Travis, whatever else could be said about him, would have provided plenty of power for a budding necromancer. But from what she'd read, a necromancer's victims just...*died*. They didn't turn into dust.

It didn't make any *sense*. If the necromancer was sane enough—despite drawing a vast torrent of power through his mind—to hide, why not destroy the evidence completely? The victim had been in Martial Magic; no one would have questioned Travis leaving the school and going for a hike, someplace where he might have had an accident. Or perhaps he would have run away from school...it wasn't uncommon. God knew *Emily* had been seriously considering it after the third or fourth hex thrown at her unprotected back.

But if the necromancer was *insane,* why wasn't he trying to tear the school apart?

"Good question," Lady Barb said, when Emily outlined her thoughts. "But not *all* necromancers go completely insane at once."

"But they do have problems thinking straight," Emily countered. They wouldn't even *know* that they weren't thinking straight. A dangerously-flawed plan a five-year-old child would have laughed at might have seemed a work of genius to them. It was very difficult to overcome a problem inside one's own head. "Nothing about this makes *sense.*"

She scowled. "Unless someone is trying to *pretend* to be a necromancer," she added. "But why?"

Lady Barb shot a quick look at the Grandmaster. "Discrediting you," she said. "A murder in Whitehall...that would be grounds for a formal investigation by the White Council."

"It's possible," the Grandmaster agreed. He looked at Emily. "I'd like you to help with the investigation."

Emily blinked in surprise. "I'm not a policewoman...ah, a forensic sorcerer," she said. "I don't know how I can help."

"You're the Necromancer's Bane," the Grandmaster pointed out. "Your assistance might help to strengthen confidence in the school's defenses."

And reassure people that I'm not killing students, Emily thought, feeling a confusing mixture of emotions. It was a relief to know that the Grandmaster wasn't blaming her for the murder, but oddly worrying to realize that he wanted to use her fame to help him. *She* knew better than to think she could stop a necromancer by clicking her fingers—and he should know better too. But if it was the least she could do to help...

"If you think I can help, I will," she said, finally. She *owed* the Grandmaster; at the very least, he'd prevented Master Tor from expelling her. "But I wouldn't even know where to begin."

Lady Barb's lips twitched. "Just try to look confident when someone asks what's happening," she said, dryly. "Fear will destroy us as surely as any necromancer."

"We have a necromancer running loose in the school—or someone *posing* as a necromancer," Emily said. "Shouldn't they be very, very afraid?"

"Maybe," Lady Barb said, tartly. "But we should do what we can to reassure them."

She looked over at the Grandmaster. "Under the circumstances," she added, "I believe that the restriction on unsupervised magic can be removed."

The Grandmaster turned his face towards Emily, his hidden eyes seeming to scrutinize her *thoroughly.*

"Very well," he said, finally. "But I would suggest that you behave yourself. No matter what we say, quite a few people will still consider you the primary suspect."

Emily felt a surge of intense relief and joy that almost sent her to her knees. Magic had been her delight ever since Shadye had kidnapped her, the one skill she'd developed on her own—although reverse-engineering concepts from Earth had forced her to think along lines she'd never had to explore previously. Being banned from using it outside classes—at least openly—had been a terrible punishment...and it would have been terrible even if it *hadn't* drawn a bulls-eye on her back.

"But you are not allowed to use magic directly to complete your detention," the Grandmaster added. "I suggest that you bear it in mind."

Directly, Emily thought, and nodded. Come to think of it, if she no longer had to avoid using magic outside class, she didn't really *need* Aloha to produce the makeshift vacuum cleaners. But the older girl would probably have more success anchoring the charm in place.

"I will," she said, out loud.

"Watch your back," the Grandmaster warned. He turned back towards Lady Barb. "Take Emily back to her room. There will be a formal announcement later today."

Lady Barb nodded. "This way, Emily," she said. "Come on."

Emily took one last look at the body, then followed Lady Barb out of the room and down into the network of secret passages. The school felt deserted again, completely empty; she wondered, suddenly, just what would happen if the murderer wasn't caught. Could the White Council use it as an excuse to remove the Grandmaster?

But who would want to remove him?

She looked at Lady Barb. "Does the Grandmaster have any political enemies?"

"Hundreds of them," Lady Barb said, sardonically. "The Grandmaster holds one of the most important posts in the Allied Lands. Of course he has enemies."

Emily scowled at her tone. "Enemies who might be prepared to kill at least one student?"

She shook her head. Even if one accepted that the Warden wasn't human—and that destroying him wasn't *murder*—there was still the issue of someone being prepared to kill Travis. What sort of blowback would they experience if they were caught? Travis had been part of a great magical family; his murder would be, to all intents and purposes, a declaration of war. Or had he been targeted randomly?

"That is indeed the issue," Lady Barb said. "Anyone sane would not have considered Travis a potential target."

Emily winced. Imaiqah—before her ennoblement, at least—would have made an ideal target. Her family had no political power, nor any real connections to great sorcerers or powerful aristocrats. She could be killed without major repercussions. And she was hardly the only student in Whitehall who fit that particular bill. Why would someone pick on Travis when there were other targets? Unless it was a deadly gamble. Losing Travis might spur the White Council to act faster, but it would also push them to investigate thoroughly.

"I'm going to have your trunk moved back into your room," Lady Barb said, as they stopped outside the bedrooms. "I would suggest, however, that you try not to be alone. And that you watch your back."

She opened the door and led the way to Emily's room. Madame Razz stuck her head out of her office and scowled at them; Lady Barb motioned for Emily to go into her room while she had a few quick words with the housemother. Emily hesitated, then obeyed; inside, the Gorgon looked up from her book and frowned at her.

"What happened now?" She hissed. "Why are we back in lockdown?"

"Travis is dead," Emily said, as she closed the door. She didn't bother to question if the Gorgon *knew* Travis. "And the Grandmaster wanted my help."

The Gorgon's face was hard to read, but she didn't seem convinced. Emily shrugged, picked up a book from her bedside cabinet and sat down, trying to concentrate on legal precedents for crop-sharing along the borderlands. Maybe Master Tor *hadn't* written the book, but it was just as boring as listening to him talk. What did it really *matter* which way the wind was blowing when it came to haggling over the exact border between two states?

Lady Barb opened the door and levitated the trunk inside, putting it down in front of Emily's bed. "I'd check it carefully," she advised, dryly. "And stay in the room until the Grandmaster makes his announcement."

The Gorgon leaned forward. "Is she still on restriction?"

"Not any longer," Lady Barb growled. "And I suggest that you pass that around the school."

Emily scowled, inwardly. Had it been the Gorgon who had told everyone that she wasn't allowed to do magic outside class? Perhaps; she might not have hexed Emily directly, but she'd certainly been mad enough at her to set her up for an endless series of humiliations. Except that was over now...she allowed herself a smile as she contemplated what she could do to Melissa, the next time she tried to hex her. Or one of the others who had seen a helpless target and lashed out.

She opened the trunk and recovered a handful of books, returning them to her desk. There were other essays to write; if nothing else, the enforced confinement should give her a chance to finish the first drafts. The makeshift typewriters they'd been trying to produce in Zangaria from her rough plans were yet to be completed. Irritatingly, they would probably have been able to produce them without her help, if they'd had the concept.

"I'd watch yourself," the Gorgon growled, as she went back to her book. "I *hate* having my property searched."

Emily nodded. She'd read up on the Gorgons and discovered that the desert clans, having very little privacy, valued what they had. Intruding into someone else's possessions was regarded as worse than murder, which had struck her as curious before she'd realized just how much they were forced to share with one another. The Gorgon had to think that sharing a room with *just* two other girls was the very height of luxury.

She was midway through an essay for Professor Thande when the Grandmaster's voice echoed through the school.

"Attention, all pupils," he said. His voice sounded tightly controlled. "I must confirm that Travis of House Athena was found dead—murdered—this afternoon."

The Gorgon let out a hiss. Lin, lying in her bed, showed no real reaction.

"As yet, we have been unable to locate his killer," the Grandmaster continued. "I would therefore like to ask you to ensure that you remain in groups at all times—and that you report *any* information or concerns you have to a member of staff. Investigators may wish to question you; if so, answer their questions as quickly and completely as possible. Do *not* take any risks.

"The school will remain in lockdown until tomorrow morning, allowing us time to search the school," he concluded. "Do *not* attempt to leave the dorms. Food will be brought to the common rooms by the staff. Anyone caught outside will regret it."

Particularly if they run into the murderer, Emily thought, sourly. *Or if they get accused of* being *the murderer.*

"Well," the Gorgon said. Her tone became snide. "Did you murder Travis?"

"No," Emily said, sharply. "I was out at Blackhall."

But very few students, she knew, were going to believe it. It was easy for rumors to grow in the telling—and she had already been considered strange and dangerous, ever since she had defeated Shadye. Hell, *Alassa* had known that there was something deeply odd about Emily a long time before Emily had told her about Earth. She just didn't have the cultural background shared by everyone else at Whitehall.

The Gorgon snorted and returned to her book. Emily scowled at her, then looked back at the three pieces of parchment she had written out for Professor Thande. He'd given them a set of alchemical formulas and told them to deduce what they were likely to do, without actually trying to make them. She knew what each of the components were used for—being forced to memorize such details had been a large part of first year alchemy—but it was harder to see how they would react if they were put together. One particular chemical actually did nothing unless it was mixed with another and then heated to boiling point. Another dampened magic to the point it rendered the whole concoction inert.

But that can't be the answer, can it? She asked herself. *Could it be that the recipe does nothing?*

She sighed and wrote it down, then scribbled out a paragraph justifying her decision. It wasn't enough in Whitehall to give the answer; she also had to prove that she'd thought about it, applying both knowledge and intelligence to the problem. But it was so hard to concentrate...

Shaking her head, she found a spare notepad and started scribbling down ideas from Earth instead. At least that took her mind off the image of Travis's body—and the nightmarish thought of a necromancer running through the school.

Chapter Twenty-Four

"Well," Alassa said, as she sat down beside Emily and cast a privacy ward, "it seems that half of the school thinks you killed him and the other half seems to think you'll save us all."

Emily rolled her eyes. Her experience at breakfast had been distinctly surreal, even though she'd gone early in the hopes of avoiding the crowd. Several students had inched away from where she sat, while others had gazed in her direction with worshipful eyes, as if they thought she was the Second Coming. It didn't help that the older students were loudly telling the younger students about Emily's exploits, most of which only existed in the imaginations of broadsheet editors. She certainly had *not* befriended a dragon by pulling a thorn out of its paw!

"Public opinion is fickle, my father says," Alassa added. "What *really* happened last night?"

"The body was odd," Emily said. She explained as best as she could, then went on. "I don't even know if we're dealing with a *real* necromancer."

"No one else knows either," Alassa confirmed. "My father sent me a short message this morning. Apparently, there's going to be an emergency debate in the White Council about the situation."

She leaned forward, confidently. "I think someone is trying to get you in *real* trouble," she said. "I bet it's Master Tor."

"I don't think he would murder a student and destroy the Warden just to get rid of me," Emily said, although she had her doubts. "Wouldn't he be risking everything?"

"He's a respected professor," Alassa pointed out. "It's possible he doesn't realize that his position can actually be undermined."

She shook her head. "If you're meant to be helping the investigation, perhaps you should spy on him," she added. "Maybe you could search his office..."

"And get kicked out for good when I get caught," Emily said. The tutors had taken to patrolling the corridors, watching for students trying to use more serious hexes on each other now that the Warden was gone. "Maybe I should just transform myself into the spitting image of his favorite student and see what he might tell me."

Alassa lifted an eyebrow. "That never works," she said. "*Acting* like his favorite student would be much harder than looking like him."

Emily shrugged. Was it possible that Master Tor was bent on discrediting her? He certainly had a motive; Emily had, however inadvertently, strengthened his faction's enemies on the White Council. But if he was prepared to murder to achieve his aims, why not simply kill Emily herself? Or kidnap her from Whitehall, if he intended to force her to work for his faction instead. It just seemed too complicated...he would have to have known in advance that she was about to break the rules spectacularly *and* that the Grandmaster wouldn't agree to expel her. And he would have had to kill the Warden too.

"It doesn't seem to make sense," she admitted. She smiled as Imaiqah appeared and sat down on the other side. "I think..."

Professor Eleas strode into the room and closed the door with a loud bang. He looked tired; rumor claimed that most of the tutors had spent the entire night searching the school, rather than call in investigators from the Allied Lands. Emily cancelled the privacy ward and did her best to look attentive. The handful of students staring at her didn't help.

"We have looked at several kinds of influential runes over the last two weeks," the professor said, as he took his place in front of the class. "And we have studied how easily they can be manipulated to affect an unknowing victim. Today, we look at ways to deflect the effects of such runes."

Emily leaned forward with interest. The runes he'd used to influence their behavior on the first day had been blatant; after that, the class had developed the habit of checking their chairs and desks before they sat down. Some of the others they'd seen, though, had been far less noticeable. It was alarmingly easy to imagine how they might be misused.

"If noticed, their effects can be shrugged off, even by non-magicians," Professor Eleas continued. "However, noticing their effects can be incredibly difficult. Indeed, a victim may invent reasons and self-justifications for doing what the runes tell him to do. The longer this continues, the harder it is to realize that the runes exist at all. There are quite a few case studies of people *discovering* the runes, after they have thoroughly embedded themselves, and deciding that the runes didn't work, even though an outside observer would disagree."

He smiled, rather tightly. "Please look inside your desks."

Emily opened her desk and blinked in surprise as she saw a small sewing kit; needles, thread and a tiny silver cup. It took her a moment to realize that the cup was a thimble, something designed to go over her fingertip and provide some protection from the needle. She knew better than to splash her blood where someone else might pick it up. Under the sewing kit, there was a simple sash made of silk. She brought them both out and put them on top of the desk.

"There are those who will argue that sewing is woman's work," Professor Eleas said, glancing at several of the boys. "The effects, however, are much stronger if the work is done by the intended user directly. I suggest that you save your complaints."

He clicked his fingers and a small outline of a rune appeared on the blackboard. "This is a very simple protective rune," he explained. "It counteracts the effects of most runes, simply because the runes are rarely very powerful. However, it *can* be countered itself. Most magicians prefer to use sewing to produce the protective runes because the threads start to unravel if they come under attack. It can serve to alert the wearer to a danger they may not have sensed."

Emily looked up at the rune, then back at the sash. She'd never really sewn anything in her life, not even when her clothes had started to become threadbare because there was no money for anything new. Her mother might have been able to do it, but she'd never tried to pass the skill onto Emily. Even putting the thread in the needle, she suspected, would be harder than it looked.

"You may begin," Professor Eleas said. "Be careful not to prick yourself. You will have to destroy the sash and start all over again if that happens."

They went to work. Emily rapidly discovered that it *was* harder than it looked; the thread seemed determined not to get through the eye of the needle, no matter how carefully she aimed it at the hole. Alassa didn't seem to be having any more luck; Imaiqah, on the other hand, confessed her mother had insisted that she learn to sew as well as helping her father with his business. With her directions, Emily finally started to sew the thread into the sash. She couldn't help thinking that it looked thoroughly unkempt.

"I never realized how hard the tailors have to work," Alassa muttered. Her delicate fingers seemed more capable of manipulating the needle and thread, but she was still having problems. "All the designs they marked into my dresses..."

Emily scowled. How many of those designs had actually been protective runes?

"Try to put in as many stitches as possible," Professor Eleas advised two of the boys, both of whom had been muttering rebelliously for several minutes. "The tighter the thread is bound to the sash, the stronger the protection."

Emily looked enviously at Imaiqah, who had managed to sew the rune into the sash perfectly, then went back to work. Alassa was right, she decided; the servants who produced and mended clothes for the aristocrats had a very difficult life. She knew that it was a skill she might master, if she pushed ahead with it, even though it seemed impossible. But that very feeling was a deadly trap.

"There," Alassa said, finally. "Done!"

"You need to tighten it up," Professor Eleas said, glancing down at her work. "Right now, it's too loose to last long if it was challenged."

Emily looked up at him. "What would happen if someone accidentally pulled out the thread?"

"It would stop working," the professor said, simply. "Most magicians are careful not to expose too many of their protections to outside eyes."

That made sense, Emily decided, as she finally finished the rune. It still looked oddly uneven to her, far less precise than the one Imaiqah had produced, but she doubted she could produce anything better without more practice. Sewing was definitely *not* one of her skills.

"My mother used to say that it calmed her down," Imaiqah said. "I don't think it worked."

Emily snorted. Both Alassa and she were short-tempered. The other girls seemed to take it in their stride, but the boys had real problems; Professor Eleas ended up handing out detention to two of them after they got into an argument that rapidly turned into a fistfight, while a third had pricked his finger and then tried to proceed with the rune anyway. The professor gave him an angry lecture on the dangers, concluding with the sarcastic observation that a student from a great magical family should be aware of the risks of letting someone else obtain a sample of his blood.

"Most of you have workable runes," the professor said, turning back to the class. "You will have to practice, I'm afraid..."

There was a loud snort from one of the boys. "Why are we not carving runes into metal instead of...*sewing*?"

Emily hid her amusement. Few boys would *want* to sew, regarding it as embarrassingly feminine and effeminate...unless they went into tailoring, where it was somehow acceptable to sew. In Whitehall, there would be much stronger objections to 'woman's work' than she'd ever heard on Earth, which was darkly amusing if the runes really didn't work properly unless they were created by the person who intended to use them. For all she knew, there were wives who used runes to influence their husbands.

"Because, as I explained right back in the first class, the harder the material you use to craft the rune, the stronger it is," the professor said, angrily. "In this case, if you happen to make a mistake with the rune, removing it from your skin and destroying it is easy. Something metallic, on the other hand, might be harder to remove.

"Furthermore"—his gaze swept the classroom—"a sewn rune starts to come apart when challenged. A metallic rune would not, thus leaving you unaware of the attack."

He reached into his desk and produced a sash, with the same rune sewn into the silk. "In order to use the rune," he explained, "all you have to do is wear it. The closer to your skin, the better."

Emily took the sash and wrapped it around her throat, as if it were a scarf. Other students wrapped it around their wrists or legs. It didn't seem long enough to be worn like a belt.

"There is yet another good reason to always produce your own protective runes," Professor Eleas said. "How do you know what the rune I gave you actually does?"

Alassa stuck up her hand. "It's in the textbook you wrote," she said, quickly. "It's listed as a general-protection ward."

The professor smiled. "True," he agreed. "But bear in mind that someone with bad intentions can trick you into wearing a rune that might *not* be intended to protect you, but do some quite significant harm. You cannot afford to lower your guard when dealing with subtle magic. A single mistake can open a chink in your armor large enough to bring you down completely."

His smile grew wider. "Open your textbooks," he ordered. "By the end of the lesson, I want you to have identified at least three *additional* runes you can sew into the next sash. I also want you to write a three-parchment essay on how best to ensure that you are protected from outside influences. Give examples of historical problems handled by magicians, if possible."

Emily groaned—*another* essay—but wrote down the details anyway.

"Those of you who didn't manage to sew the rune, come over here," Professor Eleas said. "Everyone else, silent study. I shall be testing you before you go."

"Another essay," Alassa muttered, as she cast the privacy ward into the air. "I thought this was meant to be an *easy* class."

"You just need to practice," Imaiqah assured her. "We can work on your sewing this evening." She looked at Emily. "Yours too."

"We're supposed to be playing *Ken*," Alassa reminded her, shortly. "We're facing Cat's team this weekend and he's far too good. And all of our surprises will be public knowledge by now."

She looked up at Emily. "Why *did* you leave the arena?"

Emily heard the hurt in her voice and felt a pang of guilt. In hindsight, she should have stayed and watched, no matter how long it took. Her friends had *expected* her to be there to support them, no matter how foolish and pointless the game seemed to her. But she hadn't really understood just how important it was to *them*. If the Warden hadn't been murdered, Alassa would have been *really* furious with her.

"I...I'm sorry," she said, miserably. She wanted to say something, but what could she say? "I..."

"Stay the next time," Alassa said, seriously. She leaned forward so she could whisper in Emily's ear. "I'm going to stick you to the chair. You won't be able to move without my permission."

"I'm sorry," she said, again. She would almost have preferred a shouting match—or an exchange of spells. Anything would be preferable to the guilt, guilt she hadn't even realized that she should be feeling. "I won't leave the game again."

She flicked through the book, locating a series of protective runes that seemed designed to protect the wearer from insects, disease and minor accidents. The notations beside the latter clarified that the rune didn't always work, unsurprisingly. There were accidents so inevitable that runes provided no protection, normally ones caused by carelessness or stupidity. The magic, it seemed, got confused if the user did it to himself. She made a note of them and went onwards, locating a set of cleaning runes. They didn't seem powerful enough to sweep up the dust from the barracks, but they could at least prevent it from settling elsewhere.

"Good work," the professor said, when he inspected their runes. "You'll be practicing with them tomorrow."

Emily nodded mutely as he dismissed the class, keeping a handful of students back to discuss their detentions. Picking up her bag, she led the way out of the classroom and back up to the bedrooms. She didn't know if the room would let her in if her roommates were out—nothing had been said about *that* restriction—but she had to try. The door opened and she let out a sigh of relief.

"Don't let them know you're off restriction," Alassa said, as they stepped inside. "You could give someone a *real* surprise if they thought you were defenseless."

Emily smiled. Some of her tormentors had taunted her, after fixing her feet to the floor or doing something else to immobilize her. The thought of striking back was an attractive one. She put the bag on her bed, then looked over at her desk...and froze. The books weren't where she had left them.

"Emily?" Alassa said. "What's wrong?"

"I'm not sure," Emily said, slowly. She stepped towards the desk, staring down at the notepad and books she'd been looking at while they had been confined to their rooms. They were definitely in the wrong order. "Someone has been peeking at my stuff."

Alassa blinked. "Did you use a protective ward?"

"...Yes," Emily said. There were books and notes she didn't want *anyone* looking at, even though she'd destroyed her concepts for a magical battery. "But they've still been moved."

She checked the ward...and sucked in her breath when she realized that it was still there. It just hadn't been effective. Maybe she was imagining things...but she was sure that her books had been elsewhere. Someone had sat down at her desk, read her notes and then...what? Who?

Master Tor? She asked herself. It was possible. She'd never realized that he had access to their rooms until he'd come bursting in to stop her from meddling with pocket dimensions. And he had searched her desk, she assumed, as well as everything else. No wonder the Gorgon had been so angry. The thought of someone pawing through her possessions was terrifying.

"Strengthen the wards," Alassa advised. "Maybe add a booby-trap or two; no one would question you using an anti-theft jinx, or even a curse."

Emily nodded and started to cast the spells, placing one on the desk, the chair and the floor underneath the desk. A second set of spells should alert her if anyone tried to break into her trunk, although she honestly wasn't sure if Master Tor had managed to search it himself. Yodel did very good work...she wondered, briefly, what had happened to him, then dismissed the thought. He could go to Zangaria and Bryon would help him find a place in Cockatrice. It was, she suspected, what he'd wanted all along.

"Done," she said, finally. "We'd better go for lunch. It's going to be a hard afternoon."

"And a hard evening," Alassa said. "Unless you want to go for a snowball fight instead of watching the practice."

Emily sighed, inwardly, as she recognized the rebuke. "I'll watch," she said. "And I'll throw balls too."

Chapter Twenty-Five

THE REST OF THE WEEK, MUCH TO EMILY'S ANNOYANCE, PROVED NO LESS SURREAL THAN the day after Travis had been murdered. Half of the students were *still* flinching away from her, while the other half were staring at her adoringly. It was disconcerting, so much so that she spent most of her time outside class in a private library room, where she could read and work without being constantly stared at. By the time the weekend rolled around, she was glad of the break.

Lady Barb had told her, in confidence, that the staff had found absolutely no trace of a necromancer within Whitehall, something that puzzled them as much as it confused Emily. Had there ever been a *real* necromancer? Or had someone finally managed to make necromancy workable? Emily kept thinking of the potential Lady Barb had seen in her planned batteries and shuddering. Had someone stolen the idea from her and made it work, now that the Warden was gone? Or had they started using a trunk like hers to store the magic?

She'd done her best to keep her eye on Master Tor—just in case Alassa happened to be right—but he did nothing, apart from casting dark glowers in her direction whenever she was in class. He didn't even call on her to answer some of the fiendishly difficult questions he posed to the class, or invite her to serve on the debate team. In fact, he seemed determined to ignore her as much as possible, although he didn't appear to be deliberately marking her down. But it was hard to be sure.

And nothing she'd done had allowed her to identify the person who'd looked at her notes.

Emily had added a dozen more spells, including some that were designed to trap the intruder and transfigure him or her into something harmless. And yet she was sure that her desk had been raided a second time, while she'd been in class. No toads had been hopping around her room when she'd returned, no one had been trapped and immobilized in front of her desk...it was a mystery. Whoever was studying her notes was a very skilled magician.

But how could she identify him?

"Remember to stay here this time," Alassa said, as they walked into the arena. "You don't want to miss *this* game."

Emily sighed, but nodded in agreement. The crowd of students were already gathering, even though some of them looked rather less than happy to see her. Down on the field, Cat and a handful of his teammates were getting in some final moments of practice. Two of them had been close friends with Travis and rather looked as though they had a score to settle. Emily was silently glad that she wasn't playing. No one had tried to hex her into next week—or the next life—but she'd been aware of cold glances from the upper years. They didn't seem inclined to believe she wasn't to blame.

"Good," Alassa said, pushing her into a seat. "And, just to be sure..."

There was a brief flare of magic and Emily found herself stuck to the seat. "Hey!"

Alassa giggled. "Don't run off now," she said, mischievously. "And don't read your book during the game."

Emily sighed. She *could* counter the charm, but doing so would reveal that she could work magic outside classes. And who knew who might be watching? On the other hand, she could simply ask someone to release her...she shook her head, tiredly. She owed it to her friends to stay and watch, even if the game *did* take hours.

"I won't," she said, noticing several students glancing at her, then carefully sitting somewhere else. She was alone in the midst of the crowded arena. "And good luck."

"Cat will need the luck," Alassa said. There was no way to tell if her attitude was confidence or mindless bravado. "And we'll be looking for you."

Emily watched her go, then sat back and pulled the book out of her pocket. It outlined magical booby traps, including some that she'd seen in Blackhall, and the best ways to counter them. Aloha had urged her to read up on how to split the task of tricking a protective ward by working with someone else, suspecting that they would be tested on the topic soon. It looked awfully complex, but doable.

I'll have to hold up my own end, she thought, cursing her limited experience. She'd asked Professor Lombardi for extra lessons to help her catch up, but the Charms Professor had flatly refused. Mastering the basics was more important, he'd said, than trying to skip ahead and failing to grasp some of the essentials. Lady Barb, when she'd asked, had agreed and told her that she might just have to repeat the second year of Martial Magic.

"You should consider yourself lucky," she'd added. "Those who go straight into apprenticeships often have it much harder."

The whistle blew as both teams jogged into the arena. Emily sighed and carefully returned the book to her pocket, mentally cataloguing some of the spells she would want to practice with afterwards. Perhaps Aloha would help, if only to ensure that she got a passing grade herself. There was no way to avoid the prospect of Emily holding Aloha back from passing the course herself.

Cat looked...grimmer than before, Emily saw, as he shook hands with Alassa. He would have known Travis...had they been friends? It was hard to imagine *anyone* being friends with him, but if he'd had a girlfriend perhaps he'd had proper friends too. Martial Magic did tend to focus on pushing people together, if only by giving them tests that could only be accomplished by working together. But Travis had been a jerk...

He might have only been a jerk to you, Emily reminded herself, firmly. *Perhaps he was nicer to his girlfriend.*

The whistle blew for the second time and balls started to spill into the arena, their colors rapidly flickering between red, yellow and green. Emily saw Alassa's team preparing themselves, sneakily gathering balls in places where they could be picked up; Cat's team seemed less inclined to hurry. But then, they knew that picking up the balls ahead of time—or when they were the wrong color—could be disastrous. And then the whistle blew for the third time and the game began.

Emily leaned forward in horror as the pattern became clear. Cat—or at least some of his players—wanted blood. They were pushing themselves forward, ignoring chances to score for chances to take out Alassa's players, either by throwing them into the penalty box or pushing them right out of the arena. She'd known that injuries were common in *Ken*, but she'd never realized how quickly they could mount up when one side was determined to cause as many as possible. They even threw a handful of jinxes and hexes when the referee wasn't looking.

She stared in horror as Alassa slammed against one of the invisible walls, then was hit by a ball that sent her into the penalty box. Cat's team had to have planned their game carefully, she realized; they were concentrating on scattering the Upstarts and playing on their weaknesses. Alassa's team simply didn't have the experience they needed to remain calm as the game degenerated into savagery.

The referee blew his whistle again as a hex was thrown too blatantly, sending one of Cat's players out of the arena. Emily couldn't help joining in the jeering and finger-pointing as the player made his way out of the field, where he was corralled by a grim-faced Sergeant Miles and dragged off towards the armory. She hoped, as she looked back at the arena, that he would have a tough time sitting down for the next few days. Nearly a third of Alassa's team was down...or injured.

"Not always a good idea to play," Melissa's voice said. She sat down next to Emily and smiled, rather unpleasantly. "Or to choose the wrong friends."

"Get lost," Emily ordered, shortly.

"But...ah, they blame you for Travis's death," Melissa said. "I think I know better. You're not a killer."

Emily turned her head, looking down towards where Alassa's tunic was stained with blood from her nose. She was surprised that her friend hadn't backed out gracefully, but it wasn't really like Alassa to simply give up. Instead, she caught a ball and threw it back with stunning force, blasting one of Cat's players right out of the arena. The ball had to have been boosted by a spell, Emily saw, but the referee didn't seem to notice. Or maybe he just turned a blind eye.

"I think you got lucky with Shadye," Melissa added. "Or something else happened and they let you take the credit."

"And where," Emily demanded, turning to face her, "were you while Shadye was tearing the school apart?"

Melissa shrugged. Emily guessed that she, like Alassa, had been pulled out of the school before Shadye started his attack. Only a handful of the first-years had been allowed to remain behind, including Emily. Everyone else had been evacuated.

"Oh," Melissa said, airily. "That *had* to hurt."

Emily followed her gaze...and winced. Imaiqah had just been fouled by an older player who'd jumped right into her. She was on the ground, gasping in pain...seconds later, there was a bright flash of light and the older player became a toad. The referee barked orders, halting the game, and levitated Imaiqah out of the arena. Moments later, the toad and the player who'd cast the transfiguration spell were dragged out as well.

"IF YOU DON'T PLAY DECENTLY, YOU WILL BOTH BE BARRED FROM PLAYING FOR THE REST OF YOUR LIVES," the referee thundered, projecting his voice so it echoed around the arena. "DO YOU UNDERSTAND ME?"

"One shouldn't play in the games unless one is prepared to win," Melissa observed, watching the two Captains. Judging by their remarkably similar expressions, they would have preferred threats of public floggings or other humiliations to being barred from playing forever. "And...my, are there no risks one should not take?"

"Shut up," Emily snapped. "Shut up or..."

"Or what?" Melissa asked. Her voice became mocking. "You'll work magic?"

Emily prepared a spell, ready to use it in front of the entire arena...but the referee blew his whistle again, distracting everyone. The second round seemed to be cleaner than the first; Emily glanced over at where Imaiqah was being tended by Lady Barb, trying to decide if she should go there. Before she could make up her mind, Imaiqah stood and headed to the stands.

"Something smelly this way comes," Melissa hissed. "Be seeing you."

She walked off. Emily hesitated, then cast a complicated repulsion charm at her back. It wouldn't be immediately obvious, but Melissa would find herself very unpopular in a few minutes until she realized the charm was there and removed it. No doubt she'd hoped to earn kudos for sitting next to an alleged murderess—or the Necromancer's Bane.

Imaiqah joined her a moment later and sat down. "Lady Barb said I shouldn't play for a few days," she said, disappointed. "What did Melissa have to say to you?"

"Nothing good," Emily muttered. "Are you sure you want to keep playing?"

"Yes," Imaiqah said, cheerfully. "Have you noticed that we're winning?"

Emily had to laugh. It was true; Cat's team had passed up hundreds of chances to score in favor of trying to evict Alassa's players from the field. Now they were nearly a hundred points behind their rivals—and trying to catch up desperately. Alassa, realizing the problem, directed her players to guard the hoops and concentrate on taking out Cat's players. She had the advantage, now that the referee was keeping an eye on the players, and all she had to do was capitalize on it.

It was nearly an hour before the game finally came to an end. Cat's team did better than Emily had expected, but they were down several players and two of their traitors revealed themselves at the worst possible moment. In the end, Alassa's team won by twenty points. Emily joined in the cheering as the remaining team members took a lap of honor, then waltzed off towards the showers. Cat's team were loudly booed.

"Come on," Imaiqah said, jumping to her feet. "Let's go see them."

"You'll have to undo the sticking charm," Emily said. She flushed at Imaiqah's expression. "Alassa stuck me to the seat."

Imaiqah snorted. "I thought she was joking," she said, as she cast the cancelling spell. "You did manage to hurt her badly, you know."

"I know," Emily admitted, bitterly.

The team was laughing and joking as they came out of the changing rooms, even though several of them had been injured and continued to play. Alassa's nose looked slightly out of shape, marring her perfect features, but she refused to accept any more immediate medical treatment. Instead, she insisted on leading the team out of the arena and out onto the snow-covered field. The servants had already set up a pavilion where the cooks were roasting whole sheep and cows, sending wonderful smells wafting through the air.

Cat caught hold of Alassa's shoulder and swung her around. "I'm sorry, all right," he said, quickly. "I lost control and..."

Alassa stepped forward and kneed him in the groin. "Apology accepted," she said sweetly, as Cat collapsed to his knees. The other boys backed away hastily. "And we won."

"Report to my office after the feast," Lady Barb ordered. There was the faint hint of a smile on her face, but it was buried under duty. "And then go get your nose fixed."

Emily smiled as Alassa led her towards the cooks, who cut slices of meat from the roasted animals and placed them inside large slices of bread. The meat smelled even better up close, while other scents drifted over from the large table of condiments. Emily took some mustard and spread it on her meat, then added some lettuce and cucumber. It tasted remarkably good.

"Worth it," Alassa said. They sat down at one of the tables and chewed their food. "Even if I don't sit down for a few days, it will still be worth it."

"That game was madness," Emily said. "I...are you sure you want to play?"

"*Yes*," Alassa and Imaiqah said, together. They grinned at each other.

"I guess I will never see the attraction," Emily said, ruefully. *Ken* just didn't seem *fun* to her. "And I thought they were trying to kill you."

"Some of the uppermost players were alarmed by how well we did in our first game," Alassa said, dryly. "I don't think they really considered us a serious threat. Even if Travis hadn't died, they would still have wanted to break us as a team."

She touched her nose, gingerly. "I think we showed them not to take us lightly," she added. "And the referee cut down on the nastier hexes..."

"Next time they'll just concentrate on scoring and not trying to actually push us out of the arena," Imaiqah observed. "What's going to happen then?"

Emily shrugged. Even she knew that players had to strike a balance between scoring as much as possible and wearing down the opposing team. It was quite possible—if rare - for a team to lose all of its players and still win the match on points. In fact, the ideal would be to spend the first part of the match racking up a lead, then eliminating the opposing team before they could catch up. It was easier said than done.

She finished her sandwich and looked towards the pit, where the cooks were frying chicken drumsticks in oil. It looked dreadfully unhealthy, but tempting; she stood up and took a handful of legs for herself and her friends. The cook's eyes opened wide as she recognized Emily, then passed her some additional bread without being asked. There were people, Emily suspected, who would enjoy seeing fear in someone's eyes. *She* just found it depressing.

"Back to practicing tomorrow," Alassa said, as she took one of the drumsticks. "And more classes on Monday."

Emily looked down at her fingers and nodded. They'd spent some time every night sewing runes, but it would be months—she suspected—before she mastered it completely. Alassa had complained more, pointing out that preparing wards and runes were what court wizards were for. Imaiqah had asked her, rather dryly, just how far she was prepared to trust any court wizard. Her father's old wizard had accidentally done serious harm to her family line.

"I suppose I'd better go see Lady Barb," Alassa said, standing. "I'll see you both in the library, won't I?"

"I can come with you," Emily offered. "And Imaiqah probably needs more medical attention."

"She said I needed to rest," Imaiqah said. "I'll see you tomorrow, probably."

"Probably," Emily agreed. "I'll escort you to your room, just in case..."

"Charming," Alassa said, dryly. "Leaving me to my fate all alone."

She shook her head before Emily could say a word. "Don't worry about it," she added. "I'll be fine, if unhappy. You make sure that Imaiqah gets back all right."

"I'm not *that* badly injured," Imaiqah insisted. "I just need a rest."

"Which you will get, as ordered by your team captain," Alassa said, firmly. "I need you ready to go back into the arena tomorrow evening..."

There was a loud scream from the direction of the changing rooms. Heads snapped around to see a pale-skinned girl staggering out of the building. Emily didn't recognize her at all, but she looked to be on the verge of panic. Sergeant Miles pushed his way through the crowd towards her, too late.

"It's Danielle," the girl screamed. "She's dead!"

Chapter Twenty-Six

"EVERYONE, BE QUIET," SERGEANT MILES BELLOWED, HIS VOICE SOMEHOW EFFORTLESSLY drowning everyone else out. "Be *quiet*!"

A wave of magic silenced the growing panic. Emily stared at the girl who'd found the body, shocked and terrified. If Travis was dead...and then his girlfriend, what did it mean?

"Start making your way back to your rooms," Sergeant Miles ordered. He caught sight of a handful of boys making their way towards the changing rooms. "*Don't* go peep at the body, just go to your rooms. *Now*."

The students obeyed. Emily caught Imaiqah's arm as the crowd pressed in around them, pushing them towards the entrance to the school. Everyone was glancing around nervously, many of them looking at Emily as if they expected her to do something. At least few of them seemed suspicious of her, although she was sure that would come in time. How could they blame her when she hadn't been alone since the game had begun?

She pushed the thought to one side as they made their way up the stairs and into the dorms. Alassa tugged at her sleeve, indicating that they should go into Imaiqah's room instead of either of theirs. Emily nodded; Imaiqah still looked tired, even though she insisted she was fine. Imaiqah could lie down, as Lady Barb had ordered, while her friends could sit next to her and chat.

Madame Razz looked deeply worried as she counted the female students back into their rooms. Master Tor, standing nearby, shot Emily an unreadable glance, but he didn't seem inclined to throw any more wild accusations at her. Emily allowed herself a moment of relief as Imaiqah's door opened, allowing them into her room. There were students who would take such accusations seriously merely because they were made by a tutor.

"Danielle is dead," Alassa said, as soon as the door closed. "Why?"

Emily scowled. "It's a pattern," she said, trying to recall what little crime fiction she had read. Serial killers had patterns...and if they were identified, their next target could be predicted and protected. "That doesn't bode well for the other girl."

"You mean Kay," Alassa said. She smiled at Emily's surprised expression. "Her father is related to King Jorlem of Alluvia—you will remember Prince Hedrick, won't you?"

Emily snorted. Alassa might have problems memorizing the thousands of different types of alchemical ingredients, but she knew everyone who had even a trace of aristocratic blood by heart. If she'd married Hedrick, Kay would probably have wound up as part of Alassa's court, even if she'd sought to decline the honor. Or, perhaps, one of her confidants who could never be fully trusted without oaths, oaths that could never be asked for or granted.

She shook her head, tired. "Travis may have been the first person to find the Warden's body," she said. "He's the next person to die. Danielle finds *his* body—and then *she's* the next person to die. Kay may be the next target."

"Except it was *you* who found the Warden's body," Imaiqah pointed out, softly. She looked very pale. "You weren't targeted."

Alassa nodded. "And if Travis was the first to actually *see* the body, not you, why didn't he raise the alarm himself?"

Emily scowled. If Travis had raised the alarm, *she* wouldn't have been blamed...but looking back at how he'd acted when she'd reported to the Hall of Shame, there had been no sense that he'd known what she would find. He'd seemed genuinely shocked when Emily had called him and told him that the Warden was dead. Besides, he *had* been interrogated under truth spells.

"Maybe they didn't regard the Warden's death as murder," she growled. It was hard for *her* to think of the Warden as anything other than human, but someone raised in the Allied Lands might take a different view. "In that case, the pattern is that Travis was murdered first, followed by the person who found the body."

She gritted her teeth, wishing that she knew more about forensic magic. Master Tor's lectures had been long on minutiae and short on any useful detail. The only thing she knew for sure was that it was impossible to raise the dead to ask questions—and that the very thought was regarded as taboo throughout the Allied Lands. Did they even know about *fingerprints*?

"It could still be Master Tor," Alassa pointed out. "He *was* the last known person to see the Warden alive."

Emily nodded. Assuming that Travis hadn't entered the Warden's office since Master Tor had left, it was possible that the Warden had been dead for some time prior to Emily's arrival and the whole scheme was just a clumsy frame. And yet both Travis and Danielle were well-connected pupils. Killing them would be certain to draw an angry reaction from the Allied Lands. Unless, of course, that *was* the plan.

"If the Grandmaster lost his job," she said, slowly, "who would take it up?"

"It would have to be decided by the White Council," Alassa said. "But the post would need to be held by a very powerful and disciplined magician. Master Tor probably wouldn't count."

"Unless he's a necromancer," Imaiqah said. "He'd have enough raw power to rip the building apart after one or two murders."

"Maybe," Emily said, "but surely he would also be showing signs of instability?"

She'd watched Master Tor during his classes, after Travis's death, but there had been no signs of madness lurking in his eyes. He still seemed to dislike her, yet *that* wasn't really a sign of insanity. After what she'd unknowingly done, it would be hard to blame him for feeling that she'd escaped being expelled through powerful connections, rather than simple ignorance.

"He does slip into boring lectures," Alassa said, lightly. "Perhaps that helps him to cope."

Emily snorted. All jokes aside, she doubted it would be that easy.

She scowled a moment later as a thought struck her. "How do we know the bodies were *real*?"

Alassa blinked at her. "You mean they might be homunculi too?"

"Or one half of someone who had used a bilocation spell to split themselves in half," Emily said, slowly. "Maybe Travis faked his own death."

Imaiqah shook her head. "He'd be sacrificing half his mind in the process," she pointed out. "The other half wouldn't be able to carry on, I think."

"And then he would still have to kill his girlfriend without someone else noticing," Alassa added. "They *did* search the school thoroughly after his death."

Emily had her doubts. Not counting the servants, there were fifty tutors on staff, nowhere near enough to search the entire building, not if their prey was moving around at the same time. Sergeant Miles might know how to catch a moving target, but the remainder of the staff wouldn't have that training. And besides, she had difficulty in understanding why someone would sacrifice half of their mind.

"Fingerprints," she mused. Maybe the killer had worn gloves, but it wouldn't hurt them to *try*. Come to think of it, how hard would it be to create a magical fingerprint test? If there wasn't anything like it already, she was sure Professor Lombardi could compose one overnight, if necessary. "We should ask them to check."

Alassa stood. "We'll go tell them," she said, firmly. She looked at the empty beds, then back at Imaiqah. "What happened to your roommates?"

"They went hiking," Imaiqah explained. "I'll be fine, if you want to go talk to Lady Barb."

"Well, she *did* tell me to report to her," Alassa said. "Emily?"

"We should probably check with Madame Razz first," Emily said. "I don't think we *want* to get caught outside the dorms."

Madame Razz glowered at them as soon as they emerged from Imaiqah's room. "Why," she demanded, "are you not in your rooms, waiting for permission to leave?"

"I have to report to Lady Barb," Alassa said, quickly. "And my friend here has some insights into the killer's pattern."

The housemother eyed them, suspiciously. "Wait in my office," she said, finally. "I will call her."

Emily and Alassa exchanged glances, but obeyed.

"Useless biddy," Alassa muttered, as soon as they were alone. "You want to bet she'll tattle to Master Tor?"

Emily shrugged. Madame Razz was strict, but she also genuinely cared for the girls under her care—and she had a heart of gold. Emily still remembered how Madame Razz had been the one to take care of her after the nightmares had started, after she'd killed Shadye. And the housemother also had a sense of justice and integrity. She'd been furious when one of Alassa's pranks had involved a maid.

She looked around Madame Razz's office with some curiosity. It was large, crammed with sofas and a single small bookshelf. Emily herself had never been homesick—there was nothing on Earth she wanted to go back to—but she knew there were other students who *did* miss their homes and families. Madame Razz comforted them as best as she could; sometimes, she even took them home for a brief visit. The books on the shelves were all moralistic tracts that promoted proper standards of behavior. Emily had been forced to read a couple for etiquette lessons and had been left with the feeling that the writers had intended to create Purity Sues.

The door opened, revealing a tired-looking Lady Barb. "This had better be important," she said, shortly. "Right now, we're searching the school again."

Emily nodded, wincing inwardly at the edge in her tutor's voice. "There's a pattern in the killings," she said, and explained. "Kay might be the next target."

"We deduced that," Lady Barb said, with some irritation. "She's currently under the protection of Sergeant Bane."

Emily allowed herself a moment of relief. She didn't know Sergeant Bane very well, but he seemed to be as tough and fearless as Sergeant Harkin, while possessing the magic his predecessor had lacked. One of the students had tested his defenses and discovered, too late, that they were designed to repel all hexes and jinxes. And then the sergeant had turned him into a pig for ten minutes, before giving the entire class a long lecture on taking all opponents seriously, no matter what they looked like.

"Good," she said, instead. "What about fingerprints?"

Lady Barb looked blank. "Fingerprints?"

Emily smiled. They hadn't wasted her time after all. "Each of our fingerprints are unique," she explained. "If I touch something, I'll leave a fingerprint behind. You need to check the blades used in the killings for prints..."

She spoke rapidly, outlining everything she could remember about fingerprints.

"I'll suggest it to the Grandmaster," Lady Barb said, when Emily had finished. "But if the killer used gloves there won't be anything left."

"It's worth trying," Emily said. "I couldn't think of anything else..."

"That's not true," Alassa interrupted. "Are the bodies actually *real*?"

"That's an interesting question," Lady Barb acknowledged. "The bodies were so completely desiccated that it is hard to be entirely sure. But there's no reason to think otherwise."

Emily frowned. What would Sherlock Holmes do? "Was Danielle killed in the same manner as Travis?"

"Yes," Lady Barb said. "And yet it should have been instantly noticeable. It couldn't have taken place outside a seven-minute span, while there were hundreds of magicians outside the changing rooms. I don't understand it."

"Me neither," Emily agreed. Two victims...the necromancer must be heading full tilt towards insanity. "There is another possibility."

She hesitated, then outlined their suspicions about Master Tor.

"He *was* questioned under truth spells, after the Warden's body was discovered," Lady Barb said, when she had finished. "And, whatever else can be said about him, he wouldn't kill students placed under his care."

"He left Emily defenseless," Alassa said, hotly. "Do you know how many hexes I had to take off her?"

"They didn't actually *kill* her," Lady Barb said, although she seemed pleased rather than surprised at Alassa's sudden protectiveness. "And there *were* good reasons for that punishment."

She shook her head. "Master Tor is unlikely to be the killer," she added. "If nothing else, he was tested quite thoroughly after the Warden died and he knew nothing about it."

"Unless he was powerful enough to shrug off the truth spell," Emily said, slowly. She'd read up on cases where the prime suspect had done just that, saving himself from punishment. "Is he that powerful?"

Lady Barb smiled, a little unkindly. "Master Tor will never be a great sorcerer—and he knows it," she said. "Nor is he ever likely to enjoy more power and influence than that which comes from teaching at Whitehall. And he wouldn't risk his position by killing students who have such powerful connections."

"Unless he's hiding his power," Alassa pressed. "He might be..."

"Unless he somehow managed to boost his power without going mad," Lady Barb snapped, "his power level hasn't increased beyond his recorded level. We *are* quite good at measuring magical power and potential at this school. Now, unless you have some actual *proof*..."

"He could be covering for someone else," Alassa suggested, sullenly. "If he were trying to frame Emily, he..."

"Would have needed to know in advance what was going to happen," Lady Barb said, her patience at an end. "I think it is highly unlikely that he is involved, save by coincidence."

Her eyes narrowed. "Do you have anything *useful* to add?"

Emily swallowed, then asked the question that had been bothering her ever since she'd realized they had to be dealing with a serial killer. "What will happen to this person, when you catch him?"

Lady Barb scowled. "Depends," she said. "If he's a necromancer, we will kill him and destroy the body. You can never trust a necromancer not to try to ensure that he can never truly die. If not, he'll be sent to face the White Council. They will determine his fate."

Emily nodded. "As long as you don't hand your jailhouse keys to unscrupulous creatures," she said, "you shouldn't have a problem."

Lady Barb gave her an odd look, then let it pass. "No one has ever been known to escape from the Garden of the Stoned Philosophers," she said. "Even *going* there is strongly discouraged."

Nothing Emily had ever read—in science fiction or fantasy—allowed her to believe in the concept of the inescapable prison, but there was no point in trying to argue. Instead, she stood and headed for the door.

"Wait," Lady Barb said, coldly. "Madame Razz informs me that you intended to make your way through the building to find us."

Emily swallowed. "Yes," she said. "We wanted to help..."

"That was extremely foolish," Lady Barb said. "Or has it escaped your attention that you are among the prime suspects? If you happened to be caught outside your rooms, it would be a great deal harder to prove your innocence. You have political enemies who will be happy to take whatever chance they can get to discredit you."

She rounded on Alassa. "And *you* are your father's sole heir," she added, tightly. "Did you realize, perhaps, that if you died here Zangaria would slip into civil war? Half of the barons may currently be dead, but the remainder would be unable to avoid making a grab for power. You risked far more than just your life when you wanted to leave the bedrooms, where you are *protected*."

"Didn't do much for Danielle," Alassa said, softly. "I..."

Lady Barb's eyes glittered with fury. "Your father, I suspect, will be horrified when he hears of your exploits," she snapped. "And so he should be. He already wasted most of your early life; now, you're threatening to waste the rest of it."

Alassa's face seemed to darken, very slightly. "I..."

"Emily," Lady Barb ordered, "wait outside."

Emily hesitated, then obeyed.

The corridor outside seemed as silent as the grave. There was no sign of Madame Razz or anyone else; she almost felt as if she were alone in the school. Even the lights had been dimmed, although there was no apparent reason. It was hardly night time. She gritted her teeth as she heard a smacking sound, followed by yelps of pain from inside the office. At least Lady Barb had given Alassa some privacy.

There was a long silent pause, then the door opened. Alassa looked tearful, one hand rubbing her rear as she made her way past Emily and down towards her bedroom. Emily hesitated, unsure of what to do, then gasped in pain as Lady Barb's hand caught hold of her arm and pulled her into the office. She couldn't help noticing that Lady Barb was carrying a wooden hairbrush in one hand.

"What you did was foolish as well as risky," Lady Barb said. "I shudder to think of what would have happened if you'd been caught."

Emily lowered her eyes. Lady Barb was right. It *had* been foolish.

"I'll suggest fingerprint tests to the Grandmaster later tonight," Lady Barb added. "And I will see to it that Kay remains under guard. The Grandmaster will, I suspect, make a full announcement tomorrow. Until then, I suggest that you keep your mouth closed. There are already hundreds of rumors running around the school."

She pulled Emily gently over her knee, tugged down her trousers and went to work. Emily gritted her teeth as the first smack struck her rear, then cried out in pain as Lady Barb smacked her again and again. It felt like hours before she was allowed to stand up again, clutching her bottom in the hope that it would somehow quench the painful fire.

"*That*," Lady Barb said, "was for being foolish and putting your own life in danger."

"My life is *always* in danger," Emily snapped, unable to keep the tears under control. "And I..."

"That's no excuse to make it worse," Lady Barb snapped. "I thought better of you, really I did."

Somehow, Emily discovered, the disappointment in her voice seemed worse than the punishment itself.

Chapter Twenty-Seven

Her rear was still throbbing when the students were awakened at eight bells the following morning by an announcement ordering them to make their way to the Great Hall. She pulled herself out of bed, careful not to sit down too hard, and pulled a loose robe on over her nightshirt. No one would notice that she wasn't wearing standard underclothes beneath her robes. She ran a hand through her hair, using magic to tie it back in a long ponytail, then splashed water on her face. It didn't make her feel better.

"Hurry up," the Gorgon hissed. "I want to know what's going on."

Emily hesitated, then walked out of the room and met up with her friends. Alassa didn't look as though she'd slept any better than Emily herself, although she was better at hiding it, either with makeup or glamors. No one else seemed to notice, thankfully. The mood was subdued, almost fearful. If two students could die in the school, *anyone* could be next.

Unless the pattern holds up, Emily thought. *The next to die will be the person who found the last body.*

She shuddered at the thought as they made their way down the stairs and into the great hall. It was crammed with students, giving them an excuse to press themselves against the wall rather than sit down. Several grim-faced men wearing white uniforms were positioned around the hall, their eyes flickering from student to student. Sergeant Bane was standing in one corner, next to the pale-skinned girl who'd stumbled across Danielle's body. She looked to be on the verge of fainting dead away. Emily felt a twinge of pity. The poor girl had never asked to be targeted by an insane murderer.

The Grandmaster strode out onto the stage as Mistress Irene bellowed for quiet. He looked almost...defeated, Emily realized in horror; he didn't seem to have slept at all since Danielle's body had been found. Few of the tutors looked any better. Apart from Sergeant Miles, who looked so disgustingly fresh that Emily was sure he had used a rejuvenation spell, they all looked tired and worn.

"Yesterday afternoon, Danielle of House Meridian was found dead," the Grandmaster said, very quietly. Enhancement spell or not, they had to strain to hear him. "Her body was desiccated, utterly ripped clean of life by magic. So far, no suspect has been found."

Emily fought to keep her expression blank as several pairs of accusing eyes turned towards her. There were hundreds of witnesses to where she'd been while Danielle had been taking her last breaths, but somehow she knew that wouldn't be enough. If people were scared, they would lash out at the closest target, regardless of guilt or innocence. She silently thanked Lady Barb for insisting that she be allowed to use magic again. It was going to be needed.

"We have searched the school again and turned up nothing—nothing related to the murder, at least," the Grandmaster said. "This leaves us with a disturbing mystery."

There was a long pause. Emily wondered, absently, just what *else* the search had turned up. No doubt students had been hiding contraband or forbidden texts all over the school for years, just as her former classmates had done on Earth. Some things were truly universal. And then there were questionable alchemical ingredients, pornographic materials and drugs. They would be serious business on any other day.

"I have consulted with the White Council," the Grandmaster continued. "It has been decided that the search will be expanded to student possessions and..."

He broke off as a low rumble of outrage ran through the hall. Emily cursed inwardly, knowing that it would give her detractors one more reason to hate her. If the Gorgon had been furious at having her possessions searched, just for sharing a room with Emily, the rest of the school would be even worse. And yet there was no *reason* to blame Emily...not, she knew, that it would matter. Mob rule was rarely logical.

"Quiet," the Grandmaster snapped. A wave of power washed through the hall, silencing the unruly students. "This decision was not taken lightly. There may be a necromancer in the school and finding him takes priority over everything else. As a consolation, of sorts, there will be an amnesty for anything we discover that is on the banned list, provided that it is sent out of the school by the end of the day.

"However, many of your families have requested that you be sent home until the necromancer is uncovered," he continued. "Those who have been called home—the lists are posted on the walls—are to report to the Great Hall in an hour to have their trunks searched before going through the portal to the White Mountains, where you will be sent to your final destination. The search will be carried out by Mediators"—he nodded towards the white-uniformed men—"but will be supervised by Whitehall staff.

"For those of you who remain, you should watch yourselves carefully and try to remain in groups," the Grandmaster concluded. "We will be teaching the first years emergency alert spells this afternoon. I suggest that later years join the classes unless you are confident that you have already mastered them. Those of you who *fail* to produce a proper emergency signal on demand will not enjoy the experience.

"The Mediators will be patrolling the school starting today. If they ask questions, do your best to answer them. Classes will be cancelled throughout the week, so I suggest that you spend the time writing essays and catching up on your reading.

His hidden eyes swept the room once more. "Check the lists, then go pack if your name is on them," he said, holding up a hand. "We will not entertain requests to stay if your parents want you home."

Emily looked over at Alassa as the Grandmaster walked off the stage, dismissing the students. Crowds were already gathering around the lists; it took several minutes before they could get close enough to scan for their names. No one had called Emily home, unsurprisingly; the closest thing to a parent she had in this universe was Void and *he* wasn't likely to call her out of danger, if he even knew she was in trouble. But Alassa...

"My father wants me home," Alassa said, bleakly. She glanced across the hall to where Lady Barb was talking to Kay. "Do you think she snitched to him?"

"I don't know," Emily said. Lady Barb hadn't *said* anything about sending Alassa home...and she wasn't a particularly subtle person. "But you might be a target here."

"And if I die...etc, etc," Alassa snarled. She looked up at the list again. "What about Imaiqah?"

"I can't see my name," Imaiqah said. "Most of the students listed are ones with aristocratic parents or other such connections."

"Your father may not have been informed," Alassa said, shortly. "I should stay..."

"No," Mistress Irene said. They jumped. None of them had realized she was right behind them. "You will not be staying. Your father has summoned you home."

Alassa held onto her temper with icy dignity. "I cannot go while my friends remain in danger..."

"That is the price you pay for being who you are," Mistress Irene snapped. "You are more than just a person; you are the representation of an entire royal bloodline. I suggest, very strongly, that you take it up with your father when you reach Zangaria. Until then, go pack your trunk and make your way to the portal.

"And you two"—her gaze moved to Imaiqah and Emily—"go eat breakfast. Now."

"We'll be there to see you off," Emily said to Alassa. She understood now precisely how Alassa must have felt when Emily ditched the *Ken* game. It was easy to feel abandoned, even though it wasn't Alassa's decision. Arguing would just get her pitched through the portal to explain herself to her father. "Don't worry about it."

"You'd better keep the team practicing," Alassa growled to Imaiqah. "I want to win the next game..."

"Games have been cancelled indefinitely," Mistress Irene said. "Now, *go*."

Emily obeyed, walking with Imaiqah into the dining hall. The students were already arguing over the Grandmaster's words, although there were more fearful glances thrown in Emily's direction when they thought she wasn't looking. There was a dull undercurrent of resentment in the air, an awareness that an aspect of the Sorcerer's Rule was about to be flouted openly. Emily wondered, as she sat down gingerly and took a bowl of porridge, if the resentment was about to turn into outright mutiny.

She saw Professor Lombardi making his way through the dining hall and realized, grimly, that he was heading straight towards her. "Lady Emily," he said, when he stopped in front of her table. "I require your assistance after breakfast."

Emily hesitated. "I need to see Alassa off..."

"Students are not allowed to be present unless they are leaving the school," Lombardi said, cutting her off shortly. "You may say goodbye to her after breakfast, then report to my office immediately afterwards."

"Yes, sir," Emily said, bitterly. There was no choice. "I'll be there."

"I'll stay with Alassa as long as I can," Imaiqah said, reassuringly. "It wasn't your fault."

Emily scowled. *None* of this was her fault and half the school blamed her anyway. The other half seemed to expect her to do something about it. At least the tutors didn't seem to believe that Emily was their only hope.

They finished their breakfast and walked up to Alassa's room. Their friend had her trunk open and was dropping clothes and a handful of books into it, although she seemed to be leaving half of her possessions at Whitehall. It was unlikely that anyone would steal from her—Emily hadn't heard of outright theft at Whitehall, not while the Warden monitored the interior of the school—but Alassa seemed to like having her clothes with her. Besides, the searchers would eventually paw through her wardrobe.

"Not your fault," Alassa said, although she still looked irked. "My father will have to explain himself to me. He should have called you two back to Zangaria as well."

Emily frowned. She had a feeling that if King Randor had asked, the Grandmaster would have refused. Besides, King Randor wasn't exactly her legal guardian.

"Don't worry about us," Emily said, giving her friend a hug. "We'll be fine."

Alassa's blue eyes met hers. "Really? I do worry about you."

"I know," Emily said. It was astonishing to see how far Alassa had come since they'd first met...but then, Alassa was one of the handful of people who knew where Emily really came from. It wouldn't be hard for her to deduce that the Necromancer's Bane was really nothing more than propaganda, put forward by the Allied Lands. "I worry about you too."

She gave Alassa one final hug and then walked out of the bedroom. Madame Razz shot her a cross look as she assisted two first-years to move their trunks down the stairs to the portal, so Emily walked past them and along the corridor to Professor Lombardi's office. The door was wide open, a silver knife and a pair of stone knives lying on the table. Emily tapped on the door and stepped inside, looking around for the professor. He was standing in front of a corner table, studying a large textbook.

"Those are the murder weapons," he said, without turning around. "What do you make of them?"

Emily shrugged. "One silver, two stone," she said. She took a closer look. "And they're unmarked. There are no runes."

"There's one carved into the handle of the silver knife," Professor Lombardi said. He closed the oversized textbook and turned to face her. "It's a fairly standard rune for a knife, intended to guide the blade towards the best possible place to strike. A werewolf may be unable to regenerate if pieced by a silver blade, but unless you hit a vital organ it may not die immediately. That would be...unfortunate."

"Because the silver poisoning would drive it berserk," Emily said. She'd read the textbooks, including one written by a man who seemed to consider himself a great huntsman. At least the werewolf would have a chance to fight back if attacked by a hunter. "It wouldn't be a wise move."

Professor Lombardi nodded. "The absence of runes on the other blades is rather curious," he said. "A practiced necromancer would be able to make do without them, but a new practitioner would probably need them to drain power properly. The condition of the bodies might suggest that something went wrong with the process, but if that was the case it was remarkably restrained. A necromantic accident would normally cause a colossal discharge of power."

Emily frowned. "Is it possible that someone could have mastered necromancy over the holidays and then returned to school?"

The professor quirked a sardonic eyebrow. "And somehow avoided detection, even with their magic spilling around them?"

He smiled at Emily's sour expression. "Most necromancers have no finesse," he said. "They have more raw power than they know what to do with—and tend to rely on brute force to compensate for the gaps in their knowledge. Even if the necromancer was sane enough to hide what he was, he would *still* have to learn to work with his newfound magic—and that would be extremely difficult. We do monitor your progress quite closely."

Emily nodded, wordlessly.

"This is the fingerprint reading spell," Professor Lombardi added, changing the subject. "If it worked properly, it should show us every fingerprint on the table."

He cast the spell into the air. There was a long pause and then a glowing green image of a fingerprint appeared over the table. Several more followed, seemingly identical...but there were none from the knives themselves. The professor repeated the spell, yet nothing materialized. Emily realized, bitterly, that the knives had been wiped clean—or the killer had used gloves.

"Interesting," Professor Lombardi stated. "We didn't pick up any magical residue earlier either."

Emily looked at him. "Magical residue?"

"Traces of the spells used by the killer," the professor explained. "Most sorcerers have a unique signature of their own, matching their own specific way of casting spells. There isn't anything on the blades at all, which simply doesn't make sense. Destroying the Warden so quickly should have been impossible without powerful magic. And the blades should be drenched in power if they had been used by a necromancer."

"I see," Emily said, slowly. She took the parchment he'd used to write down the spell and studied it. It seemed to be perfect, although she knew better than to think she could match Professor Lombardi in *anything* relating to charms. "Did he take in *all* of the power?"

"Every necromancer we have known had problems containing *all* of the power," Professor Lombardi said. "It's rather like trying to drink from a bucket of water. Plenty of water goes into your throat—and more ends up spilling down your chest. Only the faerie, we assume, were able to contain it all." He shook his head. "The only theory which seems to make sense is that someone is trying to *fake* a necromantic rite...but that doesn't explain the condition of the bodies."

Emily hesitated, then cast the fingerprint spell for herself. Nothing new was revealed. Carefully, she pressed her finger against the table and then repeated the spell. Her fingerprint appeared along with the others.

"This could have interesting applications," Professor Lombardi said. "Or it could prove surprisingly easy to fool. I shall have to give it some thought."

He looked at Emily. "You have a long essay to write," he reminded her. "I suggest that you go to the library and start researching for it."

"Yes, sir," Emily said, reluctantly. A quick glance at her watch told her that she was probably too late to wave Alassa off as she stepped into the portal room. "Can I keep the spell?"

Professor Lombardi shrugged. "I suppose it can't do any harm," he said. "By the way, how did you intend to complete the tests?"

Emily blinked. "I beg your pardon?"

"You suggested finding fingerprints," the professor said, "which was a good idea even if it failed. But how did you intend to find out which fingerprints belonged to which person?"

"The normal procedure would be to test every suspect and see whose fingerprints matched the ones found at the crime scene," Emily said. "Or if you don't want to tip them off, you test something you know no one else has touched..."

"The Warden could have tested the entire school," Professor Lombardi said, ruefully. "It may be months before a new one is ready to take his place."

Emily scowled. How many students would be dead by then?

"Go to the library," Professor Lombardi ordered. "If I can't hold classes, I can at least insist on excellent essays."

And you get mad if we make a tiny mistake, Emily thought.

She shook her head. It was hard to blame the professor. Advanced Charms was a fundamental requirement for students who wanted to become full-fledged sorcerers and picking up bad habits, or even misconceptions, could make it impossible for a student to proceed. Even Void, who normally showed little interest in her education, had told her to make sure she did well at Advanced Charms.

"Yes, sir," she said.

Outside, there was a pair of Mediators patrolling the corridors. One was young, no older than Jade; the other looked old enough to be his grandfather. They both eyed Emily suspiciously, then nodded and let her pass. She felt their gazes burning into her back as she walked past them and up the stairs to the library. Inside, it was blissfully quiet and empty.

"Welcome back," Lady Aylia said. "Do you want to help return some books to the shelves?"

Emily smiled. At least one person wasn't paying attention to rumor. And sorting books was relaxing as well as educational.

"Sure," she said. "I'd love to."

Chapter Twenty-Eight

If there was one good thing about the whole situation, Emily decided over the next few days, it was that cancelling classes gave her a chance to catch up with the mountain of homework that had been handed out by almost all of her tutors. Most of the other students seemed to agree, although they still seemed torn between the conviction that Emily was a murderess and the belief that she would save them all. When she wasn't dodging hexes aimed at her back, she was trying to avoid older students staring at her with disturbingly worshipful eyes.

She spent most of her time in the library while Imaiqah tried to keep the Upstarts practicing in the arena. Imaiqah didn't quite have Alassa's charisma or sheer bloody-minded determination to press on, no matter what, but *Ken* provided a distraction from the team's worries, as well as the chance to be with a large circle of friends. Emily still preferred the library, or cleaning out the barracks. The work seemed never-ending.

The Mediators had questioned her the day after Alassa left, but none of their questions were anything other than routine. They, at least, seemed confident that Emily wasn't the murderess—or a necromancer. She'd told them what she could, yet she doubted that it had been very helpful. And then they'd thanked her and told her not to leave Whitehall. Emily hadn't been able to stop herself from laughing at the thought.

"I charmed the hoops, as you suggested," Aloha said, four days after Alassa left. "The activation word is *soot*. They should suck up dust into the bags."

Emily smiled and thanked her, then carried the hoops and a piece of runic chalk up the stairs to the barracks. Inside, the dust seemed just as thick as ever, no matter how hard she brushed and scrubbed. Fixing one of the bags to the hoop, she muttered the activation word and smiled as the makeshift vacuum cleaner went to work. Large torrents of dust were pulled off the floor and into the bag. When it was full, Emily cancelled the spell, sealed the bag and fixed the next one onto the hoop. An hour later, she could actually see the floor properly. It was bare concrete, pitted by the weight of whatever military equipment had been stored inside the barracks. Emily honestly couldn't understand why they hadn't put the barracks outside the school, or at least closer to the armory.

Once the floor was clean, she took the chalk and carefully drew out the anti-dust rune on the concrete. If placed carefully, she had calculated, the runes would slowly push any remaining dust into the corners, where it could be swept up tomorrow. She placed a sealing charm on the bags, just in case someone tried to kick them, and dragged them out of the barracks. The servants would pick them up later, she had been assured.

The washroom still smelt funny, even after she vacuumed up everything on the floor. She cursed Master Tor under her breath, then went back and retrieved a bucket, a mop and some soapy water. There were stains on the floor that smelt nasty—she didn't want to even guess at what they were—but she wiped them up anyway. It took nearly another hour to get the washroom into something resembling a decent appearance, a task that could have been done very quickly with magic. She had to admit that Master Tor had chosen a very inventive punishment.

There was yet more dust in the other half of the barracks, forcing her to use the vacuum hoops again. In the corner, where the spiders lurked, she drew a simple pest repulsion rune and left it to take effect. According to the textbooks, the spiders should feel an urge to move from the spot, although it hadn't been clear how long it would take before they actually heeded the subtle command. Hopefully, they would make their way out of the castle and find a new home in the forest.

She sat back and surveyed her handiwork. It was almost done; all she would really need to do was sweep up the remaining dust, then finish mopping the floor. The bunks would need to be replaced, but she wasn't sure if that was part of the punishment or not. She'd looked at the bunks carefully enough to know that they really needed to be replaced by something newer.

Master Tor might complain that she had cheated, she knew; he hadn't specifically forbidden her from using charmed tools, but a case could be made that she had violated the intent of his instructions. Emily found it hard to care after spending several weeks on her knees, trying to loosen and remove as much of the dust as possible. Maybe she had deserved the punishment—and she'd certainly done something idiotic, if through ignorance—but she'd had more than enough of it. She really didn't want to think about what the dust might be doing to her lungs.

And Lady Barb hasn't covered that yet, she thought, as she sagged against one of the walls. It needed a new coat of paint too, but that was something she suspected could be left to someone else. *I wonder what other diseases are festering in the toilets.*

Emily's entire body was aching, her muscles twanging uncomfortably. It would have been unpleasant in any case, she was sure, but it was worse after several hours of physical training from the sergeants. She felt as if she had run for hours, followed by sessions on the assault course—and then concluding with hand-to-hand combat against the other students, watched closely by the sergeants. Her body simply wasn't strong enough to fight the boys directly.

I need a hot bath, she thought, sourly. There *were* spells designed to help work out muscular kinks, but she wasn't sure who she dared trust enough to ask them to cast the spells on her. Imaiqah was still playing *Ken,* she assumed, and the Gorgon spoke to her as little as possible. And Lin seemed to have merged into the shadows and vanished.

The door opened and she looked up, surprised. Melissa peeked her head into the room, then came inside, grinning unpleasantly. Emily was fairly sure that no one else knew about her detention duties—enough people blamed her to ensure that her handiwork was undone the night after she cleared the floor—but just one person was bad enough. The red-haired girl smirked at her, then eyed the runes on the floor nastily.

"That's *cheating,*" she said, in a prissy little girl voice. "I could call Master Tor."

"Who would then have to admit that the runes don't actually use my magic," Emily pointed out. It seemed logical—to her—that a magician could charge runes personally, rather than waiting for them to gather ambient magic, but all of her research suggested that wasn't actually possible. "I didn't cast any spells directly in this room."

"Really," Melissa said. "Should I test that?"

Emily—hot, sweaty and tired—felt her temper flare. "If you want to call him, you can," she snapped. "I have no doubt that he will be pleased with you for wasting his time."

She glared at Melissa. Tensions had been running high in the school since a third of the pupils had been called home, with fights and hexing contests breaking out in the corridors despite the presence of the Mediators. She'd seen a stream of unhappy-looking students being marched to the infirmary by the tutors, several with injuries or magically-inflicted disfigurations. The student with the ear growing out of his forehead had looked particularly unhappy.

"I don't think he likes you," Melissa taunted. "Maybe he wouldn't consider it a waste of time."

"And maybe he would send you to help me," Emily responded, clenching her fists. "Call him or go away. I don't have time to listen to you."

"My friends have been taken out of the school," Melissa snapped. "But they left me here."

"I cannot imagine why," Emily sneered. She knew very little about Melissa's background, save that it had produced a girl who was almost as bratty as Alassa had been, before she'd met Emily. "Perhaps they didn't *want* you home."

Melissa started forward, eyes flaring with anger, before she caught herself. "And King Randor clearly thought better of ennobling you," she snapped. "He could have called you home too..."

Emily scowled. She'd heard nothing from Alassa—and her friend should have reached Zangaria within a day through the portal network. Perhaps King Randor had grounded her for mouthing off to him—Imaiqah had said that Alassa had been furious when she'd walked into the portal hall—or perhaps it was something more sinister. But there was no way to know.

"But really, who gives such power to a seventeen-year-old girl?" Melissa demanded. "He probably wanted to give it to someone who..."

"You are a spoilt brat," Emily snapped, feeling her temper boiling over. "You..."

Melissa lifted her hand and cast a freeze charm towards Emily. Emily deflected it, effortlessly.

"You can't use magic," Melissa spluttered. "You can't..."

Emily shaped a spell in her mind and hurled it at Melissa's face. Melissa jumped to one side and the spell shot past her, vanishing as it struck the stone wall. Emily threw a second spell, and then a third, drawing on her training in Martial Magic. Getting off just one spell was unlikely to work out well, the sergeants had told their class. Nor was standing still while hurling spells, as if the enemy was going to be gentlemanly about the whole affair.

"I can use magic," she hissed, as one of her spells sent Melissa crashing to the floor. "And I have had *enough* of you!"

Melissa rolled over, just in time to dodge a spell that would have turned her into a slug. She twisted and threw a blinding flash of light at Emily, forcing her to squeeze her eyes shut—and winning just enough time for Melissa to get back on her feet. Emily expected her to run, but instead she threw several nasty hexes at Emily's face. Emily gritted her teeth as a burning hex struck her cheek, leaving her feeling as if she'd been badly sunburnt. She ignored the pain as best as she could and threw a force punch towards Melissa. The girl was picked up and flung against the far wall by the force of the blast.

"Get up," Emily snarled, feeling her frustration bubbling up inside her. "Get up and fight."

Melissa stared bleakly at her, then threw a half-hearted hex that missed Emily by nearly a meter. Emily ignored it as she reached down, grasped Melissa's shirt and hauled her back up into a standing position, slamming her against the wall. Melissa let out a cry of pain as Emily held her, then tried to stamp on Emily's foot. Emily sidestepped it and glared down at her enemy. After the way Melissa had treated her, she wanted to smash her, to humiliate her so utterly that she never dared look at Emily again. And yet...was it right?

Guilt boiled up in her mind as she stared at Melissa. Lady Barb had taught her not to hold back, but her anger had led to her almost killing Melissa. She let go of the redhead, watching as the girl slumped to the floor. It would have been easy to finish the job...and yet she couldn't. Melissa didn't deserve to die...

"I'm sorry," she said, softly. She couldn't tell if Melissa could even hear her. "I..."

Melissa muttered a word in a language Emily didn't recognize, but it didn't sound pleasant.

She felt tears welling up in her eyes and angrily pushed them away. There had been nothing to show her just how far she'd advanced ahead of the other second year students through attending Martial Magic. She knew that she was physically strong, but she'd always compared her spellwork to Aloha and Jade, both of whom had been years ahead of her. It had simply never occurred to her that she needed to do more than simply refrain from using the nastier spells against her fellow pupils. She needed to hold back more.

"Damn you," Melissa said, as she tried to pull herself to her feet. "You should..."

The door crashed open. Emily looked up to see Sergeant Bane advancing into the room.

"And what," he demanded, as he peered down at the two girls, "has been going on here?"

Emily struggled to explain as he tended to Melissa. The sergeant listened, even as he cast a series of healing spells, then pointed Melissa towards the infirmary. Emily read trouble for herself in his face and wondered if he would point her toward Lady

Barb or find an even worse punishment duty for her. Maybe hunting Death Vipers...

"Wipe that mess off your face," the Sergeant ordered, once Melissa had left the room. He reached into his uniform and produced a scrap of cloth that might have passed for a pocket handkerchief. "What were you thinking?"

Emily wiped the tears from her face, bitterly. They were stained with dust.

"I have had enough of watching students lose their tempers," the sergeant continued. His voice was loud enough to make her ears hurt. "It's bad enough that I just had to thrash a dozen idiots for trying to kill each other in the corridors, but now I find one of *my pupils* trying to kill one of her friends! What the hell were you thinking?"

Emily drew herself upright. "I was thinking that she started it," she said, no longer willing to just stand there and take the blame. "Or was I not supposed to defend myself?"

The sergeant looked at her, sharply. "By breaking three of her ribs? You're damn lucky that you didn't do any worse damage. Magic can't heal *everything*."

He stalked over to the door and beckoned for her to follow him. "Come with me," he snapped. "You can come back and fix the rest of the mess later."

Emily glanced behind her. One of the buckets had been tipped over, spilling water all over the floor. Several more bags had also been punctured, scattering dust everywhere. The runes on the floor had largely been destroyed. She wanted to ask if she could take the time to repair them, but she knew better than to think she would be allowed. The sergeants had warned her, right back at the start, just how dangerous it could be to lose control.

She winced, remembering the moment she'd slammed Melissa into the wall. The practice duels she'd fought with the Sergeants and Lady Barb had included immediate medical care. She'd broken bones more than once, but the damage had been healed and she'd been pushed back into the duelling ring. Melissa hadn't taken Martial Magic. Chances were that she'd never been hurt in Defensive Magic.

I didn't mean to hurt her so badly, she thought. But another part of her mind reminded her just how good it had felt to lash out at Melissa...and to watch her fall. If the sergeant hadn't entered the room would she have lasted out again? How far would she have gone? Would she have been overwhelmed by the desire just to hurt Melissa until she fell silent forever?

She didn't want to think about it. But there was no choice.

The sergeant led her down a long sloping corridor, passing a series of open windows that looked out over the forest below. Emily stopped, remembering the first view she'd had of her new world from Void's tower, after he'd saved her from Shadye. After this...would she be allowed to stay in Whitehall? Or would she be expelled? It wasn't as if she didn't have anywhere to go. Hell, she had enough money to hire tutors, if necessary.

And then a thought struck her.

"Sergeant," she said, slowly, "aren't you supposed to be with Kay?"

The Sergeant stopped and turned to face her. "And do you think that *I*, a male tutor, would be a suitable companion *everywhere* she went?"

Emily flushed, helplessly. Of *course* Kay wouldn't want the sergeant sharing her bedroom, or accompanying her to the toilet...no doubt Lady Barb or Mistress Irene had taken over, at least long enough to let them both have a break. It had been a stupid question and yet...something was nagging at her.

"Kay is quite safe," Sergeant Bane said. There was more than a little absolute conviction in his voice. "And..."

Something *changed*. Emily sensed it, although she was unable to tell *what* it was she was sensing. The magical field surrounding Whitehall had changed since the Warden's death—it was no longer so focused or precise—but this was different. She caught herself glancing around nervously, unsure of what she was looking for. Something was very definitely wrong.

"What do you think you're doing, girl?" Sergeant Bane demanded. "Come with me!"

Emily hesitated. The sense of *wrongness* was growing stronger, as if something was beating on the walls of reality itself. She couldn't move; instead, she glanced around, convinced that something was trying to sneak up on her. The glowing lights on the walls seemed to be fading, leaving the sunlight streaming in through the open windows as the only source of illumination. Sergeant Bane seemed, for a long chilling moment, suddenly lost in the shadow.

"Girl," the Sergeant thundered. His fury seemed to be growing worse. "Come! Now!"

But Emily couldn't move at all.

The sergeant stepped forward, one hand raised as if he intended to strike her...and then he stopped. Something was wrong with his face, Emily realized slowly, although her mind had difficulty in even realizing that something *was* wrong. It was almost as if she weren't quite able to comprehend what she was seeing. Her head hurt and she wanted to twist away, but something kept her feet firmly pressed to the floor...

...And then the sergeant dissolved into an eerie haze of multicolored light.

Chapter Twenty-Nine

MIMIC!

Emily stared, rooted to the spot, as the entity slowly glided towards her, pulsing with utter malevolence. There was no discernible face, nothing to suggest an expression...and yet she was sure that it *hated* her. She lifted a trembling hand, trying to send for help and cast a protective ward, but nothing happened. The mimic was interfering with the magic...or maybe she was too scared to cast the spell properly.

It had been *months* since she'd seen a Mimic. One of them had been kept in Whitehall's zoo, trapped behind extremely powerful wards...and had vanished, after Shadye had attacked Whitehall. Everyone had assumed that it had killed, eaten and replaced one of the orcs or goblins that had fled into the countryside after Shadye had been killed; no one, as far as she knew, had seemed particularly concerned. Besides, even *finding* a Mimic was supposed to be almost impossible. Had it been hiding in Whitehall ever since the attack on the school?

The Mimic seemed to be expanding...or perhaps it was simply growing closer. Glowing tendrils of mist reached towards her, the world seeming to fade as they neared. It was draining her, she realized numbly, copying everything that made her what she was in preparation to assume her form. And then it would kill her and take her place...or would it? The pattern didn't seem quite right...

Sheer panic blasted through her and she stumbled backwards, regaining some strength as she staggered away from the Mimic. It didn't seem to care; it merely glided after her, pushing her down the corridor. If it had killed and replaced Sergeant Bane—she'd never heard of a Mimic simply being a shapeshifter, although she didn't know *much* about them—it wouldn't have any trouble doing the same to her. Desperately, she lifted her hand again and threw a hex at the Mimic. The spell passed right through the entity, as if it were made of fog...or if it weren't really there. An illusion?

She'd used an illusion of a Mimic before, but she hadn't managed to duplicate the sense of being drained. How could she?

Emily forced herself to concentrate and threw another spell, one of the handful of completely lethal spells she'd been taught—and warned never to even *think* about using, unless it was a matter of life or death. There was a brilliant flash of red light, but when it faded the Mimic was still there, advancing on her. Emily panicked and cast the first spell that came into her head, the magic detection spell. The Mimic lit up with bright light.

For a moment, it seemed to hesitate—as if the spell, unlike something far more lethal, had done real damage. And then it resumed its path towards her, billowing out to block her line of retreat. Emily gasped, then swore as she bumped into the wall and started to press her way towards the window. She hadn't even realized that she was being herded until it was too late.

Do something, her mind yammered at her. *Get out...*

The Mimic's pulsing was almost hypnotic as it reached out towards her. Emily could feel its magic humming as it prepared to dine, to absorb everything she was... it was clear, now, why it had claimed the Warden as its first victim. Without his constant monitoring of Whitehall's interior, the Mimic could pick off the students and staff one by one—and remain completely undetectable. No one had come to investigate the lethal spell she'd used, any more than they'd realized when she'd freed herself from Melissa's hexes. Master Tor hadn't realized that his order was largely unenforceable...

Her life started to flash in front of her eyes as the Mimic touched her mind. Her first memories, the few moments of happiness she'd had, her abduction from Earth... somehow, the thought of Void and Shadye gave her strength. She was not going to allow the Mimic to get the better of her, even though everyone knew them to be almost indestructible. There *had* to be a way out. She looked over at the window, then pulled herself forward. It felt as if she had been walking for miles—the Mimic was already draining her life from her—but somehow she made it to the window and stared out over the forest. Behind her, she felt the Mimic closing in for the kill.

There was no time to be careful. She climbed onto the ledge and lost her footing, falling out of the window. She caught a brief glimpse of the Mimic, filling the corridor like fog, then she plummeted down towards the ground. Her mind cleared the moment she was away from the Mimic, but it was hard to cast spells—any spell. The creature had drained her magical reserves, even if it hadn't managed to kill her. She tried to grab hold of the wall, only to be repulsed by a burst of magical power. Whitehall was designed not to let someone climb up the walls.

Transfigure yourself, she thought, desperately. If she could turn herself into a bird, or something tough enough to survive the fall...but she barely had enough magic left in her to light a candle. The ground came up with terrifying speed and she knew, with absolute certainty, she was dead...

And then something caught her and slowed her fall at the last possible moment. She still hit the ground hard enough to hurt, badly. The world spun around her and faded from view...

"Emily," a voice snapped, out of the darkness. It sounded familiar, although the haze of pain made it hard to recognize it. "Can you hear me?"

Emily nodded, weakly. Her entire body felt as if it had been smashed into jelly; there was a faint haze in her mind that made it hard to think. It took her several seconds to remember what she'd seen...and what she'd done, in order to escape. Jumping out of a window nine levels above the ground...if she hadn't been desperate, it would have been near-suicide.

"You've been quite badly hurt," the voice said, "but we've fixed most of the damage. Can you open your eyes?"

Emily hadn't even realized that they were closed. There was a flash of blinding light as soon as she opened them, forcing her to screw them tightly closed again. A hand touched her shoulder lightly, then tapped her forehead. Emily opened her eyes again, squinting against the glare, and saw Lady Barb leaning over her. The combat sorceress looked badly worried.

"You took an insane dive out of a window," Lady Barb said, tartly. "If one of the Mediators hadn't managed to catch you, you would have smashed yourself to a pulp. As it was, you broke about a dozen bones when you hit the ground. I've fixed the damage, but you really should stay in bed for the next few days. What were you *thinking*?"

Emily hesitated, unsure. She was in the infirmary, but what had happened to get her there?

And then she remembered the Mimic.

She caught Lady Barb's arm. "Mimic," she said, as clearly as she could. Her voice sounded mushy to her ears, as if her jaw had smashed by the impact. "There's a Mimic in the school."

Lady Barb paled. "Are you *sure*?"

"I saw it," Emily insisted, through the haze threatening to cloud her thoughts. "It killed Sergeant Bane, took his place..."

She remembered the pattern she saw and swore, inwardly. They'd deduced that the killer was targeting the people who discovered the bodies, but the killer had *already* killed them and taken their place. Danielle had to have *been* the Mimic when she reported finding her boyfriend's body; Kay had to have been the Mimic when she'd been right next to Sergeant Bane. And a Mimic wouldn't have had any trouble posing as the person it had killed until it encountered its next target.

Somehow, she forced herself to keep speaking. "Didn't anyone *see* it?"

"You dived out of the wrong window for that," Lady Barb said, grimly. "I have to speak to the Grandmaster."

"It was up by the barracks," Emily said. How long had she been in bed, unconscious? Had the Mimic found someone else to consume after Emily had escaped? "You have to find it!"

"Finding a Mimic isn't easy," Lady Barb said. She reached out and touched Emily's forehead, very lightly. "This hasn't been an easy term for you, has it?"

Emily shook her head, mutely.

"I'm going to put you back to sleep," Lady Barb added, briskly. "You really need time to rest and mend."

"No," Emily said, frantically. Panic bubbled up in her mind, again. "It could come for me..."

"I think it won't risk coming after you when there are so many people nearby," Lady Barb said, shortly. She pointed a finger at Emily's chest. "And you really need to heal."

The next thing Emily knew was that she was surrounded by the Grandmaster, Sergeant Miles, Master Tor and Lady Barb. There was no longer any sunlight streaming through the windows, she saw, as she looked towards them. Instead, there was an inky darkness that seemed somehow too dark to be real. She'd always admired the night sky from Whitehall—there were no lamps or anything else to cause light pollution—but she couldn't see the stars. There was nothing outside at all.

"We found Kay's body," Sergeant Miles said, curtly. He sounded exhausted. "But we haven't managed to locate Sergeant Bane at all."

"The Mimic took his place," Emily said. Her thoughts still weren't very clear, but she could remember his form dissolving into the pulsing mist. "I don't know *what* happened to it."

"We checked the barracks carefully, finding nothing," Sergeant Miles said. "You were the only one who *saw* the Mimic."

Emily stared at him. Didn't they *believe* her?

"Finding a Mimic isn't exactly *easy*," the Grandmaster said. "I don't believe that it has *ever* been done successfully."

"But this one is behaving oddly, even for Mimics," Lady Barb added. "They don't normally leave bodies behind, let alone bodies with knives in them. I don't understand why it would even *bother* leaving the bodies as anything more than dust."

"Everything else fits, though," the Grandmaster said. "The bodies were completely drained of energy. Even a necromancer wouldn't produce such an effect."

"But I have never heard of a Mimic trying to frame someone else," Sergeant Miles argued. "We assumed there was a necromancer because the bodies appeared to have been killed by a necromantic rite. But why would a Mimic try to *hide*?"

Emily remembered—dimly—the handful of classes she'd taken last year on Magical Creatures. Mimics couldn't be killed, if she recalled correctly—or at least no one had ever tried to do it and come back to report. They killed someone and copied their body so precisely that they could take their place for weeks, perhaps months or years. And, as they copied their victim's memories and personality too, the change was almost impossible to detect until the Mimic resumed its natural form. They were the stuff of nightmares.

"I wish I knew," she said, out loud. "Can we track it down?"

"Maybe," Lady Barb said. "No one knows much about them, but there's a general consensus that they can go quite some time without having to change their form. This one, however, seems determined to kill every few days."

"Maybe it's injured," Emily mused. If it had attacked the Warden...it suggested a certain level of intelligence. "Are Mimics intelligent?"

Lady Barb gave her a sharp look. "No one knows," she admitted. "They certainly seem capable of posing as their victims..."

The Grandmaster held up his hand. "For the moment, I have altered the wards and sealed us within the school," he said. "We will be unable to leave until we find and contain the Mimic."

Emily stared at him. "You're locking us all inside with that...*thing*?"

"Watch your tone," Sergeant Miles growled.

Emily flinched. Sergeant Miles had lost his best friend when Shadye had forced Emily to stab him—and now he might have lost Sergeant Bane too. He might well blame Emily for Sergeant Bane's death, even if he knew it wasn't her fault.

"There's no choice," the Grandmaster said. "The Mimic could be any one of us."

"And none of the students will be welcome in the Allied Lands until they are proved to be *human*," Lady Barb added, tartly. "Or us, too."

"You can't be serious," Emily said, in disbelief. "We can't *all* be the Mimic..."

"Emily, people are *terrified* of Mimics," Lady Barb said, softly. "And with very good reason."

Emily nodded, unhappily. If a Mimic could replace a person so exactly that there was no easy way to spot the substitution, the first real sign might come when it dissolved into mist and searched for its next victim. She could imagine a wife sleeping next to a husband...and then waking up to see her husband resuming his natural form. It made her wonder if the Mimic kept the memories of those it had killed, or if it forgot what it had been when it returned to its natural form.

"It must forget," she mused out loud. "Or why would it play at being human?"

Lady Barb quirked an eyebrow. "Emily?"

"The Mimic," Emily said. "While it isn't in its natural form, does it remember what it really is?"

Travis had been interrogated, Emily recalled, and nothing had surfaced to suggest that he was anything more than the jerk he'd seemed. But if she assumed that the Mimic had killed Travis and taken his place during the Battle of Whitehall, when the wards were down, it suggested that the Mimic had been able to pass for a student... simply because it had forgotten it was anything else. Master Tor's lectures on truth spells and their limitations suggested that a liar couldn't be detected if he didn't *know* that he was lying.

"No one knows," Lady Barb said, softly. She looked down at Emily, thoughtfully. "Can you cast a spell for me?"

Emily blinked. "Which one?"

"Any," Lady Barb said.

Something *clicked* in Emily's mind. "You think I'm the Mimic?"

"It's a possibility," the Grandmaster admitted. "Danielle would have been replaced; it was the Mimic who reported finding Travis's body, not his former girlfriend."

Emily stared at him in absolute horror. If *she* were the Mimic, would she even know that she was? Might she have been replaced *before* she hurled herself out of the window? She hesitated, then cast a simple light spell. The ball of light shimmered into existence and hovered over her bed.

"But that may not prove anything," Sergeant Miles said, grimly. "If Travis was replaced when the Mimic escaped, he still would have had to perform magic in classes. I know he was studying and using spells in Martial Magic and I really don't see how he could have faked them."

Lady Barb nodded in agreement. "So that proves nothing," she said. "The Mimic could be *anywhere*. Or anyone."

"I am not the Mimic," Emily said, sharply.

The Grandmaster gave her a sympathetic look. "Would you know if you were?"

"We've had to seal the school," Lady Barb said, changing the subject. "Could that have been the objective all along? Did someone introduce the Mimic into the school?"

"There is no known way to control a Mimic," the Grandmaster said, flatly. "It is much more likely that we're hunting the Mimic that escaped the zoo during Shadye's attack on Whitehall. And we have to find it before it wipes out everyone in Whitehall."

He turned and made his way towards the door, then stopped. "Lady Emily," he said, "thank you for alerting us to the threat. Stay here, get better...then see if you can think of any way to trap the creature."

Sergeant Miles followed him, leaving Emily alone with Lady Barb.

"You can't think that I'm the Mimic," Emily protested. The very thought was terrifying. "I told you about it..."

Lady Barb shrugged. "There's no way to know just what it might be thinking," she said, "assuming that it is thinking at all. We know so little about them. No one even knows where they come from. Gorgons and orcs and other such creatures are warped humans, but a Mimic is something else entirely."

"A monster," Emily said. From what she could recall of the lectures, even the *suggestion* that someone might be a Mimic had led to that person being lynched—or worse. It was stupid, given what a Mimic could do, but it happened. Maybe she should be glad she was in the infirmary. What would her fellow students do if they thought *she* was the Mimic?

"Quite," Lady Barb agreed. "The Grandmaster is currently working on ways to trap it. There are wards that can be used to confine it, then we can seal it in a trunk like you did with the Cockatrice."

She smiled. "I need you to go over everything that happened since Sergeant Bane revealed his true nature to you."

"That he'd been replaced," Emily corrected. Sergeant Bane had an alibi for the Warden's death, she was sure. Even if he didn't...it didn't prove that he'd been the Mimic all along. "It could be anyone now."

"Yes," Lady Barb agreed. Her voice was very flat. "It could."

Emily shook her head in disbelief. A Mimic. Why couldn't it have been a bloody basilisk? A giant snake with a weakness for rooster cries would have been easy to find and kill. A Mimic, on the other hand...

No one even knew if they *could* be killed.

Chapter Thirty

Emily looks down at her hands. They seem normal, yet she knows there is something badly wrong. A thought is nagging at the corner of her mind. It is...what? She cannot focus; the thought isn't really there. And yet...her hands are shimmering with light. As she watches, they dissolve completely into glowing mist. A terrible hunger fills her and she turns, searching for her former classmates. Now, they are nothing more than sources of food...

Emily snapped awake, staring around her desperately. A nightmare. It had just been a nightmare...and yet there had been something about it that had reached down inside her and touched the very core of her being. Her entire body was soaked with sweat, even though she was wearing nothing more than a light hospital gown. The nightmare had left its mark on her soul.

She looked around. The infirmary appeared to be deserted, apart from a couple of first-years who were both fast asleep. There didn't seem to be anyone else in the ward. Emily swung her legs over the side of the bed and stood upright, despite feeling shivers running through her entire body. She clung onto the bed until the shakes faded away, then staggered towards the large mirror and peered into it. Her own reflection looked back at her.

Emily had never been particularly vain—any tendency she might have had towards vanity had been drummed out of her by exposure to Alassa, who never managed to have so much as a hair out of place—but she was still shocked by her own appearance. Her face was pale, while her hair was stringy and unwashed and there were bruises all over her body, barely visible through the gown. She touched one lightly and felt a brief ache, before realizing that the healer had fed her numbing potion. If she hadn't, her entire body would be hurting.

"You've looked better," a blunt voice said from behind her.

Emily spun around to see Kyla, the healer, scowling at her.

"I've looked worse too," Emily said, tartly. "When can I leave the ward?"

"You really need to eat and then lie down for another hour or two," Kyla said. "After that, I think you could probably leave if you wanted to. But it isn't very pleasant out there."

Emily looked over at the window and shuddered. The darkness was still there. Her internal clock had improved radically since she'd come to Whitehall, even though she'd been given a clockwork watch, but it was hard to tell just what time it was. A glance at the clock hanging over the door told her that it was early morning. It felt like the middle of the night.

"Sit," the healer said, pointing to a chair. "I'll have food brought up to you in a jiffy."

"Thank you," Emily said, sitting down. "What's happening out there?"

"Absolute panic," Kyla stated. She peered down at Emily, casting a series of medical charms. "The Mimic could be *anyone.*"

"And we're trapped," Emily finished, glancing back at the window. "How many hexes have been thrown in the last few hours alone?"

"Too many," Kyla said, darkly. "I've spent too much time fixing idiots who have been hexed by their classmates."

She walked over to a cabinet and reached inside, removing a tray of food. "Eat this," she ordered, passing it to Emily. "And make sure you eat until you're bursting."

Emily nodded. The food didn't *look* very appetizing, but it smelled remarkably good. Lady Barb had talked about Healer's Mush, a porridge-like substance that helped the body to heal quickly; Emily realized, as she dug into the food, that Lady Barb hadn't exaggerated the effects. Every bite made her want to eat more, until she had definitely eaten as much as she could. And yet she still wanted more.

"Most of it will help fuel your recovery," Kyla informed her, as she ran a series of checks on Emily's body. "I'd advise you to try to take it easy for the next couple of days. Your body was badly depleted of magical reserves even before you jumped out a window."

"Take it easy," Emily repeated, rolling her eyes. "How am I meant to do *that*?"

A thought struck her as she looked down at the bruises and she felt a stab of guilt. "How is Melissa?"

Kyla didn't seem surprised by the question. "I fixed the remaining damage and sent her to bed," she said, flatly. "I believe that she was...rather unhappy with you."

"Sergeant Bane healed her," Emily said, and then scowled. That wouldn't have been the *real* Sergeant, but the Mimic. It *could* perform magic, then. Did it copy the magical skills of the person it replaced, or did its powers grow as it moved from victim to victim? "I'll talk to Lady Barb about it later."

"Indeed you will," Kyla said. She passed Emily a new set of robes. "I suggest you go back to your bedroom, take a shower and then get some more sleep. And watch your back out there."

"Thank you," Emily said. She pulled on the robes and inspected herself in the mirror. They didn't fit her perfectly, but it was hard for someone to notice unless they looked very closely. "I will."

She stepped out of the infirmary and headed down the corridor, unable to escape the sense that something was terribly wrong. There was hardly anyone, apart from the Mediators, in the corridors. The handful of fellow students she saw gave her a wide berth, as if they thought she were contagious. It wasn't any better being thought a Mimic than a murderess and apprentice necromancer. By the time she reached the dorms, she felt thoroughly depressed.

Madame Razz glanced at her as she entered the corridor, then nodded towards the common room. Emily peeked inside and saw a handful of students who were reading a list of instructions from the Grandmaster. Students, he said, were to take an emergency charm and trigger it if they saw the Mimic. There was a dire warning added to the bottom stating that anyone who triggered the charm as a practical joke would be expelled. Under the circumstances, Emily couldn't help wondering what they intended to do to get someone out of the building. The wards were almost completely impregnable.

The students gave her fearful looks as she scanned the list of instructions, depressing her still further. She knew that she had never been entirely popular—even before she became a baroness, she'd beaten a necromancer—but this was different. At least they weren't aiming hexes at her back, she told herself, as she took one of the charms and headed out of the room. Maybe, after she'd had a rest, she could go to the library and look up whatever they had on Mimics. There had to be a clue there, something they could use to find and trap the creature before it killed them all.

Or before we run out of food, she thought. Whitehall's students consumed a vast amount of food every day, far more than anywhere in Zangaria. How long would it be before the kitchens ran out of food supplies? They'd have to go on rations as soon as possible.

She pushed the door open and stepped into the room. The Gorgon was seated at her desk, working her way through a set of papers, while Lin was lying in her bed, reading a book. Neither of them paid much attention to Emily, for which she was grateful. The last thing she wanted was more attention—and suspicion. She sat down on her bed and started to pull off the borrowed robe. It would have to be returned to Kyla before the end of the day.

"I heard you jumped out of a window," the Gorgon said, turning to face her. She looked utterly inhuman, the light catching her snakes in a manner that chilled Emily's blood. "What *really* happened?"

"I jumped out of a window," Emily said, tightly. "It was the only way out."

The Gorgon lifted an eyebrow. "Why didn't you run down the corridor instead?"

"It had me trapped," Emily said defensively. There had been something about the whole experience, she decided as she considered everything that had happened in retrospect, that suggested that the Mimic had effectively hypnotized her. She'd read, somewhere, there were predator animals that could mesmerize their prey, but she'd never heard of it happening to humans. "I couldn't think of another way out."

She finished undressing and walked into the bathroom. Some of the Healer's Mush had already worked, she realized as she glanced into the mirror. Most of the bruises had disappeared, although the remainder looked as though they would take much longer to fade away. She hadn't been so black and blue since her first session of hand-to-hand combat with Lady Barb. Shaking her head, she stepped into the shower and allowed the water to wash the sweat from her body, then washed her hair. By the time she stepped out, she was feeling almost human again.

"Walking around naked isn't a good idea," the Gorgon said, dryly. "They've been searching our rooms at unpredictable intervals."

Emily snorted, wondering if they thought that would do any good. A Mimic was impossible to distinguish from its victim until it was too late; random searches might trap a necromancer or someone experimenting with forbidden magic—or drugs—but she doubted they would actually help solve their problem. She hadn't even realized that male tutors were allowed into female bedrooms until Master Tor had come charging into her room...although she did have to admit that he'd had a very good reason.

She pulled on her underpants and the bra—made in Zangaria, a threaded note proclaimed—and then pulled a basic robe over her head. Somehow, she didn't feel like dressing up when there was a Mimic on the loose. Besides, she wasn't going to go back to the barracks, at least not for a few days. If they were going to be trapped with a murderous Mimic, the detention seemed to have become more than a little pointless as well as cruel.

And educational, she thought, sourly. *It certainly taught me a few lessons.*

Shaking her head, she sat down at her desk...and froze. Someone had been rooting through it again...and the spells she'd used to protect it had completely failed. Emily swore out loud, checking where she'd left the books. Someone had moved several of the textbooks, hunting for something else. It wasn't as if any of her textbooks weren't carried in the school library.

The Gorgon gave her a sharp glance. "Language," she snapped. "Watch your tongue."

Emily rounded on her. "Have you been touching my desk?"

"Why," the Gorgon sneered, "would I touch your desk?"

"*Someone* has been touching my desk," Emily snapped back. "And what do you care about my language anyway?"

"If one of us gets in trouble, we all lose room points," the Gorgon said, in a voice she might use to explain something elementary to a baby. "I happen to want something a little more comfortable than this rickety chair. *Your* little exploit, whatever it was, cost us every point we had. We currently do not have the points to get *anything* when the time comes to turn them into furniture."

Emily scowled. It seemed like a simple trick to push the students into behaving themselves—and policing one another, at least when they were in their rooms. *She* could afford to outfit every room in Whitehall with fancy furniture, as could many other pupils. But it was against the rules.

"At the moment," she said, controlling her temper with an effort, "it doesn't really matter."

"Maybe it doesn't matter to you, baroness," the Gorgon hissed. "And maybe it doesn't matter to a Child of Destiny. But it *does* matter to those of us who don't have vast fortunes or places to go after they graduate."

Emily flushed. She knew what happened to most students when they graduated from Whitehall, but where would the Gorgon go? Would she fit in with her fellow Gorgons after leaving Whitehall? Many students from poorer backgrounds were seduced into joining the establishment by attending Whitehall and having proper plumbing and food for the first time in their lives. Emily might well be the only student whose living conditions had taken a step downwards since coming to the school.

But then, the company is better, she thought, ruefully.

"If we get out of this alive, I'll try to be a better roommate," Emily said, tiredly. She couldn't blame the Gorgon for being angry with her, but this was going too far. "Do you know who has been touching my desk?"

"Touching someone else's desk is bad manners," the Gorgon reminded her. "I wouldn't have touched your desk unless it was on fire."

Emily scowled, but accepted the rebuke. In Whitehall, touching someone's personal possessions and notes was a severe breach of etiquette. It was rare for someone to even grant permission for someone else to touch their possessions. In all of her time at Whitehall, Emily honestly couldn't remember someone allowing someone else to open their trunk and retrieve an item. Alassa and Imaiqah certainly had never told *Emily* that she could use their trunks.

She swung back around and stared at the desk, then cast a series of revealing charms. The wards and hexes she'd placed on it were still there; they'd just failed to bite at all. Emily inspected them as carefully as she could, but if there was something wrong with them it was beyond her ability to detect. And that meant...

"Gorgon," she said, "would you mind testing the hexes?"

The Gorgon eyed her through snake-like eyes. "You don't trust your own handiwork?"

"No," Emily said, as she stood up. It was humiliating to admit it, but there was no choice. "I think I messed up the charms."

"Fine," the Gorgon said.

She stood, walked over to Emily's desk and sat down on her chair. There was a flash of light and she froze solid. Even her snakes stopped moving. A skilled magician could probably break free, even if they couldn't move their hands, but she doubted that a second-year student could.

"It works," Emily said, as she performed the counter-charm. "I'm sorry..."

"Perhaps now you can shut up," the Gorgon said, tartly. She stood, her snakes hissing around her, and headed back to her desk. "And *don't* lose us any more points."

Emily sighed, wondering just *who* was poking through her desk. Master Tor? He certainly *should* have the skills to take her wards down and then rebuild them—or at the very least neutralize them long enough to search her desk. But why would he need to spy on her when he could search her possessions at any moment? Why would he run the risk of being caught in a female bedroom alone? Surely Madame Razz would ask a few pointed questions if she caught him.

She scowled down at the desk, mulling over her options. The fingerprint detection charm might work, if she could remember where she put the note. She'd wanted to copy it into her own spellbook, but there hadn't been time. Instead, she'd left it in her desk. Carefully, she searched through the set of papers and blinked in surprise when she realized that she couldn't find it. The spell was completely missing.

Her blood ran cold. Fingerprint detection charms were unknown in Whitehall... or at least they had been unknown, until Emily had suggested using one. If someone had taken it, did that mean that they knew what the charm was intended to do?

Had they hoped it would prevent Emily from recreating it? But that seemed absurd. Emily could have recreated her own work—and in this case, all she had to do was ask Professor Lombardi for a second copy.

She ran her hand through her hair, then looked to see what else was missing. Nothing was, as far as she could tell. They'd *only* taken the fingerprint charm. And that meant...what?

"I told you to be quiet," the Gorgon said, sharply. "Do I have to turn you into stone to shut you up?"

Emily flushed. She hadn't realized that she'd been mumbling aloud.

"I'm going to the library," she said, and stood. "I'll see you at dinner time."

"Take someone with you," the Gorgon said. "*Not* me."

Emily looked at Lin, who barely looked up from her book. Her silent roommate clearly wasn't going to come with her, or get involved in the argument. Shaking her head, Emily picked up a handful of books she'd intended to return to the library and walked out the door, then headed three doors down the short corridor to Imaiqah's room. It was closed and, when she pushed her hand against the charm, it refused to open.

"I think she's playing Kingmaker with some of the others," Madame Razz said, from behind her. "They're in the games room, if you're interested."

"Thank you," Emily said. There was no point in disturbing her friend. Imaiqah loved Kingmaker and had taken to Chess like a duck to water, after Emily had introduced it. "I'll find her later."

She walked to the door and headed to the library. There had to be something there, she told herself, some way of finding a Mimic before it could kill everyone in the building. And there *were* ways to trap them...but they had to be found first. She was so intent on the possibilities that she didn't even notice the Mediator until she walked right into him.

"You should watch yourself, girl," he said. "This isn't a safe place any longer."

"No," Emily agreed, quietly. "It never was."

Chapter Thirty-One

THE LIBRARY WAS ALMOST EMPTY, EMILY DISCOVERED WHEN SHE STEPPED INSIDE, APART from a couple of sixth-year boys who were working their way through a pile of textbooks. They gave Emily sharp glances, but apart from that they completely ignored her. Emily was silently grateful as she walked over to the desk and smiled at Lady Aylia. The librarian looked as tired as everyone else.

"Half the books in the library are out," Lady Aylia said, by way of introduction. "What can I do for you?"

"I was wondering what you had on Mimics," Emily said, lowering her voice automatically. "Is there more than I saw in the textbooks...?"

"Mostly restricted," Lady Aylia said. "I shall consult with the Grandmaster."

Emily nodded and wandered over to the shelves, looking for anything that might be interesting or helpful. She couldn't help noticing that almost all of the books on hexes, jinxes and practical jokes had been taken out; the recent spate of infighting, she guessed, had encouraged the students to do more research. The only discipline that didn't seem to have been raided was history, something that struck Emily as sad. She had always *loved* history, if only because it had been an escape from her life. And the history of Whitehall was fascinating.

It was hard to be sure, but she suspected that *real* history didn't really go back as far as Professor Locke suggested. There were so many myths and legends about the time of the faerie that it was difficult to know what might be real and what might be myth, all the more so because there had been so many deliberate purges of knowledge over the years. Officially, the records dated back over three thousand years, but Emily suspected that they were only reliable up to about five hundred years ago. But there was no way to be certain.

She felt a tug and turned to see Lady Aylia waving her back to the desk. "I spoke with the Grandmaster," the librarian said, when Emily approached. "He has authorized me to allow you access to the books."

"Thank you," Emily said.

"Go into study room five," Lady Aylia ordered. "I'll bring the books to you there."

Study room five was larger than the study room she'd used last year, when the Grandmaster had allowed her to read a series of texts on necromancy. It was empty, apart from a table, three chairs and a poster on the wall threatening dire consequences for anyone who tried to remove the books without permission. Emily had done enough work in the library to know that trying to remove a restricted book would trigger the wards, which would immobilize the thief until he could be dealt with. There was no way to know if the Warden's death had affected *those* wards.

Lady Aylia entered seven minutes later, carrying a stack of books in one hand. Most of them looked to have been recently handled, probably by the Grandmaster or Lady Barb. Thankfully, none of them felt as evil as the books on necromancy, just dusty and old. The librarian put them down on the table, worked a series of charms to remove the protections on the books and then left the room, leaving Emily alone.

Carefully, she picked up the first book and read the title. *A Mimicry of Mimics.*

The author, she very rapidly decided, had never actually encountered a Mimic. Most of the text seemed to be a list of reported sightings, complete with some attempt at analysis. Emily skimmed it carefully, but saw nothing that she hadn't already known. The only oddity was a report that some Mimics, in human form, behaved oddly before reverting to their natural state. But there was no clear idea of what was *odd.*

Did Sergeant Bane act oddly when he was a Mimic? She asked herself. *Should he have done something other than dragging me off down the corridor?*

It was impossible to know. Instead, she read the rest of the book, frowning at some of the nastier comments about people who might be Mimics. The writer had suggested that someone who acted oddly should be scrutinized, just to be sure they weren't Mimics...which probably didn't help people suffering from mental illnesses. Someone unpopular could be lynched because the locals believed that he or she was a Mimic, just as suspected witches had been burned in Spain under the Inquisition.

Irritated, she looked at the next one and realized that it was more of the same, although the author did include an incredibly colorful account of an encounter with a Mimic that—he said—had sparked off a lifelong interest in the creatures. It hadn't done anything for the writer's mental stability, she decided, after reading the next few chapters. He'd come to the conclusion that *everyone* apart from himself was a Mimic and he'd eventually been locked up to stop him performing Mimic-detection tests. Emily read the description of the test in the hopes that it would be something workable, but it didn't take long to realize that it was about as useful and impartial as dunking witches.

Both books agreed, however, that all *verified* Mimic attacks were spaced out by months, at least. The Mimic had been able to take someone's place and pose as them—perfectly—for a long time, perhaps even forgetting what it really was. It *had* to forget, Emily decided, unless there was something utterly inhuman about its mindset. How could it be happy posing as someone else?

But it didn't quite make sense. Emily could understand why one human would wish to take over another's life. Everyone believed that the grass was greener on the other side of the hill. Taking someone else's life, if it were possible to pose as them so completely, might seem an ideal solution. But why would a Mimic, an inhuman creature, want to be human? How the hell could something like it have evolved?

The Gorgon might want to be human, Emily thought, slowly. *But why would a Dragon—or a Mimic?*

Dragons, she suspected, had evolved to use the magic field to their own advantage. It was the only way something their size could fly. A Mimic might have done the same, but it still seemed odd. What sort of possible evolutionary advantage would pretending to be something else so completely grant it? It was such a complete pretense that its personality was utterly subsumed in the host. Assuming, of course, that it *had* a personality.

She remembered the sense of pure malevolence from the Mimic and shivered. They *did* have personalities. And they hated humans.

She picked up the third book and smiled in relief when she realized that it was far more practical. There was *no* decisive test for a Mimic, but a Mimic couldn't change its form and hide without something to copy—and there seemed to be limits on just *what* it could copy. It didn't seem to be able to turn itself into an object, or anything smaller than a puppy—and anything smaller than a human didn't last very long. If the Mimic remained in that form while devouring life energy, it would return to its normal appearance within a few hours.

But a human form could be assumed for weeks, perhaps months...

Except that wasn't what had happened. Travis had died and the Mimic had replaced Danielle. Danielle had died and the Mimic had replaced Kay. Kay had died and the Mimic had, somehow, replaced Sergeant Bane. If Emily had managed to escape, she found it hard to understand why Sergeant Bane had been caught, but perhaps he'd simply been trapped. The notes made it clear that running *through* the Mimic would have meant instant death.

But all of those deaths had happened within a few days of one another.

She glared down at her notes, convinced she was missing something. Why had the Mimic even stayed at Whitehall? Why had it killed the Warden rather than simply leaving the castle when it began to remember who and what it was? Why had it sought to convince the Grandmaster that there was a necromancer on the loose? There was nothing in the books to suggest that the Mimics ever bothered to conceal their activities. Why should there be when they were effectively unstoppable?

"What," she muttered out loud, "am I missing?"

She'd panicked—and accidentally cast the detection charm. The Mimic had lit up brightly...

"But it can't be that simple," she mused. "Otherwise someone else would have found a way to track and identify them by now."

They'd practiced using the charms extensively in first year—and most students would light up as brightly as the Mimic. Protection charms, practice wards...all of Whitehall's students were tainted with magic. They could never be completely free of it, even if they refrained from using their powers...hell, they *couldn't* refrain from using their powers. Eventually, the magic would break free.

And then it struck her.

She flipped back through the books, checking every recorded location of a Mimic sighting. They all took place away from magical centers such as Whitehall—or the other nexus points. *This* Mimic wasn't just pretending to be human, it was pretending to be a *magician*. Just by being in Whitehall and posing as a student, it was burning up magic at a terrifying rate. And once it ran out of magic, it would be forced to revert back to its normal form.

They suck up magic to survive, just like Dragons, she thought, numbly. The Mimic was lashing out with the fury of a wasp caught in a jam jar, aided by a cold inhuman intelligence and a certain awareness of how humans thought. It had created the illusion that there was a necromancer in the school, disguising just how often it needed to feed. And that meant...

Her blood ran cold. The Mimic had attacked Sergeant Bane—and it had immediately come after her. If it had learned from him what she'd done with the nexus point, it might have decided that *Emily* was the key to a feast of magic from the nexus. Or perhaps Sergeant Bane had intended to visit her in the barracks and the intention had carried over when the Mimic had assumed his form.

And if it realized that I might have a way to make necromancy viable, it will be all the more determined to capture me, Emily thought. She swallowed a curse, then hesitated. Perhaps there *was* a way to catch it before it caught up with her again.

She took a new sheet of paper and started to scribble down notes. "Take each student into the great hall and force them to burn up as much of their power as they can," she muttered to herself. "If one of them happens to be the Mimic, they will be exhausted and revert back to natural form when they can no longer maintain the disguise."

It seemed simple, although she knew there would be objections. She wasn't too willing to burn up all of *her* power—it crossed her mind that it might be because she *was* the Mimic, all unknowing—and she suspected that everyone else would feel the same way. They would be rendering themselves defenseless and, if what Kyla had said was true, the level of hexing in the school had skyrocketed since they'd ended up trapped.

She looked back at the more practical book and worked out how it insisted that a Mimic could be trapped. The wards would have to be constructed with extreme care, then manipulated to force the Mimic back into the zoo...rather like handling antimatter, she decided. Maybe they could just leave the Mimic in its cage, sealed up forever. The books had no idea if they could *starve* the Mimic to death.

Or she could create another pocket dimension and snap the Mimic out of existence. It had worked for Shadye. Why wouldn't it work for a Mimic?

Because no one knows anything about Mimics, her own thoughts answered. *Would one even be sucked into a gravity well?*

It was hard to imagine an entity made of mist *not* being sucked inside, but she knew better than to assume something that looked like mist actually *was* mist. In fact...why did the Mimic flinch back from a detection charm, when a lethal spell had gone through it as if it were made of...well, *mist*?

"This is not going to be easy," she told herself, as she stood. "But there isn't any choice."

Lady Barb and the Grandmaster would have to be informed, then they would have to be talked into trying it, even though most of the school would object. How long would it take to test *everyone*? Emily had exhausted herself before, casting magic, but many of the remaining pupils were older and more practiced.

She gathered the books together, then called Lady Aylia and waited for her to enter the room. When she came, she was escorted by Imaiqah, who looked tired, but surprisingly happy.

"I won the match," she said, before Emily could ask why she was so cheerful. "I am now the Kingmaker of Second Year. I'm going to be playing the champ from third year tomorrow, then fourth year if I beat him..."

"Alassa is going to want you to be practicing *Ken*," Emily reminded her, mischievously. "How is the team?"

Imaiqah's eyes darkened. "We're not allowed outside the building at all," she said, softly. Under her delight at winning, Emily realized suddenly, she was *scared*. "We can't play *Ken* inside the building."

"We could probably play it in the Great Hall," Emily said. She had a sudden mental vision of balls going everywhere while the players tried to dodge, but she forced it aside with a grimace. No doubt the Grandmaster would order mass expulsions after the chandeliers were destroyed, although he couldn't get anyone *out* of the castle while the Mimic remained outside confinement. Maybe he would just turn the culprits into frogs instead. "Or the dining hall."

"There isn't food to waste," Imaiqah said. "Do you remember the food fight?"

Emily nodded. It had been started by some third years—fourth years now—before the end of last term. They'd used magic to hurl plates of food everywhere, encouraging others to fire back with bowls of soup, cakes and whatever else came to hand. The resulting devastation had ruined hundreds of robes and caused a mess that the original perpetrators had been forced to clean up, by hand. Emily had the feeling that they hadn't regretted it very much.

"Now, there's barely enough food for a few weeks, assuming we use it carefully," Imaiqah added. "I was asked to help the cooks with their calculations."

"Ouch," Emily said. Food was difficult to transfigure, let alone produce from nothing, even for magicians as powerful as the Grandmaster. Producing enough food to keep the entire school alive might be beyond even his formidable power. "How long do we have?"

Imaiqah hesitated. "A month at most," she admitted, finally. "Perhaps less. Perhaps *much* less. The cooks were talking about seeing who brought food from home."

Emily made a face. She'd never had parents who cared enough to send her food, but some of the students at Whitehall were luckier. Alassa's mother had been discouraged from sending a whole trunk-full of goodies, while other parents had sent snacks, care parcels or even pre-prepared meals. But surely even the most indulgent of parents couldn't have sent enough food to feed the entire school.

"Maybe they'll let us go out and scavenge," she said, finally. But she could easily see the Grandmaster refusing—or the Allied Lands taking steps of their own to seal off Whitehall. A Mimic was a deadly threat. "Or maybe not."

"I'll put the books back where they belong," Lady Aylia said. "If you have an idea, you might want to use it now."

Emily nodded and stepped out of the private room, casting the seeker spell in the air to locate Lady Barb. The needle appeared, pointing downwards. "Probably in her office," Emily said, as they left the library. "I think she's looking for a solution too."

Imaiqah caught her arm. "Do *you* have a solution?"

"I think so," Emily said. She hesitated, looking down at her notes. "It may work, given a chance."

The almost worshipful look in Imaiqah's eyes was disturbing, she realized. She'd been a small girl, Alassa's victim, when they'd first met, even if she had learned how to use magic to defend herself, just like Emily. And her association with Emily had brought her family money, power...and eventual ennoblement. Emily knew that her friend owed her a great deal, yet such admiration bothered her. She didn't want to spend the rest of her life casting a shadow over her friends.

But she still kicks your ass at Kingmaker, she thought, ruefully. Imaiqah had plenty of talents of her own, even if they didn't seem so spectacular. *And she's much better at handling bargaining than me.*

"This corridor should be busy," Imaiqah said, as they stepped into the main thoroughfare. "But everyone is hiding in their rooms or trying to distract themselves..."

Emily scowled. Few of the children of Whitehall had grown up in constant danger, even those born to wealthy and powerful families. They knew that the building was effectively under siege...and a Mimic was moving through the building, killing people and assuming their form. *Anyone* could be the Mimic. She couldn't really blame them for being scared, even though being alone was asking for trouble. How long did it take a Mimic to assume a new form?

"Yeah," she said, absently. "I..."

There was a blinding flash of light, directly ahead of them. And then the first hex came out of nowhere, aimed right at Emily's face.

Chapter Thirty-Two

EMILY JUMPED TO ONE SIDE, WINCING AS SHE FELT THE HEAT OF THE HEX FLASH PAST HER and smash harmlessly against the wall. Who was attacking her *now*? Melissa? She couldn't see any sign of her attacker, apart from a hex that came out of thin air and spun towards Imaiqah. The attacker was completely invisible.

A third hex darted towards her, striking her protections before she could react. Her protections glowed as they tried to repel the hex, but it clung on and started to burn its way towards her. Emily had seen Sergeant Miles cast spells that wore down a person's defenses, but she hadn't seen anyone else do the same, not even Void. She cast the counter-spell, then threw a hex of her own back towards where she thought the attacker was. It missed.

Imaiqah cast a series of tripping jinxes down the corridor, trying to expose the attacker. Emily smiled to herself—her friend was more ingenious than most people gave her credit for—and cast a spell of her own, summoning white mist out of thin air and directing it down the corridor. She would see the person moving through the mist even if they were invisible. A wave of magic came back at her and shoved her backwards, hard; oddly, it didn't seem to be focused enough to hurt. Emily kept her balance and deflected another hex as the mist rolled down the corridor. It crossed her mind, briefly, that the attacker might mistake the mist for the Mimic...

Was the attacker the Mimic? It seemed unlikely that it would risk using magic so blatantly, not if she was right about each use of magic limiting its time in a new body. But maybe it didn't *know* that about itself...there was no way for her to know. A shape appeared in the mist, smaller and slighter than Emily remembered, then another hex came darting out at Imaiqah. There was a brilliant flash of light and her friend vanished. Emily cursed inwardly and looked down. There was a tiny statue of Imaiqah where she'd been standing on the floor.

She threw a hex towards the shape in the mist, trying to make out its features now she had a rough idea of where the attacker was. Most invisibility spells, the Sergeants had explained, didn't work so well once the hunter had a good idea of where the attacker actually was. She peered and frowned, puzzled. Melissa was tall, taller than Emily; her attacker actually appeared to be shorter. And then a powerful spell blasted out of the mist and slammed directly into Emily's defenses.

Brilliant green balefire crackled over her, followed rapidly by a wave of heat that left her exposed face and hands feeling scorched. Emily swore out loud and threw back the most powerful immobilization jinx she could, then cancelled the attacker's spell before it could do real harm. She'd hoped that the wide-angle spell would be enough to catch the attacker, but it didn't seem to have caught anything. And, as the mist slowly faded away, the corridor appeared to be completely empty.

Emily didn't lower her guard. She peered down the corridor, looking for telltale signs of the attacker's presence. Who was he? Or she? There had been no hint of gender in what little she'd seen of the attacker. It wasn't as if she were short of enemies, but the spellwork seemed a little too advanced to be a second year student. She doubted that any of the first years would try to challenge a second year, not yet. They could barely master a simple jinx, let alone powerful hexes.

She knelt down beside Imaiqah and touched the statue, hoping to free her friend. Nothing happened; the spell holding her in an immobile form was surprisingly tough, beyond Emily's ability to remove. She gritted her teeth and tried again, but the spell refused to budge. That wasn't a practical joke, certainly not at second year level. The attacker...

A spell struck her legs and they seemed to turn to jelly. Emily crashed to the stone floor, letting out a yelp of pain as she banged her elbow. She rolled over and cast another spell back at the attacker, but she missed completely. The invisible attacker had to be moving as soon as he or she threw the hex that might betray their position.

"Damn it," Emily said, out loud. "Who *are* you?"

Desperately, she shaped an illusion spell in her mind, casting the image of a Death Viper and sending it hissing towards the corner where she hoped the attacker was standing. There wasn't a student in the school who didn't know what a Death Viper was, not after the Grandmaster had ordered all of them to take a good long look at the one held captive in the armory. Emily heard a very feminine gasp, followed by a scorching hex aimed right at the illusory snake. It would have killed it if the colorful creature had been *real*. She seized her chance and threw the same spell she had used on Melissa at the attacker. It was deflected back at her, the blast picking Emily up and throwing her back down the corridor.

She hit the ground again, gasping in pain. Her body remembered how badly jumping out of the window had hurt; this seemed worse, as if her repaired bones had broken once again. She grunted and rolled over, just as another spell struck her. Her entire body froze solid, leaving her utterly unable to move—or defend herself. She couldn't help wondering what would happen if the Mimic came across her right now...

The sergeants had told them that, in a real fight, they couldn't stop until their opponent was definitely out of it. Emily struggled to cast the counter-spell without moving her hands, knowing that she might be knocked out at any second. But the spell refused to work properly...strong arms gripped her shoulder and started to drag her down the corridor, before suddenly letting go. Absurdly, Emily felt an urge to laugh. She wasn't *that* heavy, was she? Besides, anyone who could cast such spells could easily use a levitation charm to move Emily's body anywhere she liked.

There was a faint sound of retreating footsteps and then nothing. Emily struggled to move, but the spell held her completely paralyzed. She cursed mentally, knowing that they were going to be humiliated when someone stumbled across them, even though she had a feeling that it was the only way to escape. The spell on her seemed completely resistant to her counter-spells—or she just wasn't casting them properly. It was much harder to shape and cast a spell without using hands to direct it. Maybe the attacker hadn't used so much power on Imaiqah...

She'd been foolish, Emily realized. Hadn't she learned by now to watch her back? But she hadn't been alone...

It seemed like hours before she heard someone coming up behind her. "Good grief," Lady Barb's voice said. A moment later, she stepped into view. "Give me a moment. I'll undo the spells."

Emily felt magic tickling over her and shivered, the spell snapping completely a moment later. Feeling completely drained, she slumped against the stone floor and closed her eyes, trying to snatch a moment of peace. The magic pulsing through the floor seemed to repel her; reluctantly, she reopened her eyes and looked up at Lady Barb, who held out a hand to help her to her feet. Her legs felt so wobbly that she wondered, absurdly, if she were feverish.

"That was a very nasty hex," Lady Barb said, as she turned her attention to Imaiqah. "Who was it?"

"I don't know," Emily said, slumping against the wall. It crossed her mind that the etiquette teacher would have had a few sharp things to say about her poise and she had to fight down a giggle. "I never saw her face."

It wasn't Melissa. She was fairly sure of that, if nothing else. Melissa wasn't only taller than the invisible attacker, she was also much less practiced. It was far more likely to have been someone from Martial Magic, except she didn't know any girls from the class who might really want to hurt her. Even Aloha had accepted her after she'd defeated Shadye.

"You might not have recognized her anyway," Lady Barb said. She was casting a series of spells Emily didn't recognize over Imaiqah's transfigured form. "These spells are fourth year level, maybe even higher. I shall have words with the Grandmaster."

Emily shuddered. They'd been warned, in no uncertain terms, that the prank wars between students were not meant to involve the students from lower years. It made sense, particularly given Whitehall's orientation on turning out sorcerers; the younger students wouldn't be able to defend themselves against the older ones. There was a fine line, it seemed, between toughening someone up and bullying them. Emily had a feeling that the line was crossed every day. God knew that Alassa had been free with malicious hexes before she'd reformed.

"My counter-spells didn't work," she said. "Why not...?"

"The spells are designed to be resistant to standard countering spells," Lady Barb explained, absently. "You need a more focused counter spell and....ah."

There was a flash of light and Imaiqah returned to normal. She was breathing heavily, but seemed otherwise normal. Emily had a sudden horrified vision of what might have happened if she'd been stuffed into a confined space, then left there until the spell wore off. Imaiqah would have died instantly when her body tried to expand...or would she have merged with the walls? She made a mental note to experiment, perhaps at a safe distance from everyone else. If two objects *couldn't* share the same place, would there be an explosion if someone tried?

"That...that was awful," Imaiqah gasped. "I couldn't cast spells at all."

"Nor could Emily," Lady Barb said, darkly. She stood and helped Imaiqah to her feet. "I think it's time we went to see the Grandmaster."

Emily shivered at her tone. She could almost feel a hint of pity for the person who had attacked them; Lady Barb would, eventually, track them down and then...? Older students who attacked younger students...somehow, she doubted the punishment would be as simple as a thrashing. Would they be expelled?

But she attacked us both and almost killed us, she reminded herself. *Should they not be expelled?*

The thought made her smile bitterly as she followed Lady Barb through the corridor towards the Grandmaster's office. There was literally nowhere to send the expelled student, not until the Mimic was captured and the wards were taken down. Perhaps the Grandmaster would have to settle for imprisoning her in her room. Come to think of it, what *did* happen to students who were expelled from Whitehall? Back home, expulsions had been a joke. Here, she suspected they were far more serious.

Lady Barb stopped outside the Grandmaster's office and tapped on the door. "Come in," she said, as the door opened. "You'll need to tell him everything."

"That isn't the only thing I have to tell him," Emily said. "I may have a way of catching the Mimic."

"Then talk about that first," the Grandmaster ordered. He waved his hand and a pair of chairs appeared out of nowhere. "Take a seat and tell me what you have in mind."

Emily sat down, suddenly very aware that she was hot and sweaty. The fight had drained her, as she had tried to cast the counter-spell again and again. And her head hurt...

"The Mimic is moving from victim to victim much quicker because it is using their magic," she said, simply. "It's actually burning up power just to pose as a magician."

The Grandmaster frowned, stroking his chin. "We have never heard of a Mimic posing as a magician before."

"Because it would need to move on quicker if it used magic," Emily explained. Although...she *did* wonder why the Mimic hadn't attacked during last term. Travis would have had to use a great deal of magic as he completed his fifth year and, assuming that he'd already been replaced, so would the Mimic. "*This* Mimic is in a place where it has to pose as a magician, forcing it to move from target to target. It faked the necromantic rites so we wouldn't know what we were actually facing."

Lady Barb leaned forward. "But why is it leaving behind the bodies?"

"I don't know," Emily admitted. All of the reports agreed that the original body crumbled into dust as the Mimic took on its form. "It might well have been injured during the attack on Whitehall, or...when it did whatever it did to the Warden. I don't think it could have replaced him, could it?"

"Perhaps we should be grateful," Lady Barb mused. "If it *had* successfully replaced the Warden, it would have had access to the nexus point as well as the wards governing the school's interior."

Emily scowled. The books had seemed to imply that Mimics were little more than beasts, if rather unusual ones, but everything she'd seen personally suggested that the Mimics were intelligent, stalking and killing their prey—and then doing whatever it took to cover their tracks. And yet there was something *odd* about the whole pattern. If the Mimic was aware of its own nature all the time, why didn't it destroy the old bodies? But if it wasn't...why didn't it unknowingly report its own murders?

But it did, she reminded herself. *The people who found the bodies were actually killed and replaced by the Mimic.*

"The Mimic must be forced into a position where it burns up its power," Emily said, leaving the puzzle alone for the moment. "If we have everyone casting spells and draining themselves, the Mimic should be revealed when it runs out of power."

"Test everyone in the school, one by one," the Grandmaster mused. "And what is to stop the Mimic from moving on to someone who has already been tested?"

"Seal off parts of the school," Emily suggested. "Once someone is vetted, they can go into the sealed part of the school and wait there until we have tested everyone else."

"Clever idea," Lady Barb said. She scowled. "You do realize that hardly anyone will *like* the idea?"

Emily stared at her. "I can't think of anything else," she protested. "Can you?"

Lady Barb shook her head. "You're asking them to push themselves to the limit," she said, darkly. "And drain themselves so completely that it will take hours, perhaps days, to recover."

"They will all be tested," the Grandmaster said, flatly. "Anyone who refuses to be tested may well *be* the Mimic."

"There will be more than one," Lady Barb said. "Unless, of course, we are dealing with more than one Mimic."

Emily had a sudden vision of everyone in the school dissolving into mist and shivered. Cold logic told her that it was unlikely, but how much did logic truly apply to the Mimics? Could there be more than one Mimic in the school? There was no way to know.

"I suppose we could have everyone bitten by the Death Viper instead," she said, sardonically. It would be about as fair as the Spanish Inquisition's favorite methods for determining guilt or innocence. "The person who survives is the Mimic."

Lady Barb snorted. "Leave making snarky remarks to the princess," she suggested, dryly. "She is *much* better at them."

Imaiqah leaned forward, nervously. "Ah...Grandmaster," she said. "How many people in the school can't use magic?"

Emily stared at her, then blanched. She honestly hadn't *realized* that there were non-magicians in the school. But she should have known. It hadn't been *that* long since she—and Imaiqah and Alassa—had gotten in trouble for involving a servant in their pranks. Madame Razz had pointed out, sharply, that the servants weren't there to be abused. And it *had* been abuse.

"There are thirty servants in the school who don't have any magic," the Grandmaster said, slowly. "And there are twenty more who have very limited magic, not enough to merit a formal invitation to study."

Lady Barb used a word that Emily was sure would get a student in real trouble if they said it in public. She couldn't blame the healer. If she was right, the Mimic could replace a servant and then wait for decades before taking another victim. By then, everyone in Whitehall would have starved to death.

"Language," the Grandmaster said, reprovingly.

Emily thought, frantically. "What happens to a Mimic if it loses part of its body?"

Lady Barb scowled. "What do you mean?"

Deep Space Nine, Emily thought. They'd been searching for Changelings...and the simplest way to do it had been to take a blood sample. When separated from the main mass the blood reverted to the alien's natural state. What would happen, she asked herself, if they did the same to a Mimic? Would the blood remain human or would it revert to gas?

"We take blood samples," she said. She explained as quickly as she could. "It might just work."

"Make it so," the Grandmaster ordered. He looked over at Lady Barb. "Take young Imaiqah and start making the preparations to test everyone's magic. Lady Emily... come with me. I have something I need you to try."

Emily nodded and stood.

"There's a different matter to discuss," Lady Barb said, flatly. "Emily and Imaiqah were attacked by an older student. They could have been seriously injured if I hadn't come along."

The Grandmaster scowled. "Do you know who?"

Emily shook her head.

"Then the best bet is to get the wards up and running as quickly as possible," the Grandmaster said. "Without them, it's hard to tell who did what."

Chapter Thirty-Three

EMILY GRITTED HER TEETH AS THE GRANDMASTER LED HER DOWN A HIDDEN STAIRWELL, plunging deeper and deeper into the bowels of Whitehall. She could *feel* the constant thrumming from the nexus point, beating like a drum inside her head. The Grandmaster looked unperturbed by the noise, as if he couldn't hear it—or as if it welcomed him. Emily had looked for information on nexus points in the library, but she'd found almost nothing. Most of them were stored in the forbidden section.

She looked at the Grandmaster as they stopped in front of a stone door. "Why are we here?"

"I have been unable to take direct control of the wards," the Grandmaster said. His voice was soft, but there was a grim undertone that chilled her to the bone. "Producing a new Warden will take months, if we could obtain the clay we needed to build the homunculus. You might be able to do better."

He faced her. "We're running out of options here," he added. "If we can take control of the wards, we can locate and trap the Mimic before it feeds again."

Emily blinked in surprise. "Again?"

"We found Sergeant Bane's body, not too far from where you dived out the window," the Grandmaster said, tightly. "And we found two more bodies the following day."

"It's eating its way through the victims quicker and quicker," Emily said, grimly. "What are you doing to keep the others safe?"

"We're trying to keep them in groups," the Grandmaster said. "But there are always idiots who go off on their own."

Emily flushed. If she hadn't been alone in the barracks, she might not have encountered the Mimic. But then, at least they now knew what they were hunting. If they'd still been looking for a necromancer, the Mimic could have feasted to its heart's content. For all she knew, she might wind up being lynched by terrified students. Or perhaps even the more doubting tutors. Master Tor would probably take the lead in blaming her.

The Grandmaster turned to face her. "There are normally years of training to go through before anyone touches the nexus points," he said. "But you've already done it once, back when you killed Shadye. I'm hoping that you can do it again."

"I was desperate," Emily protested. "I needed to find some way to strike back at him."

"And you did," the Grandmaster said. "And we are desperate now. In less than a month, we will have to lower the wards or starve to death. We have to catch the Mimic now."

He turned back to the door and started to unlock the wards, one by one. Emily watched with some admiration; the spellwork was far above her head. The last time she'd opened the stone door, Shadye had been using her as a puppet. She hadn't been truly aware of what she'd done to get inside. The memory made her shiver as the last of the wards unlocked, allowing the door to click open. She stepped forward, drawn by the power of the nexus, and into the room.

The Grandmaster placed a hand on her arm. "Be careful," he advised, softly. "Stronger magicians than you have been overwhelmed by the nexus."

Emily nodded. The nexus chamber was immense, a giant cave filled with glowing pillars that reached up towards the building far overhead. They looked almost *organic*, she realized, as if they'd grown out of the nexus and merged into Whitehall. The sense of power surrounding them was utterly overwhelming, calling her onwards at the same time as it repelled her. It made her wonder, suddenly, just how practiced the magicians who had tamed the nexus had actually *been*. They had to have been truly brilliant.

"It takes years," the Grandmaster said, when she asked. "A single flash of power can destroy all of their work in a heartbeat. They need to monitor the nexus, focus its power and then channel it into the wards. Done properly...it can be very rewarding."

And if it isn't done properly, the results can be disastrous, Emily thought, remembering how Sergeant Harkin had talked about the dangers of tapping nexus points. He'd told her about an experiment that had caused an explosion, one that had devastated the country for miles around. Given the sheer level of power she could feel in the chamber, it was surprising that it hadn't cracked the planet in half. She had the strangest sense that the nexus was actually *alive* and looking right back at her.

She staggered against the Grandmaster, who held her upright.

"I had the same reaction when I first came here," he said. "Was it so extreme when you killed Shadye?"

"I don't think so," Emily said. "But I was desperate."

The Grandmaster smiled, then nodded to one of the pillars. "I think you had a great deal of help from the spells that govern the nexus," he said. "Thankfully, the Warden wasn't destroyed at the time. But now..."

He scowled. "I need you to try touching the power directly," he added. "And be careful."

Emily looked at him. "What—exactly—do you want me to do?"

"Scan the school," the Grandmaster said. "If the spellwork is still in place, you should be able to rebuild the wards and take control."

It didn't *sound* like a very good idea, Emily realized, but there wasn't much choice. She stepped forward, eying the pillar, and gently touched the crystal with her bare hand. Strange lights ran over the structure, but nothing else happened until she tried to pull her hand away and realized that it was stuck. Moments later, there was a sudden surge of power and she was suddenly *very* aware of the entire school. Whitehall was, on some level, a living entity, one that existed on a very different plane to humanity. The sudden awareness almost sent her staggering backwards, but she couldn't break the contact...

The wards were in ruins, she realized, as she tried desperately to focus. It hadn't been so hard last time, had it? She couldn't recall—the experience had faded from her memory quickly—but she was sure that it had been easier to control and direct the power flowing from the nexus and into the school. This time, it either refused to heed her or was powerful enough to burn her mind. There was a wave of red-hot pain...

...And she found herself in the Grandmaster's arms, staring up at the crystal ceiling high overhead. Her head hurt, but the pain seemed almost illusory, as if she were imagining having a headache rather than actually having one. She reached up and touched the side of her head, feeling almost fragile. The memories of touching the nexus had already faded away.

"You were pushed out," the Grandmaster said, softly. "It didn't allow you to make contact properly."

Emily nodded. "I can try again," she said, although in truth she would have preferred to put some distance between herself and the nexus. "But I don't think it likes me any longer."

That was an understatement. The nexus seemed rather unfriendly now...perhaps it remembered how Shadye had manipulated her to attack it. Or, perhaps, how Shadye had almost taken it for his own. The thought of a necromancer wielding the almost unlimited power of a nexus was terrifying. Shadye might well have become a god—or a devil.

"Probably not a good idea," the Grandmaster said. His tone was firm enough that she knew there was no point in arguing. "Too many such contacts might destroy your mind—or suck you into the nexus. No one who has been sucked inside has ever been seen again."

Emily half-remembered the waves of endless power and shivered. It was possible that the people who had been sucked inside didn't *want* to return. If they could, of course...but the nexus was so powerful that it could do almost anything. Surely it could rebuild their bodies if they wanted out. Or maybe they had long since been destroyed beyond hope of recovery.

The Grandmaster helped her to her feet. "Thank you for trying," he said, seriously. "And I'm sorry you had to go through that experience. There was no other choice."

"No," Emily agreed. "Is there anyone else who might be able to touch the nexus?"

"Not in Whitehall," the Grandmaster said. He shook his head, dismissing the thought. "And substituting a different homunculus didn't work either. The level of spellwork that went into the Warden was quite considerable, far more than any lesser entity. I still don't understand how the Mimic managed to destroy it so quickly."

Emily frowned, considering the problem. "What would happen," she said slowly, "if the spells that gave the Warden life were drained?"

The Grandmaster turned to peer at her with sightless eyes. "Are you suggesting that the Mimic sucked the spells right out of him?"

"I can't think of any other explanation," Emily said. The only alternative was that the Mimic had replaced the Warden after the Battle of Whitehall...but if that had been the case, it should have had access to enough power to maintain its stolen form indefinitely. "Wouldn't that have killed him?"

"It might well have done," the Grandmaster agreed. "And if the spells that should have alerted the staff were destroyed too, there would have been no alert."

Emily nodded, slowly. The Mimic had presumably *believed* that it was Travis after it had replaced him...but then, it hadn't sounded the alarm over the destroyed Warden. What did *that* mean?

The Grandmaster led her through the door and closed it behind them. Emily watched as he replaced the spells, then added a twist or two that were completely beyond her comprehension. It was a droll reminder, she realized, of just how much more she needed to learn before she graduated from Whitehall. The tests in Blackhall were tough, but they were calculated to push the students to the limit. The Grandmaster's wards on the nexus chamber were designed to keep intruders out.

She asked a question that had been bugging her for some time. "Shadye was a student at Whitehall, wasn't he?"

"He used to be," the Grandmaster admitted. He inspected his handiwork thoughtfully and nodded in satisfaction. "But then he went missing for a while...until he appeared out of nowhere and took over the Blighted Lands near Whitehall. That isn't exactly uncommon, unfortunately."

Emily nodded in understanding. A known magician who was slipping into necromancy might attract attention before he was too powerful to challenge directly. Shadye might well have absented himself from the Allied Lands a long time before he made the final transformation into a mad necromancer. His humanity had been sacrificed long ago.

What were you expecting? She asked herself, silently. *To discover that he'd left a piece of his soul behind for you to find?*

The Grandmaster turned and led the way back up the hidden staircase. "I should remind you not to come down here again without an escort," he added. "The nexus can be seductive if you are unprepared for its pull. We always have to guard it carefully when newcomers are being trained."

"And you wouldn't want them in the chamber on their own anyway," Emily said. She couldn't blame the Grandmaster for being paranoid. If she had been able to create a simulation of a black hole without any prior training, what could someone do if they *did* have the training? "I won't come down here again."

But she felt the pull of the nexus growing stronger as she walked up the stairs, tugging at her very soul. It had hurt her and yet she wanted to go back and throw herself into the raging torrents of power that blazed beneath Whitehall. She felt her hands trembling and clasped them together, trying to keep them under control. The tug faded until it merged into the back of her mind, part of her ever-present awareness of the wards running through the school. And yet it was still there. She could feel it every time she remembered the nexus.

"Everyone who touches the nexus is changed forever," the Grandmaster said, softly. "And sometimes the price can be quite high."

Emily looked at him. How and why had he lost his eyes?

There were rumors, of course. Some students claimed that he'd plucked his eyes out and traded them for wisdom. Others believed that he'd been experimenting with a new practical joke hex—or perhaps something more offensive - and accidentally destroyed his sight permanently. And there were some who believed that he'd lost them battling a necromancer before taking over the position of Grandmaster. Emily wanted to ask, but she didn't quite dare. She wasn't sure she really wanted to know.

The Grandmaster led her through the main corridor and out into the Great Hall. Lady Barb was already hard at work, aided by Sergeant Miles and Professor Lombardi, both of whom were constructing wards to trap the Mimic. Behind them, Professor Eleas was drawing out runes on the wooden floor. Emily looked at the completed runes, but couldn't discern their purpose. One of them seemed to be intended to urge someone to move in a particular direction; the others were completely unfamiliar.

"We may have to start tomorrow," Lady Barb said, straightening up. "Professor Thande says that the remaining potions won't be ready for several more hours."

Emily looked over at the professor. He was standing in front of a table, messing around with a massive collection of test tubes, glass beakers and a tiny stove. Beside him, Imaiqah was watching with interest and passing him ingredients as directed. Emily had to smile at her friend's intent expression. She had always been much better at Alchemy than Emily herself and Professor Thande had even made noises about offering her an apprenticeship. But that would have to wait until sixth year.

"Understandable," the Grandmaster said, although he sounded cross. "Not the right ingredients?"

"Not for *this* level of replenishment potion," Lady Barb said, flatly. "We're going to need a dose for just about everyone, unless we get lucky and the Mimic happens to be caught very quickly. And there's no way we can get more ingredients in time."

Emily scowled inwardly. The greenhouses were on the other side of the wards—and they couldn't be extended, not that far from the school. Nor could they go to Dragon's Den or somewhere else where they might find more supplies. They would have to work with what they had—and if they didn't have enough...

"Do *not* attempt to substitute anything else for the required ingredient," Professor Thande had said, back during her first week of formal lessons in alchemy. "If you replace one with another, the alchemical reaction will be very interesting, but not what you're trying to achieve. Leave experimenting until you get into fifth year."

He'd followed up with a set of warnings, concluding with a dire threat that anyone caught deliberately altering the recipe would be severely punished—and anyone who wasn't caught would probably wish they had been, after they drank the botched mixture.

"We may be able to find substitutes," Lady Barb added, "but I wouldn't take chances with something like this."

"Probably a good idea," the Grandmaster said. "Have you spoken to the other staff members?"

"It's hard to work up a list of suspects," Lady Barb said. "Logically, it was someone who had to be alone long enough for the Mimic to kill and replace them, but how long does it take to do that?"

"Not long," Emily said, slowly. The Mimic had tried to take her place in an open corridor. It must have known that it could deal with her quickly, before anyone else came along. "Maybe bare minutes at most."

Lady Barb nodded, tartly.

"We haven't managed to identify the student who went after Emily and Imaiqah either," she said. "Whoever it was used high-level magic, including an invisibility charm, and was a short girl. But that still leaves us with several hundred possible suspects. Even if we narrow it down by only looking at students in Martial Magic, we still have at least twenty suspects."

The Grandmaster scowled. "Have them all interrogated under truth spells," he ordered. "A near-murderous attack on younger students? I'm not laughing."

"Neither am I," Lady Barb said. "But I think it's only going to get worse. Everyone is stressed, Grandmaster, and *very* fearful. I think we might have to consider moving students out of the bedrooms and into larger dorms, somewhere we can keep an eye on them."

Emily shivered at her tone.

"Go get some proper rest," Lady Barb ordered. "You'll be one of the first students to be tested tomorrow, just to help convince the others to walk into the wards and expend their magic. And we thought we'd let you explain the blood sample procedure to the servants afterwards."

"Thank you," Emily said, sourly. "I'll try and think of some good words."

Blood. No one would be happy about giving out a blood sample, even if they weren't magicians. Emily had had blood magic used against her and had studied it afterwards, even using it herself once. There were hundreds of spells that involved making use of someone's blood...and most of them were as evil as anything the necromancers had ever done. No, the servants would not be happy about giving up some of their blood. Rules or no rules, they were already far more exposed to the student body's sense of humor than they would have preferred.

"I'll escort you and Imaiqah to your room," Sergeant Miles said. "You should *not* be alone any longer. Too many idiots are still blaming you for everything."

Emily nodded, bitterly. If she hadn't been in Whitehall, Shadye would never have broken in...and the Mimic would never have escaped. But there had been no choice.

What else could she have done?

Chapter Thirty-Four

THE CLANGING OF THE BELL WOKE EMILY FROM A RESTLESS SLEEP, WHERE SHE HAD DREAMED of Shadye and Mimics and the strange pull of the nexus point. She had dreamed twice of stepping through the door and walking up to the pillar, only to snap awake when her fingers actually touched the crystal. It was a relief to wake up and dress for breakfast.

"I heard that two more students were killed," the Gorgon said. "And someone else is dead and doesn't know it."

Emily nodded, wordlessly. Could the Gorgon have been consumed and replaced by the Mimic? It was impossible to ask—and the Gorgon might not know. There was so little actually *known* for sure about the Mimics . She tugged her robe over her head, then tied her hair back into a ponytail. This wasn't a day to let it all hang free.

"Wake up, Lin," the Gorgon called, sharply. "You have to come to breakfast with us."

Lin didn't look much better than Emily felt. She sat upright in bed, clinging to the covers as if she wanted to bury herself beneath them and pretend the world didn't exist. Emily understood the impulse; she would have liked to forget about the Mimic too, even though it was pointless. Bad things didn't go away if someone wished them gone.

Madame Razz rapped on the door. "Breakfast in twenty minutes, girls," she hollered. "Be out by then or you will be unable to eat until lunch."

"I think she hates us," Lin muttered, as she pulled herself out of bed. She wore a nightgown that looked as if it could pass for regular clothes. "And she definitely hates me."

Emily shrugged. "I think she has high standards," she said. "And besides—just think of all the mischief we get into."

"You, perhaps," the Gorgon said, tartly. Her voice was thoroughly irritated. "I don't dare."

They finished dressing and walked out of the room, heading down towards the dining hall. Emily let out a sigh of relief as she saw Imaiqah waiting for her, then walked ahead to join her friend. The Gorgon followed her at a distance, catching more than a few sidelong glances from the other students. Emily felt a flash of shame and pity at their reactions and resolved to try to be nicer to the Gorgon in future. She didn't deserve to be picked on for being what she was.

Inside, there were large caldrons of porridge and small helpings of fresh fruit. Emily heard grumbling from boys—and not a few girls—who were used to starting the day with bacon and eggs, but there was none to be had. She couldn't understand where they'd bought the fresh fruit until she remembered the preservation spells she'd learned about during the long hikes they'd taken for Martial Magic. The kitchen staff probably preserved the fruit as soon as they bought it from Dragon's Den.

She finished the food and sat back, unsatisfied. There wasn't enough to keep her going for long, which might have been the point. Did the Mimic use food to produce energy too? Even if it didn't, underfeeding the students might speed up the process of draining their magic. Her eyes narrowed as she saw the sixth years guarding the doors. No one was being allowed to leave the dining hall. One particularly obnoxious fourth year had wound up with his feet firmly stuck to the floor to keep him inside.

The Grandmaster strode inside, a wave of magic announcing his presence, followed by a line of grim-faced staff and servants. A faint ripple of surprise ran through the room as the students saw the servants and wondered what it portended. It was rare for the servants to enter the larger rooms while the students were there.

Emily looked up as he stood in front of the room, waiting until he had their undivided attention.

"We have gathered everyone in the building in this room," the Grandmaster said, quietly. "One of us is the Mimic."

There was a rustle of panic, which quieted quickly as the Grandmaster scowled at them.

"We have been able to deduce that the Mimic uses up energy faster than normal by using magic," the Grandmaster continued. He didn't mention Emily's involvement, for which she was grateful. If her fellow students realized that the whole concept was her idea, she might as well try to leave Whitehall before they took their fury out on her. "When it runs short of magic, it reverts to its normal form and searches for the next victim. Our plan is to force it to do that in a place where we can trap it."

Emily frowned, puzzled. Why was he telling them the plan? Didn't he realize that he was telling the *Mimic* what he intended to do? And then it struck her. Anyone who attempted to leave ahead of time might well *be* the Mimic. It might save them some trouble if the Mimic identified itself so conveniently.

"One by one, you will go into the Great Hall and expend your magic," the Grandmaster continued. "Once drained, you will be escorted into the Dance Hall and told to wait there. Some additional food and replenishment potions will be provided. Do *not* attempt to leave the room until after everyone has been tested. This is our best chance at isolating the Mimic and we are not going to waste it."

He paused. "We found one more body last night," he concluded. "This is deadly serious. If we fail to trap the Mimic, we will be unable to lower the wards and escape. Whitehall will become a school of the dead.

"I know that many of you will object to the exercise, but we have found no other way to test for the Mimic. Please do not argue, but cooperate completely with the staff."

There was a long pause.

Emily tried to see how the other students were taking it. Some looked relieved at having a solution, *any* solution. Others seemed angry; they knew that they were going to be expending their magic, ensuring they couldn't work any spells for the next few hours. Emily wondered, coldly, if they included the person who had attacked both her and Imaiqah, but it was impossible to know. The ones shooting nasty glances at her might not include the one who had attacked them.

"When Master Tor reads out your name," the Grandmaster said, "walk through the South Door into the Great Hall. Do *not* attempt to go anywhere else."

Master Tor stepped forward as the Grandmaster, Lady Barb and several other staff members exited through the South Door. There was a long pause as he unfurled a roll of parchment and peered at the first name, then he looked up and shot Emily an unreadable look.

"Lady Emily of House Cockatrice," he said, flatly.

Emily felt all eyes on her as she stood and walked towards the South Door, fighting the urge to clench her fists or show any other sign of nervousness. The door suddenly seemed very large in front of her; she placed her hand on it and pushed it open, hearing a strange noise behind her as she stepped through. Were they admiring her bravery or were they convinced that the Mimic was about to expose itself? There was no way to know.

The interior of the Great Hall had been covered in runes and wards. Emily could feel the magic crackling around her as she stepped forward, growing stronger with every step. She could almost *see* a spider-web of magic hanging in the air, glowing with power and potential. And to think they'd assembled it overnight...

"In there," Lady Barb ordered, pointing to the very center of the Great Hall. "Don't worry about a thing."

Emily winced as the magic closed in on her. She felt trapped; there was no way to escape, not without necromancer-level powers. Indeed, there was so little space inside the wards that unleashing such power might destroy her when it bounced off the barrier. Shadye had never tried to break down Whitehall's wards directly, but what would have happened if he had attempted to unleash his full power against the school?

"Very good," the Grandmaster's voice said. "Now, start casting spells."

Emily hesitated, bracing herself, then cast the first of the most power-intensive spells she knew. Magic crackled around her, growing brighter and brighter as she pushed more magic into it, lighting up the entire chamber. She concentrated, closing her eyes as she drew on her deeper reserves of magic, feeling time slowing to a crawl...and then the magic slowly faded away. She found herself kneeling on the floor with no clear awareness of how she'd fallen—or why. Her body seemed suddenly very frail.

"Well done," the Grandmaster said. "You appear to be human."

"Thank you," Emily muttered.

She was weak, so weak that it was hard to move, but she did manage to look at her bare hand. The nightmares about actually *being* the Mimic had chilled her to the bone. Had she suggested the test, she asked silently, because she had subconsciously worried that she might have been the Mimic herself? Once again, there was no way to know.

"Come here," Lady Barb said. She was standing right next to Emily...how had she gotten there without Emily noticing? "It's all right. You're human."

Emily couldn't say anything as Lady Barb helped her to her feet and pulled her out of the wards, then—instead of going into the Dance Hall—pushed her into a small seat at one end of the Great Hall and pressed a small glass mug into her hand. The replenishment potion smelt ghastly—she recalled Professor Thande telling her that potions were deliberately made to taste awful, simply to ensure that the users didn't become addicted—but she felt better the moment she downed it.

"You might want to stay here," Lady Barb said. "It was your idea."

The next few students were all sixth years, including Cat and Bran. Emily watched, wondering why she had never been *scared* of any of them, as they expended vast amounts of power before sagging to their knees. But then, she had met Shadye—and Void. The students didn't have anything like their raw power, or experience. Not yet.

Better not let Alassa get into another fight with Cat, Emily thought, as Lady Barb helped him into the Dance Hall. *Next time he might overwhelm her with ease.*

The thought made her scowl. There was a rule against seniors picking fights with juniors, but if the juniors started it the seniors were allowed to put them in their place. In hindsight, if Alassa hadn't hurt Cat so badly in the opening round, she might just have ended up as a frog—or worse. But then, that game had brought out the worst in everyone.

Sergeant Miles came over and knelt down beside her. "They found Bane's body in a closet," he said, grimly. "The general theory is that he went inside...and the Mimic was behind him. And that was the end."

Emily nodded. Mimics were rare...but everyone was scared of them, with good reason. If a powerful combat sorcerer like Sergeant Bane could be overwhelmed, no one was safe—not even rogue talents like Void or necromancers like Shadye.

The next set of students looked more reluctant to take part in the tests, but the Grandmaster left them no option. Emily quietly made mental notes of their power levels and what sort of spells they used, noting that two of them seemed content to hurl spell after spell rather than picking one and pushing as much power into it as they could. Did that imply a lack of discipline, a shortage of imagination...or what? She couldn't help glancing at her watch and scowling as yet another student walked into the Dance Hall. At this rate, they were going to spend the entire day performing the test.

She looked over at Lady Barb as a thought occurred to her. "What happens to all the magic?"

"It gets vented out into the wards," Lady Barb said, tightly. Perhaps she remembered the experiments Emily had had in mind. "We can't leave so much residue in such a small place."

Emily blinked in surprise as she realized that Lin was the next student. Her roommate looked small and weak against the wards, her face so pale that it lacked all color. Lady Barb spoke softly to her, cajoling Lin into casting a simple light charm. The light globe blazed brightly for long minutes, longer than Emily would have believed possible, then faded away as Lin slumped down.

Interesting, part of her mind noted. *Lin has significant power reserves.*

She scowled as the thought nagged at her. She hadn't seen Lin in many classes; she seemed to have chosen very different classes from Emily, classes that didn't require much in the way of magic. It was easy to believe that Lin didn't *have* much magic, but she *had* secured a place at Whitehall—and Mountaintop. She couldn't have done that without real potential.

Lady Barb escorted Lin into the Dance Hall, then came back to watch as the Gorgon entered the trap and started to cast spells. She was good, better than Emily had realized...but then, she did have an additional year of practice. And a *lot* of anger to work out...Emily shivered as she saw the snakes, hissing and biting at the air as the Gorgon worked her magic. By the time she slumped too, the wards were positively glowing with released energy.

"Gorgons have a powerful magic of their own," Sergeant Miles said, softly. "They can be *very* dangerous opponents."

The next four students passed without incident, but the fifth seemed hesitant, reluctant to enter the wards. He was short and thin, reminding Emily of a boy she'd known from Earth who'd been the target of a very nasty gang of bullies. No one had done anything to help him, just leaving him to their mercy. He'd almost killed himself the year before Emily had been plucked away from Earth forever.

"Just cast your spells," Lady Barb ordered, calmly. "It won't take very long."

The boy gave her a resentful look—there was something in his dark eyes that made Emily shudder—and started to cast spells. He wasn't very good, Emily realized; there was something about him that reminded her of Imaiqah, before she'd become friends with Emily and started to stand up for herself. *Emily* knew little of mental health, but she would bet half of her fortune that low self-esteem contributed to poor magical skills. It was something, she promised herself, that she would research later.

But there's a taboo on exploring ways to help the mentally ill, she reminded herself. *It will need to be explored carefully...*

She sensed the sudden change an instant before the boy's form dissolved into the eerie form of the Mimic. Emily realized—as she sensed Sergeant Miles stumbling backwards—just how easily the Mimic had found its latest victim. With a student who needed to spend time alone, all it would have had to do was find him and then overwhelm him. If it could overwhelm a combat sorcerer, it wouldn't have any trouble with a weak third-year student.

"Tighten the wards," Mistress Kirdáne barked. "Hold it in place!"

The pulsing mist seemed to turn until it was looking directly at Emily. It *knew* her, Emily realized mutely; it remembered her from its unsuccessful attempt to consume her and take her place for its own. There was nothing that passed for an expression, no hint of a human face in the mist, but she could *feel* its cold hatred and abhorrence. And she was sure the creature was no beast. It had planned its hunt with great cunning.

She didn't realize she had taken a step forward until Sergeant Miles caught her, dragging her back roughly. The pain snapped her back to herself, clearing her mind; the Mimic had almost manipulated her into trying to release it from the wards. She heard a humming in her head as the Mimic glowed brightly, then a dull *twang* rang through the room as one of the wards snapped. And another.

"Replace the wards," the Grandmaster ordered. "Hurry!"

A third ward broke. Sergeant Miles let go of Emily's arm and ran forward to add his weight to the struggle, but the Mimic broke free before he could start casting wards. For a long moment, it floated in the center of the room, then lunged sideways, into the Dance Hall and out of sight. Emily heard screams as students fled in all directions, forgetting that they had to remain where they were...

"It's gone," Lady Barb snapped. She sounded badly shaken. "And so have the students!"

Emily realized just what the Mimic had had in mind—and cursed. With the students panicking, it could replace one of them and no one would be any the wiser. At the very least, they would have to run the whole experiment over again...and the wards had just proven themselves unable to hold a Mimic. But they'd worked before...

"We kept feeding it," Mistress Kirdáne said, numbly. "It never seemed to test the wards—but as long as we were feeding it, why would it bother to leave?"

Sergeant Miles clapped his hand onto Emily's shoulder. "It was a fine plan," he said, softly. "You did well, even if it didn't work perfectly. It wasn't your fault."

Emily shook her head, bitterly. She couldn't escape the feeling that it *was* her fault.

"So," Master Tor said, addressing the Grandmaster while looking at Emily, "what the hell do we do now?"

"I don't know," the Grandmaster admitted. "I just don't know."

Chapter Thirty-Five

"There's no way out," Imaiqah said. "Is there?"

Emily lay on her borrowed bed, staring up at the ceiling. Imaiqah's roommates had been lucky; they'd managed to go home before the Mimic had been revealed and the wards sealed them into the building. And she had been glad of the chance to move into Imaiqah's room, once she had convinced Madame Razz that she wasn't going to touch any of Imaiqah's roommate's possessions. Besides, it was unlikely that they were going to escape Whitehall.

"I don't know," she confessed. The Grandmaster had looked beaten, defeated, when the Mimic had vanished, leaving confusion and terror in its wake. By now, it would have eaten another student and taken their place. It could be anywhere. "If we don't dare lower the wards..."

But would the wards even hold it? They'd assumed that the Mimic was trapped in the zoo, but it hadn't seemed to have any difficulty breaking out of the trap when it had *known* that it had been caught. What if the Mimic could simply move *through* the wards once it had finished devouring everyone in Whitehall? The school would remain forever sealed, a mystery to baffle the Allied Lands, while the Mimic went on to dine elsewhere.

She looked across the room at her friend and felt a surge of guilt. It was all her fault. If she had never come to Whitehall, Shadye would never have dared attack and the Mimic would never have been released. She knew that she hadn't chosen to jump into this new world, or to be sent to Whitehall, but it was hard to truly believe it wasn't her fault.

"It could have eaten us all," she mused, out loud. "Why didn't it?"

Instead, the Mimic had broken through the wards and fled. And yet...what had it to fear? It was effectively invulnerable—she'd seen lethal curses simply passing through the mist, as if the Mimic wasn't really there—and it could have drained everyone in the Great Hall before escaping to finish off the rest of the school. Without the Grandmaster and the other staff, Whitehall would have collapsed into anarchy and the Mimic could have moved from victim to victim, utterly unnoticed in the chaos.

"Maybe it can only drain one person at a time," she muttered. *That* would certainly explain how the original capturers had caught it; there had simply been too many targets for the Mimic to choose one to drain. Or perhaps it had known better than to assume a new form in front of human eyes. Was there something about the human form that would make it vulnerable?

She sat upright. Being transfigured—into animals or inanimate objects—was a regular incident at Whitehall, even for a sixth year student like Travis. What would happen to a Mimic impersonating a human when a transfiguration spell was cast on it? Was that another way to test for a Mimic—or was the duplication so good that the spell was allowed to work perfectly? Maybe, if they could identify the Mimic's human disguise, they could trap it in stone...what would happen if the Mimic looked into the eyes of a Gorgon?

Or a pocket dimension, she thought, sourly. But the wards were too badly damaged to allow her to manipulate them for a second time—and producing her own pocket dimension risked interfering with Whitehall's interior. Maybe it was worth considering, as a desperation measure, but otherwise...she doubted the Grandmaster would be so tolerant a second time, particularly when the wards were trying to keep the Mimic *in.*

"I...I thank you for staying the night," Imaiqah said. "I didn't want to sleep alone."

Emily couldn't blame her. No one went anywhere alone now, not when the Mimic might swoop down on them and take their place. Students hid in their rooms, clutching weapons and preparing spells that might as well be snowballs, if matched against a Mimic. The hexing in the corridors had only grown worse as fights broke out, the students finally realizing that they might no longer have academic careers to protect. She had to admit that there was a certain temptation to hunt Melissa down and hex her into next week. Even with the staff patrolling the corridors and large parts of Whitehall declared off-limits, there was plenty of space for mischief—and malice.

"Me neither," she admitted. And she was sick of the Gorgon's sullen dislike and Lin's quiet passivity. Maybe they would have gotten along better if the Mimic hadn't been revealed...no, the Mimic had had nothing to do with Emily's experiments. That had been her fault, all the way. "I don't know what else to do."

Imaiqah stared at her. "You came up with a mad plan to rescue Alassa and save her Kingdom," she said. "Surely you can come up with something to face a Mimic."

Emily winced, inwardly. "My first idea worked a little *too* well," she muttered. The Mimic had been revealed...but the trap had failed utterly. Now, she rather doubted there was any point in trying again. Even if they caught the Mimic, they'd have to trap it...how? "The only other idea..."

She stopped, considering. If the blood test worked—and there was no clear evidence, one way or the other—how far did the blood have to be taken from the Mimic before it reverted to its natural form? There was nothing in the books to suggest an answer, although she was sure that Mimics would have cut themselves beforehand. Perhaps they'd simply moved on to consume and replace the person who'd seen their blood dissolving into mist. Or perhaps the magic they used was effectively a permanent form of transfiguration.

We could test everyone and move the blood as far from them as possible, she thought. *If the blood sample reverted to mist, it would identify the Mimic without it knowing that it had been caught. Or would it?*

Come to think of it, hadn't the Changelings on *Deep Space Nine* always been the first ones to suggest the blood tests? They'd had a way to fool them.

Imaiqah picked up one of her textbooks. "I wonder if there is any point in reading this now," she said. "What can we do in Whitehall?"

Emily felt another bitter pang. Perhaps she could go into the library and request books that would otherwise be forbidden, now that there was no hope of escape. She could spend the rest of the month satisfying her curiosity, even as she slowly starved to death. But part of her refused to give up hope. There was no such thing as an unbeatable enemy. She, of all the people in the Allied Lands, ought to know that a seemingly-invincible foe could be defeated.

"Good question," she muttered.

The first year was always a little chaotic, with students coming in all the time. Second year was meant to be a little more orderly. Even if the Mimic were destroyed tomorrow and the wards went down, they'd missed out on several weeks of schooling...as had the ones who had left the school. What would happen to them?

She stood and gave her friend a hug. "We'll get out of this somehow," she said, although she heard no real conviction in her voice. "Get some sleep. The world will look better tomorrow."

Imaiqah gave her another worryingly worshipful look. "I'm sure you'll think of something," she said. "But don't turn out the light."

Emily smiled, sadly, as she returned to her bed. It had taken her months to get out of the habit of leaving a light on overnight, yet another legacy from her damned stepfather. And then Alassa and Emily had been attacked in their own bedrooms, while staying at another kingdom. If Whitehall had had electric lighting, she might never have managed to sleep in the dark.

She closed her eyes and tried to sleep, wishing that she had a sleeping potion or something intended to ensure she didn't dream. But there was none; Kyla and Professor Thande had ordered that all potions were to be reserved for those who needed them to heal, rather than just have a dreamless sleep. Sergeant Miles had pointed out, when Emily had asked, that it was better to be able to snap awake instantly than remain in a slumber when someone dangerous was in the room. He was right, Emily supposed, but what was *she* meant to do about the Mimic? If Sergeant Bane hadn't been able to destroy it, what hope did *she* have?

Sleep came...and she plunged into nightmares. Shadye's face appeared in front of her, laughing even as he plummeted into the black hole and fell out of existence. Master Tor sneered at her, then somehow became her stepfather and advanced on her with his hands raised, as if he intended to beat her senseless. Melissa smiled at her and grew into giant form...no, Emily had shrunk. Her tormentor lifted a foot and brought it down on Emily...

...And the Mimic arose in her place.

Emily snapped awake, glancing around in absolute terror. There was no one in the room, apart from Imaiqah, who was tossing and turning on her bed. Sweat was pouring down Emily's body, a mocking reminder of the fear the nightmare had inflicted on her. She couldn't help pinching herself to be sure that she was awake.

Just a dream, she told herself, as she looked down at her hands. They looked reassuringly human. *Just a damned dream.*

She lay back and tried to sleep, forcing herself to recite the one thousand known uses of human blood in alchemy. Professor Thande had given them the list...and then cheerfully informed them that most of the uses were thoroughly illegal, although he did add that if they *needed* the potions, they shouldn't worry about silly little laws. Emily found it hard to imagine many reasons for using *any* of the potions, unless she had very dark intentions. Most of them were truly unpleasant as well as illegal.

Sleep refused to come, no matter how tightly she closed her eyes or tried to count sheep. The bed was uncomfortable, as if it were rejecting her despite Madame Razz carefully removing the handful of hexes and wards the previous occupant had left behind. Emily sat upright, wiping at her sweaty brow, and swung her legs over the side of the bed. She was surprised to discover, when she glanced at her watch, that it was nearly seven bells. The nightmares had lasted longer than she'd realized.

She stepped into the shower and washed, thoroughly. Her body still refused to feel clean, even if the water *did* help wake her up. But then...what was the *point* of leaving the room when there were no classes? Even the strictest tutors had reluctantly cancelled their classes in the wake of the Mimic's discovery.

Her face looked back at her as she peered into the mirror, shocking her with its gaunt appearance and grim expression. She looked almost as pale and waiflike as Imaiqah or Lin, she realized; her eyes looked almost as though she had been roughhousing with the boys in Martial Magic. Bruises and more serious injuries were not uncommon after Martial Magic, but normally they were healed instantly. These black eyes looked as though she had been fighting in the corridors.

"Emily," Imaiqah groaned, as Emily stepped back into the room. "What *time* is it?"

"Seven bells," Emily said. "Breakfast time."

Imaiqah didn't look any better than Emily herself, even after a brief shower. Emily watched as she dressed, then headed towards the door...and hesitated. It was easy to understand why; no one knew for sure what might be lurking outside their rooms. Normally, they would have been safe, but now...there was no way to be sure that the Mimic wasn't wearing a friend's face. Emily pushed the door open and stepped into the corridor, hearing the sound of Madame Razz berating a student echoing down from her office.

"You *know* you're not supposed to bring *boys* into your room," Madame Razz was thundering. "Did you *think* about the possible consequences?"

Emily and Imaiqah shared a smile. One of Whitehall's other purposes was to introduce children from the great magical families—or even lesser aristocrats—to one another and see if they fell in love. She'd been astonished by how many marriage proposals had arrived for her after the end of first year, although they'd dried up after King Randor had made her a baroness. Most of them, she'd been told, had assumed she was a new magician, just like Imaiqah, someone who might be tempted into a marriage contract. They would have been happy to share their status in exchange for her having children who would be part of the family.

Her smile grew wider as they slipped down the corridor. Aristocrats like Alassa were expected to remain virgins until they were actually married, despite the existence of both contraception spells and magical parental tests. The others...the rules were relaxed for female magicians, particularly the ones who were young and fertile. But they were still expected to maintain a certain decorum when in public. Madame Razz had good reason to be annoyed.

And boys aren't meant to be in the dorms in any case, Emily thought. It had been hard enough undressing in front of her roommates and they were both girls. The thought of a boy accidentally walking into the room chilled her to the bone.

There were hardly any students in the dining hall when they walked inside, apart from several older pupils who were staring at a map and arguing angrily over which way they should take to reach their destination. Emily recognized Cat, who gave her a nod when he saw her, but the others were strangers. She couldn't decide if they were idiots for thinking about what they could do after leaving the school or merely optimists.

"Take a seat," Emily muttered to Imaiqah. "I need to ask Cat a question."

Cat smiled at her as she walked up to his table, but some of his friends seemed much less welcoming. Emily couldn't decide if they were on Cat's *Ken* team or if they merely hated the thought of talking to a mere second-year student. Either was possible, she supposed. There was a rule that any romantic relationships between students could only involve one year above and one year below the student involved, but there was a much bigger social gulf between second year and sixth year students.

"Go away," one of the students ordered, shortly.

"I wouldn't say that to *her*," Cat said, quickly. "The sergeant is on the warpath right now, remember?"

Emily ignored the byplay. "I need to ask you a question," she said. "You knew Travis, didn't you?"

Cat glared at her. "Yes, I *knew* him," he said, crossly. "Is there a point to this?"

"Travis was consumed by the Mimic," Emily said, simply. "It must have happened during the Battle of Whitehall, I think. Tell me—did you ever see him being transfigured in the months after the battle?"

"It's one of the tests for Martial Magic," Cat said, sarcastically. "Yes, I saw him being transfigured—he once spent an hour as a toad after upsetting Danielle over something..."

"He was staring at another girl's butt," the student who had first spoken to her said. "You'd think he'd know better than to do that around her."

Emily blushed bright red at the mere thought. "Thank you," she said, embarrassed. "I just needed to know that."

She gritted her teeth at the sniggers following her as she walked back to Imaiqah and took the bowl of porridge her friend had brought for her. "No luck," she said. "I thought we had another way to track and trap the Mimic."

The thought gnawed at her as she ate her breakfast. There *had* to be another way to detect the Mimic, one that didn't involve blood samples or something else that would be considered taboo. Body wastes? The thought made her feel sick and she almost gagged on her porridge. *That* was truly an unspeakable possibility.

Other students filtered into the room, driven by hunger. They looked no better than anyone else; their eyes flickered around the dining hall, as if they expected the Mimic to reveal itself and lunge forward, intent on consuming them all. Emily looked away as several suspicious glances were directed her way, even though there were dozens of witnesses that the Mimic hadn't been wearing Emily's form. But who knew what had happened overnight?

Sergeant Miles strode into the room and marched over to where Emily was sitting. "I need you to come with me," he said, brusquely. He drew a small knife from his belt, cut his own skin enough to let several drops of blood fall onto the table and then stepped backwards, allowing her to observe that the blood didn't change to mist. "Now, if you please."

Emily looked over her shoulder at Imaiqah, then hesitated. She didn't want her friend to walk back to her room alone.

The sergeant seemed to read her thoughts. "Cat," he bellowed, loudly enough to shake the table, "escort Imaiqah wherever she wants to go, once she has finished breakfast. And *no* funny business."

Cat looked...*irked*, but nodded in agreement. Very few people would dare to defy Sergeant Miles...and no one did it twice. The sergeants had far broader authority to punish than the regular tutors, if only because of the dangers of Martial Magic. And he had a nasty sense of humor.

"Come with me," the Sergeant ordered, wiping up the blood. "Now."

Emily nodded and stood up. Maybe, just maybe, the sergeant had had an idea of his own.

Chapter Thirty-Six

"We couldn't identify your attacker," the Sergeant said, once they were outside the dining hall and walking towards the armory. "That is...*worrying*."

Emily blinked in surprise. There was a Mimic on the loose, hunting down students and consuming them...and he was worried about the mystery attacker? But it was a problem that had to be solved. The attacker could have killed both Imaiqah and herself if they hadn't fled.

"Yes," she agreed. "Sergeant...what are we doing here?"

"You're going to practice your spells," the sergeant said. "And I am going to teach you some other spells that work at a higher level."

He caught her arm as they stepped into the armory. "I should warn you," he added, "that all the normal rules about Martial Magic spells will apply to most of these, too."

Emily flushed. No one knew, she realized, that she'd used one such spell on Melissa. She'd been caught by the Mimic, not the *real* Sergeant Bane. The real sergeant would probably have dragged her to the Grandmaster's office and demanded that she be immediately expelled, or at least barred from taking Martial Magic for the rest of the year. She wondered, idly, what she should do about it. Confess and take her punishment...or keep her mouth closed?

"I understand," she said, finally.

She watched as the sergeant picked up a wooden staff and passed it to her. It was heavier than she'd expected, heavy enough to utterly crack someone's skull if it were brought down on their head. A quick glance at the head of the staff revealed that someone had wrapped the wood around a metal core that tingled, faintly, with magic.

"You will know, of course, that students are not supposed to use wands," the Sergeant said, with a hint of his old friendly grin. "Using one of them to shape and direct one's magic is a good way to wind up crippled. Indeed, the simplest way to render a wand-wielder harmless is simply to take the wand. They are rarely able to cast spells without it."

Emily nodded. Alassa had used a wand, which was why she had never been able to pass Basic Charms...at least until she'd wound up working with Emily. Without the sense for magic that magicians picked up through casting the spells themselves, she had simply been unable to advance further towards becoming a sorceress. Emily might well have saved far more than just her life.

"This is a combat staff," the Sergeant explained. He took it from Emily and hefted it in one hand. "I rarely issue them to students who have not already completed the third year of Martial Magic—or haven't gone on to apprenticeships. Your friend Jade, among others, will have a staff—and his Master will not hesitate to punish him severely if he starts threatening to become dependent upon it. He runs the risk of crippling his magic."

"I see," Emily said, slowly. "If that's the case, why do people *use* them?"

"Because, under the right circumstances, a staff can help direct and focus immensely powerful spells," Sergeant Miles said. "Each staff is individually bonded to a specific user, who channels magic through it to bring it to life. No one else can use your staff once it is yours. It simply won't work for them. However..."

He placed the tip of the staff against the floor and leaned on it. "I do not have the time to provide constant supervision," he added. "This staff, once bonded to you, will be stored in my personal quarters, under a set of very powerful wards. You are *not* to use it without my direct supervision. We will practice once a week, no more. Do you understand me?"

Emily nodded, but said nothing.

"The staff can easily become addictive," the Sergeant warned, "and when it does you have taken the first step towards restricting your magic. Ultimately, the person who will suffer if you lose your independence will be yourself. Do *not* attempt to take the staff or to beg me for more sessions. I will not take it lightly."

He passed her the staff and smiled, suddenly. "You'll notice that the tip of the staff is made of pure iron, which can dampen or cancel certain types of wild magic," he added. "The core is also made of iron, which makes the staff a formidable weapon if you happen to be deprived of everything else. If worst comes to worst and you poke a deadly trap with the staff, it will shatter rather than allowing the curse to strike you. But you must *not* grow dependent upon it."

Emily hefted the staff, trying to get used to the weight. "Should I be learning how to use them at all?"

"You need to advance quickly," Sergeant Miles said. "And besides, you have definite potential."

He tapped the tip of the staff. "I want you to focus your magic through the staff," he ordered. "It should bond with you at once."

Emily hesitated, then carefully pushed raw magic out of her fingertips, imagining it flowing through the staff. There was a sudden rush of energy, a sense that she had suddenly developed an extra hand or leg...and then the staff felt *alive* in her hand. It was *thrumming* with power. Holding it made her feel *powerful*.

"Well done," the Sergeant said. "Now...follow me."

He led her into the warded chamber and closed the door firmly behind them. A second later, an illusion—Emily couldn't help thinking of it as a hologram—appeared in front of her. It was a trio of battle-ready orcs, each one over two meters tall and carrying swords almost as big as Emily herself. There was none of the stench she remembered from the attack on Whitehall, thankfully. The illusion was far from perfect.

"There is a spell already embedded in the staff," Sergeant Miles said. "I want you to trigger the spell."

Emily concentrated, remembering the first set of lessons she'd had with Mistress Irene, when the tutor had taught her how to draw the magic out of her body. She smiled in sudden delight as it flowed into the staff, suddenly feeling the spell's presence embedded inside the wood, ready to be triggered. Magic flowed into the spell and...

Fire billowed out of the staff, roaring towards the orcs. They bellowed and lifted their swords, but it was already too late. The flames consumed them and raged onwards, burning at the wards and the walls and the...

Emily gasped in pain as the sergeant slapped her bottom, hard. She had been lost in the magic and the spell had just kept going. It would have burned until she drained herself dry if he hadn't stopped her.

"That spell is not easy to use without a staff," Sergeant Miles said. "But it also illustrates the danger of trying to *use* a staff regularly."

"Yes," Emily said. The sense of powering the spell had been overwhelming. She'd reached a point where she could cast certain spells automatically, but this was different. Whole new vistas of power were opening up in front of her...and would be forever lost, if she became dependent on the staff. "I see what you mean."

"You sound sullen," the sergeant said. He sounded amused rather than annoyed. "That's a very common reaction."

Emily nodded, flushing. "How else would they react?"

"I've known students break their own staffs and then refuse to even *touch* another one," Sergeant Miles said. "Others have become addicted almost at once, to the point where I had to make sure they never touched another staff until they had broken the addiction. You need to be careful."

He took the staff back and looked down at it, thoughtfully. "With some effort, you will be able to embed spells within the wood yourself for later use," he said. "There are magicians who have built up an entire armory of spells within their staffs. In a duel, they can just fire them off, one by one or all together. Their opponents have often been surprised and defeated before they could react."

His eyes narrowed. "But there are also limits," he added. "You could not direct the fire you summoned, not like you could if you worked the spell on your own. And you would only have what options you built into the staff yourself. And if you happened to rely on someone else to do the preparation..."

"You would be utterly helpless without the staff," Emily finished.

"Oh, not helpless," Sergeant Miles said. "But you *would* be in deep...ah, trouble."

Emily nodded, remembering their first lessons. Sergeant Miles and Professor Lombardi had staged a duel, each step intended to demonstrate common mistakes made by magicians who thought a little power and knowledge made them dangerous. Afterwards, they had gone through every step in considerable detail, until Emily could almost recite it backwards. One of the rules was to never assume that a disarmed opponent was a defeated opponent.

But if I were dependent on the staff, another magician could take it and then freeze me, Emily thought, ruefully. *And then I would be trapped.*

"We'll practice more with the staff next week," Sergeant Miles said, as he walked back into the armory and put it in a cupboard. "And remember what I said. *Do not* try to get your hands on the staff without my permission and my presence."

Emily flushed. The moment he closed the door, she'd felt an overwhelming sense of grief and loss. It was silly, she knew; it wasn't as if the staff had been confiscated permanently, not like some of the pictures male students had been caught passing around in class. And yet part of her wanted to sneak into the armory and steal it back before he could remove it to his quarters.

"I understand the feeling," Sergeant Miles said. "But it is for your own good."

He took a pair of short swords from the rack and passed one of them to Emily. "I understand that one of your tutors is teaching you swordsmanship?"

Emily nodded. The etiquette teacher had been dubious about teaching young women anything of the sort, but King Randor had apparently insisted. After what had happened in Zangaria over the summer, Emily found it hard to blame him. Alassa and Imaiqah needed as many ways to protect themselves as possible. Magic wasn't the solution to everything.

The thought made her shiver. There were potions that deprived someone of their magic, if only for a very short space of time. What would someone utterly dependent on magic do if they lost it?

"Such teachers are good at making you *look* good," Sergeant Miles informed her. "Does he get annoyed with you frequently?"

"Yes," Emily said. "He says I have no sense of display."

"Nor should you," Sergeant Miles said. He grinned at her. "There are two sorts of soldiers in this world, Emily. The ones who look good and the ones who *are* good. They are very rarely one and the same. Besides...didn't you see Sergeant Harkin's flying kick?"

Emily winced. Sergeant Harkin had shown them a flying kick that had come straight out of a movie featuring ninjas—or it would have done, on Earth. It had looked hellishly impressive until he'd done it again and Sergeant Miles had knocked him flat on his back. Once he'd picked himself up, Sergeant Harkin had explained that the move was designed to look good—and an opponent who didn't *care* about looking good would use it as an opening to smack the kicker down hard.

"Stand on guard," the sergeant ordered, as he lifted his sword. "And we begin."

He lunged forward, probing Emily's defenses. Emily barely managed to raise her own sword in time to block his thrust, then found herself being pushed backwards by a series of slashes that threatened to cut into her chest. He was holding back, she knew, and yet he was overwhelming her with ease. She feinted, trying to take back the advantage, but he crashed his sword against hers and sent it spinning out of her hand. It was something she'd been warned not to try in a real battle.

Emily dived for the sword, only to land flat on her face as he pushed her down to the floor. She gritted her teeth and tried to move, but he put his foot firmly on her back, trapping her in place. Escape was impossible.

"Bad habits," Sergeant Miles observed. "Why didn't you draw your dagger when you lost the sword?"

Emily flushed. "I didn't think of it," she admitted, finally. "I was just focusing on the sword..."

"There are no such things as dangerous weapons, only dangerous men," Sergeant Miles lectured, as he took his foot off her back and held out a hand to help her to her feet. "The weapon you carry may be the best in the world, charmed to help a hundred men win a thousand battles, but if you don't have the right mindset to use it...you would find yourself helpless very quickly. What do you think would have happened if you had disarmed me instead?"

"You would have still fought," Emily said.

"I would have gone for you," the sergeant agreed. "In your case, you should have gone for your dagger—or turned and fled. Running was probably your smartest option."

Emily scowled at him as she stood upright, waving away his proffered hand. "You didn't tell me that," she objected.

Sergeant Miles snorted. "Did I *have* to tell you the rules?"

Rule one, Emily recalled. *There are no rules.*

"I'm bigger than you, stronger than you and more experienced than you," Sergeant Miles said. "You need to learn to fight *smarter,* not harder. There is no way that a slight girl like you will win a wrestling match with me. That tutor will feel the flat of my blade."

Emily suspected he wasn't joking. "I'll do more swordplay with you," she promised. If nothing else, it would be a diversion from the yearning she felt in her soul. In hindsight, perhaps she should have refused to take the staff. "And I will have a few words with him myself."

"If he listens," Sergeant Miles said, darkly. He picked up Emily's sword and passed it to her, hilt first. "Clean it up, then replace it."

Emily nodded and carried the blade to the workbench. The sergeants insisted that all weapons be maintained by the students who used them, threatening dire punishments to anyone who dared mistreat a weapon. Taking care of one's weapons, Sergeant Harkin had said, was the first step towards ensuring they took care of you. She found a cloth, wiped the blade clean, then started to oil it. As always, the smell made her feel as if she were at home. She had no idea why.

"Good," the Sergeant said, when she had finished. "Where do you want to go now?"

Emily considered it. She hadn't—quite—finished the barracks, but under the circumstances it hardly mattered. Master Tor could rant and rave all he liked; there was no point in Emily working on the barracks when it was unlikely that they would ever leave Whitehall. Once the food ran out, they would all starve. She wondered, absently, how human flesh would taste, before dismissing the thought angrily. It would be better to die than eat her fellow humans.

Ah, a voice said, at the back of her head. *Will you still feel that way when you're starving?*

"I don't know," she said. "Have there been any other attacks?"

"We found another body this morning," Sergeant Miles said. "A fourth-year student, *well* out of bounds. The gods alone know what he was doing out alone—or who was there when the Mimic abandoned him and moved on to the next victim."

Emily scowled. The Mimic had yet another new face to play with and blend into the crowd. It could be anyone...

"The Grandmaster is considering trying to trap it again," Sergeant Miles added. "Perhaps if we pour additional power into the wards..."

"Maybe," Emily said. She'd had the impression that the Mimic had not found it difficult to break through the wards. "What if we used a solid barricade instead? I didn't notice it going *through* the walls..."

"Good thought," Sergeant Miles said. "I'll suggest that to the Grandmaster."

Emily gritted her teeth. What sort of creature *was* the Mimic, that it could do so much and yet behave so oddly? And yet there was a certain cold intelligence to its actions. What was it?

She stopped and stared at the crossbows hanging from the walls. What *was* it?

The realization, when it came, made her break down into giggles. Sergeant Miles looked at her as if he thought she'd gone mad. In hindsight, the answer had been right in front of her nose ever since she'd faced the Mimic for the first time. If she'd stopped to think about it, she might have realized what the Mimic actually was long ago.

"Tell me," she said, recovering control of herself, "what *is* a Mimic?"

Sergeant Miles scowled at her. "A monster," he said, shortly. "Why...?"

Emily shook her head. There was no clear proof, apart from a single observation, and yet she felt *sure* she was right. It was the only answer that made sense.

"We thought of it as a beast," she said. "A creature like a cockatrice or a basilisk, something weird, but something understandable. Why not? The world is *full* of creatures that have been warped by magic. Why not a shape-shifting ball of mist? But it isn't!"

Her giggles threatened to overwhelm her again. "It *isn't* a creature," she said, softly. "The Mimic is a *spell*!"

Chapter Thirty-Seven

"THIS IS THE LATEST VERSION OF THE FINGERPRINT SPELL," PROFESSOR LOMBARDI WAS SAYing, as Sergeant Miles led Emily into the staff room. "It'll find fingerprints—but it will also show the person who left the fingerprints, assuming they are in range. I think..."

He stopped when he saw the Sergeant. "Miles...?"

"Emily has deduced something about our enemy," Sergeant Miles said, addressing the room as a whole. "Something none of us would even *think* of. Emily?"

Emily took a breath, suddenly aware that some of the most powerful magicians in the Allied Lands were staring at her. If she was wrong...but she hadn't been wrong before, had she? Her plan had *found* the Mimic, after all. It hadn't been *her* fault that the wards hadn't been as strong as they'd thought. But it was still a lot of weight to put on her...

And Alassa will be Queen *of Zangaria*, she thought, tightly. *What am I complaining about?*

She cleared her throat. "The Mimic is a spell, a very powerful spell," she said, flatly. "It works on the same principles as necromancy, draining power from unwilling victims to fuel its passage through our world. Quite why it becomes a *copy* of the victim is unknown, unless the spell was intended to serve as the ultimate spy and simply got out of control."

"That's impossible," Master Tor said, stiffly. "A spell *cannot* act in such a manner."

"It would be very difficult," Sergeant Miles observed, "but it might be workable, if one had enough power and skill. The faerie were beings of magic; they might have created the Mimics as yet another instrument of terror. Or perhaps we should look for a more *human* creator. Someone might just have been trying to make necromancy viable and lost control of what they created."

"It flinched away from a detection spell," Emily said. "Why a *detection* spell when lethal curses just went *through* it? If I'd used the analysis spell, what would I have seen? The spell that makes up the Mimic?"

"Or it might have killed you," Lady Barb said. "If you know its secret..."

Emily nodded, tightly. She *was* a target—but then, so was everyone else in Whitehall.

"We find it, again," she continued, "and we cast the most powerful dispersal spell we have. And that should end its existence."

"Assuming that the spell isn't protected in some way," Sergeant Miles said. "There is no shortage of methods to proof a spell against being terminated. Otherwise wards would just be a laughing stock."

"But we have to try," Emily insisted. "There's no other choice."

Professor Lombardi was scribbling down notes on a piece of paper. "The Mimic might just be a combination of several different spells," he said. "All fiendishly complex, mind you, but they should go together...but you'd need a vast source of power."

"Necromancy," Sergeant Miles said, quietly.

"It may actually be overfeeding," Professor Lombardi added. He passed Emily a copy of his notes, which included the modified fingerprint spell. She glanced at it and stuffed it in her pocket. "There are too many students in the school."

"So we starve it," Mistress Irene said. "We isolate the students from it and let the monster starve."

"Assuming it *can* starve," Sergeant Miles said. "We don't know how often it needs to eat."

The Grandmaster held up a hand. "This leaves us with one final question," he said. "How do we catch it again?"

"We do the same test we did before," Master Tor said, simply. "We just get ready to cast the dispersal spell before it can break free."

"Except that there will be a riot if we try," Mistress Irene said. "And it would be hard to blame them."

Emily shuddered. The events of the last magical testing had scared everyone in the school, even the pupils who hadn't seen the Mimic directly. Mistress Irene was right; if they tried to gather so many people close together, the students would riot.

"There's another possibility," she said. "I go out alone and let it come after me."

Lady Barb snorted. "Are you out of your mind?"

"The Mimic has been going after people out on their own," Emily pointed out, carefully. "I intend to give it a target—me. It knows that I was meant to be cleaning the barracks..."

"It can't think that you are meant to go back there now," Sergeant Miles snapped.

"Why not?" Lady Barb asked. She gave Master Tor a dark look. "Someone *else* did."

"It may not think at all," Emily said. "But I can't think of any other way to catch the creature."

"And if you fail," Lady Barb said grimly, "you will be the next person to be killed and replaced."

"I know," Emily said. "But what other choice do we have?"

She listened to the argument between the tutors, surprised at the sheer level of venom that showed up in their words. It had always seemed to her that the tutors kept up a united front, even when they had private disagreements; the Grandmaster had certainly not overruled Master Tor when he'd decreed Emily's punishment. But now they seemed to be on the verge of hexing each other—or worse. If a fourth year student could take both Emily and Imaiqah, what could the tutors do? She didn't want to find out.

"*ENOUGH,*" the Grandmaster bellowed, using magic to project his voice through the room. "I see no other alternative."

"But a dispersal spell," Master Tor said. "How can it *work*?"

Sergeant Miles huffed. "Do you think anyone else has ever *tried*?"

The Grandmaster glared them both into silence. "Emily," he said, "are you truly willing to do this? To take the risk of merely being its next victim?"

Emily nodded, not trusting herself to speak.

"One of us should do it," Lady Barb said. "This isn't a task for a student."

"We all know that she is no ordinary student," Master Tor said. "I..."

"THAT. WILL. DO." The Grandmaster scowled at them. "Apart from Sergeant Bane, the Mimic has not gone after another tutor. It may fear what we could do to it, if we were pushed against the wall. Emily is the most logical person to serve as bait. Myself, Lady Barb and Sergeant Miles will be nearby."

Emily wasn't sure if she should feel honored or not. "Thank you," she said, quietly. "I'll go now."

Lady Barb came after her as she stepped out of the staff room. "You don't have to do this," she said, quietly. "I..."

"I *need* to do it," Emily answered. "Get ready to come after me."

The corridors felt completely empty as soon as she stepped away from the dorms, as if the students and staff were cramming themselves into a small part of the school. Emily looked around as she slowly made her way up the grand staircase, peering into the shadows as if they might hide the Mimic. Even the omnipresent *thrumming* of the wards seemed muted, somehow, as if the power were draining away. What would happen, she asked herself, if the school were completely dead?

She hoped—prayed—that they were following her as she reached the correct floor and glanced down the darkened corridor. There was already dust gathering on the floor, despite the wards and runes that should have kept it moving down and out of the castle. Emily wondered, absently, if the next pupil to get in trouble would have to sweep the corridors, before remembering that the servants would probably deal with it. They just didn't get paid enough to work in a magic school.

The lights should have come on as she walked into the corridor, but nothing happened. Emily hesitated, straining every sense for a hint of the Mimic, then cast a light globe into the air. The barracks door was right ahead of her, firmly closed. Emily muttered a second spell and the door opened, revealing that the dust had been slowly urged into a corner by the remains of the runes she'd drawn. Melissa hadn't managed to damage them all.

Emily reached for the mop automatically, then stopped herself and dug into her pocket for her notepad. It was almost full, she realized as she found a place to sit; she would have to have a new one sent to her by the papermakers in Zangaria. A notepad that would have cost less than a dollar on Earth was luxurious in Whitehall, even if the paper-making process was growing cheaper every month as they worked out the kinks. In time, she was sure, it would replace parchment completely.

She swore inwardly as she remembered what she had intended to discuss with the Sergeant—and then forgotten. Most spells designed to throw objects towards their targets could be easily cancelled—and the object, deprived of its propulsion, would drop out of the air. But with a little twiddling the spells could impart velocity, just like a cannon ball. It would keep going after being fired until gravity finally asserted itself—or until it hit something. *That* would be a nasty surprise for sorcerers who thought that a basic ward would keep them safe.

Carefully, she jotted down the concept. If she were consumed and replaced, it was quite possible that the Mimic would give the notepad to the Sergeant—all unknowing. Or that he would find it on her body. She added a few extra notes of her own, then wondered if she should write a letter to Imaiqah and Alassa. There was so much she wanted to say that she hadn't been able to tell them in person. And she hadn't even gone to see Imaiqah to say goodbye.

What would death be like? She'd never really been religious—it was hard to be religious when there seemed to be no justice in the universe—and she had always believed that death would be the end. There had been times when she had welcomed the thought of oblivion, back when she had considered suicide. And yet...it *would* be the end. There would be no afterlife, no heaven or hell.

Or maybe there *was* an afterlife. She'd never had time to really study the religions in Zangaria, let alone the rest of the Allied Lands, but there were a thousand different concepts of life after death. Maybe one of them would welcome her. Or maybe they would all see her as a stranger to their world. There were times when she knew she didn't truly belong.

She regretted, now, not seeking help and safety after her stepfather had started to make her life a misery. She could have escaped—or found help for her mother. But she'd never had the confidence to try. If Shadye hadn't kidnapped her...

...She might well have died on Earth. Or wasted her life.

And she waited.

She glared down at her notepad an hour later, wishing that she had thought to bring a book. It would have been better than just keeping company with her own thoughts, particularly the darker ones about the other mysteries puzzling her. Who had been going through her desk? Who had attacked Imaiqah and Emily in the corridor? And who had been spreading rumors about her...

Not that they really needed to bother, Emily thought, sourly. *There've been rumors about me ever since I arrived, carried on a dragon's back.*

Master Lombard's second fingerprint spell was a vast improvement over the first, she realized as she pulled it out of her pocket and studied the spell. Carefully, she cast it and smiled when she saw her fingerprints all over the barracks. She tested the second half of the spell and felt her smile widen as she saw hazy lines running from the fingerprints to her fingers. Given time, this spell might revolutionize forensic magic.

Until someone figures out how to break the links, she thought. *Or if they start wearing gloves...*

There was a creaking sound from the door. Emily looked up sharply as a figure appeared, peering towards her. She was surprised to realize that she recognized him as one of Cat's friends, the one who had told her to go away at breakfast. He looked thoroughly unhappy with Emily, but there was something wrong with him. His body was moving as though it were a puppet with half of the strings lost.

"You...friend...has...charmed...Cat," he said, slowly. He seemed to be flipping from one mode to another and back again with terrifying speed, as if he were caught between two minds. "He...is...with...her...now."

Emily slowly stood upright, feeling a chill run down her spine. The Mimic's natural personality—if it had one, as humans understood the term—and the human mindset were fighting for dominance. If it *was* the Mimic. Someone could easily have hit him with a spell intended to turn him against Emily.

"He was ordered to look after her," Emily said, wondering just what Cat and Imaiqah were saying to one another. Imaiqah *was* on Alassa's team, after all. "Why are you here?"

"I..."

His form started to break down into the glowing mist-like form of the Mimic. It slowly billowed into existence, a cold sense of malevolence filling the barracks as it placed itself to block all escape. Or maybe it wasn't quite real. The madman who had designed the Mimics could easily have included a spell intended to make someone *feel* emotions that weren't truly there. Emily felt the hypnotic effect starting to press against her mind, but this time she fought it off and stepped backwards. The Mimic glided slowly after her.

This time, knowing what it was, she could see a certain eerie beauty within the Mimic, something almost captivating. There was a sense that she was staring into infinity as the mist billowed, strange lights flickering through the clouds. She could almost make out hints of faces in the Mimic, the last traces of those the Mimic had killed and replaced over the years. There were hundreds, perhaps thousands of them. And yet the Mimic was almost beautiful.

So is a man-eating tiger, Emily told herself. *But it is still dangerous.*

She triggered the emergency alert spell, summoning the tutors, then shaped the dispersal spell in her mind. It was the first spell she'd mastered at Whitehall, perhaps one of the simplest spells in the world. Using it on the Mimic seemed absurd, which might well be why no one had ever tried it before. Inherent magic like the type possessed by dragons or Gorgons didn't break when exposed to the spell. And everyone had assumed that the Mimic was a beast like them.

The Mimic drifted forward, its invisible eyes fixed on Emily's face. She cast the spell, pushing as much magic into it as she could. It reared back as if it had been stung—and then stopped, dead—but nothing else happened. Emily stared, then realized—to her horror—that the Mimic wasn't really *one* spell. It was made up of hundreds of spells working together. And it was regenerating...

Emily cast the detection and analysis charm and *saw* the spells. The Mimic was a fantastically complex spell, almost an entity in its own right. It was almost as complex as the spells that controlled the nexus point, without the vast power they drew on to make themselves work. No wonder it was effectively a necromancer, she realized, as the Mimic recovered and started to advance on her again. It *needed* such vast power to work.

But it can't go mad, she thought, grimly. *Maybe it doesn't have the same addiction to power that Shadye had.*

She cast the dispersal spell again and again, watching as it picked away at the network of spells making up the Mimic. The Mimic paused, then continued advancing towards Emily, ignoring her attempts to destroy it. Her spells simply weren't weakening the bonds holding it together. Every spell she removed was replaced a moment later. Emily simply couldn't put out enough power to destroy it.

No off-switch, she thought, as tendrils of mist reached towards her. *What sort of idiot designs such a killer without an off-switch?*

The door burst open, revealing the Grandmaster, Sergeant Miles and Lady Barb. All three of them carried staffs, which they raised in unison as they cast the dispersal spell. The Mimic seemed to fray around the edges as the magic crashed into its form, cancelling more and more of the spells that held it together, then started to pull itself back together. Emily shuddered as she cast the spell again herself. Could *nothing* destroy the Mimic?

"No more," the Grandmaster said, tiredly.

He raised his staff and took a step forward. Emily felt the magic shimmering on the air and flinched backwards. She'd *known* that the Grandmaster was powerful, but she hadn't realized *how* powerful, not really. He seemed to grow larger as he stepped forward again, daring the Mimic to strike at him. Emily shivered. The wave of magic was stronger than anything she'd seen from any of the other tutors, even Lady Barb. Only Void and Shadye had ever exceeded it. The Mimic *screamed*, a cry that echoed in Emily's mind even after she jammed her hands over her ears, then started to come apart at the seams.

Emily cast the analysis spell one final time and watched, grimly, as the Mimic splintered into its component parts. The Grandmaster kept pushing at it, his magic thrumming through the air, until there was almost nothing left. There was a sudden sense of hatred, of anger and pain...and then it was gone. Emily slumped until she landed on the floor, feeling suddenly dizzy with relief. It was over.

"Well done," the Grandmaster said. "Very well done."

Emily looked up, dazed. He was kneeling beside her, while Sergeant Miles was studying the place where the Mimic had been. The floor was scorched and pitted into a series of blackened runes Emily was sure hadn't been there before, all of them completely unknown to her. Judging from the sergeant's frantic attempt to preserve them before they vanished completely, he didn't know what they were either.

"I felt it die," she said, softly. It suddenly hurt to speak. "What *was* it?"

The Grandmaster's eyes narrowed. "A spell," he said. There was a hint of puzzlement in his voice. "As you deduced."

"I don't know," Emily admitted. She was sure that the emotions she had felt were genuine...and that implied a living creature. But a living creature wouldn't have been affected by the dispersal spell at all. It was only good for destroying spells. A magical artificial intelligence? It seemed odd, but possible. "It might have been intelligent in its own right."

"The faerie have made other intelligent beings by experimenting on humans," the Grandmaster said. His voice became contemplative. "I suppose they may have created the Mimics to serve them in some way, perhaps during the wars. Or maybe a human sorcerer created them. No one really knows how much knowledge has been lost—or destroyed—over the years. Quite a few sorcerers went to their deaths without sharing what they knew—or teaching apprentices who might feel otherwise.

"But it was a killer," he added. He helped her to her feet, his grip surprisingly strong for an older man. "I think you've messed up the room again."

Emily looked around and shuddered inwardly. The dust had been scattered everywhere, her runes had been destroyed and the floor was badly scorched. They weren't going to make her clean it up again, were they? She wasn't sure she could do it again...

"I think someone else can do it," the Grandmaster added, after a long moment. He smirked at her sigh of relief. "Unless you wish to learn some useful housekeeping spells. You'll be surprised just how interesting they can be..."

"*I* think that she needs to go to the infirmary," Lady Barb interrupted, shortly. She peered into Emily's eyes, then cast a series of diagnostic spells on her. "Casting so many dispersal spells...no one really *knows* what *that* will do."

"I need to sleep," Emily said, fighting down a yawn. Now the Mimic was gone, she was sure that she would sleep better. So would everyone else. "Are you going to take down the wards?"

"Naturally," the Grandmaster said. His smile grew wider. "You should be there..."

"Let her sleep," Lady Barb suggested, although there was a hint in her voice that it wasn't a suggestion. She *was* Emily's Advisor, after all. "I can't find anything dangerously wrong with her that a good night's sleep won't cure. I'll walk her back to her room."

The corridors seemed brighter, somehow, as they walked towards the dorms. Emily couldn't help smiling as the lights came back up to full brightness, suggesting that the Grandmaster was already communing with the wards and lowering them so the students could go outside and play in the snow. She couldn't help wondering just what was going to happen to all the students who had misbehaved, thinking that there was nothing left to lose and cutting loose. What would the Grandmaster do to them?

"I think he might just give them a warning," Lady Barb said, when she asked. Her voice was carefully neutral. "Being under siege brings out the best and worst in people. I am not surprised that there were a whole string of nasty incidents."

She stopped as they stepped into the dorms. "Go back to your room and sleep," she ordered, as Madame Razz appeared out of her office. "I'll speak to Madame Razz."

Emily nodded and stepped past the housemother, walking automatically into her assigned room. It was empty; the Gorgon and Lin were elsewhere, perhaps joining the other students in the common room. She sat down at her desk and stared at her papers. Once again, someone had been peeking through them. And there were faint hints that someone had been trying to get into her trunk.

"Not this time," Emily muttered, feeling a cold flash of pure fury cascading through her. How *dare* someone go poking through her papers and try to breach her trunk? She reached into her pocket and produced the fingerprint spell. "Whoever you are, I can find you."

She cast the spell.

A moment later, she had her answer.

Chapter Thirty-Eight

LIN.

Emily gritted her teeth as she looked down at the evidence in front of her. Professor Thande was a *genius.* His spell had not only isolated the fingerprints on the desk, but also identified the same fingerprints elsewhere in the bedroom. The ones covering Emily's books were the same as the ones on Lin's desk and bedside cabinet.

But she'd never even *suspected* Lin...

A haze in her mind she hadn't even known was there seemed to snap. Emily swore out loud, then stood and walked to her bed. Lin's fingerprints were there too, as if the girl had been sleeping in Emily's bed when Emily hadn't been there. Emily hesitated, unsure if she wanted to know, then pulled out the drawers under the bed and cast a light spell, peering under the bed. Even knowing that they had to be there, it still took her several minutes to spot the runes Lin had scratched into the wood. One of them, she discovered, was intended to distract Emily from realizing that the carver was even there. No *wonder* she had never even suspected Lin.

The others were unknown to her, but she had a nasty feeling she knew what they did. She'd been careless with her notes, without even thinking about it—and Lin had had every opportunity to copy them. Another might have pitted her against the Gorgon, or directed her suspicions elsewhere...assuming that she actually realized something was wrong. She'd been wearing her protective sash when she'd first discovered that someone had been going through her desk.

She straightened upright and walked back to her chair. Another set of runes were scratched into the underside, pushing her to be careless while working harder. They'd worked perfectly, she realized, even to the point of encouraging her to ditch the *Ken* game in favor of coming back to her bedroom and running a private experiment. Lin clearly hadn't realized just how *odd* Emily was, even if she had been listening to rumor. Emily had been ignorant of basic material that every trainee sorceress knew.

"Why?" She muttered out loud. "Why were you spying on me?"

Emily paced across the room to Lin's bed and cast the revealing spell. The first set of protective spells were basic, right out of the textbook without any modifications at all, but the second set were far more advanced, buried under the first. Lin was clearly far more competent than she'd ever admitted...in fact, some of the charms protecting her bed were comparable to ones Emily had seen in Martial Magic. Breaking them was not an option, not for Emily. And that meant...

Lin had stolen the first version of the fingerprint spell. And then someone had attacked both her and Imaiqah in the corridors, defeating them both. Had *Lin* attacked them? They'd assumed that it was an older student, because the spells used had been advanced, but what if it had been Lin? She must have realized that she had come alarmingly close to discovery and attempted to distract Emily. And she had succeeded.

She went through my notes, Emily thought, grimly. She'd written everything down in English, rather than the Empire's script or the phonic alphabet she'd introduced to the Allied Lands, but a simple translation spell would allow someone to understand her notes. They wouldn't be perfect—there were concepts she'd scribbled down that wouldn't have made sense to anyone who hadn't come from Earth—yet Lin might be able to draw out information that she could use herself. How much had Lin seen?

The steam engine diagrams—if that hadn't leaked out already from Zangaria. Gunpowder weapons and tactics, assuming that they realized what gunpowder was and what it did. Had Lin seen her copy of the formula? To her, it might seem nothing more than a nonsensical mixture of chemicals. And yet there were also her notes on spells and magical concepts. What about the spell processor...or the batteries?

Emily shook her head. She'd hoped that she could keep control of some of the more advanced concepts, even though the basic concepts were spreading like wildfire. But Lin...might have passed what she'd seen on to others. Or maybe she'd just kept the information for herself.

She peered under her desk, looking for runes, but saw nothing. Not that it mattered, she realized; the two sets she had already found had been enough to cause real trouble, as long as she hadn't discovered them. But then, she hadn't really been able to *see* them until she had already deduced their presence. They'd had months to build up a charge they could use to influence her. And perhaps the Gorgon as well. How much of the Gorgon's anger had been due to her rage at having her possessions searched...or to the runes Lin had scratched out in the room?

The door slowly opened. Emily turned, raising her hand in a defensive posture, and saw Lin creeping into the room. Her roommate looked as small and waiflike as ever, but Emily could now see hints of quiet competence and determination surrounding her too. Lin might easily have cut runes into her own flesh, she realized as she stood upright. It would have helped her avoid attention while spying on Emily and everyone else.

"You saved us all," Lin said, softly. "Thank you."

Emily smirked. Lin had been trapped, unable to send messages to anyone outside the building. No wonder she had been prepared to risk exposure by attacking Emily and Imaiqah; she'd had nowhere to run. But now...Emily saw a hint of puzzlement flashing over her roommate's face and smiled openly. Lin didn't quite know what was going on.

"You were spying on me," she said, watching Lin closely. The shorter girl didn't show any visible reaction. "*You* were the one who was going through my desk."

"That is an absurd idea," Lin said. Her voice hadn't changed at all. "I would not dare to touch your desk. The Gorgon is a much more likely suspect."

Emily laughed out loud. "Your suggestions won't work now that your runes have been discovered," she said. Had Lin tried to steer her actions before? The hypnotic suggestion might have failed, now that she knew about the runes, but it might well have worked earlier. "I know that you intended me never to even *think* about you as a possible suspect."

Lin seemed to straighten upright, marginally. "And you have *proof* of this?"

Her voice tightened. "You do realize that throwing around absurd accusations could get you in real trouble?"

"Except they aren't absurd," Emily said. She knew she should have called the tutors, but she wanted to gloat. "And I am no longer suggestible."

Lin's eyes narrowed.

"And I *do* have proof," Emily added. "Your fingerprints are scattered all over my desk. The only other fingerprints there are mine. There are no fingerprints from anyone else at all. *You* touched my desk...and set aside my spells. Or did you influence me to leave cracks in the spells, all unknowing? I might not even have *seen* a damaged spell if I believed it was intact."

She remembered the fight she'd had with the Gorgon and felt her temper flare. Lin had been cunning; the runes prevented Emily from realizing that Lin was a potential suspect, so she'd blamed the Gorgon. The fight could have turned very nasty indeed. And the Gorgon might also have been influenced to dislike Emily. It simply hadn't worked until she'd been given a very good reason to hate her roommate.

"I think you don't understand," Lin said. There was an edge in her voice that hadn't been there earlier. "I think..."

"*I* think that we should go to the Grandmaster," Emily snapped. "Let *him* decide what to do with you."

Lin took a step forward. "And if I refuse?"

Emily ignored the question. "Why did you even do this?"

Her roommate laughed, unkindly. "Did you really believe that you could make so many changes and then go unnoticed? Child of Destiny, Necromancer's Bane...whatever title they end up giving you for defeating the Mimic...you've attracted attention. They're all coming to steal your secrets."

Emily flushed. "And who are *you* working for?"

Lin smiled. "Does it matter?"

"Yes," Emily snapped. "I want to know who did this to me!"

Lin's smile widened. "I'm afraid I am not permitted to divulge that information..."

She threw a spell at Emily before Emily could even realize that she was about to attack. It took everything Emily had to parry the spell, which gave Lin a chance to hurl another spell—and another. Emily flew backwards as one of them crashed right into her—her wards, she realized suddenly, were largely gone—and slammed into the wall. She gasped in pain as she fell and landed on the floor. Lin fired off yet another spell, sending a wave of fire washing towards Emily. Somehow, Emily managed to roll aside and throw back a series of spells of her own. Lin deflected them without apparent effort.

"You really need to work harder," Lin said. "You're the most valuable person in the school, yet your defensive spells are rubbish..."

I took them down when I faced the Mimic, Emily thought, grimly. She'd shredded her own protections and then failed to repair them in time. It was an oversight that might cost her everything. And she didn't dare to try to call for help now. *Damn it*!

She caught hold of the rug and pulled, hard. Lin stumbled, giving Emily a chance to pull herself to her feet and go on the offensive, throwing spells as quickly as she could. But Lin seemed to be deflecting them, all the while pushing forward while waiting for Emily to tire herself. Emily gritted her teeth, feeling her reserves rapidly draining. Between the Mimic and Lin, she had almost nothing left.

Lin's voice took on a thoroughly unpleasant tone. "I think that the Allied Lands will be safer without your presence," she said, darkly. "I won't make the mistake of allowing others to use you."

Emily's blood ran cold. She'd been in danger before, but this was different. She'd *liked* Lin...or had that too been dictated by the runes? And why did Lin care about the Allied Lands?

Lin raised her hand. "It's time..."

The door opened, revealing the Gorgon. Emily saw Lin flinch as she turned to see who had entered the room, then cast a very nasty spell aimed right at the third roommate. The Gorgon jumped aside, moving with a nimbleness that revealed her origins, her snake-like eyes open wide with disbelief. She'd been influenced by Lin, Emily realized, perhaps just as much as Emily herself. The Gorgon certainly hadn't suggested Lin as a potential suspect.

Emily threw a spell right at Lin's back, but the girl's protections prevented it from affecting her. "Run," she croaked. She tried to alert the tutors; the spell failed to form properly. "Get help."

The Gorgon's snakes twisted—and changed, becoming something so inhuman that Emily tried to look away. But something refused to let her. A wave of utterly unfamiliar power washed through the room, something so *alien* that it was hard to comprehend it. The snakes were channelling power...Lin let out a cry and cast a spell of her own. There was a blinding flash of light, which seemed to fall over the Gorgon's body. Emily saw her glowing with light and then, as the light faded away, turning to stone. It wasn't until Emily tried to move that she realized that she too had been turned to stone. There was no sign of Lin.

"Well," Lin's voice said. "Hoist by your own petard?"

There was a faint shimmer at the edge of Emily's field of vision and Lin appeared, smiling with genuine relief. "Funny thing about Gorgon petrification magic; if you happen to be invisible or simply looking away, it doesn't actually work."

She looked over at the Gorgon. "Should have stuck with the human spells," she added, nastily. "Can you free yourself from your own magic?"

Emily tried, desperately, to move. But her body refused to work at all. She wasn't even breathing or anything else...but then, she realized, what would a stone statue actually do? It felt different from the other times she'd been transfigured or immobilized; this time, there was a sense that her awareness was slowly drifting away. If the spell wasn't reversed in time...

Panic howled at the corner of her mind, demanding release. But there was no way to escape, not even through silently casting the spells that might have released her if she'd been struck by normal magic. She remembered just what she'd read in the library about how Gorgon magic was difficult to undo and shivered, mentally. Lin might just have condemned her to a slow, lingering death as her mind dissolved into madness—or stone.

"Quite an ironic ending," Lin said, as she walked past Emily. "You and the Gorgon lash out at each other, both ending up caught in the magic she unleashes. It will be easy to ensure that the Gorgon is blamed for your death. Her people will be exterminated for her crime."

There was a rustling sound as she picked up papers and stuffed them into a bag. They were papers from Emily's desk, she realized bitterly, still fighting to move. Now that she had been exposed—and the wards were gone—Lin would simply leave the school and walk down to Dragon's Den, where she could step through the portal and go anywhere. Or perhaps she had another escape plan. Not, in the end, that it mattered. No matter what spells she tried to cast, Emily was starting to think she was trapped for good. And, with the Gorgon equally petrified, there was no way she could simply undo her magic. They were both on the verge of death.

Lin moved back into view, staring up at the Gorgon. "I could smash you," she said. "I wonder what would happen to your mind if your stone body shattered. But I think that would tell them that something *else* happened. Instead...maybe they will think I was the Mimic's last victim."

They wouldn't believe that, Emily thought. Lin had been seen *after* the Mimic had been destroyed. On the other hand, would it actually matter? If she was far away from Whitehall by the time the Grandmaster realized that she'd been a spy, she would never be found.

"And thank you," Lin added, looking towards Emily. "Your notes were very helpful."

She walked out of the door, closing it behind her.

Emily kept struggling to move, but her body was completely unresponsive. The Gorgon, it seemed, had the same problem. She couldn't undo her own magic, at least not when it had affected her...how, Emily asked herself, had Lin managed to turn the Gorgon's magic back on her? The puzzle distracted her as she stared at the Gorgon's unmoving form. What sort of creature would have a magic that could be so easily turned against them?

Bees die when they sting, Emily remembered. Besides, the Gorgons weren't natural. The faerie had created them, along with so many other humanoid creatures. *Maybe the Gorgons are so painfully polite to one another because they're all constantly carrying deadly weapons around with them.*

The thought would have made her smile, if she could move her lips. All of the etiquette lessons she'd had, from Alassa and her other tutors, had been designed to ensure that she avoided giving offense. She would be dealing with aristocrats and magicians, both of whom could do her harm if they thought that she had offended them. Manners, even excessive manners, were a good way to avoid trouble.

An armed society is a polite society, she recalled. *And this society is very heavily armed. And it will get worse as guns are introduced...*

She felt her thoughts starting to drift away and struggled to hold them in place. If she lost her mind completely...she would die, her body forever trapped in stone. Perhaps they would put her in the Great Hall, she thought, perhaps with a sign memorializing her as the former Necromancer's Bane. Or maybe Jade would go off on a quest to remove the curse...she'd read a legend about a brave warrior who had done just that, although by the time the story had ended he'd been an old man and barely had time to do anything else before he died.

Or maybe in the nexus chamber, she thought. They should have a plaque there, one that mentioned Shadye's defeat. *HERE FELL SHADYE. SO THERE.* The thought caused her a bitter flash of brief amusement. If the necromancers were truly terrified of her, perhaps the Grandmaster would seek to create an illusion that she was still alive. Or would too many people know the truth? Lin might advertize it from wherever she was...unless she had a vested interest in keeping the necromancers in the dark. But then, they *were* the enemies of everyone, including each other.

There was a knock on the door. It opened a moment later; Emily heard a girl she didn't recognize gasp in disbelief, then start screaming for Madame Razz. She couldn't help feeling relief, even though she knew that it was going to be hard to undo the Gorgon's magic. At least someone knew what had happened...

Perhaps they just need Jade to kiss me, she thought, as Madame Razz ran into the room, followed rapidly by several other staff members. *It can't be that simple, can it?*

Lady Barb stepped in front of her, right into Emily's field of vision. "I know you're in there," she said, touching Emily's stone forehead. "We'll get you out. I promise."

Emily shivered, inwardly. She knew that it was a promise Lady Barb might be unable to keep.

Chapter Thirty-Nine

It took four days for the Grandmaster, working with Lady Barb and Sergeant Miles, to prepare a spell to undo the Gorgon's magic. Emily spent the time listening to lectures from her teachers, including—surprisingly—Master Tor. Somehow, the lectures helped keep her sane, even though her thoughts still threatened to wander from time to time. She had a feeling that she would be expected to write essays on them after she was returned to human form. But it was better than thinking she would never be able to write to Jade or anyone else again.

The worst moment had come when she'd heard Lady Barb suggest simply smashing the Gorgon. They *hadn't* realized that Lin was missing; they'd believed that Emily and the Gorgon had fought and they'd somehow both ended up stone. By the time Emily became human again, she had prayed endlessly that she would be able to warn them before they killed the Gorgon. It hadn't been the Gorgon's fault.

"Rest," Lady Barb said. "You've had a very unpleasant time."

"Not the Gorgon's fault," Emily gasped, as exhaustion finally threatened to overcome her and drag her down into sleep. She hadn't dared sleep while she was a statue for fear that she would never wake up. "Lin! It was Lin!"

Lady Barb stared at her, then nodded.

The next thing Emily knew, she was lying on a bed in the infirmary, with Imaiqah and Alassa sitting next to her. Her body felt stiff; desperately, she sat upright and looked around, feeling the sheer joy of movement. The Gorgon was sleeping in the next bed, her snakes curled around her head. Emily silently prayed that she hadn't heard the staff when they'd talked about smashing her. It would have traumatized her for life.

"Welcome back," Alassa said. She reached out her arms and pulled Emily into a hug. "I missed you."

"I missed you too," Emily said. "But you were lucky to get out."

"My father was mad at me for wanting to come back when he realized what had actually happened," Alassa said. "I think the thought of a Mimic being so close to his daughter actually got to him."

Emily couldn't blame King Randor for worrying. He lived in a world where impersonating someone else was easy, given the right level of magic. There were homunculi, shape-change spells, simple glamors...even potions to copy someone's memories and mannerisms. And now they knew the true nature of the Mimics. Who *else* might be a Mimic in human form?

"I'm not surprised," she said. "But we made it through the nightmare."

"Others didn't," Imaiqah said, quietly. "Forty students died before you killed the Mimic."

Emily scowled. The truth about the Mimics probably hadn't been widely shared, although she suspected that the Grandmaster would inform the White Council. They wouldn't want to encourage someone else to start trying to *duplicate* the monsters—and they would, if they knew that it was possible. *Emily* had certainly started a revolution simply by introducing new ideas to the Allied Lands.

"Forty students," she repeated. And last year Whitehall had been brutally attacked by Shadye. How many students would return *next* year? "What happened after...after I was turned into a statue?"

"They searched the school for Lin," Imaiqah said, quietly. "But they found no trace of her."

She shook her head. "I still can't believe that she was a...a spy," she added. "I never even thought twice about her."

"Neither did I," Emily admitted. But Lin had been cunning. "Subtle magic. Very subtle magic."

There was a hiss as the Gorgon opened her eyes, her snakes billowing around her head. Emily hesitated, then swung her legs out of bed and stood upright, feeling oddly unstable. But she needed to talk to the Gorgon...the snakes hissed unpleasantly as she tottered forward and stopped next to the Gorgon's bed. She didn't look happy.

"It wasn't your fault," she said, before the Gorgon could say a word. "Lin was a spy."

"They wanted to kill me," the Gorgon whispered. "I heard it all."

Emily felt a wave of sympathy for the Gorgon and reached out to take her hand. It felt oddly warm, faintly scaly. She had been isolated on Earth—and isolated again at Whitehall—but she had never been so completely alone. The Gorgon was different from everyone else in the school. There wasn't another Gorgon for hundreds of miles.

"I told them that it wasn't your fault," she said. She hesitated, then pushed ahead. "And Lin ensured that we would be fighting each other."

"She twisted my own magic," the Gorgon said. "I didn't even know that was possible."

"She's a skilled magician," Emily agreed. She waved a hand to indicate Alassa and Imaiqah. "These are my friends. Why don't you join us?"

The next hour passed quickly once Alassa located a board game for four players. Emily had never played it before and wasn't too surprised when she ended up losing, but the Gorgon proved a canny player, almost Imaiqah's match. Judging by the way they were chatting as they pushed Alassa out and started battling for supreme control of the board, they'd become friends over the game. Emily's acceptance of the Gorgon encouraged both of her friends to try to accept her too.

Maybe I can invite the Gorgon to Zangaria, Emily thought, wondering just what King Randor would make of that. But she *was* supreme in her own lands...and maybe it would help to break down the barriers between humans and Gorgons. Besides, she had the feeling that the Gorgon might be a friend worth cultivating. She already knew more about magic than Emily.

She looked up as the Grandmaster stepped into the ward. "I need to borrow Lady Emily," he said, shortly. "Emily?"

Emily nodded and followed him out of the room, hoping that the other three would keep playing on their own. Or perhaps they would move to a card game...she might not have been able to recall the rules of poker, but she had managed to introduce playing cards. It probably wouldn't be long before someone started gambling rings using them.

"You told the Gorgon you were going to smash her," she said, as soon as they stepped into the Grandmaster's office. "That was cruel."

The Grandmaster looked at her, then nodded. "We believed that she was responsible for your...condition," he admitted. "We were wrong."

"I think you owe her an apology," Emily said, tartly. Part of her mind was aware that she was ticking off one of the most powerful magicians in the world, but it needed to be said. "You frightened her to death."

"I will speak to her once I have finished talking with you," the Grandmaster said. He motioned for her to sit down. "Do you have any other reprimands you would like to offer or can I speak now?"

Emily flushed, embarrassed.

The Grandmaster smiled. "You're right," he said, "but be careful who you use that tone to, young lady. Not everyone is inclined to be forgiving."

He looked down at the desk, then back up at her. "We searched your room carefully—again," he said. "This time, we found nearly fifty runes scattered throughout the room, designed to keep you unaware of Lin's presence and to encourage you to be a little bit careless. I have been forced to have hard words with Madame Razz and Master Tor."

Emily blinked in surprise. "Why?"

"They searched your room after your little...experiment," the Grandmaster pointed out. "The runes were not found."

"But they might not have been there," Emily said, wondering at her own willingness to defend Master Tor. But then, he *had* read to her and lectured her while she'd been petrified, giving up some of his own time to help her. "Lin could have put them in afterwards..."

"They would have needed to be there almost from the start of term," the Grandmaster said, grimly. "They were missed."

Emily nodded, silently resolving to look up the runes herself, later.

A thought struck her and she grimaced. Had Master Tor put her in with Lin deliberately? He'd made the room assignments and Emily had wound up with the spy. A lucky break for Lin .. or something more sinister?

"Master Tor may not be at this school for much longer," the Grandmaster said, "but I did interrogate him under truth spells. He wasn't directly involved in the whole affair. His rationale for putting you and Lin together was sound."

Emily relaxed, slightly.

"We found nothing when we searched her bed, apart from a set of protections that should have been above her level," the Grandmaster continued. "It wasn't until we interrogated a couple of the other transfer students that we realized what she was. She was a spy for Mountaintop."

"The other magical school?" Emily asked. "Why?"

"One of them," the Grandmaster confirmed. "And as for why...are you aware of just how much you have changed the world?"

"I think so," Emily said, although she wasn't sure. There had already been unintended consequences flowing from her work, including some that had turned the world upside down. Who knew what there would be in the future? "She was sent to spy on me?"

"Yes," the Grandmaster said. "Apparently, the other students were...*encouraged* to transfer, even though Mountaintop rarely allows it. My best guess is that they were pushed into moving because Lin coming on her own might have seemed suspicious. They didn't know precisely what they were doing, of course. They were just cover."

"And she has some of my notes," Emily said, grimly. What might Lin have taken from her desk? "How advanced *was* she?"

"She was no second year," the Grandmaster said. "Potions intended to de-age someone are rare—they tend to have unpleasant side effects—but she could easily have taken one to pose as someone *your* age. At a guess, she was in fifth or sixth year; knocking you and Imaiqah down would have been easy for someone at that level. Under the circumstances, I suppose we should count ourselves lucky that she didn't slit your throat at night."

"Or smash us while we were statues, leaving the Gorgon to take the blame," Emily said, softly. It would have looked like a tragic accident. She scowled as a thought occurred to her. "Do you think she summoned the Mimic?"

"I doubt it," the Grandmaster said. "That might just have been coincidence. She wouldn't have attacked you at all—risking exposure—unless she had nowhere to go. And she didn't, while the wards kept us trapped in the school. All she could do was try to slow you down."

Emily nodded. The Mimic had acted oddly, but perhaps that was understandable if the spells that powered it worked along the same lines as necromancy. It had moved from consuming sheep and other animals to a school full of magic-users. The Mimic must have thought that it was enjoying an all-you-can-eat buffet. If, of course, it had thought at all. Did the sheer complexity of the spells that defined it allow for true independent thought?

"And she succeeded," Emily admitted. "What are you going to do about Mountaintop?"

"I have not yet decided," the Grandmaster said. "Spying on one another is not uncommon among magic-users, despite the Sorcerer's Rule. Everyone hates it—and everyone knows that everyone does it. But this is different."

He shook his head, slowly. "And then there's your guardian to take into account," he added. "Mountaintop may simply disown her."

Emily scowled. She hadn't given a single thought to the political aspects—but they were there. Lin had effectively tried to kill one of Zangaria's most powerful nobles, something that King Randor would be entirely justified in considering an act of war. And then Void might be expected to take a dim view of it too. Even if Lin had panicked and overstepped her orders, it was still going to create an unholy mess. The Allied Lands might come apart at the seams if it turned into a general war.

And then the necromancers would just walk over the mountains and complete the destruction of humanity.

"She must have hoped that the Gorgon would get the blame," Emily said, slowly. "If I hadn't been able to testify..."

"It would be unlikely that the Allied Lands would believe her," the Grandmaster admitted. "She would have made a very convincing suspect. And if you both ended up dead...Lin might have vanished completely."

"If she really was working for Mountaintop," Emily mused. "Might she have intended Mountaintop to take the blame?"

"Perhaps," the Grandmaster said. "Not everyone likes the Mage Master of Mountaintop. The great magical families are *very* cutthroat, always trying to squeeze an advantage for themselves out of every little incident. Maybe the true object of the exercise was to embarrass their leader."

His face twisted into a grimace. "We will certainly investigate," he added. "But I have a feeling that the information we were given about Lin will be more than a little misleading."

Emily blinked in surprise. "You didn't check their credentials?"

"We didn't check yours either," the Grandmaster pointed out, rather snidely. "We took Void's word for it."

He stood and paced over to the bare wall, then turned to face her. "There will be investigations," he said. "The White Council will have to be informed. Steps must be taken—and Void, as far as possible, must be kept uninvolved. We really don't *need* a major confrontation between him and Mountaintop right now."

Emily stared at him. "You trust him to do your dirty work, but not to avenge an attack on his ward?"

"Mountaintop provides a quarter of the White Council's combat sorcerers," the Grandmaster said. "If this led to open conflict, it could rip the Allied Lands apart. We need to know what is actually happening before we decide what to do about it."

"You'll have to speak to King Randor," Emily reminded him, wondering just *what* Alassa's father would say. He hadn't been able to do anything about Alassa's near-death experience; legally, could he involve himself in the affair? "And I need to get back to my friends."

The Grandmaster seemed to look right at her. "You do realize that you have... acted foolishly, this term?"

Emily flushed at his tone, but said nothing.

"I know; you don't come from this world and you lack the basic knowledge we teach newborn magicians," he added. "And we assumed that Void had taught you, as was his duty, and never really *checked* on it. I would scream at him for his oversight, if I thought it would do any good.

"But your experiment, whatever it was, could have had disastrous consequences. And it wasn't the only mistake you made. What would have happened if you had reported Lin to a tutor at once? She might have been caught before she could flee Whitehall. And you came very close to alienating your two best friends."

He looked down at the floor. "How much of this was because Lin was using runes to influence your mind?"

Emily shuddered. The truth was that she didn't know—but then, she wouldn't. She really *didn't* like wasting time watching sporting events...it was easy to understand why she might want to leave early, certainly before she'd understood just how important it was to Alassa and Imaiqah that she *watched*. There was no way to know, in the end, how much of her mistakes had come from her own stupidity.

"It isn't uncommon," the Grandmaster said quietly, "for people to react badly to stress, or to make mistakes as they come into their magic. They become so consumed by what they're doing that it just runs away from them. You, on the other hand, are rather more than just another student. You need to learn faster—and not just magic. You need to learn control and discipline."

His unseen eyes seemed to bore into hers. "We punish misbehavior as severely as we do to ensure that you *do* know the price of messing around with magic," he added. "But there comes a time when a sore bottom cannot save you from the consequences of your actions. I don't know how many of your problems this term came from Lin's runes, but you need to learn to watch yourself. You are not just *any* pupil."

Emily flinched at his tone. He was right—but that didn't make it any easier for her to hear.

"Lady Barb has, I have been told, sworn to keep what you tell her to herself," the Grandmaster said. "I think you should consider confiding in her, now that she is literally unable to share whatever you tell her with anyone else. She is your Advisor—and will be making sure that you learn what you need to know in future. Talk to her if you have any other ideas."

"I will," Emily promised.

"We are going to have to reset all of the schedules for classes, since we missed so many," the Grandmaster concluded, walking back to his desk. "Go see your friends, enjoy your time with them...and if you haven't apologized for acting so badly, I think you should."

He smiled. "And maybe you should consider playing games with them too," he added. "It will help bring you back together."

"Thank you," Emily said, as she stood. Part of her mind insisted that it would be a fate worse than death, but she knew that was being silly. "I will."

"You might come to enjoy it," the Grandmaster said. "Oh, and one other thing?"

Emily paused, waiting.

"There are already rumors about you and Lin," the Grandmaster warned, "but you might want to avoid telling anyone—apart from your friends. The more people who know the full details, the harder it will be to deal with the situation in a calm and reasonable manner."

Emily nodded and left the room.

Chapter Forty

Emily ducked the snowball Alassa threw at her, then scooped up a handful of snow and threw it back at her. A moment later, Imaiqah's snowball narrowly missed her as she ducked, but Emily slipped and fell over backwards. Imaiqah ran up to her and dropped snow on her chest, then winked down at her.

"I meant to do that," she said.

Alassa threw a snowball that caught Imaiqah in the back of the head. She yelped and scooped up more snow to throw back. Emily laughed, then caught Imaiqah's arm and pulled her down into the snow. Alassa saw the glint in Emily's eye and jumped backwards, heading towards the frozen lake. Emily used a simple spell to hurl a snowball after her.

"Missed," Alassa taunted, from a safe distance.

Emily had to laugh. Alassa and Imaiqah had dragged her out of the library and insisted that she join them for a snowball fight—and she was enjoying it more than she had expected. The Gorgon had refused to join them—snow didn't agree with her people, she'd explained—but she had promised to go over their textbooks tonight. Now that everyone was back at Whitehall, the staff was making them work hard to make up for the missing weeks. There was already a rumor going round that the coming holidays would be cancelled if the students weren't where the staff thought they ought to be by then.

She looked up at the darkening sky and thought, grimly, about Lin. The rumors going round were far off the mark; half of the students seemed to believe that she had been the Mimic's final victim, while the other half believed that the Gorgon had killed her and ground her petrified body into dust. At least no one seemed to be pointing fingers at Emily any longer, not after she'd received full credit for defeating the Mimic. But she'd still made sure to spend time with the Gorgon.

"Sunset," Alassa said. "Why don't you come with us to the Great Hall?"

Emily would have preferred to find a mug of chocolate—it had been surprisingly hard to introduce the concept of chocolate milk to the cooks—but she knew better than to argue when Alassa was in such a determined mood. Besides, they still weren't allowed to share a bedroom. The room Emily still shared with the Gorgon had been repaired—the beds, desks and wardrobes had been completely replaced—but there was no room for another roommate.

Or, rather, someone would have had to have been left out, Emily thought. *I wasn't going to do that to anyone.*

She'd come to the decision that she rather liked the Gorgon, once she'd had a chance to get to know her without Lin's subtle influence. They were very alike in many ways, both outcasts and strangers in a very strange land, although the Gorgon had been treated with love and affection by her family rather than neglect and abuse. It had been her magic that had set her apart from the other Gorgons, but they had also valued it as a gift. And they appreciated her intelligence.

They brushed the snow off their coats as they slipped through the door and into Whitehall, then headed to the Great Hall. Emily sensed the waves of magic coruscating through the building as the Grandmaster and Professor Lombardi slowly prepared a new Warden and reformatted the wards to make it harder for the next one to be killed. The monitoring system wasn't fully in place yet, but there hadn't been a single hexing since the wards had come down, somewhat to Emily's surprise. Or perhaps it wasn't a surprise. The day after the Mimic had been destroyed, she'd been told, the Grandmaster had given the entire school a scathing lecture on their conduct while under siege. He seemed to have cowed everyone.

She caught Alassa smiling as she stopped outside the doorway to the Great Hall, an odd little smile that puzzled her. Emily hesitated, half-expecting to discover that someone had left a bucket of water on top of the door, then pushed it open firmly. And then she stared in absolute disbelief.

The Great Hall was completely filled with students, but that wasn't what caught her eye first. It was a glowing set of words, hanging above their heads, spelling out HAPPY BIRTHDAY EMILY. She half-turned to look at Alassa—she had *known*—and then someone pushed a drink into her hand and pulled her into the crowd. Almost everyone seemed to want to shake her hand.

"Happy birthday," Alassa said, from behind her. "You deserve it."

Emily stared at her as Cat shook her hand, then went on to chat to Imaiqah. "It isn't my birthday..."

"But it *is* one year since you came...here," Alassa pointed out. "And besides, no one knows just when your birthday actually is, so..."

She shrugged. "Besides, it isn't just for *you*," she added. "Everyone needed a party after what happened over the last few weeks."

Emily found herself unable to speak. Part of her hated crowds, hated them all pressing in around her...and yet part of her loved the attention. They had come for *her*...tears threatened to start prickling at the corner of her eyes and she wiped them away, then took a sip of her drink. It tasted vaguely of sunshine and rainbows.

"A magician's drink," Alassa said, as Professor Thande appeared and shook Emily's hand before wandering off to supervise the punch. "A mundane who drank it would taste nothing more than water."

A band composed of students started to play a dance tune, but several of the players seemed to have different ideas about which tune they were meant to be playing and the sound rapidly became a discordant racket. Mistress Irene marched over to them and, shouting almost as loudly as Sergeant Harkin, pushed them into some semblance of order. Emily had been told that most aristocrats were taught to play *something*, yet she never seemed to have the time to learn. But listening to the band when they finally started playing together made her think that she should make the time.

Maybe if I alter the interior of the pocket dimensions, she thought, and then shook her head firmly. She'd gotten into quite enough trouble with that idea already.

She caught sight of Imaiqah being pulled into the dance by Cat and smiled to herself, although she had no idea if he was genuinely courting Imaiqah or if he was merely looking for a suitable partner. Alassa nudged her and pointed out just how star-struck Imaiqah looked, making Emily roll her eyes. The princess had danced with countless young princes only a few months ago.

"Lady Emily," Master Tor said, from behind her. "I was wondering if I could have a word."

Emily swallowed the response that came to mind and nodded, allowing him to draw her away from Alassa. She sensed the privacy ward as he cast it and frowned. What did he have to say that was so private her best friend couldn't hear it?

"I may have...*misjudged* you," Master Tor said, as soon as the privacy ward was in place. "I did not realize that you had such a father. To leave you ignorant of the fundamentals was nothing short of neglect."

It took Emily a moment to realize that he meant Void. From his point of view, Void probably *did* seem like a neglectful father, the kind of person who would teach his children dangerous spells instead of basic safety precautions. On the other hand, there were very few people who would dare to tell Void that to his face.

"And you risked your life to save all of us," Master Tor added. "I *definitely* misjudged you."

Emily couldn't think of anything to say, so she said nothing.

"I will be heading to the White Council after this year," he said. "But if I can do you a favor in response, please let me know."

He cancelled the privacy ward and walked off, leaving Emily staring after him.

"Sounds like that went well," Alassa said, taking hold of Emily's arm. "How many detentions did he give you *this* time?"

"No detentions," Emily said, still puzzled. "He wanted to apologize."

"You *did* save the school," Alassa pointed out. "Maybe he thought better of treating you badly after that."

"Maybe," Emily said.

She caught sight of Melissa on the other side of the room and scowled. No one had realized how badly she'd hurt Melissa, apart from Melissa herself. Emily was surprised that she hadn't already reported Emily to a tutor, but perhaps Melissa had just decided to keep her mouth shut. Or maybe coming so close to a Mimic, all unknowing, had convinced her that there were more important things in life than playing out a schoolgirl rivalry.

Or maybe she's just plotting, Emily thought.

King Randor hadn't told her *much* about being an aristocrat, but he had warned her that it was always a bad sign when people weren't grumbling. It normally meant that they were plotting something drastic. Emily hadn't quite dared to ask him what the barons had been saying before they'd launched their coup attempt, but she had a feeling she knew. Some of *them* had complained loudly to distract the King.

"You deserve a party," Lady Barb said, coming up to her. "I'm glad the Grandmaster saw fit to allow it."

Emily blinked. "It was your idea?"

"I thought you deserved *something* to remind them that you just saved the school—again," Lady Barb said. "How...*quickly* they forget."

"Most people are sheep," Alassa commented. There was an edge in her voice that made Emily blink. Was Alassa feeling guilty that she'd been called home? "They were quick to start accusing her of performing necromancy and they threw hexes at her whenever she turned her back."

"And then they started blaming the Gorgon," Emily added, pushing her concerns about Alassa to one side. "What should I do *next* year?"

Lady Barb gave her an odd little smile. "People have always been worried when someone has vastly more power than them," she said. "You have always attracted envy as well as admiration. And enemies."

She took Emily's arm and steered her towards a corner, leaving Alassa behind. "What do you intend to do during your holidays?"

"I intended to go back to Zangaria," Emily said. "I have a great deal of work to do in Cockatrice that I cannot leave in my Castellan's hands."

"It's traditional for students who want to serve the Allied Lands to spend a month or two working with a qualified sorcerer," Lady Barb said. "If you want to become a combat sorcerer, you might work with the military; if you wanted to be a Mediator, you might shadow one around, learning by doing. I think that you would benefit from doing it for yourself."

Emily hesitated. The chance to learn more was always welcome...if she had the time to take advantage of it.

"You would be welcome to come shadow me," Lady Barb said. "It would give you a far wider range of experience than you'd find in Whitehall—or Alexis. There are people out there who have never seen a magician, or who are scared of magic because they live too close to one of the places touched by the faerie. And they wouldn't talk to Baroness Cockatrice, not to tell you what you need to know."

"But they might talk to a roving magician," Emily said, quietly.

She could understand the problem. The peasants knew better than to annoy the aristocrats, no matter what laws the aristocrats gaily broke. Superior authority was a long way away, while the local aristocrat was right next door—and was willing to do *anything* to peasants who stepped out of line. The problems in Zangaria had only grown worse since the barons had launched their attempted coup—and, in failing, crippled their authority. Hundreds of thousands of peasants were moving off the land.

"Precisely," Lady Barb said. "It would also give you a chance to learn how to do certain things outside Whitehall."

Emily nodded.

"You don't have to decide at once," Lady Barb told her, "but I would like to know a month before Whitehall closes down for summer. That's when I have to make arrangements with the White Council."

"I'll let you know," Emily said, although she had already made up her mind. The chance to spend some time away from Whitehall—or Zangaria—would be very welcome. "And thank you for your support."

"I was surprised that your guardian hasn't shown himself," Lady Barb said. There was a dark tone in her voice, a reminder of what she'd told Emily about Void, several months ago. "It is always worrying when he does what I want him to do."

Emily shrugged. One thing she had learned about Void was that he appeared and disappeared as it suited him. No one, as far as she knew, could *summon* him, even when his ward was in serious trouble. Or had the Grandmaster actually tried to call him when Master Tor was threatening her with expulsion?

"I'm sure he knows what he's doing," she said, dryly.

The look on Lady Barb's face suggested that she wasn't convinced.

"Leaving him aside," Emily said, changing the subject, "has there been any sign of Lin?"

"None," Lady Barb said. "But she was clearly a very well-trained magician. Unless she does something stupid, she can avoid detection and make her way back to Mountaintop—or wherever she is going. We convinced Dragon's Den to make a search, but they turned up nothing. The Grandmaster is still investigating. I dare say that he will tell you what he finds out when he knows what it means."

Her eyes narrowed. "What—precisely—did Lin take with her?"

Emily hesitated. "Concepts," she said. The problem was that she wasn't entirely sure *what* Lin had seen. If she'd been poking around Emily's desk since the first day they'd met, she might have seen almost everything. And what if she'd managed to get into the trunk? "I don't know for sure."

She scowled. If Lin had been looking for technology alone, she might have gunpowder, steam engines and a dozen other concepts Emily had been reverse-engineering. She would have the diagrams for basic cannons, muskets and other weapons. But if she'd looked at the magical notes, she might well have the pocket dimension batteries too...if she could make them work. Emily's experiments had never reached the next stage...in hindsight, channelling that much power might be very dangerous. And yet Lin had already proven herself to be a sneaky opponent.

"I'll be asking you for details later," Lady Barb said. "And so will the Grandmaster."

And King Randor, Emily added, silently. She didn't know how much King Randor knew of the gunpowder project, but she doubted that Imaiqah's father had hidden it from him. Not when he was a noble himself now.

She shook her head. How far could Lin and her backers go with what they had? Emily had already been surprised by how fast Zangaria had advanced from what she'd told them. How far could others go *without* her help? There was no way to know.

A sudden rustle ran around the Great Hall as the Gorgon entered. Instead of wearing robes, or a human-style dress, she was wearing a long tunic that seemed to show off her inhuman attributes. It seemed to be made of snakeskin—*Gorgon scales,* Emily suspected—and showed her bare arms. They too were a strange blend of human skin and scales. Her snakes, fanning out around her head, seemed to be smirking at the crowd.

"Your friend seems to have decided to abandon her attempt to pretend to be human," Lady Barb said. She sounded approving. "Good. We need more contacts among the Gorgons."

Emily looked at the Gorgon, then smiled.

"Go enjoy your party," Lady Barb said. "You earned it."

Emily nodded and walked over to join the Gorgon, noticing the half-admiring, half-fearful glances some of the male students were directing at her. It was impossible to avoid noticing that the Gorgon had a kind of eerie glamor, a beauty that drew their attention towards her scales—and snakes. She couldn't help wondering which of the boys would be the first to ask the Gorgon to dance.

"Thank you for coming," she said, as she took the Gorgon's hand. "It wouldn't have been the same without you."

The Gorgon winked at her, then nodded to a stuttering third-year who was trying to ask her to dance. Emily couldn't tell if he was merely immature or if he was scared of the Gorgon as well as being attracted to her. She fought down a laugh as the Gorgon led him onto the dance floor, moving with a grace that rivalled Alassa's.

"Come and dance," Alassa said. "This day won't last forever."

"You taught her," Emily muttered. "Didn't you?"

"Father taught me that you can either apologize endlessly for being what you are or you can just rub their noses in it," Alassa said, with a nod. "I decided to show her how to do the latter. She doesn't *need* to pretend to be human. And look! They're all falling over her."

Emily felt her smile widening as her friend pulled her over to a group of boys. Maybe it was strange to wish otherwise, to wish that the day would last forever, but—despite everything—she was content.

She was home.

The End

About the author

Christopher G. Nuttall is thirty-two years old and has been reading science fiction since he was five, when someone introduced him to children's SF. Born in Scotland, Chris attended schools in Edinburgh, Fife and University in Manchester before moving to Malaysia to live with his wife Aisha.

Chris has been involved in the online Alternate History community since 1998; in particular, he was the original founder of Changing The Times, an online alternate history website that brought in submissions from all over the community. Later, Chris took up writing and eventually became a full-time writer.

Current and forthcoming titles published by Twilight Times Books

Schooled in Magic YA fantasy series
Schooled in Magic book 1
Lessons in Etiquette book 2
Study in Slaughter book 3
Work Experience book 4
The School of Hard Knocks book 5

The Decline and Fall of the Galactic Empire SF series
Barbarians at the Gates book 1
The Shadow of Cincinnatus book 2

Chris has also produced *The Empire's Corps* series, the *Outside Context Problem* series and many others. He is also responsible for two fan-made Posleen novels, both set in John Ringo's famous Posleen universe. They can both be downloaded from his site.

Website: http://www.chrishanger.net/
Blog: http://chrishanger.wordpress.com/
Facebook: https://www.facebook.com/ChristopherGNuttall

CPSIA information can be obtained
at www.ICGtesting.com
Printed in the USA
BVHW03s0149011018
528924BV00001B/41/P